Praise for *Karen Memory*

Named one of *io9*'s Mi... ...e Fiction
and Fantasy Books t... ...t For in 2015

"Elizabeth Bear is known for her excellent stories, and her new steampunk novel has gotten a lot of praise from all over the place. We can't wait to get our hands on this one."

—*BuzzFeed*

"Bear's rollicking, suspenseful, and sentimental steampunk novel introduces Karen Memery. . . . Bear gives Karen a colorful voice, sharp eyes, and the spunk and skills necessary to scuffle with bad types as well as to win over people whose help she needs. Her story is a timeless one: a woman doing what is needed to get by while dreaming and fighting for great things to come."

—*Publishers Weekly*

"Bear pumps fresh energy in the steampunk genre with a light touch on the gadgetry and a vivid sense of place. Karen has a voice that is folksy but true, and the entire cast of heroic women doing the best they can in an age that was not kind to their gender is a delight. Ably assisted by a U.S. Marshal and his Comanche posseman, Karen and the ladies kick ass."

—*Library Journal* (starred review)

"*Karen Memory* is a book that gets going right away and never stops. Surreally captivating, Bear's latest melds the genres of steampunk, fantasy, adventure, and dime-store Western together perfectly, thanks mostly to the charming voice of the protagonist. Karen's rough edges and obviously wicked intelligence are highlighted by nuanced details that establish

her already likable voice as even more relatable; her charming (self-taught) misuse of phrases and terminology, and reflexive bravery and morality are just a few examples in this fantastic read." —*RT Book Reviews* (4½ stars, Top Pick!)

"The story swiftly knots itself into steampunk-ishly surreal complications, with dauntless (and, by this point, love-stricken) Karen in the thick of the action. Supplies all the Bear necessities: strong female characters, existential threats, intriguing developments, and a touch of the light fantastic." —*Kirkus Reviews*

"Bear [pays] homage to the dime novels of the era, forerunners of pulp fiction packed with larger-than-life heroes, scheming villains, and gritty action. But she's subtly subverting this tradition, just as much as she's giving steampunk a gentle, loving twist. . . . It's clear that Bear is making a point about the way history, like literary subgenres, can steamroll over anyone who falls outside the norm. She makes that point engagingly and effortlessly. *Karen Memory* breezes by at a leisurely pace, a bracing yet charming adventure yarn that never feels forced, despite the brassy confidence of its delivery." —NPR

"*Karen Memory*, the latest novel from prolific, award-winning author Elizabeth Bear, is a book I have come to love with a surprisingly passionate intensity. . . . Despite dipping into the aesthetic of steampunk, this is a novel that challenges many of steampunk's most common assumptions, and one that's in dialogue with many different genre traditions. At its heart, though, this is an adventure story. . . . *Karen Memory* will be among my favorite novels of 2015." —Liz Bourke, *Locus*

Karen
Memory

ELIZABETH BEAR

TOR

A TOM DOHERTY ASSOCIATES BOOK

NEW YORK

KAREN MEMORY

Copyright © 2015 by Elizabeth Bear

A Tor Book
Published by Tom Doherty Associates, LLC
175 Fifth Avenue
New York, NY 10010

www.tor-forge.com

Tor® is a registered trademark of Tom Doherty Associates, LLC.

Library of Congress Cataloging-in-Publication Data

Bear, Elizabeth.
    Karen Memory / Elizabeth Bear.—First trade paperback edition.
      p. cm.
    ISBN 978-0-7653-7525-4 (trade paperback)
    ISBN 978-1-4668-4634-0 (e-book)
I. Title.
    PS3602.E2475 K37 2015
    813'.6—dc23

                        2015017104

Our books may be purchased in bulk for promotional, educational, or business use. Please contact your local bookseller or the Macmillan Corporate and Premium Sales Department at 1-800-221-7945, extension 5442, or by e-mail at MacmillanSpecialMarkets@macmillan.com.

First Edition: February 2015
First Trade Paperback Edition: January 2016

Printed in the United States of America

10 9 8 7 6 5 4 3 2

This book is for Karen Memery Bruce,

who is not actually a seamstress

but who is a librarian and a puppeteer.

Karen Memory

Chapter One

You ain't gonna like what I have to tell you, but I'm gonna tell you anyway. See, my name is Karen Memery, like "memory" only spelt with an *e,* and I'm one of the girls what works in the Hôtel Mon Cherie on Amity Street. "Hôtel" has a little hat over the *o* like that. It's French, so Beatrice tells me.

Some call it the Cherry Hotel. But most just say it's Madame Damnable's Sewing Circle and have done. So I guess that makes me a seamstress, just like Beatrice and Miss Francina and Pollywog and Effie and all the other girls. I pay my sewing machine tax to the city, which is fifty dollar a week, and they don't care if your sewing machine's got a foot treadle, if you take my meaning.

Which ain't to say we ain't got a sewing machine. We've got two, an old-style one with a black cast-iron body and a shiny chrome wheel, and one of the new steel-geared brass ones that run on water pressure, such that you stand inside of and move with your whole body, and it does the cutting and stitching and steam pressing, too.

Them two machines sit out in a corner of the parlor as kind
of a joke.

I can use the old-fashioned one—I learned to sew, I mean
really sew—pretty good after Mama died—and Miss Francina
is teaching me to use the new one to do fancywork, though it
kind of scares me. And it fits her, so it's big as your grandpa's
trousers on me. But the thing is, nobody in Rapid City sells the
kind of dresses we parlor girls need, so it's make our own patterned after fashion dolls from Paris and London and New
York or it's pay a ladies' tailor two-thirds your wage for something you don't like as well.

But as you can imagine, a house full of ladies like this goes
through a lot of frocks and a lot of mending. So it pays to know
how to sew both ways, so to speak.

Really pays. Miss Francina and me, we charge less than
the ladies' tailors. And it's easier to do fittings when you live
with the girls. And every penny I make goes into the knotted
sock in my room for when I get too old for sewing. I have a
plan, see.

The richest bit is that the city and the tailors can't complain,
can they, when we're paying our sewing machine tax and our
guild and union dues, too. Sure, fifty dollar'd be a year's wages
back in Hay Camp for a real seamstress and here in Rapid City
it'll barely buy you a dozen of eggs, a shot of whiskey, and a
couple pair of those new blue jeans that Mr. Strauss is manu-
facturing. But here in Rapid City a girl can pay fifty dollar a
week and still have enough left over to live on and put a little
away besides, even after the house's cut.

You want to work for a house, if you're working. I mean . . .
working "sewing." Because Madam Damnable is a battleship
and she runs the Hôtel Mon Cherie tight, but nobody hits her
girls, and we've got an Ancient and Honorable Guild of Seamstresses and nobody's going to make us do anything we really

don't want to unless it's by paying us so much we'll consider it in spite of. Not like in the cheap cribs down in the mud beside the pier with the locked doors and no fireplaces, where they keep the Chinese and the Indian girls the sailors use. Those girls, if they're lucky, they work two to a room so they can keep an eye on each other for safety and they got a slicker to throw over the bottom sheet so the tricks' spurs and mud don't ruin it.

I've never been down there, but I've been up along the pier, and you can't hear the girls except once in a while when one goes crazy, crying and screaming. All you can hear up there is the sailors cursing and the dog teams barking in the kennels like they know they're going to be loaded on those deep-keel ships and sent up north to Alaska to probably freeze in the snow and die along with some eastern idiot who's heard there's gold. Sometimes girls go north, too—there's supposed to be good money from the men in the gold camps—but I ain't known but one who made it away again ever.

That was Madame Damnable, and when she came back she had enough to set herself up in business and keep her seamstresses dry and clean. She was also missing half her right foot from gangrene, and five or six teeth from scurvy, so I guess it's up to you to decide if you think that was worth it to her.

She seems pretty happy, and she walks all right with a cane, but it ain't half-hard for her to get up and down the ladders to street level.

So anyway, about them ladders. Madame Damnable's is in the deep part of town, and they ain't yet finished raising the streets here. What I mean is when they started building up the roads a while back so the sea wouldn't flood the downtown every spring tide they couldn't very well close down all the shopping—and all the sewing—so they built these big old masonry walls and started filling in the streets between them up to the top level with just any old thing they had to throw in there. There's dead horses down there, dead men for all I know. Street signs and old couches and broke-up wagons and such.

They left the sidewalks down here where they had been, and the front doors to the shops and such, so on each block there's this passage between the walls of the street and the walls of the buildings. And since horses can't climb ladders and wagons can't fly, they didn't connect the blocks. Well, I guess they could of built tunnels, but it's bad enough down there on the walkways at night as it is now and worth your life to go out without a couple of good big lantern bearers with a stout cudgel apiece.

At Madame Damnable's, we've got Crispin, who's our doorman and a freed or maybe a runaway slave and about as big as a house. He's the only man allowed to live in the hotel, as he doesn't care for humping with women. He hardly talks and he's real calm and quiet, but you never feel not safe with him standing right behind you, even when you're strong-arming out a drunk or a deadbeat. Especially if Miss Francina is standing on the other side.

So all over downtown, from one block to the next you've got to climb a ladder—in your hoopskirts and corset and bustle that ain't no small thing even if you've got two good feet in your boots to stand on—and in our part of town that's thirty-two feet from down on the walk up to street level.

When the water table's high, the walks still flood out, of course. Bet you guessed that without me.

They filled up the streets at the top of town first, because the rich folk live there, Colonel Marsh who owns the lumber mill and Dyer Stone—that's Obadiah, but nobody call him that—who's the mayor, and such. And Skid Road they didn't fill in at all, because they needed it steep on account of the logs, so there's staircases up from it to the new streets, where the new streets are finished and sometimes where they ain't. The better neighborhoods got steam lifts, too, all brass and shiny, so the rich ladies ain't got to show their bloomers to the whole world climbing ladders. Nobody cares if a soiled dove shows off her underthings, I guess, as long as the *underthings* are clean.

Up there some places the fill was only eight feet and they've got the new sidewalks finished over top of the old already. What they did there was use deck prisms meant for ships, green and blue from the glass factory up by the river as gives Rapid City its name, set in metal gratings so that when there's light the light can shine on down.

Down here we'll get wood plank, I expect, and like it. And then Madame Damnable will just keep those ruby lamps by the front door burning all the time.

The red light looks nice on the gilt, anyway.

Our business mostly ain't sailors but gold camp men coming or going to Anchorage, which is about the stupidest thing you ever could get to naming a harbor. I mean, why not just call it Harbor, like it was the only one ever? So we get late nights, sure, but our trade's more late afternoon to say two or four, more like a saloon than like those poor girls down under the docks who work all night, five dollar a poke, when the neap tide keeps the ships locked in. Which means most nights 'cept Fridays and Saturdays by 3:00 A.M. we're down in the dining room while Miss Bethel and Connie serves us supper. They're the barkeep and the cook. They don't work the parlor, but Connie feeds us better than we'd get at home and Miss Bethel, she keeps a sharp eye on the patrons.

Sundays, we close down for the Sabbath and such girls as like can get their churching in.

So I don't remember which day it was exactly that Merry Lee and Priya came staggering into the parlor a little before

three in the morning, but I can tell you it wasn't a Friday or
Saturday, because all the punters had gone home except one
who'd paid Pollywog for an all-night alteration session and was
up in the Chinese Room with her getting his seams ripped, if
you take my meaning. The Professor—he plays the piano in
the parlor for Effie and Pollywog and Beatrice to sing to—had
gone home for the night already, it was that slow. The rest of
us—just the girls and Crispin, not Madame Damnable—were
in our robes and slippers, faces scrubbed and hair down, sitting
in the library when it happened. We don't use the parlor except
for working.

Beatrice, who's the only one at the hotel younger than me,
was practicing reading out loud to the rest of us, her slim, dark
fingers bent back holding the big ivory-bound book of Grimm's
fairy tales. She's a tiny bit of a thing, is Bea, and has all the
manners I don't. Her mother was a courtesan—what they call
a *placée*—down in New Orleans, and Bea speaks French better than English and has a long, straight nose, a good high forehead, and lips like a bee-stung rose.

We'd just settled in with after-dinner tea and biscuits when
there was a crash down the ladder out front and the sound of
somebody crying like her leg was broke. Given the loudness
of the thump, I reckoned that might not be too far from the
truth of it.

Crispin and Miss Francina gave each other The Look, and
while Beatrice put the ribbon in her book they both got
up and moved toward the front door. Crispin I already said
about, and the thing about Miss Francina is that Miss Francina's got a pecker under her dress. But that ain't nothing but
God's rude joke. She's one of us girls every way that matters,
and handy for a bouncer besides.

I followed along just behind them, and so did Effie. We're
the sturdiest girls, and Effie can shoot well enough that Ma-

dame Damnable lets her keep a gun in her room. Miss Bethel hides a pump shotgun under the bar, too, but she was upstairs in bed already, so while Crispin was unlocking the door I went over and got it, working the breech to make sure it was loaded. Beatrice grabbed Signor, the deaf white cat who lives in the parlor—he's got one blue eye and one yellow and he's loud as an Ozark howler when he wants something—and pulled him back into the library with the rest of the girls.

When I got up behind Crispin, it was all silence outside except the patting of the rain dripping down into the well and splashing in the puddles. Not even any more crying, though we all stood with our ears straining. Crispin pulled open the door and Miss Francina went striding out into that burning cold in her negligee and marabou slippers like she owned the night and the rest of us was just paying rent on it. I skin-flinched, just from nerves, but it was all right because I'd had the sense to keep my finger off the shotgun trigger.

And then Miss Francina said, "Sweet child Christ!" in that breathy voice of hers and Crispin was through the door with his truncheon, the bald center of his pate shining in the red lantern light. I heard him curse, too, but it sounded worried rather than angry or fearful, so I let the shotgun muzzle droop and walked up to the doorway just in time to grab the arm of a pretty little Indian girl—Eastern Indian, not American Indian— who was half-naked and in hysterics. Her clothes had never been good, or warm enough for the night, though somewhere she'd gotten some lace-up boots and a man's coat too big for her, and now they was wet through and shredded. All she had on else was a ripped-up shift all stained across the bosom, and I could tell she weren't wearing nothing under it.

She was turned around, tugging something—another girl's arm, poking out frontward between Crispin and Miss Francina where they were half-dragging her. She had a fine hand, which was all I could see of her, and the rain dripped pink off her sallow fingers. Once they got both girls inside in the light, Effie lunged forward and slammed the door. I handed her the shotgun and went to see to the girls.

"Here, Karen," Crispin said in his big slow-molasses voice. "You take this little one. Bring her after. I'll get Miss Merry here upstairs to the sickroom."

Miss Francina stepped back and I could see that the girl between them was somebody I knowed, at least by reputation. Not a girl, really. A woman, a Chinese woman.

"Aw, shit," Effie said. Not only can she shoot, but Effie's not real well-spoken. "That's Merry Lee."

Merry Lee, which was as close as most American tongues could get to her real name, I guess, was half-conscious and half-fighting, batting at Crispin's hands while he swung her up into his arms. Miss Francina stuck her own hands in there to try to hold her still, where they looked very white against all the red on Merry Lee's face and arms.

Effie said, "She's gun shot. I guess all that running around busting out Chinatown crib whores finally done caught up with her. You know'd it was sooner or later going to."

"You hush about things you know nothing about," Miss Francina said, so Effie drew back, chastened like, and said, "I didn't mean nothing by it."

"Go and watch the door, Effie," Miss Francina said. Effie hefted that shotgun and did, not sulking at all. Effie talks without thinking sometimes, but she's a good girl. Madame Damnable don't tolerate them what ain't.

The girl in my arms was as cold skinned as she was slick with rain, and all she wanted was to twist loose of me. She pulled away once and threw herself at Crispin, but Miss Francina caught her and gave her back, and honest, she was mostly too light and skinny to put up a good fight once I had a grip on her. I tried to talk to her, tell her she was safe and we were going to take care of her and Merry Lee both. I could hear her teeth chatter when I got close. I didn't think then she understood a word of it, but I found out later her English was better'n mine, so I think it was mostly that she couldn't hardly of been more upset. But something got through to her, because after a minute of twisting her wrists and getting blood all over my good pink flannel she stood still, shivering and dripping, her long face sad as a wet filly's. She let me bundle her up the stairs after Crispin and Merry Lee while Miss Francina went to fetch Miss Lizzie.

We followed them down the long rose-painted hall to the sickroom door. Crispin wanted to take Merry Lee in without the Indian girl, but the girl weren't having none of it. She leaned against my arms and keened through the doorway, and finally Crispin just looked at me helplessly and said, "Karen honey, you better bring that child in here before she cries down the roof."

She was better inside, sitting in a chair beside the bed with wool blankets wrapped around her, though it were another fight to get her to cut loose of that soaking old coat. She leaned forward—again I thought *filly*, starved and leaning on her plow collar—while Crispin checked over Merry Lee for where she was hurt worst. Effie was right about her being gun shot, too— she had a graze through her long black hair showing bone, and that was where most of the blood was from, but there was a bullet in her back, too, and Crispin couldn't tell from looking if it had gone through to a lung. It weren't in the spine, he said, or she wouldn't of been walking.

Just as he was stoking up the surgery machine—it hissed and clanked like a steam engine, which was never too reassuring when you just needed a boil lanced or something—Miss Lizzie came barreling up the stairs with an armload of towels and a bottle of clear corn liquor. She must of had her arm off for sleeping, because it was bundled up with the linens, but when she strapped it over her stump and started to turn the crank to wind up the spring I knowed it was time for me to be leaving. Miss Lizzie's narrow and sharp as one of her scalpels, and nothing shakes her: not even lockjaw, which is the scariest thing I can think of, just about, 'cepting maybe the hydrophobia. The girl weren't going nowhere, but she didn't look like interfering anymore—she just leaned forward moaning in her throat like a hurt kitten, both hands clenched on the blankets over the cane arms of the bedside chair.

Crispin could handle her if she did anything. And he could hold down Merry Lee if she woke up that much.

I slipped through the door while Miss Lizzie was cutting the dress off Merry Lee's back. I'd seen her and that machine pull a bullet before, and I didn't feel like puking.

I got downstairs just as somebody started trying to kick in the front doors.

Chapter Two

In the fuss Effie hadn't thrown the bolt, which should be second nature, but you'd be surprised what you can forget when there's blood and rain all over everywhere and people are handing you guns. The good thing was that I had handed her the gun and when the front doors busted in on their hinges she had the presence of mind to raise up that gun and yell at the top of her little lungs, "Stop!"

They didn't, though. There was four of them, and they came boiling through the door like a confusion of scalded weasels, shouting and swearing. Hair dripped down over their eyes—two of 'em had lost their hats—and their boots were mud caked to the ankles. And by "mud" I mean whatever's out in the roads, which ain't really mud except by courtesy. They checked and drew up just inside, staring from side to side and trading glances, and from halfway up the stairs I got a real fine look at all of them. It was Peter Bantle and three of his bully boys, all of them tricked out in gold watch chains and brocade and carrying truncheons and chains along with their lanterns, and you never saw a crew more looking for a fight.

The edges of the big doors were splintered where they'd busted out the latch. So maybe they'd of broken out the bolt trying to get in even if it had been locked.

"I said fucking *stop,*" said Effie, all alone in her nightgown in the middle of the floor, that big gun on her shoulder looking like to tip her over.

Miss Francina weren't anywhere to be seen, and I could tell from the sounds through the sickroom door that Crispin had his hands full of Merry Lee. Madame Damnable, bless her heart, was half-deaf from working in dance halls. She might of gone up to bed and even if Miss Francina had headed up to fetch her it would take her a minute to find her cane and glasses, which meant a minute in which somebody had to do something.

I didn't think on it. I just jumped over the banister, flannel gown and quilted robe and slippers and all, exactly the way Miss Bethel was always after me about for it not being lady-like, and thumped down on the curvy striped silk divan below the staircase.

I stepped off the couch, swept my robe up like skirts, and stuck my chin out. "Peter Bantle," I said, real loud, hoping wherever Miss Francina had got off to, that she would hear me and come running. "You wipe your damn muddy feet before you come in my parlor."

Now I ain't one of the smaller girls—like I said, I'm sturdy—and Peter Bantle is like his name: a banty, and a peckerwood, which is probably why he struts so much. I'm plump, too—the men like that—and I'm broad across the shoulders and hips, and when I came marching up beside Effie he had to pick his chin up to meet my eyes. He wore a silk hat over a greasy slick of hair. His cravat was pinned right up under his chin, fresh pressed, and he reeked of violets and lime. Maybe the fug was what made his eyes so squinty.

He frowned a little at the size I had on him.

The three in front of him were plenty big, however, and they didn't look impressed by two girls in their nighties with a single pump shotgun between them. Bantle's men had all kinds of gear hung on them I didn't even recognize, technologics and contrivances with lenses and brass tubes and glossy black enamel. The one in the very front had a bottle-green velvet coat and a bottle-blue stovepipe hat, and the patterned waistcoat to tie it together. He had the looks to pull those bright colors off—strong features and good skin. He was the only one of the three who was anything close to the usual size for human beings, being merely strapping as opposed to monstrous. I knowed him, too—Horaz Standish, who all the girls liked despite of who he worked for.

For whom he worked, Miss Bethel would tell me.

In fact, Horaz—that's short for Horatio—looked a bit apologetic at me now.

Bantle his own self had a kind of gauntlet on his left hand, stiff boiled leather segmented so the rubber underneath showed through, copper coils on each segment connected by bare wires.

I'd heard about that thing. I talked to a girl once he made piss herself with it. She had burns all up her arm where he grabbed her. But I didn't look at it, and I didn't let him see me shudder. You get to know a lot about men in my work, and men like Peter Bantle? They're all over seeing a woman shudder.

I don't take to men who like to hit. If he reached out at me with that gadget, I was afraid I'd like to kill him.

He didn't, though. He just ignored me and looked past Horaz's shoulder at Effie, who he could get eye to eye with if he stood up straight. He sneered at her and through a curled lip said, "Where's the Damnable bitch?"

"*Madame* is busy," I said. Only reason I didn't step in front of Effie was on account of she had the gun, but the urge to was that strong. "I'm Miss Memery. Me and Miss Sims here can help you. Or escort you out, if you'd rather."

Miss Bethel would of cringed at my grammar, too. But right then I couldn't afford to stammer over it to make it pretty.

Effie settled that gun on her shoulder a little better and lowered her eye to sight down the barrel. Bantle's men looked unimpressed so hard I could tell they was a little nervous. One hefted his black rubber truncheon.

"You got one of my whores in here, you little chit, and that thieving outlaw Merry Lee." Bantle's voice was all out of proportion with the weedy little body under his oilcloth coat. Maybe he was wearing some kind of amplifier in that high flounced collar of his. "I aim to have them with me when I go. And if you're lucky and give them over nice and easy, my boys here won't bust up your face *or* your parlor."

Rightly, I didn't know what to say. It weren't my house, after all, and Madame Damnable gives us a lot of liberty, but setting the rules of her parlor and offering sanctuary to someone else's girls ain't in it. But I knowed she didn't like Peter Bantle, with his bruised-up, hungry crib whores and his saddle shoes, and since he had come crashing through the front door with three armed men and a world of insolence, I figured I had a little more scope than usual.

"You're going to leave this parlor now," I said. "And shut the door behind you. And Madame Damnable will send somebody around in the morning so you can settle up for the lock you busted."

"I know they came in here," Bantle said. "There's Chink whore blood all over your hands and the floor here."

Oh, I knowed the answer to that one. I'd heard Madame Damnable say it often enough. "It's not the house's policy to discuss anyone whom we may or may not be entertaining."

"Mr. Bantle," that Horaz Standish said, "if you give these ladies a little room to negotiate, you know they might be reasonable. Nobody's at her best when her back's up against the wall." He turned his attention to me. "Miss Memery, was it? Of course we'll pay for the door—"

Bantle snorted. Then the thing happened that I ain't been able to make head nor tail of. My head went all sort of sticky fuzzy, like your mouth when you wake up, and I started feeling like maybe Bantle had a point. That *was* one of his girls upstairs, and Merry Lee *had* brought her here—or vice versa maybe—without asking. And didn't she owe him, that girl, for paying to have her brought over from India? And there was Effie pointing a gun at him.

And that Horaz was being right reasonable about affairs, the whole thing considered.

Bantle pointed that glove at me, finger and thumb cocked like he was making a "gun." I had another skin flinch, this time as I wondered if Bantle could *shoot* electricity out of that thing. And if it were healthy for him or anyone else for him to do so when he was dripping on the rug. His eyes sort of . . . glittered, with the reflections moving across them. It was like what they say Mesmeric—I think Mr. Mesmer was the fellow's name?

"Do it," Bantle said, and God help me if I didn't think it seemed a fine idea.

I was just about reaching over to grab the barrel of Effie's shotgun when the library door eased open off to my left. Through the crack I could see Beatrice's bright eyes peeping. Bantle saw her, too, because he snarled, "Get that Negra whore out here," and one of his stand-over men started toward her.

I had just enough warning to snatch back my reaching hand

and slap my palms over my ears before Effie jerked the gun up and sent a load of buckshot through the stained glass over the door panels that didn't never get too much sun no more anyhow. The window burst out like a spray of glory and Bantle and his men all ducked and cringed like quirted hounds.

I just stood there, dumbfounded, useless, as full of shame for what I'd been thinking about doing to Effie and Madame Damnable as some folk think I ought to be for whoring.

I wondered what the trick up with Pollywog thought was going on down here, and if he'd hightailed it out the window yet. We're not supposed to know, but one of Pollywog's regulars is Dyer Stone, and he's the mayor of Rapid City. He sneaks in the back and never sits in the parlor, of course.

"I got four more fucking shells," Effie said. *"Go on and get her."*

The bully who'd started moving couldn't seem to make his feet work all of a sudden, like the floor'd gotten as sticky as my head had been. Without looking over at Beatrice, I said, "Bea sweetie, you go run get the constable. It seems these gentlemen have lost their way and need directions."

It'd be better if we could call for help on that handsome mother-of-pearl example of Mr. Bell's telephone sitting on the table beside the striped divan. But the city council hadn't voted the constabulary money to install a set of their own, and honestly there was almost nobody in Rapid City we could even call, as yet. But we did have a line to the switchboard, and you could talk to the operator any time you liked.

When it was coming out of my mouth, I couldn't believe it. The words sounded calm and smooth, the opposite of the sticky fuzz I'd been feeling a moment before. I even saw one of the bully boys take a half step back. It didn't impress Peter Bantle, though, because while the library door was closing across Beatrice's face he started forward. Effie worked the pump on the shotgun, but he looked right at her and sneered, "You don't have the *balls,*" and then he was reaching for me with that awful glove.

Horaz Standish had his hand stretched out like he might try to stop Bantle, but also like he hadn't made up his mind to do it yet. I didn't know yet if I was going to scream or run or try to hit him, or if Effie was really going to have to learn to shoot a man dead that night.

But a big voice arrested him before I had to decide. "Peter goddamn Bantle, just what the pig-shitting hell do you think you're doing in my house?"

Madame is quick to correct Effie's mouth when it gets coarse. But I know where Effie done learned it.

Peter Bantle didn't have the sense to turn around and run when he heard the ferrule of Madame Damnable's cane clicking on the marble tile at the top of the stair, even though Horaz's hand finally reached his sleeve and tugged him backward. He did let his hand fall, though, and stepped back smartly. Effie's breath went out with a sound like surprise. I looked over at her pale, sweaty face and saw her move her finger off the trigger.

She really had been gonna shoot him.

I stepped back and half-turned so I could watch Madame Damnable coming down the stairs, her cane in one hand, the other clenching on the banister with each step.

She was a great battleship of a woman, her black hair gone all steel color at the temples. Her eyes hadn't had to go steel color; they had started off that way. Miss Francina was behind her on the one side and Miss Bethel on the other, and they didn't look like they was in any hurry, nor in any mood for conversation. "You got one of my girls in here, Alice," Peter Bantle said.

She reached the bottom of the stairs and Miss Bethel fanned

off left to come take the shotgun from Effie. "You speak with respect to Madame," Miss Francina said.

Bantle turned his head and spat on the fireplace rug. "I'll give a tart what respect she deserves. Now, you're going to give me my whore back. Aren't you."

Madame Damnable kept coming, inexorable as a steam locomotive rolling through the yard. She was in her robe and slippers, like the rest of us, and it didn't one whit make her less imposing. "I'll give you your head back if you don't step outside my parlor. You may think you can own folks, Peter Bantle, but this here Rapid City is a free city, where no letter of indenture signed overseas is going to hold water. The constable's on his way, and if you're not gone when he gets here I'm going to have him arrest you and your boys for trespass, breaking and entering, and malicious mischief. I pay more in taxes than you do, and most of the law would rather be with my happy girls than your broke-down sad and terrified ones. So you know how that's going to end."

That, I thought, *and the mayor just slid out an upstairs window. Unless he's still in bed with the covers over his head.*

Well, I hadn't seen Polly. Maybe the covers was over her head, instead.

Madame gestured to the broken door and the busted-out window. "The evidence is right there."

"Your own girl shot out that window!" Outrage made his voice squeak.

I had to hide my laugh behind my hand. Effie squeezed the other one. She was shaking, but it was all right. Madame Damnable was here now and she was going to take care of everything.

Peter Bantle knowed it, too. He had already given way a step, and when you were faced with Madame Damnable there was no coming back from that. He drew himself up in the doorway as his bully boys collapsed around him. Madame Damnable kept walking forward, and all four of those thugs slid out the door like water running out a drain.

Their boots crunched in the glass outside. He couldn't resist a parting shot, but he called it over his shoulder, and it didn't so much as shift Madame Damnable's nighttime braid against her shoulder. "You ain't heard the last of this, Alice."

"For tonight, I damn well think I have."

He took two more steps away. "And it's Hôtel *Ma* Cherie, you stupid slag!"

I wrote down in my journal that the big grandfather clock in the parlor chimed three as he slammed the doors behind him, but I don't remember now what it did that particular night. The clock is a particular project of Miss Lizzie's. She's clock-worked the thing up so it has about a hundred different mechanicals and figurines and cuckoos in it and near as many chimes and bells. The gears have some kind of offset that makes 'em perform different combinations of actions and sounds every time. Miss Lizzie says it ain't really random, but it sure seems that way. I do remember that one time she had it playing "Time Was When Love and I Were Well Acquainted" off a piano roll, so if you like, that's what you can imagine.

She probably ought to get her inventor's license and pay the city its Mad Science Tax—which is less than the sewing machine tax, actually—but that's a hard life for a woman, too. And I'd hate to see her leave Madame's house.

The chimes died down, and over the last echo we finally heard the boots on the broken ladder. Madame Damnable breathed out and let herself look around at us. "Well," she said cheerfully, "what a mess. Effie, fetch a bucket. Miss Bethel, put that gun away and find the broom, honey. Karen, you go tell Crispin when they're done with the Chinese girl he's to come down here and board up this window and sweep up the glass.

He'll just have to sit by the door until we can get in a locksmith. Miss Francina, you go after Beatrice and tell her we won't
need the constable."

Miss Francina bit her lip. "Are you sure, ma'am?"

Madame Damnable's hand glittered with diamonds and ru-
bies when she flipped it. "I'm sure. Go on, sweeties, scoot."
She paused. "Oh, and ladies? That was quick thinking. Well
done."

When I came back up the grand stair with coffee in the china
company service, the sickroom door was still closed, but I didn't
hear any screaming, or any steam engine chugging through it,
which could only be a good sign. If Merry Lee was still under
the knife, she would of been screaming and the machine would
of been whining and wheezing away, and if she had died of it
I thought the girl would be screaming instead. So I rapped kind
of light on the frame, on account of if Crispin or Miss Lizzie
was busy in there I didn't want to startle them. It took me two
tries to make my hand move, I was still that ashamed of myself from downstairs.

Crispin's voice floated back. "It's safe to come through." So
I set the tray on my hip and turned the knob left-handed, slow
in case there was somebody behind the door. The sickroom's
different from our company bedrooms. There's no wallpaper
and the sheets ain't fancy, and the bedstead and floor and all
is just painted white. It makes it easy to bleach or paint over
again if there's a bad mess, and you'd rather paint stained wood
than throw out carpets with puke or pus or crusted blood in
them any day.

The knife machine kind of hangs in one corner on a frame,
like a shiny spider with all black rubber belts between the gears
to make the limbs dance. It's one of only three or four in the

city, and it needs somebody skilled as Miss Lizzie to run it, but it don't hesitate—which when you're cutting flesh is a blessing—and it don't balk at some operations like other doctors might. And you always know its arms and tools is clean, because Crispin boils 'em after every use.

When I stepped inside, that whole white room looked like it had been splashed about with red paint, and none too carefully. Crispin looked up from washing his hands in a pink-tinged basin with clotted blood floating like strings of tide-pool slime around the edges. Merry Lee was laid sleeping or insensible in the bed—on her side, clean sheets tucked around her waist and a man's white button shirt on her backward so you could get to the dressings on her back. There was a mask over her face, and Crispin's other big enamel-knobbed brass machine that handles all those sickbed things that the steam-powered knife machine doesn't was kind of wheezing and whirring around her, its clockworks all wound up fresh and humming. The bloody sheets were heaped up in the basket and the Indian girl was perched on the chair by the head of the bed, holding Merry's sallow hand clutched between her olive ones and rocking back and forth just a tiny bit, like she was trying with all her might to hold herself still.

I picked my way between smears of blood. Crispin looked up, grinning instead of grim, so I knowed Merry Lee was going to be just fine unless the blood poisoning or the gas gangrene got her. "Karen honey, you are a delivering angel." He nodded to the tray. "This here is Priya. She helped me change the sheets."

I got a good look at her and at Merry Lee while I set the coffee on the cleanest bureau. Merry was a lot younger than I would of expected from the stories, fresh faced and sweet as a babe in her sleep and maybe seventeen, eighteen—not more than a year or two older than me.

Given she's been a thorn in the side of Peter Bantle and the rest of those cribhouse pimps for longer than I've been working, she must of started pretty young. Which ain't no surprise, given some of Peter Bantle's girls—and boys, too—ain't no older than your sister, and given that before she got away from him Merry Lee is supposed to have been one of them.

The Indian girl had dried her hair and Crispin or somebody must of given her a clean shift. She must of warmed up some, because she was sitting in the blankets like a nest instead of wrapped up in them.

Now I could see her arms and legs and neck, she was skinnier than anybody ought to be who wasn't starved to death. I sat there watching the knobs of her wrists and elbows stick out and the tendon strings move in the backs of her hands. I guess sailors and merchantmen don't care so much if the slatterns and stargazers they visit are pretty so long as they're cheap, and it's dark in a whore's crib anyway; plus, I guess if Peter Bantle underfeeds his girls they're easy keepers.

Still, as I sat there looking at her, her tangled hair with the blood drying in it and her long face and her cheekbones all sharp under skin the color of an old, old brass statue's, it more and more griped me thinking on it. And it more and more griped me that I'd been going to let Bantle have her.

That weren't like me at all.

Unless it was, I thought, sickened, and I was just making comforting noises at myself now.

There was plenty coffee in the pot, cream and sugar, too, and I'd brought up cups for everybody. But it didn't look like the Indian girl—Priya—was going to let go of Merry Lee's hand and pour herself a cup.

So I did it for her, loaded it up with cream and sugar, and balanced all but one of the biscuits I'd brought along on the saucer when I carried it to her.

She looked up surprised when I touched her hand to put the saucer in it, like she might of pulled away. She weren't any older than me, either, and this close I could see all the bruises on her under the brown of her skin. Layers of them. There was red fresh scrapes that would blossom into something spectacular. That might of been from dragging Merry Lee bleeding across half of Rapid City. There was black-purple ones with red mottles like pansy blossoms. And there was every shade of green and yellow, and you could pick out the hand- and fingerprints among 'em. And the red skinned-off slick-looking burns from Peter Bantle's electric glove, and some white scars, too, which made me angry and sick in all sorts of ways I couldn't even find half the words to tell you.

She was a fighter, and it had cost her. My daddy was a horse tamer, and he taught me. Some men don't know how to manage a woman or a horse or a dog. Where a good master earns trust and makes a partner of a smart wife or a beast, acts the protector, and gets all the benefit of those brains and that spirit, all the bad ones know is how to crush it out and make them cringing meek. There's a reason they call it *breaking*.

The more spirit, the longer it takes to break them. And the strongest ones you can't break at all. They die of it, and my daddy used to say it was a damned tragic bloody loss.

He probably wouldn't think much of me working on my back, but what he taught me kept me safe anyway, and it wasn't like either of us asked him to get thrown by a horse and go dying. Which just goes to prove it can happen to anyone, no matter how good and how careful they are.

Priya looked up at me through all those bruises, and I thought *filly* a third time. I could see in her eyes what I saw in some of my daddy's Spanish mustang ponies. You'd never break this one. You'd never even bend her. She'd die like Joan of Arc first, and spit blood on you through a smile.

My hand shook when I pushed the coffee at her. "I can't take that," she said, and that was my second surprise. Her English weren't no worse than mine, and maybe a little better. "You can't wait on me. You're a white lady." "I'm a white tart," I said, and let her see me grin. "And you need it if you're going to sit up with Miss Lee here. You're skin over bones, and how far did you carry her tonight?"

I thought she'd look down, but she didn't. Her eyes—you'd call 'em black, but that was only if you didn't look too closely. Like people call coffee black. And her hair was the same; it wasn't not-black, if you take my meaning, but the highlights in it were chestnut-red. I knowed I weren't supposed to think so, but she was beautiful. "She got shot coming out from under the pier," she said. "She told me where to run to."

Madame Damnable's. Which were near on a half mile off, and uphill the whole way. I poked the coffee at her again, and this time she let go of Merry Lee's hand with one of hers and lifted the cup off the saucer, which seemed like meeting me halfway. I leaned around her to put the saucer and the biscuits on the bedside stand. I could still hear Crispin moving around behind me and I was sure he was listening, but that was fine. I'd trust Crispin to birth my babies.

She swallowed. "I heard Mr. Bantle shouting downstairs."

There was more she meant to say, but it wouldn't come out. Like it won't sometimes. I knowed what she wanted to ask anyway, because it was the same I would of wanted if I was her. "Priya—did I say that right?"

She sipped the coffee and then looked at it funny, like she'd never tasted such a thing. "Priyadarshini," she said. "Priya is fine. This is sweet."

"I put sugar in it," I said. "You need it. In a minute here I'm going to head down to the kitchen and see if Connie or Miss Bethel can rustle up a plate of supper for you. But what I'm trying to say is Madame Damnable—this is Madame Damnable's house you brought Merry Lee to—she's not going to give you back to Bantle for him to starve and beat on no more."

I'm not sure she believed me. But she looked down at her coffee and she nodded. I patted her shoulder where the shift covered it. "You eat your biscuits. I'll be back up with some food."

"And a bucket," Crispin said. When I turned, he was waving around at all that blood on rags and his forceps and on the floor.

"And a bucket," I agreed, making sure not to look where he pointed.

I took one glance back at Priya before I went, cup up over her face hiding her frown, eyes back on Merry. And then and there I swore an oath that Peter Bantle was damned sure going to know what hit him.

On récolte ce que l'on sème.

That's French. It means, "What goes around comes around." So Beatrice tells me.

Chapter Three

I never made it back up to Priya that night. Connie and Miss Bethel was both up—the whole house was up by now—but I didn't see Miss Bethel and Connie took one look at me and poured a cup of sweet chocolate laced with whiskey down my throat and sent me up to bed, promising to feed Priya only if I went willing. Though I suppose it won't surprise you none that when I finally made it to my room I weren't in no condition to sleep.

What might surprise you is my room, though, if all you've seen is the downstairs or the company bedrooms of a parlor house like Madam Damnable's. My room's maybe no bigger than a dockside crib—I can touch both walls with my hands outstretched, and one's just chimney brick with a coat of whitewash. But there's a little white table with a lamp on top, and a shelf between the legs for my books and my little wooden horse. My room is all whitewash except the ivory moldings, and it's all mine.

It'd be a monk's cell except there's a rag rug on the floor

that I braided and sewed from scraps of our party dresses, so it's every bright color you can fathom all wound around one another. The bed's a straw-tick cot I can just about turn over in, soft and clean and hay sweet, and nobody sleeps on those sheets but me. We work downstairs, in the fancy chambers. My room's a dormer, and it's warm from the heat rising from the kitchen, and best of all, it's got a little glazed window I can see over the rooftops from, to the Sound. I can't see the street, because of the roofline blocking my view, but that's all to the good the way I figure.

It was light, which ain't so unusual for me going to bed, but my window faces near to west as makes no difference and anyway, the rain was coming down through a thick gray pall like a dirty fleece. I drew the shades and the curtains and pulled on my nightshirt, but when I laid myself down I couldn't sleep a wink. I just stared up at that dormer ceiling and picked at my cuticles with my thumb, which is a terrible bad habit.

I could feel every stem of rye in my usually cozy straw tick as if they was laid across my skin like flogging stripes. You'd think I'd never hemmed nor ironed the sheets, nor pulled them tight, there was that many wrinkles gouging me every time I rolled over.

Eventually, I pulled myself over the side slat—which was a mite more challenging than it should of been—and fetched my diary from its hiding place under a half-loose floorboard. The diary's a little book I sewed the pages of myself, and stitched a pretty calico cover for. I got a pencil off my table and I balanced the little book on my knee to write. I should of given it cover boards, for sure, but I'm still working out how to bind those. I think I might need the big sewing machine, and maybe some kind of special needle.

Writing settles me, like, and I figured if I could get the night down I might be able to get it out of my head for a few hours and get some rest. My eyes burned and my joints ached, I was that tired, and maybe a little dizzy from the whiskey.

But I couldn't write so good, or get anything laid in a proper straight furrow. Instead, I picked out words and sentences on the paper all wrong and in any sort of order and only realized how little sense or progress I was making when I tasted the splintery, resiny ponderosa pine of the pencil. I'd chewed through the yellow paint. That kind of pine somewhat smells like cinnamon, but it turns out it don't taste like cinnamon at all.

Anyway, I must of slept eventually because I woke with a page of my diary crumpled and damp under my cheek and my pencil on the floor by the bed. My room had gone stuffy. The rain was over, and when the sun came out it just about turned the whole city into a sweat lodge, even in winter. I knowed from the way the light hit my window that I'd missed breakfast, which Connie dishes up around one.

Miss Bethel and Miss Francina had let me sleep right through it, too, which only happens if you're sick.

I'm not sure the sleep had left me feeling any the better. My nightshirt was stuck down with sweat despite the chill by the window. I felt tacky and bloated and sore like my courses was coming on, though it wasn't time for that yet. I smoothed out my diary best I could and pressed the book out open under the ticking to draw some wet out of it, but I couldn't get the wrinkle out of the page. Then I washed my face in tepid water from the basin and found pencil lead all over the rag when I was done. I combed and corralled my hair and found a clean chemise. All part of the routine.

When I finished it, I finally let myself think about the night before, about Effie and Crispin and Merry Lee. And Peter Bantle.

And Priya.

I started to shake all over again and had to sit back down.

By the time I made it into petticoats and a country dress—I wasn't fighting my way into stays and a bustle alone—and groped my way down them narrow stairs, it was late enough that I figured I'd best avoid the parlor, me without makeup nor a company dress and all. There might be men out there any time after breakfast—luncheon I suppose it was, for some. I came down all prepared to sneak through the hall back to the kitchen and annoy Connie for whatever the news might be.

But the double doors from the hall into the parlor stood open, and the outside doors was shut. The grandfather clock by the library door said 2:20, so I hadn't really slept all that long. The rugs Merry Lee'd bled on were missing, replaced for now by some slightly worn ones that usually lived in the hall upstairs. Signor was tea-cozied in the armchair by the fire, though—the blue-and-lemon settee that I think he knows makes his eyes look brighter—and he blinked at me in recognition.

Crispin crouched down between his knees with a whisk and a pan chasing crumbs of ruby glass—you'd think they'd of all fallen outside from the gun blast, but maybe that only happens in detective stories. Street noise drifted down. Some of it sounded like chanting, and I wondered if we was being picketed by those placard-waving hypocrites of the Women's Christian Anti-Prostitution and Soiled Dove Rescue League again—though it seemed like I was mostly hearing male voices. Crispin hadn't gotten around to boarding the broken bits over yet, though his hammer hung in a belt loop and some boards lay across the outstretched arms of the unoccupied sewing machine to his left. It was a great brass armature, gears and pistons, every flat surface ornamented with curlicued gold-chased plates and carved plaques of ivory and shell cameo. A cast-iron door on the fabric coffer in its chest read: SINGER SEWING MACHINE COMPANY.

If you're going to pay fifty dollars tax per week per head on something you won't much use, Madame Damnable figures it might as well be pretty.

The sun was high enough and at the right angle to trickle in dusty rays through the broke-open fan transom. In its better shine, even down here at the bottom of the well, you could see where Effie's shotgun pellets had chewed up the fancy wood-work over the door. The light picked out rusty tones in the curls around Crispin's pate—and a sprinkle of tight-coiled gray—before bouncing up across the room to sparkle on Miss Beth-el's crystal, on the looking glasses in the back bar, and off the gold threads in the striped silk bodice Miss Bethel wore under her starched white apron, too.

She stood behind her bar, fitting the pieces of her shotgun back together after cleaning and oiling. I felt a lick of shame—Effie or me should of seen to it last night—but I reckoned it was too late now. I stopped in the doorway beside the short leg of the bar, though, and waited for her to notice me.

Miss Bethel had curly dark red hair and a spray of freckles across her turned-up nose, and though she was born in the United States, she looked as Irish as the potato famine. To my knowing, nobody ever got out of her what she was doing out here in the territories, but she was one of the ones who went to church every Sunday. She had a soft-seeming sweet round face given the lie by her chin and her disposition. Though she weren't big nor broad, she wore enough skirts to make up for it, in a silk striped between emerald moiré and white with em-erald figures. A long fall of cream lace dripped from her cuff at each elbow. The gleaming back bar—pride of Madame Dam-nable's and in fact the whole waterfront district of Rapid City—dwarfed her, but that don't signify. It would of still dwarfed her if she were Miss Francina's size: a great carved cliff of ma-hogany inlaid in borders with jet and ivory, it was figured with

wiry satyrs, centaurs with two broad chests apiece, plump cu-
pids, and embonpoint nymphs with their great spirals of carved
hair like carousel ponies' manes. They was all nude, and I'd
seen men take upward of seven minutes just to order a double
brandy at that bar, so taken were they with those voluptuous
carved bellies and thighs.

Miss Bethel finished oiling the rails of the bolt and slid it
into place with a greasy click. She frowned over her work, nodding. When she set the shotgun down and noticed me, the frown
stayed. It weren't no welcoming expression. But she tipped her
head to the rack of the bottles against the spotless looking glass
set in the carvings behind her and said, "Do you want a bit of
sherry, Karen dear?"

"I'd better have a bit of breakfast first," I said. I didn't feel
hungry, but food would likely be wise. Eat when you can, my
father used to say. You never know when can will turn to can't.
"I should of cleaned the gun. I'm sorry."

Crispin glanced over his shoulder and nodded at me. I nodded back. Signor ignored us all like a sultan.

"Fear not," she said, and bent her knees to drop it once more
across its hooks under the bar. "You'd other things on your
mind. Both of the colored girls are fine, by the way—Merry
Lee hasn't woken, but Lizzie says she's sleeping naturally and
hasn't taken a fever. The other girl won't leave her side. Connie
brought her up a cot and more food."

Miss Bethel can call Miss Lizzie just Lizzie. I'd never dare.

"Thank you," I said. "I'm glad you wasn't angry about the
gun."

"Weren't angry, dear," she said, and handed me the glass of
sherry anyway. "Connie set you aside some breakfast, I think.
You'd better go see."

————

In the kitchen, I found that Connie hadn't just set me aside some breakfast—she'd laid plans to make me some special. I set the sherry glass down on the table to wait until after I got some food in my head, and in the meantime I sipped the big mug of coffee she gave me. We save the pretty coffee cups that don't hold but a mouthful for the customers. She also gave me an even bigger mug of buttermilk kept cool in the cistern, since we was too close to the Sound to have a well. As soon as I tasted that buttermilk, I realized that "didn't feel hungry" was a lie: my stomach growled like a pit dog, and Connie shot me a sharp sideways grin from over her smoking black fry pan.

Connie was medium everything: medium size, medium color, medium featured, medium aged, medium bosomed . . . with a temper that never much varied up or down. But she had enough energy for three women. She bustled around for ten minutes and dished me up bread soaked in eggs and fried in dripping with molasses and butter on top. The salmon weren't running anymore, but there was a big piece of smoked Chinook with it, sweet and flaky and splashed with dill and cider vinegar.

It's plain farm food, sure, but I'm a plain farm girl. I like it better than the poached eggs and hollandaise and asparagus and whatnot we serve to the tricks at a 500 percent markup. They come in special for the food, and Connie's in charge of the maids as serves in the dining room and changes our sheets. Those girls don't live in the house, and a lot of 'em is younger than Madame would employ in a horizontal position anyhow.

The johns like to think they're getting treated fancy by the fancy women. I just like to eat. And if a little extra bit of molasses sort of smudged over onto the salmon, there wasn't much finer eating from here to China, in my mind.

Connie left me alone to chew in peace and went back to chopping onions for supper. She kept her nails short and clean white. Her hands were medium sized, too, and clever-quick as anything. Tendons played across the backs like the strings inside a grand piano. Like the spine of her knife as it rose and fell.

She's got a gadget that's supposed to do a lot of those things for you, but she don't hardly need it. You've never seen an onion diced so fine.

I was just clutching my coffee mug and watching her, blinking like a satiated cat, when Miss Lizzie stomped in wearing her street boots and a scowl. Her face was all pinched up around her spectacles like she meant to hold them in place by frowning, and her shoulders rode up to her ears. I could hear the piano wire tendons in her clockwork hand clicking as she made a fist with it—and Miss Lizzie ain't the sort to show her emotions that way. She's enough of a lady to make Miss Bethel proud.

I was on my feet in a second, the warmth and comfort of that coffee mug forgotten. My mouth opened, but Miss Lizzie stopped the words coming out with a look. Not a mean look. Just a Miss Lizzie look. One that didn't brook no messing about. "They're fine, Karen," she said, like she could read my thoughts.

I wouldn't put it past her.

I sat back down, slowly. Connie slid my empty plate away. "Pie, Karen honey?"

I shook my head as she handed Miss Lizzie a mug of coffee all her own. I took mine with cream and sugar; Miss Lizzie drank hers black as a cowpuncher and I bet she would of boiled it over eggshells if it wouldn't of made Connie blanch.

I did sort of want pie, but I didn't *need* it, if you know what I mean, and I wanted to hear whatever Miss Lizzie was working herself up to venting. Seamstresses get to have a good sense of when people want to talk, and if something's eating them, and even just what sort of people they are. And that hunch in Miss Lizzie's shoulders said that whatever was eating *her* was about the size and temperament of a grizzly bear.

She hooked a chair out with one boot—abrupt, but she always is—and thumped into it. She blew across the coffee, pushing lazy coils of steam into a streamer, and slurped the hot edge of the mug. "Picketers," she said.

"I heard them," I answered. I picked my coffee up, too, because talking goes easier if the other person sees you doing what they're doing. "The Women's Christian Anti-Prostitution and Soiled Dove Rescue League?"

"God no," she said. "It's the Democrats. On the street right over our heads, more's the pity. Just where anybody who wanted to pay us a friendly afternoon visit would have to walk through, and be spotted and recognized."

"We're closed anyway," Connie said, putting a sandwich on a plate in front of her. Ham, pickles, and sea beans, it looked like. On one of Connie's hard rolls.

I filched a sea bean. It crunched between my teeth, briny and grassy and good.

Miss Lizzie fixed me with a look, but she didn't mean nothing by it. She took a bite of her sandwich, chewed, drank coffee, and said, "We won't be closed all night. The glazier just got here. And guess what mayoral candidate those Democrats are supporting?"

Connie shook her head. "Not Dyer Stone, I take it?"

I hid a smile behind my hand, because we wasn't supposed to know about Mayor Stone's occasional visits. Anyway, he was a Republican—the party of Abraham Lincoln and Rutherford B. Hayes.

"Peter Bantle," Miss Lizzie spat, and crunched into her sandwich vindictively.

Chapter Four

Since we was closed and since it weren't raining, after I just about licked my plate Connie took advantage of my gratitude to send me to the market. I wanted to check on Priya—and Merry Lee, sure, but really mostly Priya, and I wasn't sure if I liked myself more or less for being honest enough to admit it— but Miss Lizzie got that line between her eyebrows and told me that neither girl was to be disturbed before midnight at the earliest. When I, of course, would probably be hard at work stargazing. Or ceiling gazing, since you can't see much in the way of stars through plaster, or Rapid City's constant fog and clouds.

So Connie claimed I needed a distraction and put a pile of net bags in my hand and sent me off to the market with Miss Francina to shop for supper. Even though it was sunny—albeit already getting on toward evening, this late in the year—I hooked an umbrella on to my arm. I was wise to the ways of Rapid City. We had accounts with some of the merchants, but Miss Bethel—who kept the books—signed me out a fistful of paper dollars. I'd heard some in the old Confederacy wouldn't touch the hundred-dollar notes with their portraits of Abraham Lincoln, but given gold rush prices all up and down the waterfront I was happy to fold up a couple and shove them in my button pocket. She also handed me a pile of pennies and trimes and cartwheels, for making change with.

Miss Francina and I walked along beside the cart, to stretch our legs and because it was more pleasant than jouncing. The road was fair enough dry—I skipped over a few stinking puddles—and all around on the horizon the mountains were out in every direction, looming up out of blue distance like genies standing in their smoke.

The Bayview Market is two lies in just one name—Rapid City has a Sound, not a Bay, though what the dictionary difference is I couldn't be the one to tell you, and you can't see the water from it anyhow on account of the shipworks dry docks—but it is just about hard enough by to smell the sea, and it's about my favorite place on earth, barring my own private bedroom. It's a long redwood building the size of those dry docks, up on stilts and with the doors guarded by wooden stairways on account of maybe flooding, what with where it sits. Redwood stands up to a soaking, anyway, and it was built long before the street-raising plan went into effect. Now it's just eight feet up from the road instead of thirty, even if the road isn't quite finished yet.

You used to be able to row to it when it flooded. Now there's talk of putting in stone steps, the better for folk to fall down 'em and split their heads when the granite slicks up in winter. Still, it's full one end to the other with market stalls. There's hothouse flowers in January, and oranges from China and alligator pears from Mexico, and the freshest seafood you ever tasted in your life. Scallops as big as your hand, that you cut and eat like a filet steak. Oysters by the gross and by the dozen, plain briny honest fare for whores and tradesmen alike. Agate-red salmon and agate-green lobsters that turn a whole different, brighter red when you boil them. Saffron, cinnamon, nutmeg, peppercorns. Sea salt in great soft, sticky flakes. Cheese from as far away as Vermont and France. Blackberry wine and good brown local ale. Fresh-baked bread, coffee beans like green pearls, tea that's come from as far away as Priya did. Anything you have ever eaten or wanted to eat, basically, and a slew of other things besides—baskets, cloth, Singer sewing machines right out of the Sears catalog. Even made-up clothes for the prospectors heading north who didn't bring nobody to sew a thing for them. Really sew, I mean, though I suppose most wives know a bit about the other kind of sewing, too.

I could spend a week walking the sawdust-strewn planks of that place, nibbling samples of sardines and candied salmon. So it's a good thing Connie sent me with a list, because otherwise I might wind up bewildered and wandering the aisles until I wasted away to a haint. (There is more than a few stories that the Bayview is haunted. Mostly I think they're jokes. Mostly.)

Miss Francina and me bought three kinds of bread—which I stuffed into a net bag—and two kinds of cake. She took charge of those. We also split a small apple pie as a snack. Most of the other fruit was only good as preserves by now, though you could buy some ready canned in glass jars as pie filling, but the end of the apple harvest was still coming in and the pie tasted like paradise with ginger sugar sprinkled on top. So I guess I got my pie anyway, and you know it turned out I did need it after all. We got ten pounds of onions, half-white and half-yellow, and arranged with a butcher to deliver fifty pounds of fresh beef and venison, and similar provisioning from a fish-monger. The potatoes would be delivered, too. The greengrocer had some of those Chinese oranges with the real soft skins, and I filled up a bag with 'em and another bag with Brussels sprouts. They're just fancy cabbage, but the johns will pay extra for 'em and I like cabbage well enough.

The eggs and the milk came to the house on delivery, so we didn't have to worry about those.

By the time I'd sent Miss Francina back to our hired cart for the third time to drop off packages, I was feeling quite pleased with myself. Miss Francina is nothing but good qualities, but none of those good qualities is the patience to cook well or do the kind of picking over potatoes for green spots it takes to handle the marketing. I'm good at it—it's no fussier in detail than grooming horses—and I was feeling pretty smug about my good work and Connie's trust as I shouldered a net bag of onions with one hand and picked over mushrooms in a bin with the other. I think I was even humming to myself— some fashionable tune that Pollywog, who was opera struck, had been playing on the parlor baby grand while the Professor wasn't looking.

I'd never take so little care now. But the hand on my wrist caught me by complete surprise. Of course, I flatter myself that my enemies—and now I know I got enemies, which weren't a word I would of used in those days—wouldn't do anything so careless now, neither. They'll have learned a little respect.

But as I said, I wasn't expecting nobody to grab me just then. I guess I was young yet and not too smart. I just stared at that hand on my wrist in shock. It was big, scarred across the back, curls of coarse tawny hair sprouting between the knuckles. Exactly the sort of hand you might expect to grab you unexpectedly, except for the woman's dainty gold ring on one pinky.

I followed the broad bones of the wrist up to the elbow and the rolled-up calico sleeve. Home-sewn, it looked like. Somebody cared enough about this fellow to hem his clothes with care.

As for me, I didn't care much for him at all. He was squeezing my arm something fearful.

My eyes snapped up to his face. He wasn't as tall as his hand predicted, but he was even broader. He had bad teeth and good skin, dark blond hair greased into ringlets, a red silk kerchief inside his collar tied in a fancy knot. I didn't know for sure he worked for Peter Bantle, but let's say I could guess.

"You're one of that Damnable woman's tarts," he said. He had a pleasant light voice. I thought Pollywog would of called it a tenor. He sounded more surprised than mean. "Well, you'd better come along with old Bill now."

Nobody nearby seemed to notice he was grabbing me. Or if they noticed they didn't care, even though I wasn't tarted up just then. I was wearing my plain blue muslin country dress and a carriage coat for marketing, and no paint. Amazing what people can fail to see when it's a man doing it to a woman, even a respectable-looking woman.

I hit him across the kisser with ten pounds of onions and he let go of my arm.

The net bag held, to my surprise. A couple of his teeth were less sturdy, as I surmised from the way he staggered back, clutching at his mouth, and then worked his jaw, doubled over, spat red—my stomach lurched—and grimaced. Around us, people withdrew in a circle—some watching, some walking hastily away. Behind me, the greengrocer pulled the boxes of mushrooms out of harm's way.

Bill blinked tears from his eyes, then fastened his gaze on me. "Bitch," he snarled—why they never think of anything cleverer I'll never know. When he lifted his hand up again, this time there was a fighting knife glittering in it.

But by then, I had the umbrella in my right hand, the wrist still red and burning from knocking his clenched hand loose. A knife's sharper, but an umbrella has reach, and mine has a pretty good steel ferrule to the tip. He was a lunge-and-slash fighter and he had the weight and reach on me, but Bruce Memery taught me to brawl when he taught me to shoot—and to ride—and when Bill stepped to his right to dodge my umbrella's swat and swiped at me again I surprised him by not jumping back but instead spanking him across the hand with the onions again. It worked—his hand went up—and I jabbed him in the breadbasket with the umbrella. I might of gigged him like a frog except the ferrule struck on one of his canvas braces and so it just made him *oof* like a mule when you deflate her for saddling. More's the pity.

He went skidding backward, buying me a couple of seconds, but the Spanish notch on the back of the Bowie snagged in the net and the onion bag ripped. Onions bounced everywhere.

I heard myself panting, watching the onions roll. A quick glance left and right didn't show me anything else I could use to foul the knife, and the umbrella wouldn't stand up to more than one or two cuts. There was no sign of Miss Francina, and even if she heard the cries going up and came at a run she'd hit the press of people going the other way. It would take her too long to get to me. With the knife out, the crowd was pulling back farther, and still nobody stepped in to help me. I could try to jump the greengrocer's stand, but a bustle and petticoats weren't designed for acrobatics.

Bill looked at the torn bag in my hand and smiled, showing the teeth I'd busted. A little spit-thinned blood dripped down his chin. At least he shaved; I think I would of puked for sure if it were trickling through stubble.

I wasn't stronger, and quicker only helped me so far. I supposed I just couldn't get lucky enough for Bill to trip on the onions and break his fool neck. If I was going to live through this—or get out of it without getting dragged to Peter Bantle's

house, and from there God knows what might happen—I'd
have to be smarter.

As Bill stepped up—careful of his footing between the rolling skunk eggs, damn him to sixteen different hells (one for
each piece)—I looked him in the eyes and pinned a smile to
my face like I planned to appliqué it there. "So—" I panted.
Each couple of words came out between a gasp. "I'm betting
Peter Bantle don't know one of his toughs goes about waving
knives at women in the Bayview."

Somebody in the crowd heard me. I knowed by the gasp I
heard that wasn't my own. I was just afraid that Bill might be
too het up to realize he was doing something stupid—or too
het up to stop doing it, even if he noticed.

I never had to find out.

Somebody pushed out of the crowd and stepped between
us. It weren't Miss Francina, neither.

I got a confused impression of a man's big shoulders: black
hair in ringlets on a black coat, black hat, tan deerskin range
gloves, black boots chased with silver thread. Whoever he was,
he was built on the scale suggested by Bill's hands. I couldn't
see over his shoulder.

But even from the back, I recognized the gesture he made
as he lifted his left hand to his lapel and ran his thumb under
it, flaunting a star that must be on his breast. He flipped the
wing of his duster back, and I saw his right hand cross his body
and hover over the holster tied down to his left thigh with a
rawhide string. There was another holster on his right thigh,
but the butts of his guns faced the wrong way—forward. My
da would of blanched to see that cross-body draw, but some
people said it was faster.

"U.S. Deputy Marshal," he said. A big voice to go with a
big man, and I'd put him in Texas or Arkansas. "If I were you,
mister, I'd put that knife away."

Bill drew himself up, but he didn't cringe. Pity. It'd make my life easier if he was cowardly as well as stupid. His voice dripped scorn and disbelief as he sneered, "*Marshal.*"

He lowered the knife, and the gun didn't come out.

Bill said, "This slommack broke my teeth!" His voice came out hissy and bad, on breath flecked with red spit. I ducked back behind the Marshal so I wouldn't have to see. It'd probably impress my rescuer less if I shot the cat all over his shoes.

"Is that so?" said the Marshal. He didn't look back at me. "This little thing?"

There aren't a lot of men who can get away with calling me a little thing. But I could of walked under this one's arm, if he held it out straight, and he was about twice as broad as me. "She tried to stab me with that sword stick!"

"Miss?" the Marshal asked. "I'd like to hear your side of the story."

Well, I don't know when the last time was that a man called me miss when I wasn't buying a chicken from him. "More or less," I allowed. "Except when I stuck him with my umbrella, he was trying to cut me. And when I hit him in the face with a bag of onions, he was trying to kidnap me."

"Huh," said the Marshal, drawling. He had a good voice with that flat Arkansas accent laid over it. "I guess it goes to prove what they say. There's two sides to every story." He paused, tipped his head under the hat, and said, "Mister, I'd guess you'd like to get to a dentist."

I peeked around the Marshal's shoulder. Bantle's man's mouth did a funny thing, that must of hurt like hell over what was left of his teeth. My mama had bad teeth—they killed her when I was nine and that's why Da pretty much raised me as a mustang-camp hellion—and I had an idea of how much pain Bantle's man must be in. His eyes were glassy with it, his skin sweat soaked and pallid now that the fury was draining out of him. His jaw worked, and he swallowed—spit and blood, I imagined.

Thinking about it made me want to up my chuck. I swallowed, too.

The Marshal's gloved hand alighted on the butt of his gun. Bill's eyes followed the soft movement, and when he looked up again you could tell all the fight had puddled in his boots.

"Who gives a damned Negra a badge?" he asked no one in particular, and faded back into the crowd.

I blinked. The Marshal turned sideways, towering over me but keeping one eye on Bill's retreating back. Once the crowd hid Bill, the Marshal's hand came off his gun and he ducked down a little to talk to me more level like, so I could see more than the line of his chin.

He said, "Then I reckon my reputation don't precede me."

He was a stone handsome man, and I say that even though for me humping with men is just how I earn my crust and covers. His cheeks and chin were scraped clean around a thick, well-trimmed mustache, and his brown eyes shone. His face was also brown and shiny as a toasted coffee berry, and he smelled like fresh coffee, too. I thought he might of been about forty years old. He weren't forty-five.

"Ma'am," he said. His duster's black canvas strained over his shoulders when he tipped his hat. "U.S. Deputy Marshal Bass Reeves, at your service."

And then Miss Francina burst through the crowd in a flurry of lace and wrath. She nearly took Deputy Marshal Reeves' head off before I got between 'em, and we had some explaining to do while we picked the onions up.

Deputy Marshal Reeves had a gallant streak, and never so much as gave Miss Francina a double take—well, fair enough, a small second look, but he didn't say nothing, and Miss Francina's tall enough and pretty enough to deserve a second look under any circumstance and he didn't say nothing. He offered me one arm—I had to reach way up to take his elbow—and Miss Francina the other and insisted on escorting us home.

Since me and Miss Francina had previously discussed it and elected to walk rather than rattling along in the cart with the turnips, this was not only no hardship—it was pleasure. I informed Marshal Reeves that in my opinion, his offer was downright neighborly of him. He explained that he was up from the Indian Territory in pursuit of a fugitive—that's how he said it, "fugitive"—and it had been his pleasure to render assistance. Which is also how he said it.

He gave me and Miss Francina each a brand-new Morgan silver dollar, as a keepsake, too. I hadn't seen one before, except in engravings in the newspapers, for they was new that year and only minted in Philadelphia. A dollar weren't a lot of money in Rapid City, what with the big hissing ships chugging their way back and forth from Anchorage every couple of days, but it was a pretty thing.

The coin was large and heavy, bigger than a hub wafer candy. Much bigger than the fish-scale gold dollars I was used to, more like an eagle. It did have a woman's face on it like a gold dollar, though, side on. Profile, I think you'd say. But it weren't no Indian princess. It was a Lady Liberty, like on the gold dollars from before the war.

Except this was a different Liberty. She had a sterner look to her, a lifted chin, a good strong nose, and a plump line of her jaw. She made me feel stubborn, and like getting things done. Something about looking at her eased that funny shameful itch I'd been carrying since the night before, and I slipped her into my bodice for safekeeping.

"Karen honey," Miss Francina said, "she could be your sister."

She held her coin up beside me as if studying the likeness, and I laughed. I knowed she was just pulling my tail.

It felt good to laugh, though. At first, it felt like I hadn't done it in about a thousand years, like I was creaky and my laugher needed to be oiled, but then I warmed up a little and it flowed naturally. I did catch Marshal Reeves looking at me sort of odd and sideways, however, as if he'd caught the false note and wondered.

He didn't wonder long, because we passed what by the banners and placards must of been a Democratic Party meeting spilling out into the streets on every side of the folded former bank where the Brotherhood of the Protective Order of the Sasquatch met. There was men of every shape and size, but only men and those men only of one color, and nearly every one of 'em had a Klondike beard like he'd just landed from Alaska. They were too well fed for that, though, and they wore city shoes, though most of them didn't quite fit in their clothing.

I saw the Marshal frowning after them, and Miss Francina frowning at her boots. A black man had reason to hate Democrats, for sure, but I felt like there was more to it that I wasn't understanding. When we were far enough along to be out of earshot, I asked.

Miss Francina fluffed her lace sleeves, a sure sign of irritation, but I didn't think it was aimed at me. She chewed her lip as if trying to find the right words to explain but never quite had to. Because after a look over to her for permission, the Marshal huffed his mustache out, glanced over his shoulder, and said, "Voter fraud," in a voice that dripped frustration. "Every one of those bearded men is going to vote two or three times, in different wards, depending on the skill of the Party's barbers."

"Oh," I said. I was alive for the war, of course, but I mostly remembered it with a child's jumbled sense of uneasiness, disconnection, and lack of self-determination. And it wasn't as if I could vote. But I did remember President Hayes' election, and the scandals instantly telegraphed across the nation when because of voter fraud three different states submitted two different slates of electors—one Democratic and one Republican. Congress had to decide, and some people said Republican Hayes had made a corrupt bargain with the Democrats to get his slate of electors ratified.

It occurred to me to wonder if Marshal Reeves had ever voted in an election. He had mentioned he was in from the Indian Territory, but his voice said Arkansas. Arkansas was a state.

This Marshal might of voted in 1872, I realized. And again in 1876. It wouldn't of been possible before that. I wondered if it had made him feel different. Or if he had felt like he was *making* a difference, for that matter.

Of course, it'd never be possible for me. So when I thought about those men in the prospector's beards voting three, four times apiece and selling every one of them . . . I don't mind saying it griped me.

I was quiet while we walked, chewing that over with the rough weave of the Marshal's sleeve warm against my gloves. He seemed to be taking in the sights, and Miss Francina indulged him. There were some smells, too, but mostly those weren't so enjoyable.

All around us, Rapid City was booming. We could hear the scrape and rattle of the huge logs being skidded down Skid Road, not two blocks over, and the cursing of the men trying to control their overworked mules as the animals in turn strained to control the logs scraping over paving stones. The streets about boiled over, teeming with carriages and pedestrians and steam cars and the threat of fatal collisions. Scaffolds held up a half-constructed building on every block, and there was a steam shovel or a hydraulic crane at every site. I'd swear the scaffold and construction companies just moved 'em around from week to week as new tenements and blocks of offices were thrown up with abandon in every direction, each one taller and more gilded than the last. After the Chinese lynchings and then the riots in San Francisco the previous year, nobody had wanted to hire the Chinese ironworkers left over now that the biggest planned rail lines were built. But that was all forgotten now, qualms sacrificed on the altar of the goddess Necessity, as Miss Bethel would say.

Finally, we came to Madam Damnable's, and Marshal Reeves gallantly handed us onto the ladder, then followed us down. At the bottom, by the red cut-glass lanterns flanking the door, he paused. The locksmith and the glazier had both arrived, and the stoop was a confusion of ladders and toolboxes and boards laid across the inevitable puddles. It looked like we'd be open at dinnertime. A young rat skittered past. Trying to look lady-like in front of the Marshal, I didn't kick at it.

"Well," the Marshal said. Again, I waited for the double take, the comment. Instead, his silver star glittered in the oblique evening light as he dug in a pocket of his duster. He came out with a parchment roll with a label gummed to it that read: *Chase and Company,* and I laughed, suddenly, remembering that I'd compared the silver dollar to a candy like this.

Up at street level, I could tell by the sounds that the cart had arrived, and that Crispin was going about unloading it. He'd bring the loads in by the upstairs door around back, where there was a dumbwaiter to bring them down to the kitchen.

The Marshal stuffed his range gloves into the pocket the candy'd come out of, then peeled a hub wafer off the pack and offered it to me. Wintergreen, my favorite. It was a gift,

I knowed. But he touched it with his bare fingers rather than offering me the parchment packet to pick my own one out, and so I knowed it was also a test.

I plucked it away from him and put it past my lips, dry and starchy and sweet. It barely fit in my mouth. Soon, the edges started to crumble against my tongue. He gave the clove one to Miss Francina, and we stood around and sucked for a bit. When I had swallowed enough to talk again, I asked him, "Do you wish to come in?"

Marshal Reeves tipped his hat again. "I've a wife at home, miss."

So he hadn't misconstrued the lanterns. He just hadn't overmuch cared that my new friend Bill was telling the truth about my line of employment.

Having a wife wouldn't stop a lot of men, but I wasn't about to point that out to the rare bird who would let it. So Miss Francina tried another tack. "We have a good cook. I think Karen and I owe you some measure of thanks for rescuing us, Marshal Reeves."

His smile ruffled his mustache. I thought of draperies. But he shook his head again. "Miss Wilde. Miss Memery. The pleasure of your company has been more than adequate recompense."

She glanced at me. I made my eyes wide. She covered a smile and said to the Marshal, "We could keep a look out for your fugitive. If you came in and told us about him."

But a third time, he declined. "I'd rather word didn't get back to the desperado that I'm hunting him," he said simply. He patted my hand and Miss Francina's and, in a swirl of duster panels, vanished back up the ladder into the nascent twilight above.

I palmed Lady Liberty, warm from my bodice, and considered her stubborn profile. How much did they pay U.S. Marshals, that he could afford to hand these out like candy drops?

Miss Francina and I went around to the side door to get inside. Miss Francina went back to the kitchen to oversee the unloading. I went to give Miss Bethel her receipts and change.

In the parlor—still without clients—Miss Bethel was pouring what looked like bright chips of confetti into a crystal candy dish. I wandered over and looked. They were pink and white candy hearts, and they looked just like the hub wafers. A whole shipment of Chase and Company candy must of come in by freight train, I realized, and now everybody in the city could get some. We'd all be sick of them before the last parchment-paper roll got eaten up.

A moment later, I realized each one had some words on it. I picked one up that had bounced out of the bowl. *Married in satin, love won't be lasting.*

My mouth still tasted of hub wafer, so I flicked the heart back in with its sisters. "Suits us," I said.

Miss Bethel winked.

Chapter Five

We did plan to open for supper, and judging by the number of men halooing in the third-floor windows starting around sundown, such notoriety around town as might be attending Peter Bantle's early-morning visit and his new political ambitions weren't likely to do our trade any harm. I went up to the dressing room and got kitted, all crinolines and kilted skirts and my tits about falling out the top of my daffodil taffeta dress whenever I grabbed a breath. Bea helped me with the beauty patch and did my eyes and lips. She pulled Mr. Marcel's iron from its heater by the fire and did my hair up with bright paste combs. I did her paint for her: she wears different colors. I'm hopeless with her hair, though, so Miss Francina came over to help.

We all three made sure we was supplied with sheepskins. Syphilis is a bad way to go. Miss Lizzie's machine can handle more immediate problems, though that ain't a concern for Miss Francina—but it hurts like hell I hear and there's always the risk of bleeding out.

And I don't want no john's baby saddling me. I'm saving

up. Someday I'll own a stable and be a respectable business-woman. You'll see. The girls who stay in the trade, more often than not they keep sliding down the ladder, getting paid less and less for worse and worse work until eventually they *can't* save and they *can't* make a future. Or some of 'em drink too much, which Madame don't allow. That don't end well. Not ever.

I'm not sure why, but that silver cartwheel Marshal Reeves gave me, I tucked it inside my shoe and buttoned up over it. I could feel it there, but the pressure weren't bad; it just sat against my ankle over the stocking and was comforting, like a squeezed hand. As I was helping Bea with her buttons, the other girls flocked and fluttered in and out. Some dressed faster; some took longer. Pollywog took the longest of anybody, and you could never tell why. She did her long hair in straight blond braids like a German girl and wore what came the closest a grown woman's dresses could come to an eyelet pinafore.

Effie must of gotten ready on the usual schedule, because I didn't see her until she ducked into the room already laced into royal-blue satin with a rosette over the bumroll so big I couldn't imagine how she sat. She gave me a squeeze across the shoulders, careful of her powder, and handed me a note. It was from Miss Bethel, saying as how she'd mentioned to Madam Damnable what had happened to Francina and me and Madam Damnable has sent a card and a cake on our behalf to the lodging house where Marshal Reeves was staying, along with an invitation to dine.

He won't accept, I thought, but it was a pretty gesture. And never mind how Madame knowed where he was staying. What would of been surprising was if Madame didn't know or have ways of finding out.

"Madame wants to talk with you," Effie said. "Before you go down to the parlor."

She must of seen my eyes get big, because she patted me on the shoulder. "She's in with the colored girls. They got moved into the Butterfly Room while you was out."

Bea gave her an eyebrow over "the colored girls." Effie colored her own self—more of a sunburn red than her usual peaches and cream and freckles—and grimaced an apology. "Anyway, she's waiting on you."

I couldn't of jumped faster if I'd been an electrocuted frog. Bea caught me, wiped a lip-rouge smudge off my tooth, and then nodded as I passed inspection. She patted me on the bumroll and stood aside as I swished from the room in a profusion of petticoats.

The Butterfly Room was on the fourth story, same as the dressing room, and at the back of the building. It was across the hall to Crispin's room, too, which was a good idea if there was to be any trouble. Either from inside the room or from people come to look for them as we was sheltering.

I drew up outside it and stood, catching my breath and dignifying myself. Madame's hallways were full of mirrors, surprising no one, and I glanced into the one by the door for a last spot check. Then I drew up my shoulders and stepped inside.

Madame was seated on the red-and-orange butterfly-patterned divan off to my left, the most whorehouse thing in her whole place. Her hands rested on the handle of her cane, as if she'd just sat down or was about to heave herself to her feet. Her hair was piled on her head and Marcel curled into a fortress pinned down under a pearl cannonade. She didn't turn to look at me, just said, "Come in, Karen."

The room didn't reek of blood or sickness or rot, more's the mercy, or even of the chamber pot. Given some sickrooms I've been in, I was that relieved. There were two empty bowls and two mugs on the sideboard on a tray—bean soup, by the flecks of bacon stuck to the indigo willow ware. Mostly the air smelled like strong Indian tea.

Merry Lee lay on the left side of the big brass bed, but she was on her back, propped up, and her eyes were open. I wondered if the pillow pushing against her bandage made it hurt worse or less, like when you push a cloth against a cut to soothe the pain. She looked even thinner awake, but other than that . . . bigger, somehow. Even though she was greenish with loss of blood.

She had a face shaped like an oval shell cameo and a barely there button nose, and her straight black hair—real black, not rust-black like what was left of Crispin's—was cropped off shorter than a boy's, like that of a woman who's had scarlet fever. I didn't think they'd cut it because she was shot, though, since I recollected it had been like that when she came in last night. It looked fetching, wisps framing her gamine eyes. It was probably practical for running across rooftops, but I had to pull my fingertips away from my own hair, never cut, and still a shudder.

"Gamine." That's another one of Bea's words. It means waif-like, only more so and in French. Which I reckon makes it double.

Merry Lee's right hand had reached out and it clutched Priya's left. I was that shocked. I would never have expected the legendary Merry Lee to show human need to anyone, which just goes to show how young I was then. Priya stood up beside the bed, though somebody had thought to bring her in a straight-backed chair with an upholstered seat. She looked to me like a spoon bent back and forth between your fingers until the bowl's ready to snap off the handle. Work hardened, but brittle.

She'd bathed and changed, but she weren't wearing a dress. She'd on braces and men's tweed trousers too big and too long for her, though not big and long enough to be Crispin's. Left behind by a trick, no doubt. The cuffs was rolled up to show knit socks and carpet slippers, and she wore a white button shirt under a cardigan that probably *was* Crispin's, because it fit her like a smoking jacket. And my heart skipped a beat to look at her.

I was staring. She stared back, challenging—angry—and I looked down. *Blast.*

"I don't blame you." My voice, and my lips were moving, which meant it must of been my words, but I didn't remember deciding on 'em.

"I'm sorry?" She didn't sound any less cultivated and for-bidding than the night before.

I picked my chin up again—I could hear Miss Bethel lectur-ing in the back of my head—and met her gaze. "For not want-ing to wear a dress. I don't blame you."

I could feel Madame's bright gaze moving between us. I didn't know if I should say more, or if it meant I had already said too much. I bit my lip and hesitated.

The corner of her mouth twitched. She wouldn't care if I did. "Madame says one of Bantle's men tried to snatch you away today, Miss Memery."

My mouth stuck half-open, slack as a child's. I hadn't been about to tell her. I guess maybe I had thought I was protecting her, that she didn't need to know. That she would somehow *not* know that everybody here was taking a risk protecting her.

"I told Madame that I'll move on," she said.

"No!" It left my mouth before I had a chance to stop it, be-fore I had a chance to realize that maybe Madame had *told* Priya she had to move on. That this was Madame's house and I had no say here and if I wanted to defy her it meant I wanted to leave. And if I wanted to leave I wasn't going to find an-other place as comfortable. I could work in a factory or go blind doing real needlework . . . or work in a house that wasn't Madame Damnable's and didn't take care of the girls the same way.

"Karen?" Madame asked, with that look on her face that meant she was weighing up my crimes and deciding what she was going to do about the tally.

"I'm sorry, Madame," I answered. "If you think Priya should go—"

She snorted. "Don't be ridiculous. You're the one who got involved in a fucking knife fight this afternoon, child. You get to have an opinion on whether you're continuing to risk your life on this matter."

Risk my life.

I hadn't actually thought of it. Effie should be here, too—no, Effie had come with the note. She'd already given her verdict, then. And I thought I could tell from the pinch at the corners of Priya's eyes what it was. She and Madame were waiting on my feelings.

So Effie had said she thought they ought to stay. And it wasn't as if Merry Lee could travel. And I knowed weren't none of us giving either girl back to Peter Bantle, that day or evermore.

Unless Madame was asking our opinions and making her own decision when it was all in. Which meant I didn't know what Effie had said and maybe never would. Which, to be honest, would be what I expected of Madame. Just as it was only fair for her to make me say whatever it was that I intended to say in front of Priya. I chewed up, for a moment, how *unfair* it was, too—that Priya's life could be decided by people she'd only just met. But that was everybody's lot, I supposed. Or at least every woman's.

Priya in her trousers and braces seemed to have forgotten she wasn't supposed to look me in the eye. She stared right at me, and I didn't want to be the sort who would inflict what Miss Bethel would call The Agony of Expectation on anybody, much less somebody as brave and bright and wonderful as Priya. But I weren't thinking too fast, somehow. And I was talking even slower. And Priya's fierce expression and the weight of her looking at me weren't making it any easy to twist my mind around to words.

Finally I found my tongue. "Where would I be if you hadn't decided *I* could stay, Madame? Licking radium brushes in the clock factory until my jaw rotted off? Of *course* I want her here."

Madame didn't look up from her knees, but I caught the wrinkle of her smile.

Madame heaved a big breath and said, "Well. I guess that settles it. Priya, Karen here will take you down to meet Miss Francina. She'll find you a room, and if you like you can start work tomorrow. I take thirty percent for the house and thirty percent pays for board. The other forty percent is yours to keep or spend as you see fit, though I fucking recommend you save some of it. The constables get served on the dead, I'm afraid, but we draw up a roster of who waits on 'em by turns and if they want to choose outside of it, they pay. The other ladies will help you find clothes until you can buy some of your own." She did look up, then, and weighed Priya with a glance that like swept over her. "Beatrice's dresses will be a little short, but that's no burden to a tart, and they'll fit until you start to fill out a little—"

"I won't whore," said Priya, as if every word had hooks on it. "And I won't wear skirts."

Madame stopped. She said, "Everyone in this house works. There ain't nothing wrong with honest whoring, child."

"I don't like it."

There wasn't much either of us could say to that. I liked it better than going blind in a factory sewing shirtwaists or whatnot. But we ain't all put together the same, and I suppose God made us different for a reason.

Merry, who had been watching with that fuzzed-over expression people get when they're full up on laudanum, roused herself to say, "We'll find you work, Priyadarshini, if you want work."

Priya smiled sideways at her, then took a big breath and said to Madame, "I can do other things. I can cook, and tend hens, and make a bed. I can't sew fancy, but I can mend. I can garden. I'm a good weaver and can do sums. And I speak Sanskrit, Hindi, Tamil, and Chinese. Northern and Southern."

Madame cocked her head to one side and said, "Cao ni laomu de lanbi!" I could tell whatever she said, it weren't no nice thing.

Priya's lips twitched. In a completely decorous tone, she answered, "Ni ma shi guisunzi, ni ba dai lü maozi!"

Madame stared at Priya for a long moment, then grinned. She rocked back and forth to start heaving to her feet. I itched to give her my hands, but I knowed she wanted to do it on her own, so I grabbed my wrist behind my back and stood tiptoe, looking at Priya as the safer option. *Safer than what?*

Well, it was where my eyes wanted to rest anyway.

Standing at last, Madame said, "You'll ruin your hands scouring pots, girl."

Priya shrugged. "No more than I would if I were married."

Madame made a little moue with her lips and nodded kind of sidewise, conceding. "We'll see. There's certainly enough cleaning to do, and I imagine Connie needs the help. You'll get wages as a domestic, though. You understand that."

"Room and board, too?" Merry asked, eyes bright.

"And room and board," Madame agreed, a wry smile twisting her mouth.

Priya nodded. She crossed the room to me in quick, small steps, then stopped. She turned back toward Madame and wrung her hands in the knit of her giant cardigan. "Madame—"

Her voice broke in a way I didn't understand. Hadn't Madame just given her permission to stay? Even if she didn't want to take in alterations? Me, I'd rather whore than scrub floors; it's easier work and the money's better. But I could see how after Bantle you might not want any man's rooster making up to your birdie, so to speak. What more could she be wanting?

"Speak up, child," Madame said. Not cruelly, she continued, "I can't fucking abide fucking mealymouthed women."

Priya's back straightened. I laid a hand on her elbow, realizing too late that I should of asked her first, but she seemed to stand up straighter at the touch, so that was all right, probably. Her throat rippled with a swallow. Nobody was ever braver than Priya.

"I have a sister," she said. "I don't know if she's still with Bantle, or if he sold her on. She's two years younger. Her name is Aashini."

That wrinkle of a smile on Madame turned into the furrow of a frown. She said, "I'm sorry."

"I want to get her out."

"I'm sure you do," said Madame. She glanced at Merry. "But there's not much *I* can do about it, child. None of those crib-house pimps would sell her to me, not with the way things now stand between us. And it's one thing to shelter an escaped whore. It's another to go steal one." She paused, brows beetling. "Do you even know if she's alive?"

Priya looked at her feet.

Madame nodded. It wasn't a kind nod, but it weren't cruel nor satisfied, neither. It was a tired, just-what-you'd-expect-then nod. Her eyes didn't look as bright as I was used to. "Well then," she said. "I'll take on Peter Bantle if he comes to my house, never fear. But going after him in his den might stretch my resources, young lady. And without more to go on . . . Still. Maybe we can find out something about young . . . Aashini. But I wouldn't hold my breath about it, and doing more may take money."

Money Priya wasn't going to earn as a domestic. That much went without saying.

"I understand," Priya said.

I knowed from the set of Madame's jaw that she was considering ordering Priya not to go looking on her own, neither— and realizing that it would be useless. My da would of said that a good master keeps his authority in part by not asking for the impossible except when he really has to. If he does that, then his horse won't realize it's impossible when he asks for it.

"Go on then," Madame said. "Get on with you."

Priya gave a glance to Merry Lee. Merry Lee nodded wearily. "Go rest," she said in a cracked voice. "I think you'll know where to find me."

It's God's truth that she didn't look like she was getting far, anyway.

I led Priya out the door, shutting it carefully, and showed her where the back stair was. What would of been the servants' stair in most houses, but we used it for getting around without the tricks getting in our way, when the house was working. We rattled down. I should of been eager to get to the parlor before the other girls got all the sober men, and the ones with good breath—there's nothing duller than trying to charm up a snake that won't rise due to whiskey. I like to do my work and get it over with. But Priya seemed to move in a warm glow of comfort, like a good fire on a cold day, and walking along beside her made my heart lift.

We hadn't made the second landing when I thought of something. And as I tend to, I said what I thought before I thought about it enough. If you know what I mean. "A lot of men come in here," I said with a rush. "Most of 'em won't be the same ones that go to the cribs. At least not regular. But one of 'em might . . . know your sister. Or at least have heard of her."

Men brag, I didn't explain. Didn't need to, by the spark of understanding on Priya's face when I turned to look at her.

"Madame said you couldn't help me."

"Madame said *she* couldn't help you." I knowed it was a fine distinction, but wasn't that what the whole profession of lawyers made their living off? "She didn't say nothing about me. Besides, it's just listening. There's no harm in it."

Listening and maybe asking a question or two. But wasn't that part of a whore's job? Being the sort of ear that lonely men could turn to?

I wondered who lonely women paid to listen. As with so much, it seemed as if the world had a solution for the one but not the other.

Priya had stopped walking down the stair, so I stopped, too. A step lower, so our heads was level. She stared at me suspiciously.

"What do you want?"

"I want to help." Which was the truth. I wanted to kiss her, too, and slide my hand over the warm skin under that white shirt. But that was probably a conversation for another day. Maybe a day after I had a better idea how Priya might feel about French favors and the rites of Sappho.

She stared, still. I shrugged and went back to descending. "You'll like the bedrooms," I said.

Chapter Six

Well, it turned out Priya didn't like the bedroom when I brought her up to the one Miss Francina had suggested was clean and empty. She didn't say so—too polite or too scared—but when I opened the door and held the lantern up I could see from the way she looked at the narrow cot with its clean white sheets and the narrow room with its clean white walls that she was six inches, maybe less, from bolting.

"There's a window," I said, walking in to show her how to pull the shade. I had to set the lantern down on the side table to free up my hands. Priya followed me in. The path beside the bed was so narrow she couldn't stand beside me, so she peered around my shoulder.

"It opens," I added. I demonstrated how to work the casement. When I glanced at her for approval, her frown was a little less pinched. Just a little.

"I like the window," she allowed. She still looked like bucking, though.

"Hey," I said. It dawned on me that maybe this narrow room

didn't look too different from the cribs she was used to, if more freshly painted and probably with cleaner sheets. If Bantle even saw to it that they got sheets. I think I said about how some girls just lay a slicker down. "You never have to have anyone else in here, unless you want to."

"The walls are close," she said helplessly. Then, again, "The window helps some."

I thought about where she'd come from. What she'd lived through. I thought about third-class berths on steamships from India. I thought about how I could maybe make a living gentling—it was work I might be able to get, even as a girl, because I was good at it and had my father's name. And people could pay me less.

Except I couldn't bear to be around horses anymore. They reminded me of Da.

Well, and I couldn't bear not to be around them, either. Because they reminded me of Da.

I reckoned I was going to have to sort that particular conundrum by the time I opened my stable and gave up on sewing.

I tried *not* to think about the cribs and how I heard some of the girls down there never left them. Dead or alive.

"Look," I said finally. Helplessly. "This is what we've got. What would make it better for you?"

That stopped her dead, as if she'd never paused to consider it. She blinked, licked her lips, stepped back—and tripped when the edge of the cot caught the backs of her calves. Like I said, it was that narrow.

She sat down hard, the bed catching her. A puff of clean alfalfa smell surrounded her as her bum smacked into the ticking. We'd dragged all the mattresses out and restuffed them in September. Somebody had filled this one with hay and not straw. Softer, but wasteful. Still, I figured she'd earned it. I wondered if I could find her a featherbed somewhere to go over the ticking.

I realized I was staring again and her face was steadily flushing. Mine must of flamed red—even redder, being paler to start—and I covered it by holding my hand out to help her up. She didn't take it.

Instead, with an expression of some surprise, she settled sideways across the cot, her arms spread wide and her feet still dangling off the side. Her neck was bent at an awkward angle, her head against the wall—the cot was that narrow. She gazed up at me and I—well, I'm ashamed to say I just gawked at her.

"This is comfortable." Her voice was as surprised as her expression. "Well, bugger me!" Then she clapped a hand across her mouth and giggled.

"You won't find none in Madame Damnable's house as doesn't know that word," I said. "Though Miss Bethel may pretend she don't."

I knowed she was giddy with exhaustion and I knowed I should swing her around so her head was on the pillow and her feet were on the bed, but I didn't want to leave her just yet. "May I sit?"

"Sit," she said. She tried to drag herself upright and made it to her elbows. I took the opportunity to stuff the pillow under her head before she collapsed again. Now it hurt my neck less to look at her.

There was no chair, so I sat on the bed. "What would make it better?" I asked again.

"Colors," she said. "Fabric. Some brightness. Paint." Her face crumpled. "I think I missed Diwali already. I don't even know."

I wanted to ask if Diwali was a person, but it made me feel ignorant and stupid, so I held my tongue. I know better now; Diwali is Priya's people's festival of lights. It celebrates the triumph of good over evil and light over darkness.

I reached out automatically and took her hand. She squeezed my fingers hard enough to hurt me. I didn't care.

"At least I have new clothes," she said—or kind of mumbled. Every blink she took was longer than the last one. "Well. New to me."

I was thinking about the sewing machines downstairs and about my rag rug. And about what it would take to make another and maybe a patchwork hanging or curtains or a duvet out of scraps. Not too much, I thought. And most of it, save thread, I could get out of the ragbags.

"Wait right here," I said. "Leave the lamp," she muttered.

Before I left, I poked and prodded and coaxed Priya until she was lying the right way along the bed at least. I couldn't get her under the covers, but I pulled off her carpet slippers and I sort of folded the quilt up around her. Then I ran down the hall to my room and dragged the braided rug out from under my table and two legs of the bed. I had to lift the bed to do it, and once the rug was up I realized I hadn't been doing too good a job of sweeping under it. I could see the pattern of the braids in the dust on the floor.

That could wait, though. I shook the great heavy, awkward thing out and bundled it up in my arms. I had to back out the door and then sort of edge sideways into Priya's room. She didn't say anything as I turned to her—

She was sound asleep on her side, mouth open and eyes closed, knees drawn up as if she were thinking of kicking out at somebody. I snorted at myself.

Well, the rug would just have to be a surprise for when she woke up.

I spread it out on the floor—she never stirred—and I made sure the brighter, prettier side was on the top. It glowed softly in the lamplight, all greens and golds and ruby brocade and the sapphire-blue of Effie's old threadbare silk gown. We went through a lot of party dresses, did Madame's girls. And about twice as many petticoats.

"There," I said when it was done. I pulled the covers back up around Priya, left the lamp—as she had asked—turned down to just a satiny glow, and went downstairs to see what I could salvage of my work for the evening.

It started off as an uneventful working night. I think we all expected Priya to sleep until sunset the next day, if not the second night through, too, and Merry Lee had a bell to ring for Connie or one of the day girls who kept house and served food and helped Connie in the kitchen—who was night girls at Madame's, really—if she'd need. Custom was steady but not too strong, and I spent my time between goes sitting in the parlor, listening to the Professor chat up the tricks when he wasn't barrelhousing out hot tunes on that baby grand of Madame's.

The Professor—his name was Shipman, but nobody ever used it—was average height and slender, a white man with strawberry-blond hair and a red mustache. He had knotted on a gray silk cravat—he wore a different color for every night of the week—and the only time he ever took his matching kidskin gloves off was to play the piano. He looked gentlemanly, or at least gentle, with his wire-rimmed glasses and his mild expression, and there was something aristocratic about the way the bones of his thin nose turned into the arch over his eye. His handkerchief was folded into four points.

His cheeks was dotted along the stand-out bones with old, round pox scars, and you could see the knife scars across the back of his left hand. Between tunes, he got up and sauntered over to the game room to keep an eye on the faro and billiards tables. He weren't big, but he could handle himself in a whorehouse fight as it came necessary.

Most of our business came by way of what they call referrals. Appointments and introductions. The johns stayed overnight more often than you might think, if all you've ever been in is a regular bordello. Not most of 'em, mind—which suited me fine. Madame and Miss Francina know I prefer to sleep alone, even if it means sewing more than one coat of an evening. Pollywog, Effie, Miss Francina—even Bea—they'd rather one and done, because if they want you for all night they pay for all night. And you know for all men like to brag up their prowess, ain't but one in twenty of 'em going to keep you up too late. But me, I like to sit in the library with the ladies and maybe get a little reading of my own done before I turn in.

Anyway, like I said, it was slow custom, and I was in the parlor with the Professor and Miss Francina and Pollywog. And Miss Bethel, of course, but all she was doing was polishing her glasses. Pollywog was singing along with something the Professor was playing, and her French was even worse than mine. Miss Francina was playing Patience and losing. Miss Lizzie came down, seeing off her last john, and settled in with a cigarette in an amber holder and one of the little clockworks she fidgets with sometimes. This one was no bigger than Bea's fist, and when you wound it up it walked on clattering ivory thimbles. I think it was supposed to be an elephant or a rhinoceros, but if I'm being honest the likeness weren't striking.

I was spending the time with the notebook I don't care if people see, sketching away at my idea for curtains for Priya. I'd do those first, I decided, though they'd need lining to hide the seams between the patchworks, because they was just rectangles. They'd serve as practice for the duvet and maybe for cushions.

It was all busywork, of course, to distract myself from what I was really thinking. That I needed—*needed*—Priya to stay.

So she had to want to stay. So it was up to me to make her comfortable. To make her like it here.

And of course I was all at the same time painfully aware that if I made it too obvious I was scrabbling after her I'd just drive her away. Anybody who just wants a dog to kick isn't somebody you'd want to be loved by, my da used to say. Nor somebody you'd ever give a dog, Mama would always answer.

Time went by, and people drifted in and out of the parlor. By three on the big grandfather clock by the library door, the last of the johns had either done his business and gone out or settled in for the night with the girl of his dreams. Those picketers we'd had earlier apparently didn't stay up past ten, so they was long gone, too, and in their absence custom had picked up a bit. Me, I was just starting to think about some supper—I could smell the mutton with garlic and the huckleberry sauce wafting out from Connie's cookpots every time the hall door was opened—when, muffled through the brick walls, I heard Pollywog start in to screaming out in the alley.

I say I heard, but we all did. "Christ, what now?" Miss Francina said, heaving herself up from the chair where she'd been bootless, toasting her socks by the parlor fire. Crispin was already on his feet, grabbing up an old train signal lantern we keep beside the door. Miss Bethel ducked under the bar pass-through with her shotgun ready. Effie jumped up beside me, and so did Miss Lizzie. Madame's office door creaked and I heard the thump of her cane, but Crispin was already out the door and I wasn't letting him and Polly face whatever it was alone for as long as it might take for Madame to get down the stairs. If Polly needed rescuing, then by God we were there to effect her rescue.

I bolted out behind him, in between Miss Francina and Miss Bethel.

Pollywog's real name is Mary, from which comes Polly and therefore, by the irrefutable logic of affection, Pollywog. She's got that straight blond hair like I described, and maybe not a whole mess of common sense, but she ain't in general a screamer. She's got a lot of regulars; the johns who want her usually *only* want her, and I think it is as much to do with her big blue eyes and her listening expression and her trick of petting their hair back as it is to do with her trick hip.

There weren't nothing in sight from the front stoop. I looked this way and that—and up the ladder, for good measure—but them red lamps burned steady in the still air and there was nobody in any direction. Polly screamed again—breathier this time, like a balloon running out of air—and I caught sight of the colored-glass glow of Crispin's signal lantern vanishing around the corner to my right.

I lit out after him, Miss Francina and Miss Bethel on either flank, Effie at our heels. Miss Francina was still stocking foot, but that didn't seem to slow her none.

"Aw, shit!" Crispin's voice, and I braced for a crash or a thud of fist on flesh, but all that came was Pollywog's sobbing. I rounded the corner in time to see that it muffled as Crispin pulled her face into his coat. In the light of the gas lamp beside the kitchen door, I could make out the dustbins we lined up against the scaffold holding the street fill back. There also was a pile of rags and a spilled pail of peelings—Pollywog must of dropped it—beside them.

We lot all planted our heels and piled to a halt like characters in a funny strip. Fortunately, it was Miss Bethel who bounced off my back, not Miss Francina. And fortunately, she did it with her forearm and not the shotgun. Half-carrying Pollywog, Crispin started drawing her the way we'd come, back toward the front door. Her face never came out of his shoulder.

"She hurt?" Miss Francina asked as they passed our little huddle by.

"Look to the girl on the ground," Crispin said. "If there's any use to it."

"Fucking shit," said Effie, echoing and enhancing Crispin's sentiments. I didn't say it myself because my mouth had dropped open and was hanging there as if I was a hooked fish, gasping.

The dustbins were dustbins. The dropped pail of peelings was exactly that. The pile of rags . . .

It was a girl. Or a woman.

Miss Francina, unsurprisingly, got herself together first. She darted forward, heedless of the peelings and her stockinged feet, and dropped a knee beside the prone figure. As if her moving freed us all from some paralysis, I stepped up, too. Miss Bethel stood over us with the gun held easily, and Effie made a sideways triangle to her, watching back the way we'd come. We all trusted Crispin to bring the folk inside up to speed and all.

I stepped around the girl on the ground. She was a sister, a stargazer like us. And she didn't have the look of one of the dockside whores—she was white, for one thing—but she weren't no parlor house girl. A streetwalker, rather, a ragged robin, sprawled half on her front and half on her side. Her face was lost in her tangled brown hair. Her boots were down at the heels and her hem was draggled and tattered.

She wasn't wearing stays, and the back of her dress was torn to ribbons and sticky brown with old blood. She'd been flogged.

At least blood that old didn't make me want to grab one of those dustbins and hide my head in it while I upped my chuck.

Miss Francina laid the back of her hand against the woman's cheek and paused a moment, head bowed. Then she looked up and found Effie's gaze. "You get Crispin back out here," she said. "And a cudgel and a lamp, and your pistol. And you and him run and get the constables, fast as you can."

"We should get that girl inside," Miss Bethel said as Effie vanished in a patter of footsteps. Two runs for the constables in two nights, that were a mite unusual.

Miss Francina shook her head. "She's past help, Beth. We should wait for the brass knuckles and their whistles."

Miss Bethel said, "This is a threat."

"We don't know that for sure," Miss Francina said, but her expression agreed with Miss Bethel. "Karen honey, would you run and fetch my boots?"

As it turned out, there wasn't much wait for the law. And it wasn't the constabulary. By the time I came back with Miss Francina's shoes—boots only by courtesy, as they was the frilliest, silliest girl shoes you've ever seen, and on the largest last—and gave her a shoulder to lean on while she put them on standing, there was a thump of much heavier boots coming down the ladder.

We all turned—we being Miss Bethel, Miss Francina, and me, because Miss Lizzie was keeping the other girls in the library for now. Which was just as well; having them all gathered around sobbing or staring or sobbing *and* staring would of been more than I could of handled. The tromp of big boots turned the corner, and—

I felt the skin around my eyes stretch as Marshal Bass Reeves stomped into view.

He'd divested himself of his duster and spurs, but he still had a pistol on each hip. Now he wore a town suit—maybe gray, in the lamplight—and a silk kerchief tied into the gap of his shirt. Still the same pair of boots, though, with the stirrup scuffs in the arches.

Under his big gruff mustache, he looked grim.

"Ladies," he said, and we parted before him like the Red Sea. He could of been our Moses, I suppose, but they say the Negro Moses was a woman and she lives in New York.

Miss Bethel is never at a loss for words, and it was her who said, "How did you know to come here?"

The Marshal crouched beside the girl. He touched her shoulder with some gentleness. The shadow that crossed his face at the sight of her ribboned back was no trick of the lantern light. He looked down again.

I couldn't read the Marshal's face, because the brim of his big hat covered it as he crouched, so I looked at the creases across the toes of his boots and wondered how many states and territories they'd seen. He pulled a glove off—they were town gloves now, pearl kidskin, such as none of us nor the dead girl were wearing—and gently took her wrist. The shreds of dress across her back rustled.

There was no wind down here in the well. It was just from him moving her. She weren't stiff yet.

"Marshal, she's beyond any help but God's," said Miss Francina.

He didn't look up.

"She's got to be dead," I said. "The blood . . . the flogging—"

She had to be dead. Did I *hope* she was dead?

Would I want to be dead if it was me?

"I've seen men survive as bad," he answered. "Women too." But as he stared down at his fingers on her floury-looking wrist, I knowed the answer wasn't what he would of wanted.

He pulled a compact out of his breast pocket and opened it. He held the mirror under her nose for two, three minutes before he shook his head.

Marshal Reeves looked up at me and heaved a tired sigh. "That's a right pisser."

"I did say," said Miss Francina. The Marshal raised his eyebrows at her, tilting back his hat. She sighed. "But you just had to see for yourself, didn't you?"

"It's a character flaw," he allowed.

Miss Bethel said, "You didn't answer how you knew to come here."

She sounded suspicious, even though the silver star glinted on his town coat just as it had the duster's lapel. Possibly because of it. You learn a little something about the law when you work on your back.

"I was on my way here, actually," he said. He smoothed the ragged robin's hair and stood. Easily, his gun belt creaking but his breath untroubled. "I wanted to talk to Miss Wilde and Miss Memery here about what happened . . . well, I guess now it's yesterday. It occurred to me that you might know something about the man I'm hunting, and I didn't think in your line of work you ladies would be abed yet. I passed your man and your girl on the street, and they saw my star. They went on to find a roundsman."

As if his words had been a harbinger, I heard a distant whistle blowing. The shrill cry was taken up by another, and another after that, until the night echoed with them—tinny, thin, and frail.

I looked at the girl again. I wanted to cover her. "She can't of been thrown. We'd have heard the thud."

"She's not one of yours, then?"

"In that dress? Madame wouldn't let her scrub floors dressed like that, let alone entertain clients," Miss Francina scoffed. I knowed it was to cover her horror—she hides the softest heart in the house, and Signor isn't the only one who knows it—but the Marshal gave her a sidelong glance.

"Look at her face," the Marshal said.

"I'd prefer not."

His lips stretched into a moment's grim smile. "Fair enough. She wasn't thrown."

I said, "So somebody got her down here—down the ladder—and left her."

"Someone did," the Marshal said. "Which makes me think even more that you might know something that could help me find the man I'm looking for."

Miss Francina twined one perfect yellow corkscrew curl around her finger—how she keeps her hair unmussed I'll never know—and pursed her lips at him. She said, "Something tells me you'd better come inside, Marshal. You and Karen go on. Miss Bethel and I will wait for the constables."

Chapter Seven

I said how Bea is a slip of a thing, all eyes and fingers and crinolines, and how she's still learning her English. What I might not have said is how she's kind and clever . . . so when I walked into the library with Marshal Reeves I shouldn't of been surprised to find her sitting with Priya on the long divan. Signor was cuddled up in Beatrice's skirts and Priya was wrapped up in a knit afghan Miss Francina had made. They were chattering away in French.

Or rather, Beatrice was chattering. Signor wasn't saying much. And Priya was answering, haltingly, and her accent was worse than mine—which was saying something, because mine was no better than wretched. But she was feeling her way through complete sentences, albeit simple ones and with the verbs all cattywumpus. At least Beatrice was laughing at her, the same's she laughed at me. But that, I reckon, was the moment when I started to figure out just how smart Priya really was. Because she hadn't listed French as one of her accomplishments to Madame, and I'd bet my toenails that she had been desperate enough to stay that she'd have mentioned anything she might be able to do that would be of the least little use at all. Which meant she'd picked up what she was doing now in whatever time she'd spent with Bea this evening—not much if she'd been roused by the fuss not a quarter hour before—and while I had been out that afternoon.

They both looked up when I came in, and Beatrice bounced to her feet wearing a worried look none of us would ever let a john catch us in. That was probably why it smoothed away again the second the Marshal stepped through the door behind me.

Girls in my profession know a little too much about men. The ones who want to know a woman as a person are fewer than you'd hope, and most of those don't even realize it about themselves. They don't care who a woman is, or what she's scared of, or who she wants to become. They think they want a woman, but what they really want is a flattering looking glass wearing lipstick and telling them what they want to hear. Easy enough for me; it's my job, ain't it? I'm not as good at it as Pollywog, but I can mostly keep my face straight on my skull.

Harder if you have to live with one and play that role all night and day, without your sisters to keep you from going starkers. I can't imagine being married to most men.

Well, maybe a man like Da. But I suspect most women don't even know that men like Da are possible.

Anyway, the Marshal came in and I saw Bea and Priya both assemble their sweet, stupid faces in a hurry. What was funny was I saw him noticing them doing it and I saw the sharp little twist of his frown when he did. He got control of it again right quick, and I was left with the strange thought that everybody in that room just then was wearing a mask for the purpose of not upsetting one another.

It was a queer thought, and it rightly unsettled me.

"This is Marshal Bass Reeves," I told the ladies. "Marshal, this is . . ." I stumbled, realizing all at once that he'd want the last names and that I did not know Priya's. Hell, I didn't know if the Indian girls *had* last names, exactly. The Chinese did their names in some kind of a funny order, and the Spanish girls had three or four last names apiece, and our Indian girls—the American ones, I mean, rather than the Oriental ones—might have last names or might not, as suited them and depending on what tribe they came from. ". . . Miss Beatrice Malvot," I finished when I realized everyone was staring at me. "And Miss Priya—"

She winked, and she came to my rescue. "Priyadarshini Swati," she said. "Priya is fine."

"Miss Swati," he said. He'd lifted off his hat and tucked it under his arm when he stepped inside, so he touched his forehead. "Miss Malvot."

"Charmed, Marshal Reeves," said Beatrice with her beautiful manners. She extended her hand like a real lady, and nothing in her face gave away that Marshal Reeves hadn't the faintest idea what to do with it after he took it. If I'd been her, it would of been endless awkwardness—but she just lifted her glove away from his after a moment, and nodded like the French Queen. If France still had Queens, which it hasn't since my da was alive, which I know because he was at pains to tell me when it happened that another great nation had become a Republic.

Whatever that means.

"Polly?" I asked.

"Miss Lizzie took her up to bed. Perhaps you would like a drink, Marshal Reeves?" Bea offered, and I realized that I should of rung for Connie already. Her accent made her sound even more regal. "Madame will be with you in a moment. I assume you're here about . . . what happened outside?"

"Yes," the Marshal said. "And a cup of Arbuckle's would

go down just fine, if you don't mind. Sleeping hasn't been much on my mind of late."

Bea would of rung, but Priya slithered out of the afghan and headed to the kitchen, still wearing her trousers and cardigan. Bea and I watched her go, then hastily collected ourselves. I was the one who remembered to offer the Marshal a chair.

I hoped Priya would be back with the coffee around the same time Madame finally put in her appearance. It'd strike a good note.

"So, Marshal," I said after we'd both found chairs not too far from either Beatrice or the fire, "I have the distinct impression that nothing in that alley much surprised you."

He'd hung his hat on his knee. Now he huffed and moved it to the floor. Signor stood up in Bea's lap, stretched his portly self six ways, and hopped down to the floor with a bump that was the shame of supposedly graceful and elegant cats everywhere. He thudded over to Marshal Reeves and began investigating his boots and hat with a pink, twitching nose.

The Marshal, meanwhile, had at first kept talking. "You'd be right, Miss Memery." Then he seemed to get stuck. His breath went in and out, flaring his nostrils, and he found that deaf cat inordinately distracting.

At last, he said, "I've followed this son of a bitch from the Indian Territory. Begging your pardon, ladies."

"If you have followed him," Beatrice said, "you must know who he is, no?"

Behind the luxuriance of his mustache, Marshal Reeves' expression pickled. "I wasn't sure I'd even come to the right place until now. I don't mind saying it, I'm half-sorry to have my theory proved."

He reached to his inside pocket, past his gold watch chain, and brought out a scrap of oilcloth tied with a bit of bootlace. He laid it on the low table and was just about to start unwrapping it when Priya backed into the room balancing a coffee tray—the same one I'd brought upstairs to her not twenty-four hours before.

She had set it down on the receiving table by the door and had just commenced to pouring when a commotion arose in the parlor. Miss Bethel's and Miss Francina's voices combined with some male ones, and through them I heard Madame's heavy tread on the stair.

I might of stayed in the library, to speak honest, but the Marshal tucked his packet back in his coat and stood. "I'll show you before I go," he promised when Beatrice and I protested.

We followed him out into the parlor, though I hesitated for a moment at Priya's hand on my sleeve. She whispered me a question and I answered, likewise under my breath.

Priya looked like the best kind of savant when she slipped a coffee cup into Madame's hand, cream and one lump, just as Madame preferred it. And I hid a smile behind my hand at Madame's brief expression of respect. I think only I and possibly Marshal Reeves noticed the exchange, but it would of been easy to miss anything in the sudden chaos and bustle of the parlor. Effie and Crispin was there, out of breath with running, and with them were Miss Bethel, Miss Francina, and three constables—two roundsmen and a sergeant. Miss Lizzie had come downstairs with Madame. And of course there was Bea and Marshal Reeves and Priya and me.

Eventually, Miss Francina got everyone settled and introduced and Priya outdid some professional butlers of my acquaintance with that tray of coffee. The sergeant—one Waterson—even sat, though the roundsmen shifted about uncomfortably, accepting no coffee and looming by the door. Waterson looked a little put out to find a U.S. Deputy Marshal already on the scene and made a little fuss about Reeves being out of Judge Parker's court district. "You're a long way off your patch," he said.

"I am that," Marshal Reeves allowed.

Nobody else paid that much mind, however, and Sergeant Waterson dropped it. After that I thought Madame was going to send Beatrice and Effie and Priya and me out of the room, but apparently it was Pollywog mostly who they wanted to talk to, so we all stayed while Miss Lizzie went back upstairs to fetch her, since she'd sent her up to her bed. It weren't all real organized like, and I wondered what was taking them all so long. And then Polly came down in her robe—not a peignoir such as we'd wear for entertaining, but a warm dressing gown— with her hair all crinkled on her shoulders from her braids— and I realized what they'd been up to.

You've never seen a whore look so scrubbed and clean and pristine.

They talked, all right. They talked for hours. Not that the talking came to much of anything.

How had she come to be out in the night? She had offered to help Connie with the rubbish, sir. How had she come to find the dead woman? "Well, she was laid right by the trash, sir." Had she seen who might of done it? "No sir." Did she know how long the woman had been there? "No sir, not that, either." What had she done when she found the woman? "Touched her, felt her cold, and cried for help, sir." Had she ever seen the woman before? "No sir." Then she'd never been employed at the Hôtel Mon Cherie? "No sir, never."

And on and on. Occasionally, a constable would poke his head in from outside and whisper to one of the men by the door. Even more occasionally, one of the men by the door would walk over and whisper to Waterson behind his hand. Once he passed the sergeant a note, which Waterson read twice, scowling.

Finally, the Marshal intervened—half a beat, I thought, before Madame had been planning on it. He said, "Sergeant Waterson, I think you'll find—if you search in the mud along the top of the well—that there are footprints there that demonstrate that this victim was lowered on a rope from above. And that someone spent some time up there, smoking cigarettes and waiting to enjoy the spectacle of his work discovered."

Waterson was a slight man with transparent hair combed over the beginnings of a bald spot. He had a high, freckled forehead and his brass star was pinned to a gray wool waistcoat over a sharply pressed shirt. It only flashed when his movements disturbed the hang of his jacket. He wore a string tie and a frustrated expression. I didn't know if the sharp look he shot the Marshal was because he didn't like being told by a black man or because he thought he knowed something the black man didn't.

I wouldn't of wagered on him being right about that second one, personally.

"We found the cigarette ends," he allowed. His voice was rich with suspicion. "How did you know?"

"I checked the top of the wall before I climbed down. I have reason to believe the guilty party is someone I've chased here from Indian Territory."

He pulled a creased slip of paper out of his pocket and handed it to Waterson. "I've a writ for his arrest."

Waterson perused it. "This says 'person or persons unknown.'"

"That's how I swore it," Reeves agreed. "I trust that's how it's written."

"You haven't read it?"

"Can't read," said Reeves. "They don't teach slaves that." He touched his forehead. "I've got a hell of a memory, though."

I liked Waterson better when he tapped his fingers on the rustling paper, handed it back, and said, "I can respect that."

Madame set her coffee on the saucer with a disciplined small click. She pinned the Marshal on a look and said, "How'd you know to come to Rapid City, if you don't know who you're chasing?"

Beside me, Beatrice looked delighted. We all want to be Madame, should we be lucky enough to achieve that certain age. And here was Madame echoing just what Bea'd asked previous.

Again, the oilcloth packet made an appearance. Reeves picked at the knot with a thick, split thumbnail and had it worried open in a moment or two. I thought he probably could have even done it faster, but he was enjoying the suspense. He balanced it on his knee and extracted two objects, though I didn't think the packet was empty yet. One of the things he handed over was a greasy, grime-rubbed ticket stub with a part of a boot print still visible on it. The other was a cuff link, mother-of-pearl in sterling. I reckoned, though I didn't touch the thing.

"The man I'm looking for killed at least two women in the Indian Territory. One in Frogville and one in Wauhillau. The same way: flogged, left to die, and dumped. I know he would have stayed to watch because he stayed to watch before. And I came here looking for him because of these. As I told these ladies earlier"—his gesture took in Beatrice and me— "I wasn't sure until tonight that I was even in the right territory."

No one else made a move for the ticket and the cuff link, so after a glance around I did. Waterson looked like he might of intercepted me, but out of the corner of my eye I saw Marshal Reeves raise a big hand—his hands belonged on a man even bigger than he was, and that were saying something—and Waterson slumped back on his chair.

The ticket stub was a rail ticket from Rapid City to Sherman, Texas, dated May 25, 1878. The cuff link was stamped on the back of one link 925, and on the back of the other was a hallmark: *HB&S RC.*

I handed both to Waterson, who frowned over them.

"Harney Brothers and Sons," Reeves said, without being prompted. "Rapid City, Washington Territory. They're on Burnside."

"You've been to talk with them, I suppose?"

"They sell these by the dozen." Reeves accepted the cuff link and stub back from Waterson. He rewrapped both carefully. "But they might be a little more forthcoming with the local law, if you know what I mean. And if I can find a man who visited the Indian Territory this year—"

"With a gold rush on? You'll find a thousand."

Reeves nodded without looking up from his meticulous fingertip job of knotting. "There's a reward in it for those as helps me. And I figure, well, this scoundrel's different from the general run of rogues blown in on the Klondike wind."

"He's been here before," said Waterson. Then, a little crestfallen: "So he knows his way around."

Reeves gave a tight smile, and the first glance he'd offered Waterson that didn't seem to imply that the sergeant was studying up to become a half-wit. "And somebody knows him. And if he's killing . . . soiled doves, begging your pardon . . . then he's got to be patronizing them, hasn't he? And not crib whores, and not ladies like you, who work a parlor. He needs privacy and time for what he's doing. Also, all his victims have been white so far. Which ain't no accident, not in the Indian Territory and not in Rapid City."

"They're streetwalkers," Madame said slowly. "Women who'll go with him without asking any fucking questions. Without a struggle."

I don't know if Reeves or Waterson could read the lines of her face, but I knowed from experience that her insides were casting up like poured steel. Maybe they felt it, because no one said anything until Madame gathered herself and continued, "I'll make sure the word gets out. And I'll make sure our sisters on rounds know to be careful."

Reeves sucked his teeth. "Make sure they know who to come to if they meet anybody who makes 'em feel . . . odd or unsafe, too, if you please?"

Miss Lizzie barked laughter. "In our line of work, sir, men who seem odd or unsafe are two-thirds of the custom."

Reeves tipped his invisible hat to her again. "Ladies, you have my solemn vow. I came nigh on two thousand miles by nag and rail, without a cook or a wagon and trailing only one posseman, leaving my seven children and my pregnant Jennie back in Oklahoma. When I leave Rapid City you have my word as a Christian that I intend to do it wearing that bastard for a hat."

Considering how polite he was to whores, I admit I wondered a bit just how Christian Marshal Reeves was. Which ain't no aspersion; I'm not so much for churching my own self. And you'd think them as follows Jesus, who befriended a stargazer, might be kinder to robins and crows.

So come to think of it, maybe he was a Christian after all, and a better one than most.

"What else is in that wrapper?" Madame asked.

The Marshal tipped his head. He handed her a little box, just folded stiff paper. "Sergeant Waterson will want to see that when you're done."

She lifted the lid and glanced inside. I snuck a look over her shoulder: there was a scrap of a hand-rolled cigarette inside.

"I ain't no expert on tobacco leaf," the Marshal said. "But that looks to me like those scraps on top of the wall. And I don't know about you-all, but I save my cigarette ends and re-roll them. There's good tobacco left in there."

Chapter Eight

After that night, it all got real quiet for a fortnight or so, so's I weren't sure whether to be apprehensive about it or grateful. We didn't hear much else from Marshal Reeves or from Sergeant Waterson, though each one came by once or twice to check on us. We took up a collection for the dead girl—nobody would admit to knowing her name—and got her buried decent, at least. When the constables were finished with her.

The world, I thought, had finished with her firsthand.

Priya settled in right smart and got into the habit of coming out to sit in the library with us girls and read by the fire when the tricks had gone home. By the sixth day, she was helping Merry Lee come downstairs, and Merry sat with us all, too. She was wobbly, sure, but she was standing—and Priya got strong quick, once we started feeding her regular.

I remarked on it to Miss Francina, and Miss Francina gave me a funny kind of look—not sad, but not not-sad, neither—and said, "They're young yet, Karen."

Nobody suggested it was time Merry got on home. In faith,

she weren't ready—I didn't imagine she could climb a ladder yet if her life depended on it, and she sure couldn't do it without tearing her wounds open again. And she couldn't do for herself yet, either—though by the end of the fortnight Miss Lizzie had her stitches out and she was healing up right sharp. Anyway, none of us was certain she had a home. We didn't ask, and she didn't offer much.

But she was a sister, or she had been; and she risked her life helping women who . . . well, there but for the grace of God went every one of us in that room. Both of 'em—Merry and Priya—took their turns with the books, too. Since it turned out Priya could read, though not as good as me—not in English, anyway. It turned out she could read Chinese just fine and I guessed probably her own language. She had a knack for tongues, like, and could read a sentence in Chinese and speak it out in English fast as anything.

Merry Lee, though, did the voices and everything. Different accents. She could sound as American as me if she wanted. Or as French as Bea. She said that after she'd escaped the cribs the next place she'd had to escape was the Education House of the Women's Christian Anti-Prostitution and Soiled Dove Rescue League. Which was maybe better than the cribs, but it were an Improving Workhouse, no mistake. And I'd heard the only way a girl left *there* was if she could find a Christian man the matrons approved of to marry her—and how many Chinese men are Christians, I ask you?

Anyway, I got the idea pretty quick that Merry Lee was prone to disguise herself. As part of her chosen work, like.

I think she figured I figured. But we held a conspiracy of smiling silence and I don't think anybody else caught on. In two days' time, she was in demand to do readings every evening after supper. And we all gathered around to hear her, too.

One night the book she had was a dime novel called *Dead-wood Dick Defiant!*, brand-new and already yellowing. It was about Calamity Jane, who was a favorite in our house. Some would say she was nothing but a camp follower, just another new-state whore. But she could ride and rope with any man, shoot better than all of 'em, and she was a hero to us.

The way I saw it, nobody thought the worse of a man who followed his pecker anywhere it sniffed, like a droopy-faced hound dog led on by his nose. So why a woman did the same should be judged different . . . well, women always is.

Judged different, I mean.

Anyway, Merry Lee was reading on about something Jane had done or was supposed to have done the year previous:

"In the spring of 1877, Calamity Jane was riding her sorrel pony out on the range between Cheyenne and Crook City. She spotted a roil of dust on the horizon and rode hard to investigate.

"Before long, she caught sight of the Cheyenne to Dead-wood stage, running flat out with horses lathered and a band of Indians in hot pursuit. The driver was nowhere in sight, the stage horses starting to slow with their reins flapping wild. She reined her sorrel alongside and spotted the driver, facedown in a pool of blood in the boot of the stage, an Indian arrow between his shoulder blades!

"Calamity Jane knew she could waste no time! She jumped up on the saddle of her running sorrel, standing on the horse's back like an Indian herself. In a hail of arrows and bullets, she leaped across the gap to the stage. Swinging wildly from the rail, she got her foot on the step. Her hat blew back on its laces as she caught the reins of the stagecoach four, found the whip, and urged them on.

"Her rifle was still in the sorrel's saddle holster. One of the six passengers climbed up the rattling, swaying exterior of the stage to take the reins, and Jane managed to lean out and retrieve the Winchester at risk of her own skin. A bullet creased the running sorrel's shoulder so close that blood spattered Jane's shirt cuff.

"Having retrieved the rifle, she mounted it to her shoulder and from the jouncing seat of the stage, returned fire against the galloping, whooping band of Indians. They fell away, and then under Calamity Jane's care, the stage and its passengers made it safely into Deadwood.

"The driver survived."

Merry turned the page and held up the book so we could all see the engraving of the woman on the next page. She leaned back on a bench with one foot kicked up, flourishing a Winchester rifle. She wore buckskin chaps, a fringed coat, an open-creased hat, and a good white neckerchief folded well. I liked her scowl and I liked her freedom to wear it.

Martha Jane Canary, it read underneath. *"Calamity Jane."*

Priya bounced on the edge of her cushion, as pleased as a pup with two tails. "I want to be like her!"

"She drinks, they say," Miss Bethel said, but kindly.

Miss Francina snorted. "A woman in the West? You show me one who doesn't drink, and I'll show you one that wants to."

Well, as I was saying, Priya settled in right quick, and half the time I'd come down to breakfast to find her in the parlor with Miss Lizzie, taking apart that Singer sewing machine. With all her other smarts, she had a knack for mechanicals, too. Sometimes they had to race to get the thing put back together before the trade showed up, and I know once or twice there were pieces that got left off for a day or two when they ran short of time—because in *my* spare time I was sewing.

I didn't tell her what I was sewing on or that it was for her, but I spent all day Sunday on that patchwork coverlid, a wedding ring pattern in orange and red, and with the machines and all it was finished by suppertime. Even quilted. I got to use the big machine for the quilting, stitching spirals with my right hand and measuring with my left. It was easier inside the frame, because the machine did all the measuring and math for you and kept the circles even and whatever they'd done to it made it work smoother even with the thick layers of fabric. I filled the quilt with wool bat instead of cotton, too. Priya being so skinny, I reckoned she wouldn't mind the extra warmth.

I found some grosgrain ribbon I'd bought to make over an old dress and never gotten around to using and folded the quilt up, then tied it into a fancy package—pretty as you've ever seen. I didn't want to embarrass Priya or make her feel beholden by giving her things in front of others—and also I was a little shy. So after dinner, but before we all gathered in the library, I tracked Priya down in the pantry where she was inventorying flour and cornmeal and suchlike, and I brought it to her.

I must of crept up behind her softer than I meant to, because when I rapped on the open door with my knuckles she about jumped out of her skin and left it straggled out on the boards. She squeaked and pirouetted, arms crossed over her apron.

It threw me off my stride, I don't mind saying. I stood there gawping at her while she skipped and stared like a startled filly. You could have used her pupils for stove lids.

"Careful, now," I told her. "It's just me."

Slowly, pretending I didn't notice her chest heaving up and down, I held out the coverlid all packaged up with its bright blue ribbon. Even folded up, it was colorful and pretty. I'd picked the brightest scraps from the ragbag, greens and pinks and purples and reds in addition to the oranges. It mightn't match much else—it didn't match itself, in point of fact, though I loved the way the green and the vermilion played off each other on that one patch—but it was a gaudy great, wonderful pile of cloth.

Priya kept her hands at her sides and caught her breath as she looked at it. "That's beautiful."

"It's for you," I said. I bounced my hands a little. The quilt was getting heavy. "You're supposed to take it now."

"Oh!" Her eyes couldn't possibly have gotten bigger, but they seemed to. She put her hands on her mouth instead of reaching out. "I can't—"

"You'd better," I said. "I got no use for it."

"But the rug—and—"

"I like taking care of my friends," I told her. I took a step forward, and she didn't move back. "This isn't getting any lighter, you know."

"Oh!"

Priya didn't so much reach for the quilt as let me put it in her hands when they came down again. But once she had it, she clutched it like the mane of a bucking horse. Her hands made little fists on the fabric. "Karen, I—this is too nice."

"So you do something for me someday," I answered. "Friends don't keep score."

Because friends don't have to keep score, my da would of said. Friends just pitch in as needed, as they can.

Thinking that made me notice something else. To wit: she was wearing the same clothes she'd had on since she got here, the cuffed-up trousers and shirt, and they were all starting to get a bit dingy. She'd washed them, I knowed—we all had a hell of a laundry day once a week, boiling big vats of water with lye soap in Connie's kitchen for all the underthings and the linens tough enough to take more than airing and brushing. Shifts and bloomers and Crispin's shirts and suchlike. But

I knowed Priya'd borrowed a shift from Beatrice to wear while her shirt was being boiled. And that she didn't have much else.

"Tomorrow," I said, "we're going shopping. If you're going to wear trousers, they're going to be trousers that fit. And you need shoes before winter gets worse, and more than one shirt and one pair of skivvies."

"I haven't saved the money yet," she said.

"We'll buy cloth. I'll loan you for it. You can pay me back in cash or chores, your option."

"I don't sew that well—"

I waved at the coverlid. "I do. We'll get you ragged up proper in no time at all."

The look on her face was the most complicated thing I've ever seen. She just stood there, canisters of flour and meal on the counter all behind her, hugging that quilt like a cat with only one kitten. I was afraid she was going to cry, and I was afraid I was going to beat her there.

"Tomorrow," I said. "We'll get up early."

Early, in this case, was before noon. I was afraid I wouldn't be able to find Priya when the time came to go—I'd already learned she had tricks for making things she didn't want to happen not stand a chance of happening without putting up no kind of a fight. But I woke up instead with her bouncing on my bed like a puppy. Connie was just putting the bread she'd risen overnight in the ovens, but there was some stale from the day before, and she dipped it in egg and fried it in dripping for us so there was something to eat for breakfast.

We gobbled it up, and I wish now I'd been more mindful of my gratitude. Connie had a way of doing such—putting herself out to make things a little easier for all while being so quiet about it you never think to stop and appreciate the kindness.

But I was too wrapped up in Priya to pay proper attention. Mama would of been ashamed.

I'd noticed Priya didn't eat beef or pork by itself—she'd eat around it, not making any fuss—but it seemed more of a philosophical objection than a physiological one. Which was for the good, because ten out of every eight things Connie cooks is fried in dripping.

In return for the early breakfast, Connie gave me a shopping list of her own. "And this time, try not to pre-chop the onions."

I could feel Priya watching. When I looked at her, she gave me a flicker of a smile. I wondered if she was figuring out how, in this house, we lived together mostly by doing one another favors. I mean, I know there's houses where it's every girl for herself, and constant knives in the back. But Madame won't cotton to that, and any girl who tries to import that sort of behavior and don't take a warning or two winds up plying her trade elsewhere. Madame's even less keen on mean than she is on drunk. She might *forgive* a girl who miscalculates how much liquor she can hold, as long as she don't do it regular.

I loaned Priya a pair of my boots and three sets of socks to keep 'em on her feet. It weren't perfect, but it was better than nothing. Then we checked the barometer, which was uncharacteristically heartening, and I flipped open the morning paper to check the Mad Science Report. No experiments were scheduled, and no duels had been announced—at least among the Licensed Scientists—but you never knowed when a giant automaton was going to run rogue unscheduled. Mostly the city makes the inventors keep to the edge of town. Mostly. And there's always those as won't pay the licensing taxes, and while that's illegal, it's hard to track them.

So I guess what I'm saying is that both looked fair for now, but both was always subject to change without notice.

Blinking in the unaccustomed sun and with Crispin for an
honor guard and to help haul dry goods up and down the ladders, we set out with baskets and sacks to get some marketing
done.

First I took Priya down Threadneedly, in and out of shops
that sold gingham and muslin and wool. We had to walk the
long way around to get there, as two big construction armatures had the Deucy Street sidewalks blocked off. They was doing the work of six steam shovels, each lifting a block of granite
the size of a boxcar into place to shore up one of the raised
street walls, and we all stopped to gawk for a minute. They was
like the sewing machine's much, much, much bigger cousins,
and you could hardly see the operators embedded inside the
framework of the big things' chests. One operator must of
caught us looking, and the hue of my primrose day dress,
because once the rock was placed he began cavorting in his
armature, making curled arms like I was supposed to fly up
there and feel his big machine's hydraulic biceps.

The Threadneedly end of town was nearer the rich folk's
homes and the airfield than the docks, and one big airship
drifted over while we walked, shadowing us from the rare winter sun. It was a gaudy thing, gold and vermilion and peacock
blue and parrot green, and as the docking boom reached up
into the sky to snag it and it tilted slightly, I read the words
Minneapolis Colony appliqued up the hydrogen bag. I spared
a thought for if that was a port of registry or the name of the
thing—neither seemed likely. Still, it caught the light, and I heard
Priya catch her breath at how it glittered.

"Colors like home," she said when I glanced at her.

The homesick in her eyes made me wonder if I could live in
India. And it made me think maybe I'd been right to pick those
bright, bright colors for her quilt. I know I'd meant to do the
curtains first . . . but the ring pattern was more fun, anyway.

Priya'd need a coat, I reckoned, and two pair of trousers. A pair of boots that could stand up to the wet. Shirts. There was a good wool check in black and yellow that I liked and she liked, too. We smiled over it conspiratorially: we'd both seen the dime-novel covers with Tombstone cowboys wearing shirts of that stuff. She liked a bright pink gingham with little green sprigs, too, which was more ladylike than I would of taken for her. I decided I could make a shirtwaist of it, for fancy, and there was no law saying she couldn't wear a woman's shirtwaist with men's pants.

Actually, there was a law saying so, but the same law said she couldn't wear trousers at all—and Miss Francina couldn't wear sixteen yards of crinoline and skirting. I didn't see it as about to slow down either one of 'em.

The boots were harder, but in the third shop we found a pair ready-made that were narrow enough for her. They was boy's boots, for walking, not for riding, in dark blue leather. They cost about the earth, but I didn't let her find that out. I just paid while she still had 'em on her feet and was admiring. She wore 'em out of the shop. She seemed to have given up protesting.

Crispin winked at me conspiratorially while I handed him loaded baskets and my old pair of boots Priya'd given me back, along with four out of six socks. I wasn't getting nothing past Crispin. But then, he knows pretty well that I feel exactly the way about women he don't, and I didn't think most anybody could have missed me mooning over Priya. Except possibly Priya. Who was pretty and clever and a wit . . . about everything except me being falling-down in love with her, apparently.

We was only halfway down the block and hadn't yet found the right wool for trousers when she stopped stock still on the boards and stared. I followed her line of sight, and I ain't ashamed to say I cussed as well as staring. There on the wall beside a barbershop and dentist's was a big printed placard in two colors of ink, advertising the mayoral candidacy of Mr. Peter Bantle, Democrat and local businessman.

I liked to have turned my head and spat, but I remembered at the last minute that I was out on the street and ought to comport myself as a lady. Cussing aside, but it was too late to rein that wagon.

Crispin, coming up behind us, didn't seem too much more pleased. He lifted a sagging basket out of Priya's shocked hand, though, and made a little production of redistributing his loads. I thought it was probably intended to hide whatever he happened to be thinking.

"Can he do that?" Priya asked, waving her now-freed hand at the sign.

"He can't win," I said. I looked at Crispin, and I knowed my face was begging for him to offer an opinion backing mine. He made an attempt at it, but I could tell the encouraging expression was spackled on. "Madame pays more in taxes than he does. Half the city council are her customers. She . . ."

"Greases the right palms?" Priya asked, grinning wickedly.

"So to speak." I laughed softly. Even in my desperate denial, I felt better for her humor.

But then her face fell. "Bantle *can* win."

I glanced at her for an explanation. No explanation was forthcoming. Just tight lips and a curt, quick shake of her head.

Crispin said, "There's them as would give Bantle money. Just to spite Madame. Or because they think it'd be good to have the mayor owe them. Or for half a dozen other reasons. Who's running for the Republicans? Is it going to be Mr. Stone again?"

It was a good question, and I wished I'd thought of it. The Republicans were the party of President Hayes, and I knowed a lot of people didn't like him because of the way he'd been elected. But they were also the party of President Lincoln, who people still talked about in hushed tones as a martyr. Of course, here in the Washington Territory we couldn't vote for President and being a woman and under twenty-one, I couldn't vote at all.

I didn't know a lot about politics. But I did know that even just within the confines of Rapid City, we elected a lot of Republicans. "He can't win," I said. "He's a Democrat." A sick thought came up in me like water up a drilled well. "He's just doing this to get back at Madame."

Priya's brows bunched up over her nose, shading those deep-textured eyes. "How does this . . . get him back at Madame?"

I winced and looked at Crispin. He was studying on rearranging those baskets, still. None of us was supposed to know about Mayor Stone and Pollywog. If my mouth was a mare, I'd put her on a curb bit.

Priya was just looking at me like it was a matter of life and death that she understand what I was talking about. And I couldn't tell her. "Just," I said, "the city council owes her favors. Just what we said before."

"Ah," she said. She thought about it for a few seconds and looked satisfied, like she'd figured something out. Priya's not just smart as a whip. I bet she got no end of practice reading between the lines, working for Peter goddamn Bantle.

"Anyway," I said, hoping to change the subject without letting on that I was changing the subject. "He can't win."

"He can win if nobody runs against him," Priya said.

"That'll never happen!" I said. "Mayor Stone would never give up without a fight, even if nobody else was running!"

Priya cocked her head at me, her braid falling over one shoulder. "No doubt," she said, "it shall be as you say."

But she was right, of course. We tracked down a fresh hot copy of the *Rapid City Journal Miner Republican* from a newsboy crying the afternoon edition in the street. He looked to be about eight years old, and I slipped him a silver quarter, which was exactly double the price of the paper. But newsboys paid for their own papers and most of them were orphans, like me—or had homes such as you wouldn't send a child back to under any circumstance.

We gathered around that rag and skimmed past stories about a gold ship sunk coming back from Anchorage and a splintercat that had done some damage up at a logging camp near Shasta. We quickly discovered that not only was Priya absolutely correct—Bantle was running unopposed—but there also was a full column of editorials discussing how Peter Bantle was undoubtedly the man for the job. In sickening and laudatory detail. And wishing Mayor Stone well in his retirement.

It weren't raining, for a mystery. But the day felt pretty dark to all of us just then, notwithstanding.

I crumpled the paper in my fist, more or less by accident, and hastened to smooth it out again. "How did you know?" I demanded of Priya.

She gave me the bleakest look imaginable. "I know Bantle. He's got his ways."

Our previous merry mood was shaken, and I hoped to recapture it. We were by that time down by the opera house, which was about the grandest building in town. It was dark green with white and brick-red trim, all gussied and hung with elaborate jigsaw work in the English style, and it was about as big as three banks put together. It was dark on a Monday afternoon, but I wandered over to look at the bills anyway.

The Fisk Jubilee Singers were prominently billed, and somebody called Anna Bichurina—we were getting a lot of Russians over, with the new fast steamers and the airship route from

Vladivostok. "Who's Ram Shankar Bhattacharya?" I asked, no doubt mangling it terribly.

Priya reached out to touch the posted bill with one finger-tip. The touch lingered. I noticed that she chewed her nails and loved her a little bit more than I had already. "A court musician," she said. "Very famous in my homeland."

I wondered, suddenly, how long she had been in the territories. How she had come here and where her family was. What had happened to them. When you meet someone in our line of work—or, I guess, my line of work, as she's out of it now—you sort of assume that if they had any family they'd be doing something else with their lives.

I thought again about the stable, about my idea for a little business of my own. I wondered if Priya liked horses.

For her, I bet I could stand to be around them again.

"How long have you and your sister been in America?" I asked her.

She shook her head. "Since last winter."

Ten months, then. Twelve at the outside. She must of seen my expression and read it flawlessly, because her spine got longer and her chin came up. "I'm quick with languages."

Crispin elbowed me. I looked at him, and he was grinning.

"Yes," I said to him. "She slapped a brand on me, all right. How kind of you to point that out."

I turned back to Priya. "I noticed," I said.

Priya was looking at Crispin and me in slight confusion of her own now, though. "He laid hands on you."

"An elbow," I said. "Not exactly the same thing."

But she looked wounded, and I took pity on her. "Among the things Madame don't tolerate is lording it over people on account of their skin."

"She was a—an abolitionist?"

Crispin patted her on the arm. He glanced around; there was nobody nearby. As I said, the opera house was dark Mondays.

"She's black," he said. "Just very fair complected. We'd say that she 'passes.' But she's got a black great-grandma, and that makes her black, by American law."

It was an interesting thing, watching the procession of emotions dawning and fading across her face like the sequence of the seasons, each replacing the last. Consternation gave way to surprise, which gave way to something else.

"She's low caste, then. But she can employ people of higher caste?"

I didn't know what a caste was, then. Now I know it's like classes, in Priya's homeland—lords and commoners and gutter scum.

"Does Bantle know?"

Crispin shrugged. "Maybe suspects. It'd be hard to prove out here in the middle of the wilderness, especially as none of us knows where Madame came from, or even her right name. We ain't never lied about it, to my knowledge. Just let people assume."

"He called her Alice," I remembered with a twist of unease. "Bantle called her Alice. He knows something. Or he thinks he does."

Priya nodded, and I could about see that glittering brain of hers work and spin. She said to Crispin, "You shouldn't of told me. You trust me too much."

He winked. "You was going to tell anybody, either way?"

She shook her head, but she didn't seem appeased. I could almost feel her thinking what a weird country we had. Rather than remarking on that, though, she seemed to steel herself and seize an opportunity for conversating. She turned to me. Quietly, she asked, "Have you . . . you've been so kind other ways. Have you learned anything about my . . . about Aashini?"

Damn. I'd been hoping she wouldn't ask. And the way she had to sneak up on her sister's name about broke my heart.

I had tried. The problem, it turned out, was finding ways to slip it into conversation. Natural like. Men liked to brag, true. But they didn't always like to be distracted.

"Not yet," I said. "I'm thinking there has to be a way to find out where she is, and maybe get her a message. But I haven't found it."

Her face fell like Connie's soufflés don't. Like when you put your lips against a vacuum tube, except as if somebody had done it to her expression from the inside. "I'll think on it, too," said Crispin. When Priya cocked her head at him, he said, "Slaves had families, too, miss. Sometimes it ain't so easy to keep in touch. We had our ways of getting word around, and keeping track of kin."

When the air came out of Priya and her shoulders fell, that was when I realized how twisted up inside she'd been and how much courage it had taken to ask that question. I thought about the burn scars on her arms.

Bantle had dozens of girls in his cribs. Surely he didn't have time to give that sort of attention to each and every one of them.

Priya, I surmised, might of been a special favorite. And the special favorite of a man like Bantle . . . well, in her shoes I would pretty fast get so I didn't let anybody know what I did or didn't care for, I imagined. Because vulnerability . . . that's the sort of thing that a man like Bantle would use against you.

Well, a man like Bantle would use anything against you that he could. And—it occurred to me—a man like Bantle might have ways of getting hold of somebody's sister, if he wanted to hurt that somebody. And, like Crispin's relatives, he might have ways of making sure word reached that somebody. Sooner or later.

"Hey," I said. "Friends do things for each other."

She stared at the toes of her new blue boots, frowning on one side of her mouth. That long face of hers made all sorts of complicated whimsies happen when she wasn't careful to guard it. I could see the leather flex as her toes wiggled restlessly beneath.

When she looked up, though, her eyes were bright. Her expression impulsive. "Let me make you a new rug," Priya said, bouncing on her toes a little, swinging her arms like a boy of seven bursting with so much excitement he has to share.

Friends do things for each other. So were we friends, or was I courting her? Did they have to be exclusionary? How did I find out which she wanted it to be? It bothered me for a whole half a second before I realized that if I was only being her friend because I wanted to get into her bloomers then I was a pretty lousy friend *and* a pretty lousy romantic prospect.

And maybe if we spent enough time being friends, I'd study out for myself if she had some kind of interest in making more of it. Or at least I'd study out if that was the sort of thing she might not care to be asked about. Because I was pretty sure I could ask . . . but I wouldn't if it would chase her away. Because I wanted Priya in my life any way she'd have me, so scaring her as to my intentions just wasn't in the plan.

I . . . grinned. And said, "I'll show you where the ragbags are. And how to work the sewer."

Best of all, when we were leaving Threadneedly Street we saw the elephants. Five of them, arranged in size from biggest to littlest, walking in a line. They wore bright blankets and caps, alternating blue with red borders and red with blue, and each one carried a man in spangled tights or a woman whose short skirt resembled a bicycle costume.

They were gray and enormous, and the patterns on their skin was like the tiny triangles on the backs of your wrist only magnified a hundred times.

Priya stood beside me, squeezing my hand until I thought my fingers might pop off. "Those aren't real," she said. "They can't be real!"

"Aw, miss," Crispin said, laughing pleasantly. "It's just that the circus is in town."

Chapter Nine

It was a few nights later when Merry Lee declared herself well enough to leave us the following day. That was the night everything changed, and not for the better. Although we didn't find out what it was about until the next day, it turned out that was the night Missus Parkins' girls took unwilling delivery of the second murdered *nymph du prairie*.

It was just Beatrice, Effie, Merry Lee, Priya, and me in the library that evening. Miss Bethel was feeling poorly, and Miss Lizzie was with her. We were all a little agitated, hoping it wouldn't turn out to be scarlet fever or God knows what, but we were also very cheered by Merry's recovery. We were drinking sherry and whiskey; Merry was reading aloud from another dime novel while Priya pawed through the pile that remained, deciding what she wanted to hear next. The one Merry was working on was about the Dodge City Marshal Ed Masterson, a Canadian who was shot down just that April by a cowboy in the line of duty but swiftly avenged by his brother Bat.

That's what the book said: *swiftly avenged*. It made me angry at first. Like avenging anything brings back the person you lost, or makes it hurt any damned less that they ain't with you anymore.

And then I thought, *But if Peter Bantle does anything more to Priya, I'll fucking kill him.*

As if she had heard me thinking of her, Priya suddenly looked up, grinning. Just as Merry finished a chapter, Priya blurted, "Here's one about your friend, Karen!"

The red-and-yellow cover she flourished held a completely unrecognizable image under lurid words that read: *BASS REEVES: THE LONE MARSHAL OF THE INDIAN TERRITORY.*

"Lone?" Effie scoffed. "Don't Marshals always got a posseman?"

"Marshal Reeves mentioned one," I allowed. Still, I itched to get my hands on that book. But I knowed better than to let Effie see me eager. She didn't mean ill, but she'd never let me forget I cared, either. And she'd try to make it as if I was romantically inclined toward him, which just weren't the case.

Maybe a little fascinated. And maybe a little envious as well.

Priya leaned forward. She wasn't playing Effie's game. She handed me the book.

I flipped it over. *Shootist. Legend. Master of Disguise. Lawman in a land without law!*

For the law-abiders in the Indian Territory, Deputy United States Marshal Bass Reeves is the Last Recourse.

"Master of disguise." I riffled the pages.

"We can read that one next," Beatrice said. She had a grin on her face, too, but not a teasing one. I started to think maybe she liked the Marshal as well as I did. And he hadn't even saved her life.

Bea has pretty good horse sense when it comes to who to trust and who not to, and I took a note. Sure, I liked him. But if Bea liked him, that meant something. "Master of disguise," I muttered again.

Now they was all looking at me.

"Priya, I might know how to get a message to your sister. Maybe even how to bust her out."

"First you have to find her," Merry Lee said, lowering the book about the Mastersons—there were three of 'em in all, Mastersons and lawmen, that was.

I tried to hold in my grin, knowing it weren't appropriate. But it crept across my cheeks as irresistibly as dawning before I let myself say, "If this works, Peter Bantle hisself will tell us right where to find her."

I looked up right after I said it—and right into the wide, wide gray eyes of Miss Francina, who was leaning in the library door. She blinked them, and I jumped up from my chair and opened my mouth to explain. I'm not sure I've ever thought so frantically in my life, saving right when Da died.

Miss Francina held up a finger and said, "Shh." Just like that. Like it was a word. She looked us over, one by one. Not a one of us had the moxie to pipe up to her.

Then, shaking her head, she continued, "Oh, you girls. No, not a word more. I don't know what you *are* thinking . . . and I want to be honestly able to say I *didn't* know what you were thinking, either, if you follow me."

The door clicked shut behind her on a last glimpse of jiggling yellow corkscrews, and Beatrice, Effie, Priya, and me all looked back and forth at one another.

It seemed like we had a friend.

Priya watched the door shut, then put her elbows on her knees and hunched at me like a hairy-shouldered buzzard. Whatever demand was in her pose and her expression didn't make it into her voice, though. It was hesitant, afraid to hope. "You have a plan."

"We need to talk to Marshal Reeves," I said.

As luck would have it, he came by just after breakfast the next day—or maybe the meal was luncheon for him. I wasn't sure the Marshal ever slept. Or if he did, maybe it wasn't on any kind of a regular schedule. He kept long hours, I guess I'm trying to say.

Crispin came in to tell me I had company while I was still sitting in the dining room after everybody else had gone. The funny thing is, I was writing out a note to the Marshal to go in the afternoon post and wondering who he'd find to read it and trying to phrase everything so there was nothing suggestive in it. Suggestive the wrong way, I mean: I didn't care if people took it as a proposition. That was as good an excuse as any.

The Marshal had left us the address of the hotel he was staying in, and I guessed they'd have a concierge or somebody who could read it out loud. Anyway, I wanted to get it done fast, because I didn't want anybody to catch me writing it and it was cold in my room for writing.

This time, the Marshal wasn't alone. He had what looked like a full-blood Indian with him, and not Priya's sort of Indian, either. And they asked for me special, at the door.

Crispin led them into the dining room, where I was the last one at the table, having pushed aside plates once piled with Connie's flapjacks and bacon and sausages to write. "Karen," he said, "the Marshal'd like a word with you."

I snorted at my failed letter in amusement.

"Thank you, Crispin."

He winked at me—*Karen's got a special* friend—and left again without comment. I'd take it from Crispin in a way I wouldn't from Effie, because I knowed Crispin didn't feel no need to fix me, file off my edges to make me more comfortable to be around.

The Marshal took my hand and stood to one side to introduce me to his companion. "Tomoatooah, this is Miss Karen Memery. She's helping with our inquiries. Miss Memery, this is Tomoatooah, my posseman. He's a Numu. You'd say Comanche."

"Hello, To . . . Tomoatooah," I stumbled over his name, and tried again. "Tomoatooah?"

He corrected me. The vowels weren't quite shaped like any sounds I was used to hearing. I tried again.

He shook his head and said, "I wish a good day to you, Miss Memery."

I looked at the Marshal curiously. "*I'd* say. You wouldn't?"

Marshal Reeves smiled tightly. "I lived on tribal land for a long time, between when I ran away and the end of the war. I speak some Indian." I could tell by the way he said "Indian," ironic, that he meant he spoke several kinds of Indian. You might not know this, but it's a fact that they have as many languages as white folk has. Maybe more.

Tomoatooah had a Roman nose, narrow and arched, like a warm-blood stud's. Full cheeks and a small chin, but a strong jaw that made his face look square in profile. Eyes like jet beads, glittering, and hair chopped at the shoulders except for two longer braids. He wore a lady's hat that would of been plain and black except there was a pale blue muslin scarf with black polka dots tied around it as a band, and he wore a gray wool coat over a red sprigged cotton shirt and buckskin trousers. But his real glory was the necklace, or breastplate, or what have you: long stark white Campbell hairpipe beads, hung horizontal between smaller bits of silver and wampum. It rustled a little with each breath he took, and I thought it very fine.

I asked him, "What does your name mean?"

His eyebrows arched as he replied, "What does yours?"

I hadn't thought about it until he said something, but his question was as good as mine, weren't it? "Karen," I said. "It's Danish. From my mom. It means 'pure.'" I held my hands up flat and shrugged. It was what it was. "And Memery, that's Irish. My dad's dad was a horsebreaker in Ireland before the potato famine. They came here to escape. I don't know what it means."

"Escaping famine," he said. "My people too have traveled for that. Thousand miles, or more. And horsebreaking, that's a good trade. My own name means 'Child of the Sky.'"

"Does that commemorate a deed?"

"Of my namer," he said. "Not of my own."

"Won't you sit?" I asked. "Have some flapjacks and bacon?" The servers still rested on the table.

"Don't mind if I do," the Marshal said. He proceeded to pull a plate from the warmer and load it up, finding some beans that I'd missed. "Oh," he said, discovering the sausages. "Mysteries!"

He handed that plate to Tomoatooah and filled one for himself. The two men fell to as if they hadn't seen food in a week. Maybe the Marshal treated it like sleep: a requirement of lesser men, until the need came unavoidable.

I knowed the Marshal hadn't just come for breakfast, so I weren't surprised when he got past the first flash of hunger, slowed down his fork wielding a mite, and poured himself another cup of still-warm coffee from the pot. Tomoatooah kept eating, chewing each bite meditatively before washing it down with coffee, but never slowing in his pace. Connie poked her nose out of the kitchen just then, saw that we was engaged, and backed out. I heard soft clattering behind the doors and wondered how long it would be before another piled-high covered platter appeared. Connie liked to cook for folk with an appetite.

"Miss Memery," the Marshal said. He paused and sipped coffee and started again. "Another girl's dead."

My mug rattled on the table when I set it down. "Who?"

He pursed his lips and shook his head kind of sideways. Judicious, like. "We don't rightly know. She was dumped outside Missus Parkins' kitchen door last night, or more like early this morning. Done up the same way as the other." That last he said with particular distaste.

I looked at him again—the weather-beated creases at the corners of his eyes, the tight-curled hair oiled and combed into a crinkle, pressed flat in a ring where his hat usually sat. Wrangler tonsure, my da would of said. His skin looked gray under his eyes. Maybe he weren't so immortal after all.

As I studied the Marshal, I was aware of Tomoatooah studying me. The Marshal broke the triangle, though, gazing off into the distance as if his eyes tracked an invisible killer across an invisible range.

We might still have been there if there hadn't been a thump and a creak—familiar to me, if not to the gentlemen. I started anyway, tossing my head up like a high-strung colt, and I swear the Marshal actually reached for his gun. Tomoatooah just folded another rasher into his mouth. That was the correct reaction; it was just Signor opening the door with his trick of jumping at the handle. He sauntered in, purring in a self-pleased fashion that about rang the crystal, and proceeded on a circuit of the table. He put a paw into my lap—he was big enough so it wasn't much of a stretch for him—and butted his big, round head against my elbow. He was begging for my bacon scraps, of course—but the wobble of his belly made a pretty convincing argument that he didn't need any.

Still, it broke the tension and made me able to talk again.

"You think there's a reason the killer's doing that," I said. "Dumping the dead girls that way."

The Marshal glanced at me, then forked another flapjack and a couple of mysteries onto his plate. "I think it was good fortune and happy happenstance as led me to you, miss. And I think I've been an idiot not to realize before now that there's some link between your nemesis and my murder writ."

I knowed the word "nemesis." It turned up in Bullfinch's *Age of Fable*, which I'd read cover to cover about five times. I pushed Signor down gently. He reared up again, purring all the harder. In a minute, he'd start to caterwaul louder than a puma. Being deaf as a stone, he didn't know his own power.

I said, "My nemesis . . . you mean Peter Bantle."

"Given how he seems determined to threaten you lot, and you in particular, miss—and the fact that the first dead whore, begging your pardon, was dumped in your rubbish? I'd say it's a fair guess he's got it in for you, miss, personally as well as categorically."

That made sense. I nodded, and when I followed Tomoatooah's gaze back to his face I found him nodding, too.

"I did tell him to get the hell out of my parlor. And I didn't let him see I was scared of him, neither."

The Marshal looked at me with the same look he'd given when he'd said he'd seen folk survive worse floggings than the dead sparrow'd gotten. Like maybe he knew something about folk who needed to see you scared of them. He said, "He'd hate you for that."

We were briefly interrupted by Connie with a fresh pot of coffee and a plate of corn cakes, of which I took one just to be companionable. I weren't too hungry, having just had breakfast and all, but a hot corn cake fried in grease, with a good drip of molasses, ain't to be missed.

Once I'd gotten myself around a good forkful—the rest weren't going to waste, not with the Comanche's dedicated trenchermanship at hand—and poured myself some of that fresh coffee, I starched up my nerve and said, "Marshal . . . I had an idea."

At this point, Signor determined that he'd get no satisfaction from me and went to bother the Marshal. I winced, thinking of sharp claws and of white fur on black trousers and of how some range men ain't tolerant of pets. But as I was trying to figure out what order to put the coffeepot down and get my feet under me in, so I could retrieve Signor and eject him from the dining room—not that that ever lasted—the Marshal lifted his arms, leaned back, and made room for the cat in his lap.

I watched in wonderment as all stone and a half of Signor thumped into the Marshal's lap and tea-cozied up, purring even louder.

Reaching carefully around the cat, who was now rubbing his face against the Marshal's waistcoat buttons, the Marshal put his cup out. I switched the stream of coffee from my cup to his.

"He don't usually cotton to strangers," I said, nodding to Signor.

The Marshal fed him a bit of bacon. "I like critters," he said. "Can't be a good horseman if your horse don't take to you."

I stared, blushing. That was it, I realized. Though one was black and the other Irish, this man reminded me of my da. It took me several good seconds before I could manage, "Well, you've got a cat for life, now. Or at least as long as the bacon holds out."

The Marshal smiled, sipped his coffee somehow without dragging his mustache through it, and said, "I'm all ears."

"You're all mustache," Tomoatooah corrected, and they shared a tired grin.

"Let's hear the lady's plan," the Marshal said. When I set the coffeepot down, he poured for Tomoatooah and we all drank silently together for a few moments as I collected myself.

"It requires an awful lot of you," I started hesitantly.

His mustache did that thing I was starting to learn was a silent laugh—a kind of quiver, as if his upper lip was writhing behind it. "Miss," he said, "I believe I told you how I came twelve hundred miles—as the crow flies; I'm pretty sure I covered half again that—by rail and pony and mule and my own two feet—"

"And mine," Tomoatooah added between bites. He talked with his mouth full. I'd better make sure Miss Bethel didn't see that.

Fortunately, she was still abed with her gripe. I only say "fortunately" because she was already feeling better from the night before, you understand.

"Anyway," Reeves added, pushing his polished plate back. There was still one smear of butter and molasses on it: he picked up a corner of flapjack off Tomoatooah's plate and scrubbed it away, then disposed of the evidence. "I've already given an awful lot of me to this case. I can only hope that Judge Parker will still pay my expenses when I get back, and they'll probably only do that if I get my man. Now, I ain't no Texas Ranger—"

Tomoatooah worked his jaw as if he meant to spit, then recollected the dining room rug and took a swig of coffee instead. I was getting to like this rough man. Comanche had a reputation as the fiercest of Indian braves; I knowed even the other Plains tribes was afraid of them, though I thought they was all supposed to be on reservations since that Quanah surrendered a few years back. And this one might of been a hardened killer—but so was the U.S. Marshal sitting across from him, and I was finding myself more and more enamored of both their senses of humor.

"Tell me your plan," Marshal Reeves finished.

I hid my scorching cheeks behind my hands, thereby losing any chance of pretending it was just the cold in the room growing as the fire died down. "I read in a dime novel that you was a master of disguise," I said. "Now I know them books ain't worth the dry yellow paper they're printed on. But . . ."

The Marshal's mustache was doing its little burlesque shimmy on his lip again. "Master of disguise? You know not to believe what you read—"

Tomoatooah leaned across the table and jabbed him in the shoulder with the handle of a butter knife. "She's got your number, gunslinger."

I had to finish on a rush, because otherwise I just wasn't going to get the words out. Quickly I told him about Priya's sister. I finished, "So. If you was to go to Bantle's crib," I said. "And say you was to say you'd heard he had a girl called Aashini that gave a real good ride. And wanted to have a go . . ."

"But according to what you just said, your friend Priya said she didn't know if she was at Bantle's, last she knew."

"You don't know Peter Bantle the way I do. Priya meant something to him. Nothing good. But she got away, and so he's gonna get his hands on her sister to punish her. Same as he'll do whatever he can to punish Madame, and me. And Effie too, I don't wonder. I'd wager Aashini Swati's in Bantle's crib now, because he knows it'd make Priya suffer."

It was a little while before I recognized the look on Marshal Reeves' face, though it silenced me. It was respect, and I hadn't seen that from a man who weren't Crispin since I don't know when. "That's not half-bad," he said, having chewed it over for a bit. "And it might of worked, too. Except Bantle knows I'm here, now, and he knows I'm looking for . . . well, not him, maybe. Unless he's out of town often, on a lot of long trips . . . ?"

"Sorry," I said. "I wish I could say so. Hell, I wish he was gone so often we'd never heard of him."

"It was too much to hope for, really. And I'd still be glad to help you, on account of your friend's sister might be able to tell us a thing or two about Bantle and his friends. But anyway, the meat of it is, he knows I'm here. And while I know a few tricks—making myself look smaller in the saddle and the like—I can't change out my nose for another." He tapped it with a forefinger. "More's the pity."

"Damn." I looked at Tomoatooah. "Maybe you—"

"Only thing lower than a nigger is a savage," he said, shaking his head, the long muslin tails of his scarf rustling over his beadwork. "It wouldn't work. Even crib whores aren't for sale to Indians."

"Goddamn."

"Karen, darling. Language, dear."

A horrible shock seethed through the pit of my belly, cold and sharp. I turned in my chair to see Miss Francina pushing the hall door Signor had cracked the rest of the way open, frowning down at me.

"How much of that did you hear?" I asked her.

"Enough to know what a bad plan it is," she said. She pursed her lips and shook her head. Signor purred at her from Marshal Reeves' lap, arching his neck to see over the table.

"But Priya—" I started.

Miss Francina held up one kid-gloved hand. "Yes, Priya. I'm not insensible, sweet child." She flipped a glorious waterfall of golden ringlets behind one white shoulder, baring the delicate line of her collarbone and the creamy swell of her little bosom. I didn't know how she managed that effect, but I knowed some small-chested girls who might kill to find out.

She tapped her fingers on her lips. Then she sighed and said, "Well, there's nothing else for it. I'll do it." And as we all three gaped at her, she smiled with one half of her mouth and said, "I can pass for a man, sugar. I've known enough of 'em. Besides, it's for Priya."

We determined to strike while the iron was hot. Having helped Merry Lee pack up her few things—and let her into the plan, because we could think of nobody in all Rapid City more qualified to lead a daring rooftop escape if we should need one—we resolved to do the thing that very night.

We also agreed not to tell Priya just yet. It would be cruel to get her hopes up while there was still so much that could go wrong. We couldn't bring Aashini back to Madam Damnable's, either. She hadn't expressly forbidden it, but she had not beaten around any bushes in making it plain that she didn't wish to work her way any further into Bantle's bad graces.

Merry Lee said she had a place and Bantle had never found it. And that he never would find it, she figured, since Chinatown residents didn't have much to say to Peter Bantle. "He had his girls led through the streets in collars once a week," she said. "To show off the wares. It's the only sunshine most of 'em get."

There was not much any of us could say to that stone look in her wide-set black eyes. So we all sat dumb, and after a while she took pity and said that she'd feel safer all around if rather than telling Miss Francina where her safe house was, she just waited for Miss Francina and Aashini to make their escape and then guide them to it.

"Well, I'll wait with you," the Marshal said, which kicked off a brief argument that wasn't settled until he agreed to let Tomoatooah and me come with him, too. He looked dubiously at me at first, but I reminded him that I could handle a gun, and he finally tipped his head and shrugged in that way he had. "Well, ain't you a regular little Annie Oakley."

Once that was settled—and I make it sound easier than it was, but there ain't no point in regurgitating fifteen minutes of circular arguing—Miss Francina raked a hand through her curls, snagging her fingers on a jeweled comb. "All right then," she said. "We won't meet here."

"There's a bar down by the docks," the Marshal said. "It's called the Lion's Den. You know it?"

Miss Francina smiled. "I know it," she said. "I'll see you there at three A.M."

But then Marshal Reeves looked at me, kissed air, and said, "Miss Memery, can you ride?"

I purely don't mind saying my heart fell through to my boots. No, well. Actually, I do mind saying it. But that's what happened, all the same.

I just concentrated on keeping all my doubt and confusion and sadness off my face while I figured out what I was going to say.

"If I gotta," I answered at last, and the Marshal was kind enough to leave it at that.

Chapter Ten

We knocked off work a little after two, it being early in the week, and Miss Francina and I both separately pled tiredness and headed upstairs. I changed myself into plain clothes and no stays and no crinolines. Remembering what Marshal Reeves had called me, I'd taken a few minutes to tack up the hem of my sturdiest navy broadcloth day dress almost to the tops of my boots—just like Annie Oakley wore. I envied Priya her trousers and might almost have borrowed a pair, but they'd never stretch over my hips and anyways, she'd want to know what I planned on using them for.

I slipped the Marshal's Morgan dollar back into my boot top, though. For luck.

When I sneaked back down and met Miss Francina out by the dustbins, I could hardly credit my eyes. I mean, standing there gave me a shiver, like that poor dead girl's half-flayed corpse was still cooling on the stones. But the real shiver was because of the tallish, slender man with his blond hair slicked back in a plait and dropped down the back of his collar. He

looked so familiar . . . and yet so strange. He had narrow, aristocratic features—the sort you'd expect from a Bostonian,
maybe. Or an Englishman. The eyes were deep set and drowsy,
gray under a pronounced curve of bone. The nose was long
and elegant.

He wore workman's togs, though—dungarees and a check
shirt with a dingy red bandanna for a cravat—and hard boots
laced to the mid-calf. And when he talked, he talked like me,
or any of the girls who ain't yet learnt all Miss Bethel has to
teach 'em.

It was like meeting a good friend's hitherto-unexpected kin.
It gave me a good hard unsettle, that I don't mind reporting.

"Do I pass?" Miss Francina asked me. And then she smiled,
and it was her again, just dressed up in men's kit.

"I'd not have recognized you on the street," I admitted. Then
I said, "Your teeth and your skin are too good to be visiting
Bantle's girls."

"Some like rough trade that can afford better," Miss Francina said sourly. "And some like a girl who'd like to fight back,
but can't afford to."

"Gah," I said, though of course I knowed it. "How are we
going to find you, once you're in?"

She dug in her big coat pocket. "I borrowed this from Lizzie."
When she held out her hand, there was something like a min-
iature wireless telegraph set in it, except it had some dials set
in the front and two antennas. I tapped on a dial with my fingertip; the needle stayed pointed right at Miss Francina. The
other needle seemed to be pointing at the first dial.

"Slip that in your reticule," she said.

"What is it?"

She flipped her coat open and showed me a brooch pinned to
the lining. "It tracks this," she said. "The left needle points toward the brooch. The right needle swings toward the left needle

depending on how close the brooch is. And the brooch has a switch in it so if you click it the right way, it'll make a light light up on the dingus. Merry Lee will be waiting for your signal. So when I have Aashini, I'll click the switch. You wave Merry in to take the girl. I'll get her up to the roof."

I felt my forehead crinkle right up like a ruched skirt when you draw the strings. "That's genius."

"That's Lizzie," she replied.

I don't mind saying I were on pins and tenterhooks and broken glass the whole way down to the Lion's Den. It ain't a nice saloon, by any means, and when I walked in on Miss Francina—I mean, Alias Zach Murphy's arm, a lot of heads turned to see the lady. Nobody commented on my tacked-up dress, though, even though there weren't a lot of other sets of skirts in there.

Merry Lee was nowhere in sight, which was probably wise. Some of these men might get the wrong idea about a Chinese girl walking in here, and that would end badly for everyone. But Bass Reeves was elbowed up to the bar. He had a shot of whiskey on the plank before him, black enough that I wondered if it was wood alcohol darkened up with some coal tar. I might of warned the Marshal, except he didn't seem to have any intention of drinking that stuff.

A real western saloon ain't the kind of dusty tavern with swinging doors they write about in the dime novels. I mean, sure, there's some barrelhouses ain't got more than a plank laid over sawhorses to serve on, but the balance of 'em have got carved mahogany back bars—ours ain't even the nicest I've seen—mirrors, Oriental carpeting. Glass windows, some of 'em have.

Except for this place, apparently. There was nothing on the

bare splintered floor but sawdust and eyeballs. The bartender's stock was on a couple of plank shelves against the back wall, none of it looking too appetizing. Sawhorses would of been a step up: the plank bar balanced on empty barrels, and the clientele apparently used 'em as spittoons.

I followed Murphy as "he" cut through the crowd to the bar, bellied up, and in a raspy monotone told the bartender, "Kill me quick!" "He" laid a shiny silver trime on the counter; it was quickly superseded by a shot as black and tarry as the one in front of the Marshal we were pretending not to know.

"Anything for the lady?" the barman said, looking at me dubiously.

"No, thank you." Under my breath to Murphy, I said, "You know they call it that for a reason."

"He" nudged his shot of "kill me quick" with a thumbnail, then picked it up and downed it. The grimace that followed was as elegant as "his" voice when he rasped out, "Turpentine," quietly enough that only the Marshal on "his" right and me on "his" left might hear "him."

"Well," I answered. "My guess was coal tar. Have you gone blind?"

"No, more's the pity." Murphy gestured to the piss-stained sawdust on the floor. "He" called for another shot of the coffin varnish and let this one sit, much to my relievedness.

After a bit, I edged in between Murphy and the Marshal and we engaged in a bit of business with money changing hands. I left with Marshal Reeves. The plan was for Murphy to come out after us and proceed on to Peter Bantle's cribhouse. Marshal Reeves and me would stay with the horses, since I'd allowed as I could ride. We were Miss Francina's way out. And the distraction, and the backup plan. We hoped we could hand Aashini off to Tomoatooah and Merry Lee, who should already be in place on a nearby rooftop. They would whisk her away, and the Marshal, Miss Francina, and I would be able to lose our pursuit in the rat's nest of alleys down by the docks, or in the shantytowns that washed away whenever the summer storms got bad.

Merry still wasn't in any shape for daring escapades, and I was passionately worried about her. She'd not been willing to tell us where her safe house was, though, and so she was in whether we wanted her to be or not.

I would just have to count on Tomoatooah to defend her. Given the fearsome reputation of the Comanche, I didn't expect him to disappoint me. But I was still worried. For him, too, of course. For Marshal Reeves and me. But chiefly for Miss Francina—I mean Murphy. And for Merry Lee.

It was overcast, and that was our friend. But it was starting to rain—lightly, but enough to render roof tiles and cobblestones slick as ice. That might be our friend . . . but it was just as likely to be our enemy.

I hoped Aashini could climb and run. I hoped she was as tough and smart and stubborn as her sister.

I was worrying about that and a dozen other things when the Marshal and I made it back to the horses. He'd paid a pair of small Negro boys to watch them, and I waited in the shadows until he'd given them each a pinky-nail-sized flake of gold—for urchins, the very large wealth of a dollar. The urchins (children with homes to go to weren't running wild in the streets at three in the morning) vanished into the same shadows I emerged from.

There were four horses, a gelding and three mares—Bass Reeves' and Tomoatooah's mounts and remounts. They looked mighty fine to my eye, all four of 'em, and it filled my mouth with sick water just catching wind of their warm, horsy scent. I wanted to go run and throw my arms around their necks, I'd missed horses so damned much. And I wanted to go punch each of 'em in the throat for what had happened to my da.

I knowed that was stupid, and my hands shook with not trusting myself not to take out on 'em what wasn't their fault—and what wasn't even the dumb animal fault of the colt that killed Da.

Da would always say you don't blame an animal for being an animal. Not when we're men and God gave us reason and made us custodians. And then he'd usually mutter something uncomplimentary about folk who didn't use that God-given gift, and who still thought they had the right to boss around God's other creatures.

Every time I started to get killing mad at that colt, I tried to remember him saying that. It helped, mostly. The colt lived past me, anyway.

But it occurs to me now that maybe I was being a bit two-faced when I said earlier that I didn't understand coveting after revenge. I guess in honesty it's more that Mama and Da raised me to think things through before I did 'em, mostly. And mostly, I do.

So I bit my lip and made myself look over the horses without flinching or making faces.

The gelding and one of the mares were big for my taste, but Bass Reeves is a big man. They both carried good muscle. The gray—the gelding—had a neck that made me sad he was gelded, and if he was a bit straight behind he had the muscle to make up for the lack of leverage. The sorrel shoved a soft nose at me as soon as she saw me, and nibbled around my pockets for a treat. I pretended like I'd forgotten to bring any, and looked at her shoulders, which were strong and sloped just right.

I thought the gray was probably a pretty light-colored horse, in his own right, but judging by the streaks he was starting to

show from the raindrops, Marshal Reeves had blacked him up
a bit with soot so he wouldn't show so much in the darkness.

The other two mares were Indian ponies, and some people
use that to mean scrub horses, but those people is just plumb
ignorant. Mustangs was what the Pony Express used, and
nobody—not the fanciest eastern racehorse farmer or the can-
niest western cutting-horse rancher—knows more about breeding than the horse tribes do. When Indians don't have good
horses, it's because their good horses was killed by the army
or taken away when the Indians was moved on. Their ponies
are smart and strong and though they're little, nothing makes
a better cutting horse. My da used to itch to get his hands on
Indian ponies.

He would of traded his eyeteeth and his last pan of biscuits
for these. One was a sturdy-looking paint, a black tobiano with
one brown eye and one china blue. She had the smartest ears
I'd ever seen, perked up and touched almost tip to tip, and a
dished face that made her look like a Barb. She might be, part-
ways. There's Barb blood in those Indian ponies, because they
come from the Conquistadores' horses and those come from
when the Moors conquered Spain. She also had a big chest,
for a mare, and clean, straight forelegs. All four of her hooves
was dark. I don't hold with the idea that a white-footed horse
is necessarily worse than one with dark hooves, though I know
some do. But I could see that her hoof edges was clean, though
she'd never known shoes.

The other was a dun—the kind of dun the Indians get, with
the stripe down her spine and the stripes on the lower part of
the legs, like maybe her grandaddy was a zebra. It wasn't the
prettiest color I'd ever seen—dull in the gaslight and like somebody had rubbed red earth all through a gray horse's hide—
but she grinned at me like a mule when I came up to her. It

might of been a mean expression, except her ears stayed up. I've knowed a few horses learned to smile back at people. They always seem to be the damned smart ones.

My Molly was a grinner.

I finally "found" the carrots and parsnips in my pockets and broke bits off for everyone. Until I felt the whiffle of whiskers across my palms, the nibble of soft lips, I didn't realize how much I needed it. Something tightened up in my chest. But something bigger eased—a band cracked open. Like the iron straps that coop a barrel together, it split, and everything I'd been holding in came boiling up, trying to get out and splash all over. Like that beer flood over in London you've heard of, near on forty years before I was born, where all the people drowned in cellars when the brewery's vats exploded.

It would of been about that much of a mess, too. I could feel my lip quivering, my eyes starting to burn. I was going to collapse in the mud in a second and be no use to Priya or Miss Francina or Aashini or Marshal Reeves or anyone. And it was all down to that warm snuffle on my palm, such as I hadn't felt since I had to sell off my father's stock. And give up Molly. I still can't help but feel like I betrayed her, though I found her the best home I could and it was better for her than starving with me would of been.

That stock money didn't go near as far as I expected, in a place like Rapid City. And weren't many willing to hire a girl of fifteen to break horses for 'em or even as a stable hand.

And that's how I wound up seamstressing for Madame Damnable.

"Miss?" Marshal Reeves said behind me. His hand on my shoulder was warm and solid, and somehow I used its weight to pull myself together instead of crumpling completely. It were a near thing, though. "Miss Memery? Second thoughts?"

I couldn't bear to have him think me a coward. I jerked my head up as if I could toss the tears back into my eyes, sniffed hard—hoping it sounded like disdain—and said, "No sir."

I wanted to tell him that my da had horses. That I grew up in the saddle. But if I'd been going to tell him that the time to mention it would of been when I'd told him I could ride.

I hadn't said a word about how I hadn't touched a pony in more than a year. It wouldn't do anything for his confidence in me to bring it up now.

"What's her name?" I asked, of the piebald mare.

"That's Scout," he said. "The dun is Adobe. The sorrel's Dusty, and this here gelding is Pongo. You'll be on Scout."

I nodded. I was glad she seemed friendly, and I could see from the condition of her lips and the easy bit she was wearing that she reined well—and that Tomoatooah had a gentle hand. "I'm looking forward to it," I said, and it was half a lie and half the bitterest truth I ever mouthed. I scratched behind her ever-so-pointy ears and gave her another bite of parsnip. "Good horse."

His teeth flashed in the dark. "You'll have to give her back when you're done with her."

"How're you going to catch me?" I asked, grinning back. I kicked my shortened skirt up and swung into the rig before I could think about it too much more. Scout stepped right once, then steadied. She *was* little—I was looking over her ears, not between them—but she didn't so much as duck under my weight.

"You'll do," he answered, forking his own rig—the one the sorrel wore. "Come on. I got our stakeout all selected. There's some cover, and it's even out of the wind."

I followed on the clopping of the hooves leading me toward the pier. Adobe's rein was looped on Scout's saddle biscuit, and he trouped along with his nose on her shoulder like they did this daily. That seemed likely, actually.

My da wouldn't of approved of that name—Adobe. He'd say you couldn't yell it well enough, and every horse, dog, and child should have a name you could holler clearly through a hurricane. But it suited the horse and she wasn't *my* horse, so I weren't in any hurry to rename her.

Marshal Reeves pulled up, and I saw he hadn't oversold his hidy-hole. But he hadn't much undersold it, either. It was a nook, was all. A bit of alley with a bend at the back and no gas lamps. And nothing to stop the sky dripping on us, neither, though he was right in that it was more or less out of the wind.

We hunched under our hats, angling our heads so the rain didn't drip off the brims down our backs. We stayed mounted, and I imagined we was both anonymous and shapeless in our oilcloth capes. He smoked under his hat, cursing occasionally when the rain put his cigarette out. The horses didn't waste their energy shaking or stamping. They just stood, ears only a tetch droopier than their heads, and occasionally heaved great horsy sighs profound enough to make Marshal Reeves' spurs jingle.

We waited.

And waited—long enough for the butterflies in my stomach to start tying knots to pass the time, long enough that I started at every sound, expecting shouts or gunshots. Much, much longer than I had hoped or expected—or so I guessed. I had a little watch on a chain that had been my mother's. I didn't dare pull it out and check the time for fear of it being ruined by the rain—and it was too damned dark to see it anyway. I was trying to keep from checking Miss Lizzie's tracker, too, other than glances under the cape to see if its light had come on, since I didn't know how that would respond to being doused, either.

Even less cheerfully than the horses did, that was my supposition.

I did look at it once, shielding the whole thing with my oil-cloth, but I had to edge over close to the gas lamp to see it at all, and while I kept the gadget dry, I got rain all down my back in the process. As near as I could figure through the dark and the rain stinging my eyes, Miss Francina was off in the direction of the cribs and some distance away. Right there where she was supposed to be, in other words.

I gave up on the gadget. Might as well save its juice for if she got kidnapped and we had to chase her down and save her.

Despite my being on edge and my checking over my shoulder approximately every thirteen seconds, I still would of screamed and fallen off Scout's saddle when Tomoatooah appeared if it hadn't been for Scout giving him away in advance. But by her pricked ears and turned head I knowed somebody was approaching, and by her pleased expression I knowed it was someone as she knowed and liked. The Marshal, of course, wasn't taken by surprise at all.

I already had Adobe's reins unlooped from my biscuit and extended when Tomoatooah came up on us. He weren't running, though, and he didn't reach for 'em, so I dropped 'em back over the horn and waited to see what happened next.

We both knowed something was wrong. The Marshal didn't bother asking, just turned his head and looked down at Tomoatooah from the height of his saddle.

Whatever the question was, it must of been contained in their prolonged association. Because Tomoatooah nodded. He started to say something in what might of been Comanche, then glanced at me, pitched his voice lower, and replied, "There were men with rifles on the rooftops. Who would post sentries over a crib-house?"

"Somebody who had more in there than starved, beat whores," Marshal Reeves said. Then he glanced at me. "Begging your pardon, Miss Memery."

"Wait," I said. We were all talking—not in whispers, because whispers carry. But in low conversational tones. "There *were* men with rifles?"

Despite the dark, I made out Tomoatooah's modest shrug, and wondered if he'd ever be getting around to naming some young cousin Kills on Rooftop. The chill that gripped my spine had nothing to do with the drip of rain.

Then he grinned and said, "I imagine they'll get out eventually. Wet rawhide stretches, and I used my second-best knots."

The Marshal's posture eased a little; in the dark, I couldn't see his face. But he sounded relieved when he said, "Counting coup on Bantle's men is a dangerous pastime, Sky."

"That's the point of coup," Tomoatooah said. "Killing is easy. There's no face in it. Any sign yet of our friends?"

The men exchanged another look I couldn't read—couldn't barely *detect,* in the rain and the gloom. Then—I thought for my benefit—the Marshal said, "Five more minutes and we leave the ponies with Miss Memery and go in after them."

I might of protested. But somebody did have to stay with the ponies. And having just seen Tomoatooah move down the alley like a panther on greased ice, I couldn't justify any argument I came up with to me, let alone the Marshal. Besides, I *knowed* I could handle the horses. I'd be a help here, and not an impediment.

The Marshal checked his revolvers—careful to keep them dry under the shelter of his hat—and I swear I heard him singing under his breath: "Two herring boxes without the tops on / Just made the sandals of Clementine. . . ."

Damnedest thing I ever witnessed, but I supposit we all got our ways of keeping the wolves amused if we can't keep 'em at bay.

It didn't take five minutes, though. I was counting one-Mississippi two-Mississippi for the third time and Marshal

Reeves had just finished up with Clementine and was moving on to, "Fare thee well, Fare thee well, Fare thee well, my fairy fay," when that shouting I'd been afraid of broke out. It was a ruckus that should of invited the squeal of police whistles except there weren't nothing legal about the way Bantle kept his girls. The constables weren't going to cross him and go in after any Indian or Chinese whore, I mean—but they weren't going to help him get one back, neither.

Some of them constables had used to be slaves before the war, too, I heard tell.

Before I really knowed what was happening, Tomoatooah was up in Adobe's saddle. He leaned way out, so one knee hooked the saddle bow, and lifted the reins off Scout's pommel before I did more than start reaching to loose 'em.

The Marshal was already pushing Dusty into a canter. He tossed me Pongo's reins as they passed—as if to make up in a weird sort of way for me losing Adobe. I grabbed those reins and held on: the gelding wanted to follow his stablemates, and Scout had to turn in a circle a time or two to convince him otherwise.

By the time me and the horses was sorted, the Marshal and his posseman had about vanished into the rain. They were just big, bulky black shapes in the gas lamps of Commercial Street, and as I nudged Scout up to the edge of the alley I could make out the grim dull lights of Bantle's cribhouse at the end of the block.

A cribhouse, if you ain't seen one, is sort of a stable for people. It's one or more long buildings, a single story tall, not built to keep the weather out. And rather than having stalls that open on to a central corridor, it has cells that open out to the outside, built side by side and back to back.

Well, one of those cells was open and grimy lamplight spilled out on to the street. A tall figure, strangely lumpy on thin legs, was half-running and half-staggering toward Marshal Reeves and Tomoatooah, booted feet stomping big splashes out of puddles. Behind him, a hue and cry was swirling out into the street—half a dozen men at least, though some of them seemed the worse for drink from how they was staggering.

The horses' hooves rang or thudded, as the state of their farriering dictated, and the foremost running figure hurled itself toward them. They charged past, and I realized suddenly that if that was Miss Francina, then the plan was changing and I needed to get Pongo up there *tout suite,* as Beatrice would say.

I gave Scout my heels—just a touch—and she responded like an angel. Like an avenging angel, jumping forward through suddenly heavy palls of rain. I hoped Merry Lee could hear the commotion, and had sense enough to take herself off.

And then we had other problems and I lost the leisure to worry about any of 'em.

Scout had the build of a good cutting horse, and it turned out she had the wits of one, too. She seemed to know what we were after better than I did, and shouldered the bigger Pongo to a halt just steps from running over Miss Francina. And it *was* Miss Francina—hat blown off, hair draggled and lank, rain dripping off the tip of her long nose. The strangely bulky appearance was on account of she had a girl bundled up in her arms.

A girl she hoisted up to me, straight armed. Now, I knowed Miss Francina was strong as hell, but seeing that I wasn't surprised that the person I pulled onto Scout's saddle behind me wasn't much more than twine and broomstraws wrapped up in a wet cotton nightshirt and Miss Francina's Alias Murphy coat.

Miss Francina thrashed up into Pongo's saddle and I tossed her the reins, then stole a glance back at Tomoatooah and Marshal Reeves.

They'd reined in and now sat their horses two abreast across
Commercial Street, blocking the way. The Marshal had his Winchester rifle out and his head bent over it. Tomoatooah had put
a shotgun to his shoulder.

The Marshal called something to the men swarming out of
the cribhouse. I couldn't make the words, but the tone echoed
with command. The men coming up on him and Tomoatooah
stopped. One reached for a hip holster but then danced back,
sparks flying from the wet stones by his feet. A split second
later the sound of the gunshot reached my little party. Pongo
and Scout both took it with equanimity, but the girl against
my back, who was probably Aashini Swati, made up for it by
startling enough for all of us.

"Aashini," I said over my shoulder to the shivering girl, "hold
on tight. Your sister Priya sent us."

Not exactly true. But close enough, and I needed to save
on explanations. And from the way she clutched at me, she
wanted to believe it.

"Karen honey," Miss Francina said, "not to needle you, but
we should be going."

As we turned the horses, I called out to Miss Francina, "Why
didn't you use the gadget?"

She was wrestling the reins. Fortunately, Pongo knowed what
he was doing. She yelled back, "I tried! It didn't work, now,
did it? And they must of twigged right off that something was
up, because there were two men right outside the door. I
knocked 'em down on the way out. But they seem to have got
up again."

We couldn't run the horses on these wet cobbles—not and
expect them *and* us to live. But Tomoatooah and the Marshal
were buying us time. I let Scout have her head, trusting her to
pick her own pace. She settled into a lope that was less pell-
mell than I would of liked but inexpressibly safer.

I glanced back over my shoulder. I had a confused glimpse of somebody pulling some strange sort of helmet on—big goggles on it—and then crying out and pointing after Miss Francina on Pongo. "He can see in the dark!" I yelled. I got a sense that he was gesturing for the benefit of unseen watchers, and felt a great relief at Tomoatooah's removal of those same.

The Winchester cracked again. I missed seeing it—I'd glanced back forward. But I felt a sudden, shocking tug as a bullet touched my collar. I gasped. Aashini huddled tighter under my oilcloth, making herself tiny against my back. I heard cursing behind me—the Marshal's voice—and then the shotgun roared once. I hunched down as close to Scout's neck as I could manage and urged her to pick up the pace, if she felt able.

When I glanced back again—under my armpit this time to keep from lifting my head—I saw something that chilled me. Peter Bantle was out in the street, standing under the gas lamp by his office door. I knowed him by his stature and his coat and because . . . because he had that glove on, and it snapped and sparked blue in the rain, but that didn't seem to trouble him. He was making a beckoning gesture to the Marshal, and the Marshal reined toward him—

I should turn back. I should turn back and help Marshal Reeves. What kind of a pissant coward was I, riding off when that brave man needed me—

That brave man who had just shot at me?

My hands lifted the reins as if moving of their own volition. My seat bones shifted in the saddle. Willing, generous, Scout slowed and turned.

"Dammit, Karen!" Miss Francina yelled back at me. But I didn't register it. Her words didn't mean any more than the heavy plop of the rain. Nor did it mean anything to me that Aashini yelped and twisted, seeming to try to figure out if she could slide down out of the saddle without breaking a leg.

Marshal Reeves rocked back and forth in his saddle, first urging Dusty forward, then clutching at the reins. The mare was getting mad at him, too. She skittered and hopped and thought about a buck. Her manners held though, for now. He pushed her a step forward. I could see he'd dropped his rifle—

He was five steps from Bantle now, in among Bantle's men. One—not the one with the bug-eyed helmet—stepped in to take his reins—

There was a bloodcurdling whoop, and in a flurry of hooves and streaming tail Adobe charged through the middle of the gang of men. I didn't even see Tomoatooah on his back, stuck as he was like a bit of sticking plaster in her mane, but I saw the result. The gang of men scattered, shattered. Dusty reared, kicking out at the one who had been about to grab her rein. And Tomoatooah must of leaned out of the saddle and grabbed Peter Bantle by the coat collar, because suddenly he was flailing along beside the running dun—running! On these roads!— with his boot heels bouncing off the stones and his arms flailing this way and that.

Tomoatooah had grabbed him on the off side—with his right hand—facing the other way. So Bantle's evil electric glove was on the side of his body away from Tomoatooah and Adobe, sending its sparks harmlessly into the air.

What am I doing? I thought suddenly—just as Tomoatooah let go of Bantle's collar and Bantle fell heavily on the stones. *What the hell am I doing here?* The Marshal, sitting in his saddle with his head shaking back and forth as if dazed, seemed to be wondering a similar thing. I saw him reach for his Winchester and look down in surprise to find it not in its saddle holster.

"Marshal!" I yelled back at him. *"Run!"*

I didn't stick around to see if he was listening but turned Scout back after Pongo and gave her a bounce to let her know I had returned to my senses and wanted to get gone.

What the hell were you waiting for? her ears said with a saucy flip.

I wished I had some kind of reasonable answer.

Chapter Eleven

It took us an hour and a half to get to where Merry Lee was supposed to be waiting if we needed our backup plan, because we rode in circles looking to befuddle any pursuit.

Tomoatooah and the Marshal caught up with us about a quarter hour after we all left the dockside, though. Tomoatooah had picked up the Winchester, but he didn't give it back to the Marshal straight off. He must of leaned out of the saddle and snatched it up off the stones. There was a chip out of the hardwood stock, but it was otherwise serviceable. A deal of what they say about Indians is goose grease, but I'm here to tell you—there's no goose grease in the stories of how Comanche ride.

And the Marshal couldn't stop apologizing for having taken that shot at me. "I had no intention of it. But my hand just came around—I just managed to jerk the gun up before the trigger pulled. You must believe me—I could not be more sorry. I have no idea what possessed me. It was as if someone else had control of my hands."

"I believe you," I said at last. "I don't think you miss unless you aim to. And—"

He shot me a sharp look. Miss Francina, off on my left, shot me a sharper one.

"I might know something about it," I allowed. "Let's talk later, when we're dry and not looking for killers on every corner."

Aashini might of fallen asleep against my back. Or she might just be huddled up like a mouse in the faint warmth of the oil-cloth. Miss Francina's shirt was plastered to her body, transparent as a jellyfish. Even the horses was grumbling with the wet and cold, and half the time we was picking down the darkest alleys imaginable and they was practically feeling their footing out with their whiskers as they went. The lit streets wasn't any better, seeing as I kept expecting Bantle's bullies to jump out and confound us.

Me, my shivering was half on account of I couldn't stop thinking of the shame and horror I'd felt after Peter Bantle broke down Madame's door. I could see that reflected in the stricken look Marshal Reeves kept shooting me.

And I also couldn't stop thinking about how sure Priya'd been that all sorts of people might vote for Bantle, whether he seemed like the right choice for the job or not.

I reined back beside the Marshal and reached out between horses—and way up, given the relative heights of Scout and Dusty—to put a hand on his arm. Wet wool rubbed my fingers, and his startled glance rubbed my face.

"I think maybe I got an idea what's going on," I said. "But let's talk about it back at Madame's."

He nodded. I could tell that much by the bobbing of his hat against the lesser dark of the walls behind him. When I let Scout head forward again—she was pretty obviously the lead mare in this bunch, for all Dusty was a sight bigger—I caught the speculative look Tomoatooah was giving me under Dusty's neck. Maybe he thought I had designs on his partner.

Maybe he was just wondering how much I knowed.

When we got to where Merry Lee was supposed to be waiting if things went cattywumpus, she was nowhere in sight. We rode up under an awning, though, glad for a bit of shelter from the constant drip drip of the rain. It didn't have the decency to really belly up and piss down on us. I missed the thunderstorms back in Hay Camp something awful. Here in Rapid, it just rained. There weren't no romance nor suspense to it.

We paused there, and it was quiet just long enough for Aashini to start to uncoil against my spine. I could feel her back there, all bones and elbows. Skinny enough to take a bath in a shotgun barrel. She straightened and poked her head up but didn't otherwise move. All of the rest of us just started exchanging unsettled looks. We had no way of knowing, see, if Merry Lee had gotten clear, or if she had fallen off a rooftop, or been gobbled up by a hidebehind or a gumberoo, for that matter. (Though I didn't rightly know if such critters of the lumberwoods ventured this far into town, not having grown up local. I'd heard the polar bears in Anchorage would walk right up to front doors, so people laid nail strips across their porches to prevent it. But our own native hodags back in Hay Camp are shy and won't come out where people can see 'em.)

We was in among some of those premade cast-iron buildings, the ones they ship in on barges and can get up in three minutes with the big armatures if they're being paid by the piece, not the hour. They sure is pretty, though, with their big fine windows and slender columns, and the painted iron on the front makes for a fine, elegant facade. All those curlicues and rosettes was casting funny shadows in the gaslight, though, and I was full of evil thoughts. I saw every flicker of motion as evidence of Bantle and his bullies, heard every shift of rain as stealthy footsteps.

And the damn rain just kept dripping down, dull and unpunctuated.

Unlike the rain, it turned out, Merry Lee had a fine sense of the dramatic. I was just getting antsy enough with the waiting that Scout started stamping and tail-swishing from catching my nervousness when Merry came spidering down a cast-iron drainpipe on one of those tall buildings just exactly like someone who hadn't had a bullet dug out of her back three weeks previous.

"She's gonna rupture herself," Marshal Reeves muttered as Merry set her boots neatly in the mud and turned to face us.

"Good to see you all," she said. Her cap of short hair was plastered down. As she came up by Scout, her eyelashes glittered with raindrops in the gaslight. "You got our friend away safe?"

The funniest thing is, by then I had to wake Aashini up to explain to her that we were handing her on to Merry Lee. She'd fallen asleep with her head on my shoulder, and as I turned in the rig and shook her gently I wondered how long it had been since she'd had an uninterrupted kip. I'm sorry to say it, but after everything, her blinking awake, bleary and terrified—and then sharply grateful when she saw my face and that of Merry Lee—that right there might of been what it took to crystallize my hate for Peter Bantle from something hot to something cold and despising. I felt mean and recognized that mean, because the only other time in life I felt that way was about the colt that killed Da.

Difference being, the colt was a colt and didn't deserve a ration of loathing. But Peter Bantle was a man.

I handed Aashini down and slid after, Scout waiting patiently while we sorted ourselves—though she allowed herself a little ear flicking and a snort over the clumsiness of riders.

"This is Merry Lee," I told Aashini when she'd gathered herself a little. The men—and Miss Francina, who was dressed to look like a man—stayed well back in what was most likely a wise decision. "She helped your sister Priyadarshini, and she's like to help you. Will you go with her?"

Aashini looked back and forth between us. I didn't doubt she understood me well, because whatever expressions crossed her face, confusion wasn't one of 'em. She seemed to weigh what I said, and then she answered, "You give me a choice?"

"From now on," I said, "you have choices. I can't bring you home with me, though—Madame wouldn't like it."

She flinched when I said "Madame," and I thought I knowed why. She pictured someone like Bantle. It didn't seem like the time to argue with her, so I let it slide.

For a moment, she chewed her ragged thumbnail and considered. I'd given her my oilcloth, and along with Miss Francina's coat it made her look like . . . not so much like a waif as a ragged old tree with a ripped-up tent draped over.

Then she nodded. "I'll go with Merry Lee," she said.

The Marshal and Tomoatooah—and Scout and Pongo—even got Miss Francina and me home in time for breakfast. For Connie's breakfast, that is. Not for the house's. Connie gets up earlier than everybody.

We drew up on the street above, opposite the upper-floor windows. When I swung my leg over the cantle and slid down Scout's side, though, I nearly fell down. Sure, my legs ached—a year out of the saddle will do that to you. But more than that, my whole belly ached with loss. I hadn't felt a grief like that since Da died, and I didn't rightly know what to do with it. So

I buried my face in the mare's pied mane for a bit and I gave her a big hard papa hug.

So maybe I could stand to be around horses again. Or maybe this horse, anyway.

For her part, she craned around and knocked my hat back on its strings to whuffle my hair, so that was all right then. The rain ran down my back, but I was so soaked already, who cared?

In truth, I had to hang on to her neck for them other reasons, too. It had been a good long time since I'd sat a horse, and the insides of my thighs were telling me all about it. I'd never had a lot of sympathy for the saddle sore before now. But it sunk in just then that maybe I'd just never felt real saddle soreness, having about grown up on a horse and been hardened off at a young age.

"I'll see to getting the horses back to the stable," Tomoatooah said to Marshal Reeves, "if you want to take the ladies inside."

The Marshal nodded. Miss Francina took my arm and guided me toward the ladder. Just looking at it made me bite my lip in anticipation, given that I was walking like somebody'd dropped red-hot iron wires down the inside of my bloomers. But I still heard Tomoatooah ask the Marshal if he wanted him to leave Dusty and the Marshal allowing as how she probably needed a hot mash and a rubdown more than another hour in the rain.

"I'll walk," he said, and even managed to sound cheery about it.

Somehow, we made it down the rain-slick ladder—I'm not too proud to admit I whimpered some—and into the kitchen door. Connie about dropped her spoon when she saw us, or in particular Miss Francina in her male clothes. But Connie gathered herself up fast enough and pretty soon we three was seated around her kitchen table with rags for our hair and with no questions asked, but plenty of hot coffee and hot biscuits and butter and honey being parceled out. Connie's kitchen gadget scrubbed and sliced and stirred and scraped, its octopus arms going every which way, and Connie herself presided and tasted and spiced and tweaked the knobs. I'd have thunk the clattering would drive her mad, but she just kept on smiling and lifting pot lids to sniff.

I don't know when Connie sleeps. Maybe she's related to the Marshal.

Speaking of sleeping, I knowed I needed to go upstairs and wake Priya and tell her her sister was safe and with Merry Lee. But I just didn't have the strength in my legs to walk up the stairs, or the strength in my heart to make myself do it anyway. Some coffee, and a biscuit or two, and a sit and I'd make myself get on up there. My legs would be screaming all the more when I got up again, I knowed. But maybe my moral fortitude would of regenerated. And if Priya was asleep, well, it weren't hurting her any to wait.

I thought about Scout and sipped my coffee. I had nearly four hundred dollars in gold and silver saved. I figured I needed a thousand to be safe, to buy my ranch and stock it and keep it running. I didn't think Tomoatooah would sell me Scout. But maybe someday he'd sell me one of her fillies.

I'd ridden a horse that night. And it hadn't broken me wide open to do it.

That was as comfortable and comforting in my belly as the coffee was, and I clung to it so as not to start crying over having to give Scout back to Tomoatooah. I always did fall in love hard and quickly. Da used to worry about it so. I remember this one sickly orange kitten. . . .

But that's a terrible story, and I don't feel like telling it today. I'd rather think about Molly, and Priya, and Scout.

Connie was kneading loaves on the other end of the table—she could have had the gadget do it, but she swore the results weren't as good. I watched her muscles play under medium-brown skin as she put her weight into it. Miss Francina was watching her own hands on the coffee mug, staring down her long nose like a hunter thinking over a jump. The Marshal was watching Connie, too, but from the faraway eyes and the little smile on his lips, I thought maybe he was thinking about another woman somewhere else. He'd said something about his wife . . . his Jennie. That was her name. His Jennie.

I wondered what it was like for her, being married to a man gone so often and so far away, dodging bullets and hunting bad men. I wondered how she trusted he'd come home or if she had plans laid in case he didn't.

Miss Francina sighed but didn't look up. The Marshal had one hand under the table, and I could see he was fingering the strap securing his pistol. He frowned and looked down, as if his reverie were broken. I wondered if he was feeling that same filthy grief I had, after I nearly grabbed the shotgun away from Effie.

I thought maybe I should manufacture some conversation.

"Why do you think the cribs was guarded like that?" I asked. It wasn't what I had intended to say . . . but I wasn't actually sure what I *had* intended to say and it was the easiest to talk about of all the things that was weighing on me.

"Not to keep in the girls," Miss Francina said. "They got bars on the window for that."

Connie could hear every word, of course. But she was Connie, and never a more trustworthy soul was hatched. She gave us a look, though, like she was thinking hard about what we said. In case she had some answers squirreled away somewhere, like the chocolate she could produce at any provocation.

"He's hiding something," the Marshal said. "Something . . . more than just the killer. He's got an armed camp there, and those whores are just . . . camouflage. Moneymaking camouflage," he amended.

"I hope," I said softly, "that Aashini's strong enough to make it."

The Marshal frowned more deeply at his coffee. "You ever seen a three-legged dog? Most times they get around just fine."

"I don't follow," Miss Francina said. But she looked interested.

The Marshal seemed to realize then what his hand was doing and resolutely plucked it up and reached for another biscuit. It steamed as he broke it open, which encouraged me to take a third myself. It was every bit as fluffy and fantastical as the first had been.

Connie, still working away, didn't look up as I complimented her. But she did mutter a "thank you."

She got the machine to do the biscuits, and I wondered what the difference was between them and the bread. I'd asked her once, and she'd said something about keeping the butter cold. Which made no sense to me, because weren't it all going in the oven?

Marshal Reeves, one hand on the butter knife, resumed speaking. "So you've got a crack in you," he said. "A scar. A spot where the light don't shine. That's all right. Creativity comes out of that. Endurance."

"Don't tell me I'm better off for being an orphan," I scoffed.

His face was serious, though, and he didn't take offense. "No more so than I'm better off for having been a slave."

Whatever I'd been about to say died in my mouth, and it didn't taste so good in there, either. Of course he was talking about himself. Or out of his experience, anyway—and his experience related to mine, and to Aashini's . . . and to Miss Francina's and to Connie's, too, for all I knowed. At least, based on the *um-hum* noise Connie was just then making.

Marshal Reeves swirled his coffee in his mug. "My life'd be easier if I had my letters, sure. But I had to exercise my mind and learn ways around it. Now I got those ways, and they serve me."

He put the mug to his lips and took three long swallows. He set it down again. Miss Francina topped it up while he continued, "The means you figure out to bridge your lacks, those'll serve you, too, Miss Memery. And it'll serve that poor little mite we half-drowned this night, as well."

His voice trailed off. I heard what he heard—mayhap keener, as my ears was younger. The rising trill of constables' whistles. An idea they'd gotten from London, England, so I heard tell.

Heavily, the Marshal stood. He settled his pistols in their holsters.

"They're playing my tune, Miss Memery, Miss Wilde. Miss Connie," he said, and sat his front-creased hat on his head with a courtly nod.

I made up a plate with some of those biscuits, wrapped up in a napkin to stay warm, and some butter and honey as well. With a pot of coffee and a mug clutched by the handles in my other hand, I climbed the stairs to Priya's room. I'd been right about what the steps felt like. I had to rest every few, and I wished to bejesus I'd been smart enough to put the food on a tray so I could balance it on one hand and use the other to haul myself up the banister. At least I'd taken the back stair and at least the house was still abed, so no one noticed me.

On the landing I paused and leaned against the wall for a moment before persevering.

The second flight was worse than the first, but eventually I found myself before Priya's door. That was when I realized I'd left myself no way to knock.

I couldn't quite bring myself to kick at the panel, although I'd left my soaked, filthy boots in the mudroom. But in a moment of ingenuity, I stepped up to the door and thumped my forehead on it lightly.

A half second later, I realized I could have used my elbow. But too late, and it was enough. I didn't even hear the patter of sock feet on the floor or have time to step back before Priya was swinging the door open.

"Sorry to wake you," I said softly, though she didn't look like she'd been asleep. She wore a flannel nighty and nightcap and the woolen socks I'd guessed at, with a plaid dressing gown pulled haphazardly on. Looking over her shoulder, I saw the shade was up and there was a copy of *Huckleberry Finn* on her night table.

"You didn't," she said, confirming my surmise

"I brought breakfast," I said unnecessarily, lofting the plate.

She stepped aside. "Have you been up all night? Out in the rain, also?"

I nodded. She shut the door, and I set the food and coffee on her little table. The pot and mug took a little juggling, as my fingers had fair gone numb on the handles. I took the chair when she gestured me to sit; she perched on the bed. The room was chill but bright—her windows faced east. "Only one mug," she said, pouring.

"For you. I ate already. It's right reverent coffee, good and thick. Keep you warm." I took a deep breath, and waited until she'd set the coffeepot down, because I'm kind that way and also because Connie gets stern about breakage and Miss Lizzie gets stern about burns. "The first thing I have to tell you is that your sister is safe. She's with Merry Lee. We'll make sure you get to see her as soon as can be, but I can't take you right this instant."

I got it out on a rush, before she could stop me. Not that she tried: she just stopped, blinking, staring at me with one hand reached out to the coffee mug.

"You—" she creaked, at last.

"Me and Miss Francina. And the Marshal. And Tomoatooah. And Merry Lee, of course, but I already said her."

Her hand fell into her lap. She sat for a second and then shuddered. And then sat again. Finally, she looked up at me.

"You did this for me."

"I did."

"It was dangerous."

I nodded.

"Madame told you not to."

I nodded again.

Very calmly, with that same calm she'd shown the first night we met, she took up her mug and sipped at it. When she set it down again, she said, "Why?"

Because I love you.

I just sat there, mouth hanging open. How do you even answer a question like that?

"Because it needed doing," I said, which was also true and a hell of a lot less frightening.

Chapter Twelve

Priya jumped up off her bed, suddenly decisive, animated. "We should go right now!" She started rummaging around, finding shoes and her trousers, sniffing the armpits of shirts.

"You should drink your coffee," I said.

"You can't just sit there—well, maybe you can. I can't just sit here!"

"I don't know where Merry Lee's safe house is," I said reasonably. "Do you?"

She shook her head. Her olive complexion took on a greenish cast. She said, "And I don't want to."

"Neither do I," I answered. "And I bet we have the same reasons."

She watched me like a prairie dog watching a coyote, and I hated myself for the expression on her face.

It didn't stop me from saying, "You know something about how Bantle makes people do things they ordinarily wouldn't, don't you?"

Her eyes widened incrementally, but she didn't blink.

"Besides the electrocuting folks, I mean."

"Don't make me—" she said.

"I ain't going to make you *do* nothing, Priya. You're your own woman. But it'd be a damn big help if, if'n you knowed anything about how to fight off Bantle's mind control machine, you passed it along before me or the Marshal or somebody got wrangled into *actually* shooting somebody, instead of just nearly so!"

I hadn't realized as I was angry until it come out of my mouth. And once it come, I weren't angry anymore. Especially because her face froze and she thought about it and then, if anything, she turned greener.

Her hands came down, trailing her trousers on the floor. "I'm sorry," she said.

I went on in a much softer tone—I hadn't been yelling before, just forceful. Da didn't hold with raised voices. "You didn't think it was important to tell us this?"

"I was ashamed!" she blurted. She dropped her clothes on the bed. "I was ashamed, all right?"

I reached out toward her, but either I was smart enough not to touch her or I was too cowardly to push through being scared. My hand hovered, though, and I said, "You got nothing to be ashamed of."

"Nothing? He used that glove on me, and he used that machine. And he made me . . . do things."

Things she didn't want to do. And I didn't need to know what they were to know how it'd hurt her. I could still taste my own shame as hot and fresh as if it were just yesterday that I'd nearly grabbed that shotgun away from Effie. And I'd seen the Marshal's crooked feelings last night.

"It ain't the same," I said after a time, sitting back down again. I didn't remember having stood up. "I know it ain't the same as being held by him and hurt again and again. But I maybe sort of understand, Priya. He . . . nearly made me hurt Effie. And he nearly made Bass Reeves shoot me."

It was harder to get those words out than it had any right to be, but I did it. And then I stayed there with Priya while the sun spilled brighter and brighter through the clouds and her curtains, just thinking and sitting and breathing the same air.

It helped some. Both of us, I'm thinking.

I pulled my jaw closed and squared up my shoulders and proceeded to spin her a tale of midnight raids and derring-do until we both forgot to be strange, and eventually she laughed and rocked and ate biscuits and hugged me a whole lot of times.

But though we didn't say it, we was also thinking about Peter Bantle and about him running for mayor and how we and Merry Lee and everybody at the Hôtel Mon Cherie would keep safe if he got the votes he seemed in line to get. Not to mention how anybody would go about finding the man killing our frail sisters if the mayor himself were to run Marshal Reeves out of town.

"Do you think he's the Marshal's murderer?" I asked.

Her eyes got strange—opaque, as if they was suddenly made of jet rather than dark coffee amber. Her face went still and cool as the water down deep in a well, and all I could think was, *I shouldn't of asked her that.*

Whatever she was thinking of—whatever awfulness I'd stupidly made her recollect—she came back from it quickly. She tipped her head and a wisp of hair fell across her forehead. I wanted to smooth it back so bad I had to sit on my hand.

"I've never seen him flog a girl," she said at last, forcing the words out. "That doesn't mean he hasn't, but it doesn't seem to be what he's looking for. If you take my meaning."

I did, when I thought about it. Bantle liked to hurt girls, sure. But he liked to do it up close, with his hands. Tying somebody up and flogging her—that'd be too much remove for him. He'd want to make her come close with that filthy glove of his, and then put it on her.

"Can you think of somebody else it might be?"

Priya sat back and crossed her sock ankles. I heated her coffee for her. She held the cup in both hands and rested it on her belly but didn't drink. "I should teach you to make *masala chai*."

I repeated the words. My tongue tripped over them.

"Spiced tea, you'd say. It has cinnamon, cardamom, black pepper, ginger. Milk and sugar."

"It sounds like cake."

"It tastes like cake," she replied, and smiled.

"You're changing the subject."

"It's—" She shrugged. "Habit. I don't know as very many of Bantle's men are really . . ."

"Most of 'em ain't the sharpest, it's true." My private opinion was that old Bill whose teeth I had broken was about characteristic: not but one in ten could tell skunks from barn cats, and I'm being overly generous with that tenth one. Old Peter Bantle didn't hold with too much creative thinking in his hands.

"There's his engineer," she said. "Goes by Bruce Scarlet. But that ain't his real name: he's a Russian. He built Bantle's glove, and some of the other things he . . ." She swallowed and shook her head. "He's a good builder. He could get work anywhere. But Bantle lets him have the run of, of the girls."

"Did he ever hurt anyone?"

She sipped her coffee and swallowed it and set the cup aside. Then, she nodded.

"I wonder if we can find somebody to put some questions to Standish," I said. "Draw him out a little, like."

"Standish travels a lot. We hated it when he went to India or China," Priya said. "Everything is better in Bantle's cribs while Horaz is home. You can talk to him, and, well . . . he treats the girls like livestock, don't get me wrong. But he treats us like . . ."

"Like you needed to be fed and warm to be healthy?"

"And clean," she said. "Horaz didn't care about us. Doesn't care about us. As people or as whores, you take my meaning."

"He don't like girls that way?"

She shrugged. "Or he doesn't like Asian girls. But he cares about . . . taking good care of property, I guess. Not wasting. And Bantle respects him enough to follow his advice. But when Horaz's gone, Bantle . . . does what's easiest, I suppose."

She glanced at her coffee but didn't pick it up. I sighed and settled back in the chair. She wasn't done talking, though—she was just changing the subject again. "Karen . . ."

"Yes, Priya?"

Her forehead pinched between her sleek black brows. "I need to ask you something, and I need you not to be mad at me if I've got the wrong end of it."

"The only way I'd be mad at you is if you wanted to ask me something and didn't."

She nodded, lips tight. She said, "I get this sense that maybe you have feelings about me."

I don't mind saying that the whole bottom fell out of my breadbasket at once. If I'd been standing up I would of sat down, and sitting down I think I doubled up, as if somebody had thumped me a good one under the ribs. I couldn't look at her face, so I found myself staring at her knees. *Good work, Memery. Make her think you're ogling her legs.*

I couldn't breathe enough to talk, so I nodded.

Gently, Priya put her hand on my cheek. And gently, she tipped my face up. And gently, she brushed her lips against mine.

She pulled back, looking at me—and from being unable to look at her face suddenly I couldn't stop gawking at her. My eyes sought into hers like there was a horizon inside her. And then I kissed her back, hard, sudden, and uncalculated, with all the fury and loneliness I'd ever felt pouring out of me. She liked me, too. She liked me *back*!

When I came up for air, she put a hand on my shoulder and set me back a bit. I went, mostly willingly, and we wound up sitting side by side against the wall, breathing heavy.

She glanced over at me sidelong and caught me looking at her profile, and she grinned while I blushed.

"Karini," she said, and didn't have to tell me it was an endearment the way her people would put one together.

"We gotta get Bantle," I said. "We gotta keep Bantle from getting us. And Madame. And Aashini. And Miss Francina. And Dyer Stone. And God knows who all else."

"We have to wreck his machine."

"His thought control machine?"

Priya nodded.

"It ain't the glove?"

"The glove is just a . . . how you say . . . focus." She waved her hands around as if at a loss. Finally, though, she folded them in front of her, so they fell in her lap as she sat. "It's a big machine," she said. "Bigger than the sewing machine Lizzie's been teaching me to modify. He keeps it at his house, not where . . . where the girls are."

"You've seen it?"

She looked at those folded hands. "How can we get in there?"

"Sneak?" I asked. "We got Merry Lee on our side."

"And then what are we going to do? How are we going to keep him from just building another one?"

"We're awful smart," I answered. "We'll think of something."

Her thready smile made me wish I believed it as deep as I made it sound like I did.

Merry came for Priya that afternoon, while she was up helping Miss Lizzie take the surgery spider apart, to clean and oil
it all. Priya's instincts were developing her into a pretty good
mechanic—or so Miss Lizzie and Crispin both said—and I
made a note to myself to get her a pair of dungarees. I bet she'd
look cute as anything in those. Never mind how unfair it was
that Priya should be extra-good at languages *and* machines.
At least she didn't know a damned thing about horses. I'd have
to try harder if she were better than me at *everything*.

Merry Lee came in by the kitchen door and Connie said that
at first Merry Lee gave Connie a bit of a start, her disguise was
that convincing. She was done up as a street urchin, in a soft
cap and trousers too thin for the weather, and if I passed her on
the street I never would of knowed her.

Connie called me in from the parlor to run upstairs and tell
Priya to come down when she was done helping Lizzie. Merry
Lee was settled in a corner of the kitchen with a mug of choc-
olate to wait it out.

"I shouldn't drink this," she said. "It gives me indigestion
something fierce. But I do love it so."

I grinned at her. I felt the same way about mincemeat pie.
Then I scampered up the stairs. Madame wouldn't give me a
hard time for taking time off during the day now and again,
but she would give me a talking-to if I weren't carrying my
share of work. And taking time off wasn't contributing to my
savings none. The fact that my rouge and kohl was covering
up for not having slept more than two hours notwithstanding.
I'd washed down two aspirin tablets with my coffee, and I was
fixing to find a couple more before much longer. Being saddle-
sore wasn't lightening my toil that evening, if you take me.

Miss Francina had just gone back to bed after breakfast, her
face peaked and drawn, muttering something about the resil-
ience of the young being wasted on 'em. I could tell Madame

knowed something was up from the rubber look she bounced between the two of us, but she decided either to let it pass or—more likely—to drag it out of us when she'd amassed more evidence. Unsettling thought, and I didn't dwell on it.

I'd make the sleep up that night. Or the next morning, to speak more rightly. As long as I didn't actually snore at a john, the most of 'em would never notice I was tired. I stifled a yawn before tapping on the surgery door, just the same. "Merry Lee's here to see Priya," I said when they summoned me in. The whitewashed floor was covered with a canvas drop cloth, and all the gears and bits of the surgical automaton were spread out in the tidiest fashion you could imagine, sorted by size and color and position and probably function, too. Priya was kneeling to one side with a greased rag, wiping down clockwork innards. Miss Lizzie was doing something to a spring no wider around than the cord of the telephone downstairs. She held it in her personal hand—the one she grew, I mean—and fiddled at it with her clockwork armature while squinting through a glass mounted on a pair of spectacles.

"Are you souping that up, too?"

Priya looked up, but at Miss Lizzie, not at me. "Miss Lizzie won't let me modify this yet," she said with an easy smile. "Not until we've rebuilt the sewing machine a few thousand more times."

"We'll be able to use it for construction work, too, when we're done," said Miss Lizzie.

I was busy trying not to stare at Priya. Priya, who had kissed me.

If I had my way about it, I'd drag her off right now and get back to practicing that. I wondered if she could learn to like horses. I wondered if the horses would mind if part of the barn was a big garage for Priya to work in, and whether it was likely she could get paid to do repairs.

Half what a man half as handy at it could, probably.

Well, two half wages was one living, and folk were always saying that two could live as cheaply as one. I waited for a smile to reflect what I was thinking on Priya's face, but Priya only had eyes for Miss Lizzie.

"Finish greasing those bits," Miss Lizzie said to Priya's questioning look, "and you can go down. Thank you, Karen."

"Welcome," I said, and shut the door. I knowed my feeling stung was just the raw flinching skin of infatuation, where every gesture feels six times as important as it should. And I knowed that Priya was thinking of nothing but her sister and getting away from Miss Lizzie as fast as she could and maybe hiding our conspiracy and the reason for that eagerness—and that's why she stared at Miss Lizzie. She hadn't *kissed* Miss Lizzie, after all. She'd kissed *me*.

I still felt it. These feelings ain't nohow sensible. They just is.

I had to glance in the mirror to smooth the thoughts off my face before I went back down to the parlor. Men don't like women with too many thoughts.

At least, the men such as come into whorehouses doesn't.

It weren't no good night, neither.

I mean, it started off just fine—typical weekday evening, with the trade slow and steady. A few of the men just came to sit at Miss Bethel's bar and drink and order a plate of oysters from Connie's kitchen. Most of 'em, though, sooner or later they wanted a tumble, though that's not the only service parlor houses offer. In addition to the gamblers, and a few that comes to hear the Professor play piano, and the eaters, well. We get some gold miners in for a bath, too, and some of 'em want a bath attendant. Or two.

I got one of those to start the evening off, and then a little lull. Miss Francina gets almost nothing but regulars and special requests, and Miss Francina's requests don't want any of the other girls. Pollywog was in demand, as she always is, and Effie too—redheads is popular. By the time they were pretty busy, my own trade started to pick up some and Effie was on an all-nighter. So I did my share, and took care of two regulars—both of 'em, for a giggle, named Adam. Though the second one could have gone by Goliath: he had rusty hair and furry, freckled arms and might of made another half a Crispin stacked on top of the first. Scots and Swedish, I think, and come out west as a convert to one of them new religions. Though he tipped well.

When the trouble started, I'd just come downstairs from fixing my stays after the second one. I was nibbling on a little sandwich at the bar while flirting with an easterner just off the Overland Route from the old states. I didn't think he'd be spending any money on a girl that night—he had the rail-carriage-glazed look of a tourist and the wide eyes of a man who's never been in a nanny shop before and just wants to take it all in. We get those sometimes, men who just want to claim as they've seen inside a real Wild West gold rush vaulting-house saloon like the Hôtel Mon Cherie—without actually getting inside it, if you take my meaning—and they're easy work. We keep 'em company, drink pay-mes (which are mostly unsugared cold tea) while Miss Bethel serves them the real stuff, and encourage 'em to talk about their sweethearts back home.

Not that I'm one to judge.

Hell, I ain't in no position to. And that's possibly the *only* position I ain't been in.

So I was soft-selling all my soft soap: "Is this your first time, honey?" to this easterner with his slick boots and slick togs, and his name, for a wonder, weren't Adam. He claimed Jonathan Smith, but don't they all? I thought the Jonathan was a nice touch, anyway. Showed a little creativity. He'd been sneaking up on grilling me about my job—out of curiosity and prurience both, I reckoned, like most of 'em. And I was engaged in weaving him what Miss Bethel refers to as The Usual Tissue of Pleasing Lies. You can hear the capital letters when she says it.

Anyway, he was on his fourth whiskey and I was on my third cold, bitter tea. I was actually starting to think I might unwind him enough to get him upstairs—or at least that I was making a close enough friend that when he came back—and about half of 'em do, pluck up their courage and come back—he might ask for me special. And he was clean and smelled fine, so I didn't mind none.

My house name's Prairie Dove, on account of being deep bosomed and having that Hay Camp accent. I was trying to make sure he'd remember it when he woke up the next morning with the inevitable hangover. I leaned my head back on his shoulder, careful of the curls Bea had slaved over and also not to stab him in the neck or the eye with a hair comb or a pin.

I had just about gotten comfortable perched on his bony knee—the petticoats help, thank Jesus—when with no more warning than a snaky-mean horse biting, he jumped up, dumped me to the floor, and roared.

I don't mind saying it knocked the wind out of me. I landed flat on my butt and banged my tailbone on Mr. Jonathan Smith's boot toe, which is an exquisite sort of agony I can't even begin to describe. I lay there—well, half-lay, half-sat, propped on my elbows and wheezing with pain and disbelief—as Smith yanked his foot out from under me and snatched up the tufted bar stool he'd been sitting on. I had the clearest view ever of the red velvet seat dented under his smooth white hands, and I couldn't even raise up a hand to shield my face.

And that sound he was making! Sweetness, half roar and half wail, like a bear crossed with a panther.

I won't lie. I thought I was dead. Dead, or crippled. I thought he was going to break that chair over my head, and I couldn't even scream. I knowed Crispin would be coming, and Miss Francina too, and Miss Bethel diving under the bar for her gun—and I knowed weren't none of them going to be fast enough to stop him doing whatever he was going to do to me. It was like a time I went out to halter Da's new sorrel gelding and nobody told me he was head shy on account of having been twitched and beat, and when I pulled the noseband over his lip he went straight up on me and I was too surprised to let go and wound up dangling from the lead rope between his legs while his hooves beat the air to batter around my head. I was too surprised to be scared, though I think Da was scared enough for the both of us, from the way he hugged me when I got back down.

This time I had the time to be scared, though. Because Mr. Smith stood over me for long enough for me to think real hard about that stool, and how solid it was joined together.

Then, with a grunt, he turned and hurled it over the bar. I heard Miss Bethel yelp—I couldn't see much from the floor—and then I heard it hit, and the crash of all the glass in the world.

"Son of a bitch!" somebody yelled, and Mr. Smith was suddenly airborne as the second Adam, who hadn't headed home yet—and who, being Mormon, was sober as a preacher—reached right over me, picked him up by the forearms, and threw him across the parlor with his arms pinwheeling like the legs of an upturned bug.

Well, some men can't resist a slice of cake and some can't resist tobacco and some can't say no to a glass of whiskey. Or a cup of coffee for that matter. And then there's some who just can't turn down a fight.

A peculiar number of that sort of men wind up working lumber, running traplines, or panning gold. In preference to the kinds of jobs, you understand, such as come with garters to keep your sleeves out of the ink and visors to keep the light out of your eyes. Or in preference to the kinds of jobs where you have to show up punctual for a sixteen-hour shift and try to keep your fingers on your hands and not raise your voice to the overseer all day. And such as requires you to be polite to a job lot of strangers all day long. Or in preference likewise to farming, which takes a steady hand and a kind of patience with slow-growing things and cantankerous weather and slow-shifting seasons that's in short supply in Rapid City. As you might guess by the name.

My da had that patience, and it's why his horses was tamed more than broken. Crispin has it, to sit by the door quiet and attentive and calming and always be ready when Miss Bethel needs a hand with a customer as has overindulged in the fruit of the whiskey tree. And I see it in Bass Reeves, too. I suppose you have to have some such, to trail such men as you've got writs for until you find 'em, and then to stalk 'em until you get the opportunity to take 'em in safe. The Professor? He ain't got it at all. He'll cut a man soon as look at him, if he feels he's being trifled with. But he's always kind to us girls.

Women have more of that patience, as a class. That ain't because we're born with it, though. It's because we're schooled to it and taught early that if we don't have it we won't never win. I think Crispin was the only man in that room that night with any such patience. Because before I even collected my wits and got my feet under me, the whole room was throwing furniture and insults—with none of the usual windup.

I dragged myself up on the next stool over, wincing and shaking but determined to get off the floor before somebody up and trampled me. The Professor was standing between the mob and his piano, brandishing a pool cue. No one was spoiling to challenge him, neither. By the time I was up on the stool, Miss Bethel had grabbed her shotgun, straightened up, and shaken the shards of broken bottles and shattered looking glass off her shoulders. I heard them crunch under her boots as she stepped forward, craning her neck this way and that to get the lay of the battle.

Most of the girls was in full flight, making their escape to the corners of the room. Crispin was wading in, and so was Miss Francina. Which meant Miss Bethel couldn't shoot into the crowd even if she wanted to. And despite their best efforts, the melee was spreading. I ducked a thrown chair, so it thudded into the front of the bar and missed me entire.

The funny thing was, they seemed to be concentrating their efforts on property damage. Smashing furniture and the like. For example, I saw one of them taking the fireplace poker to that striped divan, which seemed like an odd waste of time in a brawl.

Miss Bethel glanced dubiously upward. I wouldn't want to shoot a second load into Madame's ceiling in the same month, neither, but I wasn't sure what her other options were.

Then her gaze crossed mine. She said, "Karen honey, give me your hand."

I held it up, steadying myself on the bar with the other one. She grabbed it, and—still holding on to the shotgun southpaw—used my support to lever herself up onto the polished top of the bar.

Her little boot came down on it as if it were a dance hall stage. She shucked that shotgun with a sound that cut through the crowd like a snake's mad rattle. And she yelled out—my hand to God—"*What the Sam Hill do you all think you're doing?!*"

You've never seen a room that noisy get quiet that fast. The man taking the hot poker to the divan turned around; I saw coils of smoke curling up from the batting. *Fire.*

Nothing terrified me more, I tell you frankly. Fire in a largely wood-frame city like Rapid . . .

It was a horrifying idea.

Then I saw that the man with the poker was Adam. My less-sober Adam. You learn not to get attached, but . . . it was a hoof in the breadbasket, and no mistake.

And worse, when he brandished that poker with the smoking wool bat seared on the tip and yelled, "Peter Bantle sends his regards!"

I was so mad I hopped up onto that bar, right behind Miss Bethel, and I looked him in the eyes, and I yelled, "Adam Wainwright, what on God's earth do you think you are doing?"

Well, he blinked. And he gave me a look I purely recognized from the inside out: confusion, and shame, and wild-eyed something-or-other. The poker sagged; he realized a second before it scorched the rug what he was about to do and jerked it up again.

All around him, other men were glancing about with dazed expressions, like they were just realizing where they were and couldn't imagine how they'd gotten there or what they thought they were about. Beatrice darted out of the library and tossed a wool shawl over the smoldering divan. I imagined I heard the shawl emit a small sigh like a sleeping kitten as the smoke was quenched. The burning wool smelled like a festival in Hell. Crispin had one miner off the ground by his shirt collar and braces and just held him there dangling as if waiting to see if he was going to take another kick or swing.

I was minded of a mother dog scruffing a puppy, using no more force than is necessary.

The silence was thick and heavy, and it lasted until it was punctuated by Madame's unmistakable boot on the stair.

She stopped there and surveyed the damage. I felt her eye tick across me, even though I couldn't bear to meet it. Then she took the kind of deep breath that plumped her battleship prow up over the top of her stays, and let it out again. Say what you will about the formidable Madame Damnable, but I can see how she made her money in Anchorage. She's got to be fifty-nine, and she's still got a balcony you could do Shakespeare from.

"We're fucking closed," she said in a voice that was heavy and tired and still brooked no argument. "If you don't work here, get the ever-loving black bastard Jesus *fuck* off my property."

There followed a general exodus, and Crispin waited to bar the door behind them while Miss Francina climbed the flights to roust a few customers who might still be in upstairs rooms. Madame came the rest of the way down the stairs and then she just waited, hands folded over her cane. Pollywog fetched her a bar stool, which was like Polly, and Madame leaned back on it gratefully, easing her bad foot, and said, "Thank you, darling."

When at last we were all assembled—all us girls, at least, and Crispin; Connie stayed back in the kitchen, and I think Priya was still out visiting her sister with Merry Lee, for which I was more grateful than I can say—Madame looked us all over, from Beatrice clutching Signor to her like a rag doll big as her chest to Miss Francina, whose face was as stubborn and stern as I have ever seen it. Then she sighed and twirled her cane. "I believe I overheard something about that no-account Peter Bantle?"

I stepped forward before Miss Francina could and shot her a look that said, plain as day, *This was my doing and it's my problem.* At least, that were the message I meant to put in it. Miss Francina's scowl in return told me it weren't too well received.

"Madame," I said. "I maybe have some things to tell you about."

"My office," she said. "Right now."

Chapter Thirteen

Of course, Miss Francina weren't about to let me get away with taking the fall for her, and she followed me right down the hall to Madame's office and stood with me inside the door. Madame watched her do it with an expression of exactly zero surprise. Madame didn't follow us right on, and I didn't know whether she was making us sweat or taking a closer survey of the damage. Either way, I was pretty sure none of it looked good.

I wanted to say something to Miss Francina, but I wasn't sure what. The door was closed, though, and she was eyeing me like maybe she was trying to reckon out what to say as well.

"It was my plan," I said. "I should be responsible for the results."

Miss Francina scoffed at me, "Ain't you a martyr, just like our Lord. 'Cause I sure as hell didn't volunteer myself as a grown free woman, and you're the only one in the room as cares about Priya."

Well, when she put it that way.

I frowned and twisted the toe on my boot on Madame's blue-and-cream knotted silk rug. Her office is made to look like a boudoir, all lace and mother-of-pearl and silk draperies. "Damn me to hell," I said. "I'm as self-important as Da always said I could be."

Miss Francina shrugged. "You have your good qualities, too."

Whatever we might of talked about next, we never got to it. Because there was a hitching tread in the hall and the door swung open, then closed again as Madame stepped into the room and shut it behind her. She walked between Miss Francina and me, went around her gilt, scrolled desk, and sat heavily in the armchair there, using her cane as a prop to lever herself down.

"You girls sit," she said to Miss Francina and me.

We sat.

Madame stared at us for ten seconds or so. I could hear her desk clock ticking. Then she looked from one of us to the other and sighed and said, "All right, then. Which one of you wants to explain what exactly just happened in my parlor?"

We looked at each other, Miss Francina and I. Apparently it was one thing to volunteer. And another entirely to actually carry out the task you had volunteered for.

When we broke, though, we both started to talk at the same instant. Then I knuckled back and let Miss Francina have it, but she'd quit also. We stared at each other.

Madame sighed. "Karen," she said. "You first. Though by rights I should be interviewing you separately. So you don't get your stories straight."

Miss Francina looked righteously hurt at that. "I have never lied to you."

"Nor do you tell me everything," Madame said. She held up her hand, forestalling further protest. "God help me, nor do I *want* you to, Francie. I want to hear from Karen, please."

No way through but both feet in, I reasoned. I said, "Peter Bantle has a machine that lets him change people's minds."

"People," Madame said. "Voters?"

I nodded. "And it can make people do hasty things. Hurt people they don't mean to hurt. Get in fights with friends."

When she sucked her teeth like that it was unsettling, because I knowed it meant she was thinking. She said, "That's what happened downstairs, then? He . . . influenced a passel of *my* clients to wreck up my parlor?"

Miss Francina nodded. I bit my lip.

"How do you know this?"

"Priya told me," I said. "About the machine. And he used it on me, when he chased her and Merry Lee in here. I just about took Miss Bethel's shotgun from Effie and pointed it at her. And I know he's used it on the Marshal, too—"

I choked up before I could tell her what had happened the previous night. We'd gone against her direct orders, and I knowed it. But whatever I was holding back—and I meant to tell her, I swear I did. I just . . . choked on it.

But Madame gave me a canny look anyway. "So why'd he pick today to have another go at us?"

"To scare us," Miss Francina said quickly.

Madame shot her a warning glance. She subsided, but not without a sigh.

"Karen?"

I fixed my gaze on that carpet and stared at it like to set it on fire. "What I said about him using that machine on the Marshal?"

"Yes?"

"That were last night," I said on a rush. "Marshal Reeves and his posseman and Merry Lee and me went and busted Priya's sister out of the cribs."

"And I," Miss Francina said dryly, so at first I thought she were playing Miss Bethel and correcting my grammar, but then I realized she was putting herself in the rescue party, too, when I'd intentionally left her out.

"Francina, dear," Madame said. "Fetch me that decanter, please?"

Miss Francina rose and did it and brought her a snifter, too. She set both on the edge of Madame's desk blotter. As Miss Francina sat again, Madame poured two inches of brandy into the bottom of the balloon glass, and knocked it right back. Then she poured a second, smaller glass, closed up the decanter, and held the snifter under her nose for a long minute or two.

"I'm not overjoyed with either of you," she said, unnecessarily in my holding. "Do you know what Bantle can do to this house—to all of us—if he makes mayor?"

I didn't, really. Not know. But I could come up with some pretty chilling fantasies. And Miss Francina nodded, so I did, too.

Then she put the glass down. "But it can be fought off?"

"The men who started the fight," Miss Francina said. "They were the ones who had been drinking the most, or smoking a little hemp. Maybe their idea of what was wrong and right had gotten a little . . . malleable."

"That's true," I said. "None of the girls was drinking much. And none of the girls went crazy. And when he tried it on me, before . . . I was sober. And I could kind of . . . see around it?"

We didn't drink much, on duty, in Madame's house. She thought it weren't safe to cloud our wits that way while dealing with customers. And she didn't want no woman whoring for her who had to get herself tangle footed to get through it. "And you *and* the Marshal both shook it off on your own."

I nodded. "And Mr. Jonathan Smith, who started it all downstairs—he could have kilt me with that stool he was waving around. But he just waved it around for a bit and then threw it at the back bar. And he'd *had* several whiskeys."

"So maybe it ain't too powerful."

"I'm unsettled to point out that I've only ever witnessed him use it when he was right near whoever he was aiming at," Miss Francina said. "Priya says it's a big machine in his house that does the dirty work, but it seems to my observation as if he has got to focus it through his glove. If I'm right about that, he was right here. Right outside, maybe. Might still be, although I sadly expect he's got more sense than that."

"It sounds more like an urge than a compulsion," Miss Francina said.

"Or he uses it on some drunk who already thinks it might be a good prank to bust up a whorehouse. Or dump a whore on her ass for laughs, especially if he ain't none too comfortable around the sisters," Madame said, as if she was thinking out loud. "So he's got enough to sway somebody who thinks it's their own whim. Like whether to run for mayor, or for whom to vote."

"Especially," I said slowly, "if there's also some blackmail in train. You know, for the old-fashioned kind of attitude adjusting."

I didn't say *Dyer Stone,* and Madame couldn't fault me on that. She nodded, though, and flicked a fingernail back and forth against the stitching of a leather-bound book that was resting on her desk. I weren't used to seeing it there, but that didn't signify: she kept the ledgers locked up when she was out.

"Well, that's a shit sandwich and no mistake," Madame said.

It got worse by morning. Priya still weren't home—I hoped somebody had sent her a message to stay away, and nobody seemed upset that she wasn't there, so I expected she'd sent Miss

Lizzie or Miss Francina a note—but when I went out for Connie's eggs I could feel the eyes of strangers following me. I was wearing my plain walking dress—I wasn't out trying to drum up custom, and my hair was barely braided, to tell the truth—so it weren't my stunning appearance of beauty drawing the attention.

I reckoned word of the fight had gotten around and tried to ignore the stares and the heads bent in mutters, and I didn't have to leave the neighborhood. So it was the corner grocer Mr. Mulligan who shook his head at me and said, "Have you heard what they're saying about that Negro United States Marshal of yours?"

I almost said, *He's not mine,* but Mr. Mulligan wouldn't of understood it the way I meant it, and his misunderstanding would make me feel disloyal. So I fingered the lucky silver dollar that was in my pocket now and I said, "What are they saying?"

He sucked his teeth and added two extra eggs to my basket, tucking 'em well into the padding straw. Brown ones. I missed hens, but not as much as I missed horses. "The frail sisters started dropping dead of an overdose of horsewhipping right about when he and his pet Comanche came to town."

A chill crept through my belly. *Of course they were saying that.* Because Peter Bantle was putting ideas in their heads.

"You know," he continued, "them Comanche are savages. Things they do as a matter of course would chill normal folk. Skinning, scalping, roasting people alive. They cut folks up—babies, women—and torture 'em just for the fun. And word's gotten around that those two have been coming and going at Madame's place. You might want to pass the word to her that some people aren't too pleased about it."

He dropped his voice down low. "Some people is even saying that Madame's a colored girl herself, what's been passing, and that's why she lets all these"—he flipped his hand back and forth, like there was a word he weren't going to say in front of a lady—"scalawags come and go as they please. Course, old Mrs. Mulligan and me, we don't believe that for an instant."

I thought of the shiny healed burns on Priya's arms, the dog-fights down by the docks, and I held my peace, though what I wanted to say was, *Does it seem to you that one race in particular holds the patent on savagery?*

But I didn't want to argue with Mr. Mulligan right now, especially if he was defending Madame in the court of gossip. What I wanted was to drop that basket of eggs and go running down the street shouting for the Marshal.

I didn't do that, either. What I did do was pay for Connie's victuals and smile nicely when Mr. Mulligan threw in some butter, too, and then I lifted my heavy basket up and went out to try to climb the ladder at the end of the block without spilling any eggs.

Made it, too. Without cracking any of the four dozen plus two. And once I'd delivered them to Connie, I went back out again, climbed up the ladder, and walked two more blocks to the telegraph station.

The telegram I sent was just: *WE MUST TALK SOONEST DONT COME TO THE HOUSE,* because I didn't want to say too much where it would get around town. And I spent the rest of the afternoon and evening in a sort of agony, twisted up left and right and inside and outside and upside down with not hearing from the Marshal. But of course I didn't know if he'd gotten the telegram yet or if he'd even been back to his rooming house. All my wild imaginings of him clapped in irons or lynched from a lamppost were just that. It's a real particular twisting razor, having a bad intuition and no news as such. At least Priya had returned by the time I came back, and she was hard at work sweeping the parlor carpet with Madame's newfangled suction engine that didn't half work half the time.

The good—or bad—news kept coming, in that the only visitor we had all night other than a messenger was the john we're not supposed to know about, and he went upstairs with Pollywog and neither one came back down. So us girls and the Professor entertained ourselves in the parlor playing cards and playing piano. Bea told fortunes from tea leaves for half an hour—my leaves looked like storm clouds breaking, she said, and that meant good fortune out of bad, but what I saw in them was a herd of mustangs running. The Professor said he was going home, fooling no one, and wandered out before the witching hour to find a card game for money. Most of the Misses was in bed not half an hour later.

I crinkled the note in my pocket, not much more crumpled than when the messenger had handed it to me, and didn't even bother to change my dress. I pulled on street boots and buttoned them, though, and fetched my heavy coat. It was getting on December by then, and the air through the door when Crispin had opened it earlier had been sharp. I wasn't sneaking out, not exactly—I told Priya where I was going and why; she worrited at me, but she didn't nag or naysay, and I had that good feeling again that I hadn't had since Da was alive—that somebody sensible cared about me and wanted to help me on my path rather than bending me to their own. I collected a kiss from her for luck and good measure. I could still feel it tingling on my lips long after the cold should of wiped it away.

I slipped out the kitchen door, because Connie had sent the day girls home and gone to bed herself already and because Bea and Effie was still playing bezique by the parlor fire with cups of Miss Bethel's best sherry, pretending—if I'm not mistaken—at being the ladies of their own homes.

When I clambered up to the street, the abject dark of the

sidewalks gave way to flickering gaslight. I was nervous being out alone, no mistake—but I didn't think I'd have to go far. The Marshal's note had said he'd be waiting for me, and the Marshal hadn't let me down once yet. Which put him right up there with Crispin and my da and Madame, and damn few anybodies else. I felt bad for telling him to stay away from Madame's, but I had thought of what Mr. Mulligan had said about how folk were talking and I had realized that I had even more of a duty to Madame and Crispin and the girls as I did to the Marshal and Tomoatooah.

Being a growed woman, it turned out, was harder work than it looked. But that's a thing, too, ain't it? Them as work hardest get no respect for it—women, ranch hands, sharecroppers, factory help, domestics—and them as spend all their time talking about how hard they work have no idea what an honest day's labor for nary enough pay to put beans in your family's bellies is all about.

I got less and less patience for any of that talk, the older I get, lessen it comes from a miner or a picker or some such.

I was standing in the dark on the cobbles, knowing it was safer out of sight even though every scrap of my soul—if whores got souls—wanted to go stand under a streetlight where every robber or rapist for ten miles could mark me. The light would of felt good, but you see I knowed it wasn't safe.

So I lurked in the dark, pinching my coat closed across my bosom with my left hand, and I waited for the Marshal to show.

Hoofbeats told me he was coming. I didn't turn my head; if somebody *was* watching me, even here in the shadows, I didn't want to look like I was looking. Or worried about anything. But I knowed Dusty's hoofbeats from the other night, and I didn't expect anyone else would be on her.

Nor were they. The Marshal pulled the chestnut up under the hissing streetlight, letting the light flicker and fall on every side. His spurs jingled, and I knowed from their pure tone they was silver. I may have smiled a little over men and their vanity.

He just sat there, slouched under his hat, the collar of his duster mostly hiding his face. He waited. I was sure he hadn't spotted me, for I was in the shadows and waiting very still. Also, he was looking in the other direction.

I didn't keep him waiting long. Just a half a moment, in which I reviewed what I needed to tell him and got it all ordered out in my head. Then I stepped out of the dark and strode toward him, letting my boot heels make noise.

The walking boots didn't go with the skirts I was wearing, but sometimes being fashionable ain't a priority. Even for me.

He turned at my first footfall. You know how sometimes you can see the tension go out of somebody? Like their shoulders fall and they sit up both more straight and less, simultaneous?

Well, the change in the Marshal as he caught sight of me was the opposite of that.

As I came up on Dusty, I noticed she had a red-and-blue Indian blanket under her saddle, and Marshal Reeves held out his hand and pulled his foot out of the stirrup. "Swing up," he said. "Let's not all talk in one place."

Well, I wasn't kitted for riding astride, but the thing about my working dresses is most of 'em's slit to the hip bone. That makes it a pile easier to do all sorts of things in 'em, and it turns out one of those things is jumping up on a horse.

I swung up over the cantle and settled myself. It might of been cold, but the coat kept the gap in my skirts covered. At least, as long as we was moving slow. If Dusty was given cause to canter, it might come to be a different story.

"Bantle's trying to get you lynched," I told the Marshal, once the mare was under way. "You and Tomoatooah both."

"Is that so?"

I was trying not to press up against the Marshal's back,

mindful of what he'd said about his Jennie. But he was warm, and my being there didn't seem to faze him. Also, the pitch of the saddle made it well-nigh impossible to hold myself back.

"He's spreading the rumor that the murders started just when you and Tomoatooah happened to arrive in town."

"Well," the Marshal allowed, between the slow clop of Dusty's hooves, "that ain't a misrepresentation."

"Because you was chasing the killer here!"

The Marshal shrugged. "In an ideal world, more folks would see it that way."

"He'd get you both killed soon as look at you. He's mean enough to eat off the same plate with a snake," I opined.

"And ugly as a burned boot," the Marshal agreed. "This don't change anything, though. I still have a writ of arrest to serve. It just means the clock's ticking."

"What do you mean?"

He rolled his shoulders. "The clock on how long Tomoatooah and me can stay in town. And stay in a boardinghouse. Instead of laying our heads on velvet couches somewhere out in the hills and hoping no bounty hunter don't find us."

"A velvet couch" was a cowboy's term for his thin and usually smelly woolen bedroll. "Bounty hunter?!"

"Sure," the Marshal said. "He'll have a bounty on us next week, at the latest. He just needs enough time to convince enough people that the case against us is incontrovertible." (I didn't know the word then, but I looked it up when I got home that night.)

"So you've got to catch the murderer before Bantle finishes laying his trap."

Marshal Reeves turned his head and smiled so I could see it. He laid one finger alongside his nose. I was nervous and sick, and the Marshal seemed pleased as a pup with two tails. "We've learned something useful, though," he said.

"What's that?"

"The killer's somebody Bantle has a percentage in protecting," he said.

"Right," I said. "Damn it. Priya said that Bantle's mechanic, a Russian alias Bruce Scarlet, might fit the bill. She said all the girls were scared of him."

"I'll bear that in mind," the Marshal said. "I can ask Tomoatooah if he will tail this Scarlet and see where he drinks. Maybe we can find a way to have a word with him outside."

"If he drinks."

"Mechanics all drink."

"Not Miss Lizzie." I grinned, and the Marshal tipped his hat at me in surrender.

I was just about to rummage around for something else to twit the Marshal's dignity with—just being near him, and his calm boredom at Bantle's machinations, was taking the edge off all my worry—when we were both startled by a scream and the almost-immediate shrilling of constables' whistles. I grabbed for the Marshal's waist as he raised the reins and jingled his spurs at Dusty.

He sure didn't need to stick her with 'em, because just the ring sent her forward like a scorched weasel. The horse went, and he went, and a split second later I went, too—and a damn fine thing I have a practiced seat, or I'd have been rolling in the cold cobbles clutching my tailbone and wondering what happened. Speaking of the tailbone in question, it weren't none too fond of its new accommodations, being enmeshed in recollections of its recent encounter with Mr. Jonathan Smith's boot toe. I was determined not to whimper in front of the Marshal—or behind him as the case might be. So I held on and tried to grip as good as I could with my thighs, having no stirrups.

Thank whoever looks out for whores and cowboys that Dusty's canter was as smooth as they come. You get that in a real strong horse sometimes; they catch themselves, like, and let themselves down easy instead of just hitting the ground. Feels like they got springs in their step for literal like.

Well, Dusty was about the strongest horse I ever rode. I could feel all the muscles moving under me—not bulky, but no yielding in 'em at all. I worried after her in the dark, on the could-be-slick stones, but I figured the best thing I could do to help was just to hang on, try not to throw her balance, and let her be about her business.

Best plan I ever had, letting Dusty take care of me. Pity I can't talk that mare into doing my tax paperwork.

She cantered and I suffered for maybe two minutes and not more than four, though it seemed a hell of a lot longer. The whistles shrilled up sharp and then dropped off for a bit, started up again more hesitant like for a second wave and then shushed completely. I figured at that point every constable in the Frog Hollow neighborhood had gotten a chance to toot his pipe and they needed a little rest before they got up to it again.

By then, anyways, Dusty and the Marshal had found the locus of the activity, so to speak. And I recognized where we was—red lanterns outside and red velvet curtains drawn over the windows facing the street.

"Aw, horsefeathers," I said. "This is Breakneck Hill. This is Miss Pearl's establishment."

I felt the big sigh, and he nodded.

I expected Marshal Reeves would pull his foot from the iron again, so I could get down, but he just reined up into the middle of the swirling herd of constables and counted on them to clear a path for him. It worked, too.

I was starting to covet that man's authority for my very own. It wasn't that different from being with Madame; people just plain tended to did what she said, because it was her saying it. I wanted that, I realized. I wanted that respect.

The Marshal reined Dusty around, peering through the torches and over the heads of the swarm of constables all milling about like red ants. "Where's Waterson?" he bellowed.

"Right here, Marshal," Waterson said, appearing at the top of a ladder. He levered his foot over to stand and came up to Dusty, right fearless. "You want to rein that horse back? This is a crime scene."

"Where's the girl?" Marshal Reeves asked.

"Girl?"

"You get another murdered girl?"

"Yes," Sergeant Waterson said shortly. "She's down there. Whipped to ribbons, too."

The Marshal reined Dusty over, closer to the edge of the road than I thought she'd go, but she trusted him enough to step right up against it. I held my breath. There ain't no railing. Every week, a drunk or two tumbles off the edge of the street and is crippled or he dies. In the papers and over at the coroner's office, they call it *involuntary suicide*.

If I'd been holding my breath a minute before, now I squeaked. Because the Marshal hooked one knee over the saddletree and just slid right down Dusty's side, hanging there upside down with his head next to the red mare's knees. "Torch!" he yelled, and somebody brought over a lantern and held it out.

"You could dismount," Sergeant Waterson said dryly. "Because that looks more than a little ridiculous."

The Marshal flipped upright again, so smooth in the saddle he hardly even nudged me. "Son of a bitch ain't got far. Begging your pardon."

"What'd you see?" Waterson asked.

"There's a butt still smoldering there." Reeves pointed. "Right by the mark where he ran his rope to lower her." He turned in the saddle, left and right. "And we know he likes to watch the fun, now don't we. . . . Hang *on*, Miss Memery!"

I grabbed for his gun belt quick as I'd grab for a bolting colt, and I got it, too. My fingers hooked leather, spurs rang, and the next thing I knowed Dusty was stretched out running like she was after hounds. I have a vague recollection of her clearing a couple of constables and of me striking against Bass Reeves' back when she landed, but it ain't more than the memory of a story somebody else had told you.

I just put my head down and tried to hang on while the Marshal laid his rein ends against Dusty's shoulder—just once—and she somehow accelerated. "You saw him?" I yelled over Reeves' shoulder.

"I saw something!" he yelled back. "Man on foot, shadow of that building over there. Could just be a damned rubberneck, but if so, why's he lurking back there? And why'd he take to his heels as soon as I laid eyes on him?"

Dusty cornered like a cutting horse and barreled up the next street—it was River Styx Road. No, I don't know who names these damn things. We also got us a Sarcophagus Street. Anyway, as she ran it, I saw a flicker of movement up one of the ladder escapes on the building sides.

"There!"

The Marshal reined Dusty so sparks flew. "Damn," he said, "Can't shoot at him. There's people behind those windows."

He didn't bother dismounting, just jumped up on her saddle, tossed me the reins, and threw himself up at the first landing on the escape. It was a jump out across that drop-off to the sidewalk thirty feet below us that would of curled my hair if Mr. Marcel hadn't handled that already.

"Follow on the ground!" He yelled something else, but it was lost in his boot nails ringing on the wrought iron.

I grabbed the reins and did the best I could. Dusty's stirrups was too long, and no time to fix them, so I kicked my calves into the straps to keep the irons from banging her belly. She didn't think much of the change of rider, but she was too much a professional to do more than flick an ear at me and smack my thigh with her tail. She moved for me, though, and no argument, and that was the bit that mattered.

Craning my head, I could make out the silhouette of a man vanishing over the roof edge, slightly darker against the moonlit clouds. He was only there for an instant—the same instant I realized that the Marshal had left me a long arm in the saddle holster. The Winchester with the chip out of its stock. Damn it, I'd had a shot.

But I didn't know who I'd have been shooting at or if he'd committed any crime worse than running from a Marshal. Hell, I've run from an officer of the courts once or twice myself.

I felt a horrible chill at the thought that the Marshal didn't have a weapon. I almost yelled up to where I could still hear his boot heels climbing the iron, but then I'd be letting the maybe killer know Reeves'd left his gun. I was just about to expire from apoplexy when I remembered the gun belt I'd grabbed.

So he was heeled, and all I was doing chasing myself in circles down here was letting our suspect build up a lead.

I reined Dusty forward again. She went, asking for more rein than I was comfortable giving. But she took the corner easily, and in time to see somebody hurtle past overhead, jumping between buildings.

"This way!" I yelled, in case the Marshal could hear me, and gave chase.

I kept Dusty as tight to the building walls as I could without putting her in the sidewalk ditches. No bullets yet, but that didn't mean old what's-his-face up there didn't have a gun. Just that he hadn't decided to use it yet.

Dusty and me followed on, trying to track him. We saw him jump one more time, and we followed—but two or three blocks later and I had to admit we'd lost him somewhere. I was about to turn Dusty around to go look for the Marshal when I heard a rising whistle and suddenly I was just a passenger on the big red mare. She whirled and snorted, then trotted along as businesslike as you please, back the way she came.

We met the Marshal standing at the roadside, looking crestfallen as a cat trying to seem unconcerned at a mousehole.

"No luck, either," I told him. "Where the hell did he go?"

The Marshal shook his head. "I had him. I was right on him. And I slipped on a damned roof tile." He turned his head and spat. "That'll teach me to chase people across rooftops without Sky."

I offered him Dusty's reins. She weren't listening to anything I had to say through them, anyhow. "I wish the damn constables had gotten that search dirigible they're always trying to pry money out of the mayor for," I groused. "We'd have seen him try to give us the slip then."

The Marshal laughed, not sounding too happy. "I got enough of a look at him to say he's a white, at least. Not as tall as me. Hat over his hair, more's the pity, and his face all muffled up."

"It's winter," I said. "So is everybody's."

He stood there, stroking Dusty's nose. He didn't talk, but I could about smell his frustration.

I sighed, heart hurting as the excitement faded and I remembered the other business at hand. "We should go find out who's dead." I hoped it wasn't somebody I knowed, and I felt awful about that at the same time.

"Miss Memery," the Marshal said. "I make you a promise that I will do everything in my power to stop this man. I'll catch him, and if I can't catch him . . ." He shrugged. "If that's what it takes, I'll bed him down."

He meant a pine bed, and a narrow one. "God bless you, sir," I said. "Now come on, let's go see whose murder you're next to be blamed for."

Chapter Fourteen

When I walked into Madame's office the next day, she looked startled and irate. Neither of which was how I was used to seeing her. She had been bent over an account book, pince-nez slipping down her scowl, and now she closed it with a snap that made me think she might be more mad at the accounts nor me.

That weren't settling to my spirits. In fact, it plumb took me aback. But I grabbed up my courage anyway and I said to her, "I know how to fix all our problems."

She cleaned the nib of her pen, still frowning.

"That's a pretty tall order, young lady," she said. "Are you sure you know what all our problems are?"

Da would say that first you make a list of everything that needs doing. Then you figure out a plan to get it done. If you can't get it *all* done, you figure out what's most important and you do that.

"No," I admitted. "But I know the cause of most of 'em is Peter Bantle."

Her fingers tapped the leather cover of the account book. "And what's the cause of Peter Bantle?" she asked.

I must of meant to say something next, because I'd had that feeling of being on a roll you sometimes get. And with her question it was gone—poof—like so much snow falling on the ocean.

There ain't nothing quite like the sensation of standing there with your mouth agape. "And what's the reason, you think, that I haven't moved against him yet?"

"I know you ain't afraid of him."

"Afraid?" She laughed gently, which worrited me more than if she'd brayed like an ass. "I'm concerned about him. I'm wary of him. I might be a little afraid—not of Bantle, but of the crazy stupid shit a man like Bantle will do. Normal people, they're lazy. They want to protect what they got and they won't risk it. Peter ain't like that, Karen honey. He'll risk all sorts of things just for a little power, or the chance to make somebody hurt."

"But that ain't why you won't let me go put a stop to him."

"Maybe I'm the lazy one here, protecting what I already have."

I didn't have no good answer to that, neither. So I just looked at her, because she was Madame and I couldn't tell her she was full of shit.

"Everybody owes something to somebody, Karen. Bantle owes somebody, you see if he doesn't. And it's possible I owe something to somebody else." She tapped the account book again.

I had the oddest sensation, that of somebody who had always seemed invulnerable, capable, prepared—invincible—showing or admitting weakness. I won't say it was as bad as when Da died, because ain't nothing as bad as when Da died. But what I wouldn't of given for one real good barrage of profanity out of her, just then.

"He don't have to know it's us," I said stubbornly.

She tilted her head. "And just how do you prescribe to prevent him knowing?"

"Sneak," I said. I must of looked like a shooting dog leaning on the leash, because she shook her head and stared down at her hands and smiled. Indulgently, so I felt more like a child than I had in five years, or six maybe. She must of caught my consternation, because she smoothed that smile out right quick. Not quick enough to keep it getting under my skin like needles, though.

"Because he sure won't put together the folks that have been stealing his indenturees with whatever it is you've got your mind made up about? You've been out running around so much I think you don't know the constables have been here twice looking for that Comanche, and looking for any excuse they can find to shut me down."

"But . . ." I thought about how much we all paid in the taxes, about the mayor's officially nonexistent special relationship with Pollywog, about all the constables I'd taken a turn with. About how secure I'd felt that our position weren't going to nohow alter. I'd been smug. Maybe I'd let myself feel safe.

Maybe wanting to feel safe *was* a mistake.

"If that happens, then where will we all be? I'm too old for whoring on corners, miss." Madame straightened her shoulders. "Too old for whoring on corners. But old enough to know something you ain't yet learned. This too shall pass, Karen honey. The luck will swing. And if we hunker down and husband our chips, we'll still have some to play with when we get that killer hand."

"I can save us!" I yelled, forgetting that no one *never* raises her voice to Madame Damnable. "I can break his machine! Then nobody will do what he says, and we'll be safe! Priya knows where he keeps it. Her and me—"

Madame stood up, her chair scraping over the carpet with
a final sound. She leaned her hands on the desk like a school-
marm, and she let me see how disappointed in me she was.

"Karen."

I shut up. I did. And I fixed my eyes on my hem and didn't
let my lips curl the way they wanted to, I was that angry. Da
always said I had my mother's temper.

"Karen, are you listening to me?"

I made myself nod.

"You need to trust me to handle this. I can't have you running off to take matters into your own hands again."

Once again, I made myself nod, though it hurt to do it. Apparently it wasn't enough, though. Because Madame cleared
her throat and said, "Look at me."

So that was even more hard. I'm not sure how I did it. If it
were Da, I imagined he would of been working up to giving
me a hiding, but Madame didn't strike her girls. When I managed to drag my line of sight up there, I saw her staring at me
over the gold wire tops of her pince-nez.

"I value your spunk, girl. And your willingness to do what
needs done without waiting to be told. But if you go up against
Peter Bantle again—unless he directly started it—I will turn you
out in the street. Do you understand me?"

I nodded, stunned. And still a touch rebellious, to tell you
true—wondering if there weren't a way I could manage it. Leave
Rapid City; take what I had saved and maybe find work or a
way to save more. I wouldn't get another job in a parlor house
here if Madame turned me out. And cottage girls worked
harder and made less money. Maybe I could go on south to
San Francisco—

I'd hate to leave Rapid. But it would be worth it to me to
see Priya and the rest of the girls safe. And Madame too, even
if she were hell-bent on thwarting me.

Maybe she read rebellion in the set of my lips, because she looked me up and down and said, "And don't think I won't turn your friend Miss Swati out as well. I think you care more about her than you do about yourself."

Damn. "I'm listening, Madame."

"Good," she said. She came around the desk, limping heavily, but without her cane. She put her hand on my shoulder, and this time it was easier to look at her. "I've got a great affection for you, young lady. And some wisdom in the world. Please restrain yourself for long enough to let me use it."

Chapter Fifteen

It's not every night a wild Comanche tumbles in your bedroom window. Some folk might consider that sort of a pity,
but it suits me just fine. Especially since the one time it ever
happened to me, he managed it so quiet that I didn't wake up
and notice him until he was well inside and closing it behind
him.

I woke with a start to a slim man silhouetted against a gray
sky, and I probably would have shrieked like a teakettle if I
hadn't been struck completely dumb with terror. By the time
I'd gasped in a breath, I recognized Tomoatooah and that he
was holding a finger to his lips. "How did you know which
room was mine?"

There were probably other questions which bore asking first,
mind, but that was the one I managed to think of.

He smiled and pointed at the little wooden horse on the
ledge. My da made that for me when I was just little. It was a
stiff little critter with a tossing mane—and he mended the leg,
too, when I broke it.

"Guessed," he said. "Also, I peeked inside. You should lock your window."

"If I locked my window, what would I do for Comanche?" I got up, glad I was wearing thick flannel, and went to the window. "You hiding from somebody?"

He nodded and stood aside so I could get a look. I made sure not to rustle the curtain when I peered around it.

The sky overhead was graying, but the streets were shadowed and dark. Down by the waterfront—about two blocks away—I saw the flicker of torches moving around the street in a pattern that suggested a search. I heard 'em calling back and forth to each other through the mist.

"Lynch mob?" I asked.

He shrugged. "I didn't stay to ask."

"They didn't see you come in here?"

He shook his head. "I came down from the roof."

"Hm," I said. "Something tells me you ought to get out of Rapid, *pronto*."

"No flies on you."

A sarcastic houseguest. That was just what I wanted to be awakened by at dawn. I sighed.

"Well," I said. "As long as we're up, we might as well get some breakfast."

I managed to rustle up some of yesterday's bread and scrape some dripping into a pan while Tomoatooah blew up the banked fire and got a little flicker going. I fried up the bread and warmed some cold coffee without waking Connie in her room down the hall—she would have cooked us two breakfasts apiece, but she deserved her sleep as much as any of us—and we ate the greasy salty bread standing up over the plank work top, hands cupped to catch drips.

By the time we were done, Connie had woken up of her own accord, and she got Crispin to help her hide Tomoatooah under some empty coffee sacks in the back of the wagon so we could spirit him away. Crispin promised to get him to the edge of town and then personally take a message to Marshal Reeves as to what had happened and where the Comanche would meet him—Connie suggested an old sawmill up the river two miles—and when that was arranged I went the hell back to bed.

It weren't the most successful endeavor I ever undertook. Mostly I laid there with a pillow over my face, worrying. Tomoatooah wasn't safe in the city no more, not with Bantle convincing half the town he was the killer. And how safe was Marshal Reeves going to be without his posseman?

I didn't like any of it. Not at all.

Hell, for fifteen minutes I even wondered if there was any sense in going to see Horaz Standish and seeing if some kind of a truce could be brokered. He had the reputation of being a reasonable man.

But I figured Madame Damnable would consider that interfering with Bantle without her permission, and at this point I figured if I did that she might just break all my fingers for me *before* she tossed me out on the street.

So began a long, cold wait.

I read somewhere that there's little in this world more frustrating than having a plan and the desire to carry it out and being thwarted in expression. But thwarted I was, and all I could do was work, read, write, and fuss over Priya. And frankly, there just weren't that much work to be getting on with. The parlor was nearly empty most nights—there was more girls than men, even counting Crispin and the Professor. Madame came and went at strange hours, and there was three or four men I didn't know who came in, spoke right to Miss Bethel, and went up to Madame's office without further ado. Crispin walked each one up, but they came back down on their own and left likewise.

We got some business from the constables, if you can call it business when they didn't pay. In fact, I saw Miss Bethel handing at least one of them a little cloth purse as he left. Seems to me as you should take your bribe in money *or* flesh. To ask for both seems like trying to use your fat to fry and spread it on your cornpone, too. But I suppose if you're taking grease from a whorehouse, you ain't too concerned with the appearance of venality.

I kept hoping to see the Marshal or Merry Lee, but other than one quick note from Bass Reeves delivered by a street urchin, I heard nothing from either one of them. Priya didn't go back to see her sister, either, though I know Aashini sent her a letter in some language that looked to me like a whole set of brush doodles. Pretty brush doodles, but Greek made more sense. Going to see her would of been too dangerous—anybody could have followed Priya to wherever Merry had Aashini holed up. Priya, though—she was walking on air the whole time.

And Priya and me . . . well, whenever she was around I was walking on air, too. I taught her how to braid rugs, and things was so boring she made me one in about three days, to replace the one I'd given her. And there was more kissing, too, although sometimes we'd be curled up all comfortable together and she'd suddenly have to get up and pace or she'd find something needed doing right desperate like, and in a different room.

That's all I'm going to say about that except the other girls—and Crispin, even—got to treating the two of us as if we came as a set and that didn't gripe me none at all.

That note from Reeves just told me to hang tight and watch my back. Because I hadn't been doing that without his urging, nor Priya's back, neither. It hinted at progress but didn't spell none out, which made me wonder if he weren't just telling me something good to keep me quiet and out of trouble. As if I needed anything more than Madame's threat against Priya to manage that.

I tried like hell not to fuss when I didn't hear again. Maybe they was lying low or tailing Bantle's Russian mechanic and they didn't have much time to chat.

I didn't tell Priya what Madame had threatened, because I knowed what she would say. That she could take care of herself and that she'd help me go get Bantle any time I said the word. Hell, she'd lead the charge and I'd be the one holding her gloves.

So mostly I got a good big lot of sewing done. Sewing sewing, I mean. Not the other sort, though I took my turn with the constables when it came around and pretended to like it. Priya and Miss Lizzie had turned that Singer into the next best thing to a steam shovel, and the sewing went quick. Priya got another pair of trousers and two shirts including the pretty one—she hid her face in her hair when I gave it to her—and Miss Francina got the trim work done on a bodice, and I had to let down all of Beatrice's hems because she wasn't getting any bigger around, but she was shooting up like a stem.

One good thing that happened, though, was when Priya took me to the circus as a thank-you for the rug and coverlid. Mostly good, anyway. Well, the circus itself was a great idea. There was all those elephants, and a pink poodle that drove an automaton after some clowns, and a trapeze act with rocket packs. There was a tiger who jumped through flaming hoops and didn't seem very impressed with the whip the trainer kept cracking. I liked the tiger fine, and the popped corn, and the dog-faced boy—but I could have done without the whip. Given what we'd found out by the trash bins, I don't think Priya *or* me really needed the reminder.

There was some trick riding, though, that was Cossacks and the equal of anything Da could've done. Maybe better. Neither he nor I could have managed a bareback handstand. I had to look away from the horses after a while, though, and watch the girls in their tight bathing costumes sailing around under the big top on buzzing mechanical wings.

Priya wanted to go around the back after the show and see the elephants. She said she'd heard sometimes you could ride on them or feed them peanuts.

I didn't feel the need to make the acquaintance of an elephant, but I was happy to go wherever Priya led. She could look at elephants and I could look at her, and we would both be happy. I didn't want to stay too long—I was thirsty and didn't want beer, and God knew what could be in the water out here: cholera, the dysentery . . . tiny piranhas.

There was a good crowd out by the elephant pen. I say "pen," but I don't believe for an instant those split-wood rails would do one damned thing to slow down an elephant that wanted to be on the other side of them.

Priya pushed up right by it anyway, leaning on the rails, so I came and stood beside her. The elephants mostly seemed interested in their hay—they picked it up with their long curly noses and stuffed it into their mouths—and I didn't expect any trouble from 'em. Some folk had brought apples or peanuts to tempt 'em, and pretty soon one of the smaller ones wandered over to the fence and started to lift goodies from people's fingertips. One of the keepers was loitering nearby, keeping an eye on what people fed to his charge, but he didn't seem concerned overall.

Priya, though, looked stricken. And I thought I knew why. We hadn't brought anything to feed the elephant with.

I touched her on the shoulder.

She turned to me, dark eyes wide under her arched brows—the prettiest thing I have ever seen. "Wait here," I said. "I'll be back in a quarter hour."

"These are Indian elephants," she said with a smile. "I will stay right here."

I hadn't known there was more than one kind of elephant, and I made a note to myself to ask her later what the differences was. Right now, though, I threaded through the crowd, dodging at least one would-be rump squeezer along the way. There was a line at the concession stand, but I wrinkled my nose and joined it, flicking the skirts of my iris-colored day dress smooth. I'd told Priya a quarter hour, after all. And I didn't think she'd run away if I was a few minutes late—but I also realized that I hated being away from her.

Ain't love grand?

But I was set on my surprise, so I stayed in line.

There were two men in front of me talking politics and I ain't proud of it, but I made a mule ear over at 'em while all the while pretending to search in my reticule for Christ knows what. Eavesdropping's a sin, but ignorance is fatal. Take your pick.

". . . we haven't done so bad with Stone," the tall one said.

The smaller took a swig of his flask. "We haven't done so good with him, either. You think Bantle would put up with those Chinks spreading cholera and syphilis all over the city?"

You ever hear somebody blithely say something so amazingly plastered over with bullshit it just makes your eyes bug? I swear to God, I found my nail scissors in my bag and dug it into my fingertip to keep from opening my mouth. It hurt less than biting my lip. I wanted to ask him what Bantle was blackmailing him with to get him to spread such categorical lies.

"Besides," said the one with the flask, "Stone won't run. He's too afraid of what would come out. I bet he's swindled the city out of hundreds of thousands of dollars by now."

I remembered something Pollywog had said about her secret client not seeming like himself lately and bit my lip. But I was saved from whatever I might have said because they got to the front of the line and had to order. Fried dough, bratwurst, fritters, and beer. They were too busy stuffing sausages into their faces to continue the conversation when they left, thank Christ.

I got up and ordered two caramel apples, two beers, and a bag of peanuts, but when I pulled coins from my reticule to pay, a hand reached over my shoulder.

"I've got the lady's order," someone said over my shoulder.

When I turned around, I startled. It was René, a gold miner from Quebec I knowed from Madame's house. Sometimes he'd just sit in the parlor and buy Bea drinks and they'd talk at each other in two different kinds of French. He hadn't come in in a month or so, though. He was a good tipper with good breath, and all the girls liked him.

I said, "That's very generous."

He handed me the caramel apples. "How were you going to carry all this?"

"I manage," I said. We turned away. "I haven't seen you in lately."

He shrugged and frowned. "I don't know," he said. "I haven't had much gumption to come visiting of late."

I thought about how business had been falling off. "Have you been going somewhere else?"

He snorted. "You know that'd be like hot dogs after caviar, Karen honey. Begging your pardon."

I took a bite of one of the apples. The caramel was chewy and thick, the apple inside a lick of crunch and juiciness. It'd be a challenge not to eat it all. "Did you hear about the murder?"

"Right outside your door, it was, *non?*"

I nodded. "The Ancient and Honorable Guild of Seamstresses is getting up a Vigilance Committee. Patrols. You don't need to be afraid to come see us."

He shrugged, one of those eloquent Frog shrugs with a whole paragraph in it. Pity Bea wasn't there to read that paragraph to me, because it was in a language I could recognize but not speak much of. "I heard some girls went to Horaz Standish to ask for protection," he said.

I made myself swallow instead of spit, but it weren't easy. "They better be careful they don't wind up in Bantle's cribs. Oh, here we are. René, this is my friend Priya. She's . . . she's one of our mechanics."

That seemed safest. She looked down, and I held the second apple out to her. "There's peanuts for the elephant," I told her. "And I got you a beer."

You have never seen a face light up like hers when I said "peanuts," I tell you true.

René didn't seem to mind being seen with a couple of whores, or maybe he enjoyed watching the elephant's hairy, ridiculously dainty nose tip whisk peanut after peanut out of Priya's slender fingers. She even let me try once, and the prickle of fine hairs and the huff of warm breath reminded me of a horse's lip feeling for carrots so it almost made me weep. Priya and René were both generous enough to pretend not to notice, though.

Afterward, Priya and me took our leave of René and walked home slowly. It was getting on sunset but sunny and we hadn't needed our umbrellas. We were companionable and it was fine indeed—but our peace and goodwill lasted only until we climbed down the ladder by Madame's and walked into the parlor.

Nobody was there but the girls, the Professor, and Crispin. And all the girls was there—even Madame. All gathered around Francina, who sat on a love seat with her head on her hands.

I slipped up next to Bea, who was at the back of the group—or the front, depending on your perspective. Closest the door, anyway. Priya ghosted behind me. "What happened?"

Bea's lips compressed. "One of Miss Francina's specials went down with a gold ship."

I blinked, stunned. Then something awful occurred to me. "Wait, that same ship?" I remembered reading in the paper about one that had gone down some time ago.

"No," Bea said. "A second one."

"Criminy." Sure, the seas got rough in winter—but those modern ships were huge things and expected to weather anything short of a hurricane. To lose two in the space of a month was bad luck indeed. "That's awful."

"She just heard," Bea whispered.

"Well," I said. "I'm going to get her some coffee—"

But Connie had beaten me to it. She came out of the back with a tray and set it down, and started shooing girls away from Miss Francina like so many busy chickens. The Professor went back to his bench and started picking out something skipping. Crispin came over by the door.

I stood there feeling useless until Priya took my hand and led me over to sit down near Miss Francina and Miss Lizzie, where we talked about the circus and not shipwrecks at all.

Priya's not just smart about machines.

After Miss Francina got herself together, she wanted to look for conspiracies. And we had next to no johns come in that night, so talk in the parlor was all of the Russians and the Brits and rumors that they was allying up in Victoria to pincer into

Alaska and take it back, now that they knowed it was full of gold.

The Professor eventually wandered off his bench and came over to opine that the Russians wouldn't even put up with the Brits, even for all the gold in Alaska. We were working up to a good old cheerful row over that, and that color was coming back into Miss Francina's cheeks something wonderful, when Crispin jumped up to answer a knock and we all fell silent and turned.

I'm sure we didn't look the least bit suspicious at all.

Crispin opened the door, and in walked that constable, Sergeant Waterson, and one of his towers of muscle. He paused inside the door, shifting from foot to foot as if embarrassed, and said, "I'm sorry, ladies, but I'm here to investigate a complaint that there's a woman on the premises dressing in men's clothing."

He very carefully didn't look at Miss Francina, and Miss Francina very carefully kept her back turned to him. She was perched on a bar stool, leaning against Miss Bethel, and though they each took a breath, neither one of them acknowledged Waterson in any way.

Madame happened to be in the parlor herself just then, and she stood up slow, leaning on her cane. "Sergeant?" she said in her warning voice. "Who was it, exactly, that swore out this complaint?"

"It was anonymous," he said. "And you know I don't take it seriously, Madame. But you know I have to make a visit."

"Right." She sighed. "Bethel, my cash box, please?"

Waterson held up a hand. "There's no fine."

We all blinked. If he wasn't going to take a bribe, then what was this all about?

He scuffed a boot on the edge of the rug. "I can see there's nothing amiss here. I was asked—"

He quailed under Madame's advance, though, and whatever he might have said next was lost. He dug in his pocket and produced an envelope. He held it out to her.

She slit it with a thumbnail smooth as I might have used a pocketknife. It took her fifteen seconds to read the half sheet within. Then she grunted, crumbled the whole mess in her hand, and pitched it underhand into the fire.

"You tell Peter Bantle that I'll kowtow to him when he breaks both my knees," she said evenly.

"Madame—"

"And another thing, Christopher Waterson," she continued. "He ain't gonna win this. So you better decide right now which side you think you'd like to be on."

Chapter Sixteen

The fifth night after my talk with Madame, I went to bed early with a book, because there weren't nothing more I could do. Priya was still at work in the kitchen.

I hadn't been sleeping so good, and it turned out that was a blessing. When someone knocked at my door about four in the morning, I was awake and curled around the pages of Bea's copy of this French book translated from the Arabic that I'd been struggling through. I liked it a lot, when I could make head or tail of it. It was about a woman who's married unwilling to a sultan who murders each of his brides after consummating to stave off getting an heir, but she keeps him at bay every night by outwitting him, and telling him stories he can't bear not to know the end of, so he keeps letting her live another day.

So I was lying on my side with the blankets pulled up to my ears, bent toward the lamp. Miss Francina always claimed reading in the dark would ruin my eyes sure as stitchery, and she was probably right. But even she couldn't tell me nothing when

I had an idea in my head. I save all my better judgment for dealing with horses.

I got up—getting out from under the quilt was hard, the air was that sharp—and stuck my feet in my slippers as fast as I could. Of course, the slippers was cold, too, though not as cold as the floor. Still, cold enough that I hissed and limped as I scuffed over to the door.

I had my hand on the latch when I heard Priya's voice outside. "Karen, I'm cold. Let me in?"

I probably would of jumped out of bed faster if I'd known it were her, and no mistake. As it was, I yanked that door open so fast I made a draft.

Priya was bundled up in shawls over her shirt and trousers, her hair braided for bed but unmussed. She stepped out of the way so I could shut the door behind her. Then I gestured her toward my rumpled bed and she sat, sliding her sock-clad feet into a fold of the blankets. I should of gotten her slippers better than the carpet ones.

"Hi," I said, and sat down on the bed, too. Closer to the head, though. Just close enough that our shoulders brushed together. I had made up my mind early that as long as she knowed I was willing, it was going to be Priya made all the moves between us. I was giving her time, and you know it weren't easy. But like gentling a badly broke horse, I knowed I had to let Priya do most of the traveling if I didn't want to spook her away for good.

I handed her a pillow. She smiled and leaned back against it. I stuck my legs back under the covers.

"Hi," she said. She looked down at her hands, picked at her cuticle, and tucked her fingers into her armpits under the shawls while I tried not to stare at her.

A minute or two later, I said, "Did you want something?"

"Um," she said.

She looked at me and glanced away again. In the lamplight, her dark eyes seemed opaque. She dropped her head as if she meant to hide behind her hair, but the braid thwarted her.

Then she said, "Company."

I wanted to reach out and take her hand so bad I could taste it. But her hands were tucked up warm under her arms, and anyway the foot and a half between us seemed unbridgeable. I wanted to kiss her, too, but she didn't look too kissable just then. More remote, and worried.

I wished I could offer her tea. You don't think about it, but all those little fusses we make over company have their purposes. They give us something to do with our hands and our anxiousness until everybody settles in and starts having fun. It's probably why the men who come into Madame's spend so much money at the bar. Even though they gotta know—the savvy ones, anyway—that we girls is drinking soda water or cold tea. But it gives everybody something to do with their hands.

"I want company, too," I admitted. It was on my lips to say, *In kind of particular, I want your company,* but all I could see was her jumping up and scooting for the door. When people have only lured you close to hit you or throw a rope over your head before, it's hard to learn to trust the ones who aren't going to. Hell, it's hard to learn to even know which is which.

So I just sat there like an idiot, watching the most beautiful person I'd ever seen huddled up on my bed, and I didn't put an arm around her.

She pulled her hands out of her armpits and twisted them together, all pale with the chill. She had the most elegant fingers—tapered, like a lady's, even with her nails kept cropped for the domestic work she was doing. Mine were blunt and plump, though I grew my nails out to make them look more genteel.

Looking at them, not at me, Priya said, "Karen, have you ever thought about leaving here? About what you might want to do after?"

"Are . . ." . . . *you asking me to come with you?* It died on my lips. It was too much to hope, and it would give too much away.

She waited patiently, still not raising her head.

"I have," she said when I was quiet too long.

"Me too," I answered. "I'm saving. I want a stable some-day, a horse ranch. A breeding operation. Sell good cow ponies, and maybe break 'em for folks."

"Oh," she said.

She didn't sound disappointed so much as concerned, so I hurried to say, "You would always be welcome. I . . . I'd build you a machine shop, and you could fixit while I wrangled, and you could cook and I could sew. And, and we could each read to the other while we did it."

It was about the prettiest dream I'd ever put to words, and no mistaking. I held my breath while I waited to see if she was going to shoot it down.

She said, "I don't know anything about horses. My family had cattle and sheep . . . but the cattle weren't for eating. We don't eat cows at home. They're for milk and cheese and ghee."

I didn't know what ghee was and made a note to ask her. But it seemed more important to say, "I know all about horses. I practically grew up on one. I could teach you, especially if you know cattle. If you're not afraid."

"I'm afraid of all sorts of things," Priya said. "But not farm animals."

"I wish you could have known my Molly."

"Molly? This is a . . . what's the word? Mare?"

"Is, yes. As far as I know, she's still alive. I had to give her away after my da died." Horses live a long time.

"Not sell?"

I shrugged. "I sold the rest. Her . . . the person I wanted to have her couldn't pay for a horse, so I gave her to him. A neighbor's lad. My age." I knowed Lutz would give her back to me if I ever came looking. That was part of it. I didn't say that, though, because I didn't know if it would be fair to him—or to Molly—and frankly, I didn't know if I would. You grieve, it's one thing. You grieve and go back, it's another.

She gave me a sly look. "Did you love him?"

"Hah! No, of course not. I loved that mare. Though some folk would say you can't love an animal, on account of they have no souls."

"I don't believe that," Priya said.

"That you can't love an animal?"

"You can love an animal," she said. She was uncoiling a little, straightening up. Though it hadn't gotten any warmer in the room. "And animals have souls. Your religion is very strange to me, Karen. I believe that when we die, we come back on a wheel of rebirth. And depending on whether we have acquitted ourselves well—depending on our *karma*—we may be reincarnated to a good life. Or we may be reincarnated to a life where we must earn our way out of misdeeds—pain we have caused, injustice we have benefited from."

I'd been blinking at her confusedly, I'm afraid. But when she said that last, I bounced on my seat bones, ridiculously pleased to find some common ground in her blasphemy. Or was it just heathenish? Can a heathen blaspheme?

I'm a fallen woman; who am I to judge?

I said excitedly, "That's like Purgatory!"

Her lips curved so gently I'd be afraid to call it a smile, lest it fly away. "We would say it is *dharma*. It supports the natural and proper order of things." She got quiet again, and I knowed from her frown that she was wondering what her past self had done to deserve a life in Peter Bantle's cribs. But she pulled herself back together and said, "Tell me about your mare. Your Molly."

"She's a strawberry Appaloosa," I said.

Priya looked at me like I was speaking one of the maybe five or six languages on earth that she wasn't already fluent in.

I guess it was what you'd call technical vocabulary. "That means she's a roan, a kind of speckled red and gray. With a white blanket across her shoulders and . . . sort of silver-dollar-sized spots of red on top of that. And she's smart, Molly is. Smart for a horse, anyway."

Smart enough to get herself into plenty of trouble. Learning to unlatch gates and suchlike. Nearly colicked herself once, getting into the grain. I told Priya about some of that but wound down halfway through what was supposed to have been a funny story about a barn cat when the wave of longing hit me. Loneliness and missing . . . Molly, and Da. Molly almost worse than Da. Because Da was gone, and he weren't coming back, and I hadn't had no choice about it.

I hadn't had no choice about Molly, neither. Not really. But I'd had to make one anyway.

Priya waited a few seconds, as if to see if I was going to carry on. Then, as if I'd asked a question, she started to tell me about her baby brother, and her parents, and the crop failures. And how she and her sister had signed indenture papers to come to America so their family could afford to eat, not realizing that they was going to wind up in a barred crib or paraded on leashes through Chinatown weekly for their only exercise. "It was supposed to be domestic work," she said. "We were supposed to send money home."

She was picking at that cuticle again. She was going to draw blood in a minute.

"Well," I said. "That's what you're doing now, ain't it? You just got a bit delayed."

I couldn't stand it anymore. I reached out and pulled her nails away from her skin. She looked up in surprise, like she hadn't noticed what she was doing to herself, despite having been so studious over it. Her fingers was strong for being so slender, and she gave my hand a short, quick squeeze. I was half-stunned by how warm it was, and I thought—for a second—she was leaning in toward me and I thought I might get my kissing in after all.

I wondered if someday she might trust me enough to fall asleep with her head on my shoulder. Or even lie there a little while without having to get up and pace circles to burn off the anxiousness of getting too close.

All I saw was her lips as she hesitated. Then her head twisted around and her expression froze. "What's that smell?"

A second later and I caught it also. Burning—and not the clean smell of wood or coal. This was a dirty kind of stink, like a trash fire.

"I smell smoke!" Priya cried.

"Shit," I said. "I do, too."

Some good grace of God made me pry open my hiding place— right there in front of Priya—and grab out my journal and my savings. I left Da's wooden horse, though it about killed me. We pulled sheets from the bed, wet them in the basin, and wrapped them around our heads. I opened the door—Priya made me touch it first and check to see if the wood or the handle was hot, which I had never heard about before then— and we stumbled hand in hand into the corridor, me holding up the lamp.

The door at the top of the stairs was open, and ordinarily

Connie would of had the head of whoever left it so—letting all the heat run out of the downstairs like that. And the heat was sure running out now: streamers of smoke crept along the stair ceiling like foul black fingers. Hot air rushed up the steps, like holding my hand over a lamp chimney except on an industrial scale. The smoke had already left oily smears on the corridor ceiling, like the ripples on water. I stared at it, trying to think—could we get down the stairs? Could we go out the window? It was only a short drop down to the street, but it was farther to the sidewalk—much farther—and I wasn't sure I could jump the gap. And even if the fire companies were en route, which they probably weren't because I hadn't heard nobody raise the alarm of *Fire!*, it might be twenty minutes before they arrived. And then if two or more showed up, they might just have a fistfight over who got to hook up to the hydrant rather than getting to the business of dousing fires.

In twenty minutes, we might all be dead.

"Fire!" Priya shouted, thumping on the nearest door. "Fire!"

Now, that was what you call direct and functional action. Since I couldn't make up my own mind what to do, I figured I might as well follow Priya's lead.

She was pounding on Effie's door, because Effie was next door to me. I whirled around and ran down to Miss Francina's room, shouting.

Other doors were starting to open—Crispin, and Bea, and Pollywog all pouring out in their nightclothes. Crispin had grabbed boots and was stamping them on over his pajamas. That seemed like a fine sensible idea, but all my boots required a buttonhook and if I was going to die in a fire I didn't want it to be because I stopped to make sure my shoes was fastened. Or because I broke my neck trying to run in ones as weren't.

Madame's bedroom was on the floor below, behind her office. I looked up and saw Miss Lizzie and Miss Bethel coming out of the room they share, and from the way they headed to the stairs they had realized that, too. But just as they got there, I heard a door below slam open and Madame shouting up the stair, "Girls, it's a fire in the kitchen! Go out the windows at the front! Get out! Get out!"

Priya grabbed my arm. She pulled me toward Pollywog's room, which was at the front of the house. But just then, Bea darted toward the stairs. "Signor!" she yelled.

She probably would of gotten past Miss Lizzie and Miss Bethel, too, because by then they each had Madame by a wrist and was hauling her, limping, up the stairs. But when she darted past Priya, Priya let go of me and grabbed at Bea.

The air was getting thick. My head spun, even with the wet cloth over my face. I grabbed Bea's other arm and helped Priya hold her. "I'll look for him," I said. "You go with Priya."

"Karen!" Priya snapped.

I shoved my journal and my little purse at her. "Keep these safe. They're yours if—"

"*Karen.*"

"Connie's down there, too, unless she made it out the back," I said. "And didn't you just tell me animals have souls?"

She threw up her free hand in despair. "All right," she said. "All right."

And then she leaned forward, and in front of God and Madame and Effie and everybody she kissed me square on the mouth, wet rags and all.

"For luck," she said, and dragged Bea toward the windows.

"Wait!" Crispin yelled. He had a big voice. It carried through the room. I thought he was going to try to stop me, and I'm sure he thought about it—but Miss Lizzie and Miss Bethel was struggling with Madame, who was coughing like a consumptive as she came to the top of the stairs. I saw him look around, and think about the odds.

"You can catch the girls when they jump," I said. "I can't do that."

One thing about Crispin. He don't waste time making up his mind. He yanked his boots off and shoved them at me, then threw the overcoat he'd been struggling into over my shoulders. "It might help," he said. "Get Connie. I won't let them open the window for two minutes, so's you can get down the stairs."

Because once that window was open, the stairs would be a chimney. Right.

Hopping on one foot to get the other boot on, I looked him in the eye and nodded. "I'll see you outside," I said. "Shut the stair door behind me, too."

I wouldn't of gotten past Miss Francina that easy. But she was corralling Pollywog and Effie after Priya, so in the thickening haze I figure she didn't see what I was fixing to do.

It's damn hard to crawl down stairs, I don't mind telling you. I skidded down backward on my hands and knees as fast as I could, mindful of my time limit. Whenever I lifted my head, it felt like dunking it into a warm bathtub, except for upside down and strangely dry. But there was a ribbon of cooler air down by the steps, and through the wet cloth I could breathe it.

I was counting under my breath—that one-Mississippi, two-Mississippi—and I had gotten to sixty-seven when my feet thumped against the wall at the landing. I couldn't see much anymore—my eyes was streaming and the smoke was damn near chewable—and I hoped Crispin didn't count much faster than me. So I turned around and scurried faster. Eighty-Mississippi. Eighty-one. My knees were going to look like somebody'd taken a hoof file to 'em. I weren't going fast enough, and I knowed it. I think I peeled off half my senses, reaching 'em out like whiskers, trying to feel the draft that would be followed by the flood of hot air and maybe fire up those stairs.

I should of shut the door at the top. Ninety-Mississippi. But I weren't going back up there to correct the oversight now. Maybe Crispin would remember I'd asked him to. My elbows were bruised up something awful, but I was running on so much fear and excitement that they only hurt when I whacked one of 'em on something. In sorrow I report, I whacked 'em on a lot.

One hundred. Twenty seconds until Crispin opened the window. I must be almost there by now, but I couldn't count stairs and seconds both at once. One-hundred-five . . .

The door was kitty-corner to the stairs, and I kicked out as I slid down what I thought was the last few steps. So I felt it was open space. I kind of swapped ends and fell out into the hall, then scrambled forward and kicked the door shut, nearly losing one of Crispin's giant boots. I jammed it back on by stomping my foot against the doorframe.

Then I lay there on my belly for what felt like enough time for the whole damned house to have burned down around me but was probably only ten seconds or so. My breath heaved in and out like a bellows, and thank Christ there was less smoke down here or I would of choked on it. I pressed my face to the carpet and breathed through the wool fibers and the wet sheet, and it was almost like breathing air.

But the fire wanted that air, too, and when it was done there wouldn't be none left for me. Even if I didn't manage to roast alive before then. I pushed myself to my knees—damn, my knees—and tried to crawl. But Crispin's overcoat got tangled in my legs and his boots was too big, and I didn't have rags to stuff them with, so instead I laid back down and I kind of shuffle-kicked my way forward. Like a frog. *Smoked frog.*

I laughed, which I shouldn't of done, because even with the wet wrap I got a stinging lungful. But I couldn't see anyway, so coughing myself blind didn't really matter, except it slowed me down.

I couldn't afford to get lost. It was dark as pitch down here, like swimming in muddy water at night. I figured that was a good sign, because if I got in sight of the fire I'd sure be able to see that, no matter how dark it was otherwise. So I was feeling my way around and hoping I could remember where all the furniture was in the dark. Furniture we'd recently rearranged, of course, due to the riot in the parlor previous.

Down here, though I couldn't see the fire, I could *hear* it. There was a hollow, grumbling roar, like a splintercat raging in an empty barn behind a stark oak door. It came from the kitchen, and that made my stomach churn, because Connie's room was in the hall right outside. Every so often that was punctuated with crackling pings of hot metal and the thud of falling beams. I could hear something else, too—the clarion peals of Signor's loud, monotonous, evenly spaced meows, that rang all the way back from the parlor to where I huddled at the base of the servants' stair.

Maybe I should of tried to come down the grand staircase to the front, but I was thinking about Connie and—

Well, it was too late to change my mind now.

Groping, I felt a doorjamb and found the door to the back hall, where Connie's room was. Priya saved my life, because before I jerked it open I touched it.

I yanked my hand back with a real ladylike swear: my finest. Hot; sharp hot. Blistering. Then I realized I could *see* my hand, dull red through the clouds of smoke. And something like flakes of black snow was falling through that smoke, stirring eddies.

I looked up. The ceiling was on fire, flames licking from behind the door, and what was flaking down on me now was bits of blackened lath and plaster. And I could see the glare of red through the keyhole, too.

If Connie was back there . . . there weren't nothing I could do for her. All I could hope was she'd made it out the kitchen door.

I wanted to curl up and sob. I wanted to yank open that door and go running into the fire looking for her, but I couldn't even touch the cut-glass doorknob, it was so hot. And Signor was still yelling. Maybe I could get to him. And anyway, that was my only way out now.

I got up on my hands and knees and crawled.

At first, it seemed like the air was getting cooler around me, the smoke less thick. But then it started getting worse again—hotter, smokier. And when I came around the corner to the parlor, there was that awful orange flicker again.

The parlor wasn't on fire.

Just those poor much-abused front doors.

I was trapped.

God bless Signor. I think I would of frozen there in horror until the roof fell on me if he hadn't picked that moment to yell, with all the power of his deaf little lungs, right in my left ear. It shocked me into moving. And squeaking like a mouse. Like a stepped-on mouse.

Signor was standing right at the base of the grand stair, glaring at me with his one blue eye and one yellow exactly as if the whole thing were my fault. I scooped him to my chest, and the ungrateful little bastard left a bloody long trail of scratches down my forearm with his hind foot. But I hung on to him. And about squeezed him into pudding, I was so glad to see him alive.

I say "little," but Signor was twenty pounds if he was an

ounce. I crouched, hugging him, and he hid his face in my wet
sheet wrap. Flakes of burning something was sizzling out on
Crispin's overcoat, the wool adding a scorched stench to every
other awful smell in the room. I needed a way out. Anything.
I had to pick a direction, and I was terrified that whatever direction I picked would be wrong. I didn't think I was gonna get
a chance to change my mind and try something different if I
happened to get it wrong.

Maybe I could go back up the stairs? Go out a window?
Crispin would be out there to catch me now, or Miss Francina.
Or there might be a firefighter with a ladder by now—

And then my eye lit on the sewing machine to the left of the
parlor doors. That big, industrial, ridiculous, totally overengi-
neered, souped-up-to-Jesus Singer sewing machine. The one
that Priya and Lizzie had been hot-rodding for weeks, with the
ornamental metal plates all over the armature, and Miss Lizzie's
diesel engine welded in beside the hydraulics.

It hurt me to stand up. Knees, spine, everything. My lungs,
from the heat of the air, even through the wrap. The wrap was
nearly dry now anyway, all the water sizzled off into the fire.

Head spinning, breath rasping, I staggered to the sewing machine. It weren't easy getting into it while holding on to an un-
happy cat, wearing boots four sizes bigger than my feet. The
sewing machine was hot as a bitch, but I managed somehow,
and the coat and boots were a lifesaver. It burned my legs
through my socks and where my night shift didn't quite meet
up with 'em at the knee. I burned my hands some, too, in the
process but didn't drop Signor and I got about half the straps
catched.

That were probably enough. I just left the machine's left
arm hanging, because I was using that hand to hang on to Signor anyway. He quieted down a bit when I swaddled him up
in the sheet and bound him against my chest. At least it was

easier than getting a horse out of a burning barn—a job I only knowed in theory, though Da'd made sure I was good and drilled in it. Stable fires had been the worst dread of my childhood.

Turned out there was something worse.

I had the coat, and I had the big machine. And I had the cat, who had quit yowling and twisting and scratching and now just huddled against me, face shoved into my chest. The heat was rising as I sparked the boiler, hoping whoever'd used it last had left some water in the damned thing. It ran on kerosene, not coal—thank God—because kerosene was cleaner indoors.

I never would of gotten a coal engine fired up fast enough to save our lives. It took me thirty seconds that felt like six hours just to get the diesel engine cranked up so it would spark, and then and turning over—me praying the whole time that I remembered right that diesel didn't explode, then remembering the kerosene.

And it turned out to be a horrible kind of blessing that the thing was hot, because the water in the boilers might already have been near simmering. Anyway, it came up to pressure right quick, with hissing and creaking and a whole mess of noise. While I waited, I managed to force the thing into a crouch by main strength and with the torque from the auxiliary engine, so I could get me and Signor closer to the floor where there was still some air lasting.

I don't recommend any of it.

The parlor, as I said, wasn't burning, though now flames licked out from the doors into the paneling on either side. I imagined those flames inside the walls, creeping up to the ceiling—and the fire behind me, from the kitchen, chasing down the hall. I knowed rooms could get engulfed in flames in an instant when they got hot enough. But I also knowed—I *knew*—that somebody had set this fire on purpose to trap us inside.

There weren't no other reason for just the door to be burning, excepting if somebody had set it on purpose to shut us in. And I knowed the longer I let it burn, the weaker the wood would be.

And the more pressure there'd be in the sewing machine, in order to break it down.

I don't mind saying I ain't never been so scared in my life.

Finally—it seemed like hours, but it were only two minutes or so—the gauges read 70 percent pressure and climbing. When I rose up, it was a hell of a lot easier than squatting down had been. As soon as my head came up into the smoke layer, though, everything went dizzy and rough edged. I would of swayed, but the sewing machine has gyroscopes, so it shifted around me and caught my stagger. This is a good thing, because the sewing machine weighs half a ton and if you fell inside it you might never get up unless the hydraulics kept working.

And if it fell so the weight was on you, well. You'd crack a rib or three sure as if a horse fell on you. You'd be lucky to walk away without a hole in your lung, and not even Miss Lizzie can fix up that.

Now that I was decided, I had to go fast. The smoke up here was that thick. I could barely hear the roar of the Singer's engines over the roar of the fire. I might of missed the door, honestly, if it weren't for those flames glaring orange. They made such a beacon I couldn't of asked for more, except maybe a fog light.

I clutched Signor against me, turning my shoulder toward the door, and started to lumber up to a run. I aimed right at the middle, at the place the panels met. And I thought, *If Peter Bantle can break it in, by God I can break it out.*

I half-surprised myself when I came up on the edge of the flames, howled with all the strength in my lungs, and ran faster and more hard.

Don't get me wrong. I knowed I had courage. But until that moment, I didn't know I had the courage to run through a fire. We surprise ourselves all our lives, Miss Bethel would say. That is, if our lives is gonna be worth living.

The fire licked all around me, but the Singer's big grippered feet beat the flames down, and the plates Miss Lizzie had welded to the legs shielded me a little. I hit that door screaming and I busted through so hard I didn't stop until I fetched up on the other side of the sidewalk, against the masonry wall that held the street up. Rock dust powdered down around me. My scream turned to coughing, and all around me the sewing machine armature smoked in the cool air. Puddles hissed under its feet and its springs complained of the sudden change in temperature.

"Mother of God," I said, turning to look back at the house.

The second story was all ablaze. I couldn't see any higher, because smoke and flames billowed out the windows, and the narrow space of the sidewalk was near full of smoke as the inside.

I couldn't stay here, either.

Signor wasn't moving, but he was wrapped up close against my chest under the coat and I didn't have time to look at him. And the ladder wouldn't support the weight of the sewing machine.

Which left climbing.

I pulled more wrapping sheet off my head, tucked Signor into it against my chest, then strapped my left arm in with three quick jerks. If Signor was passed out—he'd better not be worse than passed out, and I didn't have time, dammit, to think about Connie—he was probably safe enough just slung against me like a papoose. And if he started to fight, well . . .

My breasts would be the first to know. I'd worry about it if it happened.

The rock wall was too smooth for climbing, unless you was

Merry Lee. But with the sewing machine, I could drive the fingers right into the mortar between the big stones, and the feet had grippers meant to anchor the thing when it was hauling cloth off bolts of denim heavier than it was. It weren't easy, don't get me wrong. And I broke three needles and blunted the scissors and awl something fierce. But length by length, I dragged me and Signor up that wall.

Effie tells me that when I hauled myself over the edge of the street and lay there suspended inside the frame, the machine scrabbling on its belly like a big turtle out of water to move forward, the first thing that happened was a cheer. I don't remember, or maybe I just couldn't hear it over the incredible roar of the fire. I was coughing and coughing and coughing, and all I could feel was the skin on my hands and around my eyes where the sheet didn't wrap, tight and sunburned hot and sore.

Crispin and Effie got me up—or guided me up, anyway. The machine did all the work. They led me at a staggering run away from the blazing building, to where the rest of the girls was huddled, staring and waiting. Crispin just looked at me—he didn't say Connie's name. I couldn't even make myself shake my head, but he must of read the answer in the way I closed my eyes. When I opened them again, he didn't say nothing. He just started unbuckling the armature. Effie was petting my cheek and crying.

She started crying harder when they unwrapped the sheet and found Signor.

I looked down, not wanting to. He looked small—ridiculously small, for a white cat—gray now, smudged and sooty—with a head as big as both my fists together. And at first my heart lurched, and I moaned . . . but then I saw his eyes was open, his ears laid flat.

He looked me right in the face and hissed like a furious teakettle, and I hugged him as hard as I have ever hugged anything in this life or, if Priya is right about what happens when we die, I am likely to hug them in the next one.

And then everybody was around me, helping me out of the sewing machine, and Bea took Signor, which was good because she's the only person on the planet who can pick up that damned cat without getting scratched. I staggered, and I stayed up because Crispin held me up. It seemed like I was doing a lot of that tonight—staying up because something else caught me.

Then he and Miss Lizzie was unwinding me, pulling his burned coat off, checking over my every limb. There was a little drizzle out here, and I turned my face up to it. There was a heavy mist, too, and it fought the smoke back and felt good, so good, on my scalded skin. "Connie," I said.

Crispin put his finger on my lips. I pushed it away. Or tried to: I missed. But he moved it back a fraction. That's what I like about Crispin. Well, one thing out of many. He leaves it to you to judge what you is and ain't capable of. Most men seem to like to decide that for a girl.

Maybe it's because he ain't preening his feathers for no woman. Maybe Crispin's just busy trying to run the lives of other men.

Or maybe he ain't. This evening, my money's on ain't.

"Somebody did this on purpose," I said. "There was fire at all the doors."

"Connie was murdered." He said it like he was getting it straight in his head.

I meant to nod; I don't know if I succeeded. The firelight was painting us all weird through the mist, stark and glowy at the same time. Like somebody draped gauze over one of those Dutch oil paintings that show somebody's face side-lit. And I don't think it was just the fog made everybody look a little hazy at the edges.

Miss Lizzie finished inspecting me. She said, "You need aloe on all of that," and then she said, "Honey, it's a miracle, but if you don't pick open a wound scratching and if it don't take a taint you're going to live without any big scars. Maybe a couple around the knees there, but stockings will cover that. Most of this ain't even going to blister."

I didn't quite make sense of it.

But she moved away, and suddenly my arms were full of Priya hugging me breathless tight, which started me coughing again. "Stupid!" she yelled at me when she stepped back. "Stupid, *stupid*!"

And before I could try to hug her back she knuckled her eyes and ran off, shoulders hunched. The mist ghosted over her. I took a step after, Crispin steadying me, but Miss Lizzie had pulled his boots off me and the cobbles hurt my feet something fierce. "I don't—"

"She likes you," Crispin said with the tired wisdom of somebody who's seen it all before. I half-hated him for his wisdom at that second, and I was half that grateful for it. "She's running away because she's scared of how much it would have hurt if you'd got killed. She'll be back, no fears."

"I'm sorry about Connie," I said between coughs. *Lord, don't let me retch.*

He kissed me on the head. "I ain't sorry it weren't you, too."

That was when, with a thunder of hooves and a clamor of bells, amid the barking of a pair of dalmatians who ran guarding the horses, the fire engine wheeled out of the mist, rampaged past us, and halted before the blaze with so much rearing and head tossing that I would of marched right over there and had a word with the driver about hauling on the horses' mouths that way. I would of, that is, if I hadn't of fainted.

Somebody caught me this time, too. But I didn't see who, because everything was black in all directions.

Chapter Seventeen

I woke up. I wasn't sure I had expected to. But I did it anyway. And where I woke up was someplace I had never been before.

It was a comfortable room, with green walls and ivory window ledges, and I was tucked up in a narrow bed. My hands and arms rested outside the mint-colored chenille bedspread laid over me. They was wrapped in gauze, which felt stuck to the skin with something slippery. Miss Lizzie's aloe leaf, I was guessing. And I was wearing a clean nightgown, too big for me, red flannel. With a frayed lace collar.

My hair on the pillow was still in its braid, though pulled all which-a-way, and it still smelled like dirty fire. My skin smelled like dirty fire, too.

I was alone.

I sat up cautiously, but the room didn't spin. My arms smarted, and the skin around my eyes. The burns on my knees from the sewing machine were welted, blistering, and I guessed before long they would scab. They were the worst of it, though, and I have never felt so lucky.

There wasn't any gauze on my face, but the skin felt sticky there, too. And it itched as well as stinging. I reached for it with gauzy fingers, then remembered Miss Lizzie telling me the scalds weren't bad and that I wouldn't scar if I could leave it alone. So instead I groaned. I might of sat on my hands—or laid on 'em, I guess—but they hurt too damned much.

So instead I put my feet on the floor and winced. I had no socks, and the boards were ivory painted and rugless, cold. Not a rich room, by any means. But not a poor one, either. The bedstead was oak, and mended. There were sprigged gingham curtains over the windows, a blue and green that went with the green of the coverlet, and the blue-and-silver wallpaper. I wondered if somebody had just taken the rug outside to beat it, though that would be weird in the winter.

Sitting up seemed to be going better than anticipated. I felt . . . well, I didn't feel dizzy. But I didn't feel all myself, either. Lightheaded, maybe. Like I wasn't quite in my own skull, but above and behind and a little to the left. Watching myself rather than . . . I don't know. *Being* myself.

I wondered if I could stand. At least my feet weren't burned, and thank Crispin for that. I put my gauzy hands down—one on the bedspread, one on the sheets—and slow as I could I pushed myself up. Now, Da would tell you that Caution ain't my middle name, but this once, honest, I was trying. There was a ladderback chair right there, too, that I could grab if I needed, or so I was thinking.

Turned out, I didn't need it at all. I stood there, rocking, and gathered my wits and my dignity—such of both as I've got—for the best part of five minutes. I knowed it was five minutes, because there was a glass and brass shelf clock ticking away on that little side table. It seems strange to me now, but right then that little clock meant the world to me. It was almost like a companion, and its polished brass case and fresh-wound works told me I hadn't been forgotten in this strange place entirely.

I guess it ain't uncommon for a person to get maudlin under circumstances such as that.

Well, when I decided I wasn't like to pitch over if I lifted a foot I did so—lifted one—and put it down again a little bit forward of its previous position. It turned out to be a blessing that the rug was up, because otherwise I might just have tripped on it and pitched right over. And that would of been embarrassing.

I made it to the window without needing to grab that chair, but then I didn't get to look out it for a spell because I had to clutch at the frame and cough up several ounces of horrible black grit. Bits of burned-up velvet draperies and knotted wool rugs that had made their habitation in my lungs, no doubt.

It didn't taste too nice.

Then I had to find someplace to spit it, because I wasn't swallowing that Christ knows what back down and I didn't appear to be equipped with a pocket handkerchief. Or for that matter any pockets. There was a brass spittoon tucked between the table and the bed, though, so I shuffled back over to it—walking was getting easier—and used it.

When I straightened up again, my eyes were watering so I didn't dare go wandering around until they quit. I wiped my eyes on the gauze on my arm and wished I hadn't; the pressure started up a raw throbbing ache underneath. *No scars,* I reminded myself, and didn't scratch it.

By the time I made it back to the window, I was in a bit better form, though the gunk coming out of me looked and tasted like well-used axle grease. I leaned my forehead on the glass pane. It was cool and comforting, but I left a smear of aloe on it and felt bad about that for the housekeeper. Oh, well. There was aloe all over the bedsheets, too.

The view out the window was something special. As soon as

I pulled the curtain aside, I knowed where I was. Well, not right where I was, in the sense of I could have told you the address.

But what I could tell you is that there was Rapid all spread out in front of me, a sweep like a lawn made of rooftops and the poky tops of trees. And there I was up above 'em all, looking down across the city like a Queen. It was a rare clear day. You could see the bristle of masts and smokestacks at the harbor, the glint of the sun off the Sound, the tumble of white that was the river moving fast over stones, unfrozen. Off to every side, mountains hovered on tails of blue distance.

I was up on the hill. And more: the gaudy-painted clapboard of the house I stood in framed the view. I could see part of a turret, a bit of wall. Lemon and sea green, with a thick row of fish-scale scalloping below the roofline banded in three different shades of turquoise. So then I did know whose cold wood floor I was standing on.

This was Mayor Stone's house.

Down close to the water, a single slow black trail meandered higher and thicker through the haze of gray chimney smoke. I knowed what it was, and I knowed it should make me feel lost, or afraid, or something like that. But all it did was make me angry. So furious that if it hadn't been for the gauze and the way my hands rocketed hot pain up my arms when my fists clenched, I would of been picking fingernails out of my palms for a month.

I knew who had set that fire—or who had ordered it set. Who had burned up our house and all our books and the little wooden horse that Da had made me. Who had probably killed Connie and nearly killed Signor and me—no. That hurt too much to think about, so instead I thought about what I was going to do about it.

And I *was* going to do something about it, too. It wasn't like Madame could put me out on the street now if I defied her.

Well, I was still standing there wishing I could ball my hand up to punch the wall when the door swung open and Miss Lizzie come in, carrying a little basket of gauze for dressings and such in her clockwork. I jumped, guilty like, because I knowed I weren't supposed to be out of bed. But she just set her basket on that side table and said briskly, "You're up. Good. We should see about getting you some clothes."

She grabbed a silver-tassled bellpull in the corner that I hadn't even noticed, it blended into the wallpaper so well, and gave it a tug with some decision behind it. Wherever the bells were, it was far enough away that I didn't hear even a faint jangle.

"There," she said. "We'll get you some tea, too. Are you hungry?"

As if my stomach was a tiger trained to come to the word "hungry," it rumbled. Miss Lizzie looked at me with her head cocked to one side, obviously wondering if I was going to try to brazen it out.

"I should eat," I allowed. "Even as I don't have much appetite right now."

"Oh, honey. None of us do. But it's wise to get what you can, when you can, if you take my meaning."

There was no telling where we'd wind up come morning.

A maid came and Miss Lizzie sent her away again, on a quest for coffee and breakfast. As soon as the door shut behind her, I asked, "Connie?" I hoped, even though I knowed there was nothing to hope for.

"They're still looking for her," she said. "I'm sorry. Everybody else made it out, though, and that's thanks in large part to you and Priya raising the alarm." *We were lucky to only lose one.*

Neither she nor I was going to say that out loud. And it was cold comfort, but I'd have taken the coldest just now. "Is everyone else here?"

"Nearly."

I waited for her to say more, but she absorbed herself in the dressings so devotedly that I knowed she was avoiding the question. The hands looked better than I'd feared—about like I'd poured boiling water on them, sure, but no worse than that. One more small mercy.

Then, just about as she got my hands rewrapped, the food and coffee came, along with a basin and water for washing and a borrowed day dress. Soft-boiled eggs weren't the best choice, it turned out. Because of my hands, she had to do the next best thing to feeding me. Fortunately, we got that out of the way before I tried on the dress.

"What happened to the Singer?" I asked.

"Downstairs," she answered. She looked at me curiously.

"It saved my life," I said. Then, heart in my throat: "How's Signor?"

"He's himself," she allowed. "Soon enough, everybody is going to forget how happy they are he's not dead."

As she was lacing me up, I reminded her, "Nearly everyone is here?"

"Priya," she admitted. I could see her in the mirror, looking everywhere but at me. "She hasn't come back. We left a message with Merry Lee where to find us—"

"How long has it been?"

"The fire was just last night."

I tried to rein my temper and my voice shook with the effort, but I managed it. "What if Bantle's got her? What if something awful's happened?"

She had my journal. And my little purse of savings. The Marshal's silver dollar . . .

I realized with a sting that that was everything and everybody

I had left in the world. All missing, all at the same time. "What if she needs rescuing?"

"What if she don't?"

That stunned me into silence. She wouldn't—Priya wouldn't do that to me. I didn't believe it for a heartbeat.

"She might of just made a run for it," Miss Lizzie said. "Collected that sister of hers and moved on. Or she might be in hiding. Odds are better that than the other, Karen honey. There." She patted my shoulder and stepped away from my laces to glance me over. "It's not the best fit, but not bad for borrowed, and for now it'll do."

"Do for what?" I asked.

"For the parlor," she said. "For the council of war we're about to have."

The character of the house changed from threadbare respectability to opulence when we left my sickroom and descended to the second floor. We used the servants' stair, and I wish I could say that surprised me. From back there, I could see how expenses had been spared, but the public rooms of the house were as luxuriant as anything Madame's had had to offer.

That thought put a pang in me, and no mistake.

What was going to become of all of us? What was going to become of Madame? Everything she'd earned and owned was in that house. And she was, as she had said, too old to go back to whoring on street corners. I'd survive, even if Priya was gone with all my savings—and I felt like a miserable weasel even for considering that she might be, but I had to consider it. There'd be enough there to get her and Aashini back to India, and if it were my sister mightn't I do just that? And feel like I had to, even if I also felt awful about it all the while?

Maybe the Marshal would take me with him and I could

get a job breaking horses in the Indian Territory. I heard they were less stiff about what women could and couldn't do the farther into the wilderness you got. That weren't without its own kinds of risks, though; people back east might think Rapid was the Wild West, but we had constables and an opera hall. There were places where the law was whose arm was strongest, and that was all.

Those weren't no places for a woman all alone.

Anyway, all my dreadful musing was brought to a screeching halt as soon's Miss Lizzie and me walked into the parlor. And I do mean "screeching," because there was Signor, stalking at me across the royal-blue, honey-gold, and ivory Oriental carpet, yelling his tiny head off until the crystal chandelier vibrated. I was surprised the crystals weren't popping like squeezed grapes, to tell you true.

Somebody had washed the soot from his coat, and he sparkled every time his little fat tummy wobbled. The colors of the carpet made his eyes look like jewels. I'd never been so damned happy to be yelled at by somebody as left a four-inch gouge down my forearm the last time we met. He twisted around my ankles, leaving the usual dusting of white fur and me feeling painful self-conscious about my lack of shoes and stockings.

I didn't try to scoop him up, though. He might be happy to see me, but I knowed better than to push my luck.

Also, I weren't half-distracted by the *people* in the room.

The sheers was drawn across the windows, so the afternoon sun shone through 'em with a soft orange glow that made everybody in the room seem not a mite otherworldly. Madame was there, and the misses except for Lizzie, who came in right behind me of course. Miss Bethel and Effie had their different shades of red heads together, Miss Bethel's arm around Effie's shoulder. Effie might of been sleeping, or she might just have been resting her eyes. Miss Francina sat in a back corner with

Crispin and Bea, and I could tell they was all trying to melt into the upholstery. Pollywog . . . well, she was on the arm of one of the other two men in the room, leaning into him with that trusting kind of . . . sincere melt that we all learn to fake first thing. She was gazing up at him out her big blue eyes and tugging at her pigtail in charming nervousness with the hand that wasn't wrapped around his elbow, and I knowed I was watching a professional at work.

She was three times the politician of old Dyer Stone, the middle-aged lump she was making up to. I remember thinking that if only she could run for mayor we'd have it sewn up.

The Professor wasn't there, though I didn't really expect him to be. He wasn't part of Madame's family, exactly, in the way the rest of us was. And that was his choice; I'd always gotten a feeling he was a man didn't like too many commitments.

The other man in the room, the one who weren't the Professor . . . well, he was the most flamboyant thing I'd seen this side of a saloon girl in full whoop-de-do. He was tall—not quite as tall as Marshal Reeves—and he had straight dirty-blond hair slicked back in a ponytail under a bottle-green tricorne hat with vermilion piping. He had the strength of feature to carry it off, too—notched chin, planed cheeks, a nose like a ice skate blade. He so resembled my mother's people, I felt a kick in my chest to look at him.

His coat was in the same shades as his hat, with the addition of plenty of bullion on the left shoulder, and his trousers was a darker green. He had—of all things—a cavalry sword belt slung about his waist. The sword was not currently in evidence, but the rig to sling its scabbard through was, the straps pattering against his leg as he stood.

I blinked at him for a moment before I realized he was standing for me and Miss Lizzie. That ain't something whores get accustomed to. "Mr. Colony," Madame said, "this is Miss Karen

Memory and Miss Lizzie Bach. Karen, Miss Lizzie, this is Mr. Minneapolis Colony."

With the airship that matched his coat! Of course. I remembered glimpsing it when Priya and Crispin and me were all out shopping for Priya's now-burned-up wardrobe. I wondered where she'd run off to, barefoot in her nightgown. I ain't the praying sort, but I prayed she was unhurt.

And somehow I managed to collect myself, keep my cool, and remember to be polite to Mr. Colony.

"Charmed," I said, and gave him my hand. "Please make yourself comfortable. You don't need to fuss on my account"

He had a gold ring on his right hand, set with seven or eight different-colored stones in a kind of wheel pattern. There was a kind of winged figure on either side of the band. It pinched my hand when he gave me a gentle squeeze. He settled back, garish on ivory silk, and I looked around for a place to settle. I wanted to hide my bare feet under my skirt hem as soon as possible. I was seating myself on a gold-and-ivory settee when Miss Bethel leaned forward, obviously resuming an interrupted conversational thread, and said, "I think we ought to consider taking Mr. Colony up on his offer of transportation."

"Mr. Colony is a business acquaintance of the mayor's," Madame said for my benefit—and maybe for Lizzie's. "He's offered to take us as far as San Francisco if we like."

"I'm supposed to be heading down there to pick up Edwin Marsh, anyway," he said.

I blinked. "He writes those dime novels!"

Mr. Colony smiled indulgently at me. "I'll tell him he has readers in Rapid. Unless you come down with me and get to meet him your own self, of course."

"Where are you taking him?" I asked, because I could tell from Bea's expression that she was dying to find out.

"He's heading out to Tucson to interview some shootist who

tracked down a road agent out there last summer. For his next book."

I watched Mayor Stone as Madame was talking. The possessive way he stroked Polly's hair, and the little lean forward while Miss Bethel was talking—he wanted us out of town, I realized. This was his idea. I wondered if he meant to have Pollywog stay on with him and if he'd marry her or just set her up as a servant or something. If I were Polly, I'd hold out for the ring. Assuming she wanted to spend the rest of her life yoked to Dyer Stone, I'm meaning.

"I'm not real keen on leaving Rapid, personally," Miss Francina said. I could see it took some courage for her to speak up against Dyer's glare, too. "We built a lot here, and we have a customer base. Some of us had our money in the bank, or got it out—and I know the house was fire-insured. Once it pays out, can't we rebuild?"

Madame lifted her chin, stretching the soft skin underneath. "Assuming the insurance company doesn't spend two years making me jump hoops to get what I'm entitled to, half the payout would go to my investor."

That took us all aback. "Investor?" Miss Lizzie asked.

Madame nodded. "Some years back—before the Gold Rush—we hit a tight patch, and I sold forty-three percent of the house to an investor. Lately, he's been urging me to sell out."

She didn't say another word, but she looked at Mayor Stone and so did all of us.

Well, that's Peter Bantle and his mind control rays again.

Stone shook his head. "Rapid's not going to be the Wild West for too much longer, girls." I could tell Madame was included in that "girls," and it put my back up. She had years and miles on Dyer Stone, and brains to boot. But he had a prick, and inherited money, and a prick. I guess that gave him the right to lord it over her.

And I thought about his upstairs bedrooms and their serviceable furnishings, and I thought that maybe he needed the insurance money more than he was about to let on. Don't get the wrong end of it: I didn't think he'd burned down Madame's house. There was more than enough candidates for that bit of evil, and all of them was named Bantle. But I realized he weren't above capitalizing on it. And if Bantle had blackmailed or mind-gadgeted him out of mayoring, he'd have to get money some other way than kickbacks and bribes from now on. . . .

"Mayor Stone," Madame said, as if casually. I'd never seen her work feminine wiles before, and I am ashamed to say that it surprised me. But she got to be Madame somehow, and it weren't by taking no for an answer. "Is Bantle blackmailing you?"

He didn't answer, but he flushed. He shrugged. Pollywog leaned in closer to his arm.

She said, "If you don't run against him, you know it'll be seen as an admission of guilt."

"So I should spend a lot of money to lose to him?" Mayor Stone asked. His eyebrows arched. "Spend money to make money," she said. "A business*man* knows when to cut his losses. Something maybe you should study up on, Alice."

"Now, Mayor," Mr. Colony said in tones that sounded like they was meant to be appeasing—or maybe the better word is "reasonable." "A beautiful woman thinks you should keep your job. Is there some shame in that?"

Stone shook his head. "I'll leave you ladies to talk it over. Mr. Colony, will you join me in the library for cigars?"

Cigar smoke being the best thing for books, of course. But maybe it made Mayor Stone feel some kind of cultured.

Madame's fingers twitched. I knew she was pining for her pipe, though she usually won't let nobody but us girls see her smoking. Mr. Colony, though, he seemed a bit reluctant. Nevertheless, while Mayor Stone was patting Pollywog's hand and making sure at her that she'd be taken care of he stood up. I thought he gave me a sly kind of wink, too, but maybe he was just tossing his ponytail over his shoulder.

They left, the door shut behind them, and Madame sighed. "I built a life here in Rapid," she said. "And I ain't gonna let Peter fucking Bantle fuck me out of it, neither."

"We ain't gonna get no help from him," Miss Francina said, her lip curled, meaning the mayor.

"Now, Francina. Our host wouldn't leave us out in the cold," Madame said. "But we're to be gone as soon as possible, and in the meantime we're to stay out of sight and stay hid." I could tell from her tone that it griped her.

I cleared my throat. "What if Peter Bantle wasn't a problem anymore?"

Everybody in the room looked at me.

I looked at Madame. I didn't want to give away more than she wanted me to—but she nodded permission, and so I gathered myself. It felt like I was pushing those words out through the weight of all those gazes on me, but I managed.

"Peter Bantle's got a machine." My voice sounded like it was being dragged over a wood rasp. Just talking hurt my throat sore, and before I could finish everybody had to wait through another damned coughing fit and me wiping more black muck off my lips. Miss Lizzie got me some more tea, and that helped— or maybe it was just the lemon and the honey in it.

I continued, "He can use it to change people's minds, sometimes make 'em do things they might not, otherwise. Maybe tell him things. Definitely vote for him, some of 'em. It might be it works especially well on drunks. He used it to make those tricks bust up our parlor, remember?"

I could feel all of 'em doubtful at me. But Miss Francina nodded and said, "I've seen it work," and Miss Lizzie—who had walked over to perch on the arm of the chair beside Miss Bethel and Effie—said, "It's theoretically possible," at the same instant.

"Priya said it was in his house. If I was to destroy it . . ."

"Karen, honey," Miss Bethel said, "that's a lot of risk."

"I think the bastard as is whipping girls to death is his mechanic," I said. "Don't it serve Bantle to have us all afraid, cowering? I could take a swing at both of 'em at once. We could change things up, maybe provoke 'em into making a mistake where we could prove something!" It all came out on a rush, which was probably a mistake, I reckoned, looking at their faces. I should of been chewing on my words some, so everybody else would have had a better chance of swallowing them.

"Madame," Miss Bethel said. "Are you listening to this nonsense? Are you really going to let her take these kinds of chances? Especially if it turned out that there is a multiple murderer working for Bantle? Do we want Karen to be the next girl flogged to *death*?"

Madame said, "She's a grown woman. She can make her decisions. And this would benefit us all."

"I can't listen to this," Miss Bethel said. She slipped out from under Miss Lizzie's soothing hand and stalked to the door. She was wearing a borrowed dress, too, and where mine strained at the shoulders, she swam in hers. "I'll be upstairs."

We all watched her go. I knowed I should say something, should maybe back down. But I couldn't think of another way to keep us together. We could go to San Francisco, go work for different houses. None of those houses would be Madame's.

And Priya was here in Rapid. And I couldn't help but be scared that Bantle had her back. I had to go find out.

So yes, I guess you could say I had an ulterior motive.

My frown stung my face, but it weren't no worse than some sunburns I've had, and I gritted my teeth and ignored it.

Before I took up sewing, I didn't used to scorch so easy, but I'm out of the sun most days now.

"Wait!" Bea cried suddenly, and darted after Miss Bethel. The door swung shut behind 'em, and I sighed and settled back.

"We're in a bad box now," Madame said. "And no mistake about it. Does anybody have a better plan?"

"I want to go with her," Effie said, shaking her red hair back. "For Connie's sake."

A lot of faces hardened when she said that, but I knowed they weren't hardening at Effie. She'd just said out loud the thing that had changed everything. Everything else Bantle had done to us—even burning down the Hôtel Mon Cherie like that and pauperizing the lot of us—weren't a patch on killing Connie. We'd get him for that, and no mistake.

It didn't even really need saying out loud, but still I felt a kind of relief that Effie'd up and said it.

Madame looked around the room. No one said anything else, though Miss Francina's stare was pretty heavy where it laid on me.

"Without the machine," Pollywog said, "I might be able to talk some sense into Dyer. If Bantle's running the insides of people's heads, that might explain some things about how Dyer's been different lately."

The silence kept on for another few seconds. Madame let it go until it was uncomfortable, and nobody was making any signs of breaking it before she nodded. "Then it's settled."

"Fetch your friend the Marshal," Miss Francina said. "If they haven't hanged him or his posseman yet, he's got a horse in this race."

"And a bounty to collect," I agreed.

After all, he'd come all this way.

Chapter Eighteen

And that's how I came to be shivering beside Tomoatooah at three in the morning, and not for the first time, neither. At least this time we was on a rooftop. You know, for the sake of variety and him not getting lynched.

I'd hate to find myself in some kind of a rut when it came to skulking. Which was perfectly likely, with Tomoatooah and the Marshal and Merry around.

They hadn't gotten hanged, or jailed, or what have you—though to hear the Marshal tell it that weren't much more than a happy accident and not for lack of trying on Bantle's part. They'd moved from the rooming house they'd been staying at and were camping up the mountain to cover their tracks. I imagined neither one of them was much enjoying the ride back and forth, but at least Rapid was still small enough that it weren't too inconvenient. You'd be riding half a day, you tried that near New York City.

Or so I imagined, anyway. I was all of a sudden struck by the urge to see it for myself.

Maybe I didn't care to stay in Rapid and environs after all. I wondered suddenly where all those dime novels came from, and who wrote 'em, and if any of those writers had ever spent a night crouched on a hoar-slick tile roof next to a wild red Indian. Maybe I was setting my sights too low, thinking about a livery stable. Because I realized then, too, that if there was a living in dime novels nobody who published or read 'em needed to know that K. L. Memery was a woman.

And maybe I could still talk Tomoatooah into selling me one of Scout's fillies.

For the first time, I realized I might not have to work in horses to *have* horses, if you see my meaning.

It was not much more than a wild hair, honestly. A fancy to keep me from thinking about how cold my damned toes were. I'd borrowed money from Francina and bought myself some used boys' togs. I could get used to lace-up boots, but I hadn't borrowed enough for good ones and the socks were thin.

And we had been up there on that roof for the best part of two hours, waiting for the last lights to go out at Bantle's house.

Effie and Marshal Reeves was off somewhere to our left, and the Marshal and Tomoatooah had some system of whistles they planned to use to communicate. So we was waiting for a signal, unless we felt confident enough to give it ourselves. Tomoatooah and me, we were meant to go in and smash the machine and look for evidence. The Marshal and Effie, they was supposed to stand watch.

It nearly worked out that way, too. At least at the beginning.

Bantle's house was the best on the street, a big foursquare Italianate in shades of amber and piney green, with a wrap porch and dull red window sashes. You couldn't see the colors by night, of course, but I knowed what the house looked like. He lived within sight of his cribs and the Sound, but far enough down Geoduck Street not to be bothered by the traffic.

Bantle'd apparently learned something about guarding rooftops from his men's last run-in with Tomoatooah. Now they
moved from place to place and met up at regular intervals. So
this time, Tomoatooah hadn't knocked any of 'em over. Instead,
he'd timed their routes and led me past 'em until we was inside the perimeter—that's the Marshal's word—and then we
hunkered down in the shadow of a chimney and stayed quiet
and small.

Quiet and small was about my speed, anyway. I guess I was
mad lucky I wasn't hurt any worse than I'd have been if I was
dumb enough to go out on a boat without a bonnet, but my
lungs still felt congested and thick, and you know how a sunburn makes you nauseous? I had a little of that, too, and spent
some time swallowing the sick water that wanted to fill up my
mouth.

I might of chattered—it all made me nervous as a brown field
mouse at a cat convocation—but Tomoatooah was like an Indian carved out of rock and I caught the silence from him. He
waited better than anybody I'd ever met, including my da. And
I would of said nobody waited better than my da, and there
was damn few as could wait *like* him.

The last light got blowed out about five minutes after three
by Ma's radium watch. Tomoatooah glanced over at me—I
caught the glitter of the whites of his eyes. It was hard dark,
no moon, just some glow up from the street lamps—and it
crossed my head kind of hysterical that this was a bad night
for a Comanche raid. That's why they called it a Comanche
Moon, when it was full and bright. They could ride their horses
by moon- or starlight better than most white men could during the day.

But maybe it was a good night for housebreaking. Tomoatooah tipped his head, an invitation I thought, and slipped away
down the angle of the roof. Not toward Bantle's house, but on

the back side. Dark or not, we didn't want to take the chance of being silhouetted.

I followed.

I expected to be scared shaking, hardly able to make myself move. But maybe I was getting a taste for all this adventuring. Or maybe my system was just in a state of saturation, having absorbed all the adventure it could hold, and so this one was just rolling off me like it was happening to somebody else. I put my rubber-soled boots down careful, and the roof slates held, and when I got to where Tomoatooah had tied a hand line I used it to lower myself over the gutter without breaking it off. It hurt my hands—there was still gauze under the too-big gloves I was wearing—but a little bit of getting hurt just didn't seem to matter much anymore.

It might of been scary, if I'd bothered to think about it. But my mind was on other things. Like where to put each foot in the dark and how much less awful this was than my house burning down around my ears and whether I'd ever see Priya again. It crossed my mind to wonder if I fell, if I'd see Connie first in Heaven or if it'd be Mama and Da. Did they come in order of how recently they'd died or how close they was related?

I'd heard some people say Negroes didn't go to Heaven, but some people said Negroes didn't have souls, and you'll pardon me if I got no truck with that. Any Heaven didn't want Connie I didn't want no part of my own self, and it wouldn't have any good biscuits, anyway.

I was so caught up in thinking about what might happen when I got to Heaven that I forgot to die on the way down at all. Tomoatooah was waiting for me at the bottom. Silently, he pointed with two fingers along the alley. I followed, stepping in his footsteps as best I could. Something brushed my leg, furry and fast—a rat or an alley cat. I didn't squeak.

Bantle's house was at street level, not below it. New built, and it showed. A lot of the land down here by the docks was fill.

We got into the shadows by the kitchen door and Tomoatooah touched me on the shoulder, a light touch moving me back into a niche behind the kitchen porch. He went up the cast-iron drainpipe like a tree octopus, leaning back and grabbing on with his feet and hands. A squirrel would have more difficulty and make a hell of a lot more noise.

I waited, counting Mississippis, and made it to forty-one before the back door came open. Bless city houses and brass hinges and capitalist pork-barrel bastards who can afford staff to keep them oiled. The leather hinges on Da's kitchen door would of let the door drag and in the wet of Rapid most metal hinges quickly learned to squeak and stick, but this door opened in silent as a jaw gaping.

And weren't that an unsettling image?

I came up the porch steps, keeping to the outside so the wood wouldn't squeak, and stepped into the dark kitchen beside Tomoatooah.

There was a fire banked in the big new fireplace, but it didn't shed much light beyond a kind of faint cherry glow that vanished once it met the bigger dark outside the hearth. My eyes was so used to the nighttime I could sort of see anyway. At the very least, I could catch the whites of Tomoatooah's eyes, the faint rose glow on his beads. It was enough to follow him.

The kitchen was deserted. Something niggled at me so I decided to risk a word, spoke low. Murmurs don't carry so far as whispers. "You don't mind a girl on an expedition like this?"

He looked over and I swear he winked at me over the palisade of one cheekbone. "Numu women ride to hunt and raid," he said. His shrug continued, *And they know when to keep quiet.*

Since I'd met him, I'd found out in my reading that "Comanche" was a Ute word, meaning "enemies." All the things I'd seen him do, on horseback and off, and that moment was the thing gave me an inkling why.

His hand gesture said, *Follow,* and I did. Conversation over.

Bantle liked rugs, the thicker the better. I followed Tomoatooah across them, both of us slinking like cats. He moved like he weighed half an ounce and was made of baling wire and bison jerky. I did my best to copy him. The India rubber soles of my boots felt squishy underfoot. I guessed I could get used to that for walking on, though they'd be terrible for riding. And probably wear out fast.

Still, they was quiet. Especially as I took care not to let 'em squeak. With luck, the servants' rooms were in the attic or at the back of the second floor, and we weren't making much noise at all.

We didn't see a soul as we picked down the corridor. Priya'd said the machine was in the parlor, and parlors were at the front of the house. My guess was as good as Tomoatooah's whether that meant right side or left, but the right side (as seen from the outside) had a bay front and piano windows—little windows up high—and I was guessing if you were going to show off your big pretty mind control machine and you didn't play piano, that might be where you'd want to put it.

I touched his elbow and pointed left. He didn't give any sign of acknowledgment, but he crossed the hall and flattened himself against the wall on that side. The door from the back of the house and the servants' stair to the atrium was closed, and he opened it softer than anything. No sound.

There was a little nook to our right—the house's left—and a short cross hallway off to the left that gave access to a cupboard under the grand stairs. Past those, the hall opened out—and upward—to a foyer. After the kitchen, the little light that floated in from the street made it seem bright.

The room I thought was probably the parlor was off to our left—the house's right—behind a set of pocket doors. Glass ones, and as we crept past the stairs I glanced through.

Something gleamed in the dimness—brass and glass and God knows what—with a faint blue spark shimmering on and off inside what might of been a big vacuum tube. I wished I was Miss Lizzie, all of a sudden, or Priya, so I might know what I was looking at.

Found it, I mouthed. Tomoatooah stepped forward, and I put a hand out to redirect him.

There ain't no such thing as a quiet pocket door.

We fell back toward that cross hallway with the closet under the stairs. There was a door there that probably led to the dining room or library, by my guess. I hoped the hinges was as well oiled as those out the back.

They was, too. Tomoatooah turned the handle, and we was just about to step into the hall when a familiar—and totally unexpected—voice hissed from the crack of that understair cupboard door, "*Karen?*"

It's a miracle I only squeaked and didn't scream. Honestly, I think if it had been anybody other than Priya I would of shrieked like a pig's bladder blown full of air. But something deep inside me responded to her voice the way horses responded to Da: with a settling kind of attention.

Some of the knots of tension all up and down my back slid away, and a few new ones came to join the remainder. Was she *locked* in that closet? Why the hell would Bantle hold her prisoner here in his house and not in one of the cribs? And what had he done to her?

The fear didn't last, though. Because she slipped out from behind the door, one hundred and eleven pounds of whipcord and attitude in men's tweed trousers, and Merry Lee with her cropped hair and her black bowler hat was right behind her.

"If I'd knowed you were coming, I'd have brought a picnic," I murmured.

Priya looked befuddled—there was just enough light coming through to make out her expression—but Merry Lee grinned and laid her finger alongside her nose like Saint Nicholas.

Suddenly I wanted to take Priya by the shoulders and shake her. She'd been fine, all this time, and she'd left me hanging and waiting and worrying, and she hadn't even sent a note to see if I was hurt bad. But then she grabbed me by the shoulders and hugged me sharp and tight, and I realized maybe she had come looking, and who was there who would of been able to tell her where I was, or what had happened to me?

So of course she'd gone to Merry Lee, and she'd talked Merry Lee into coming here, to smash Bantle's machine.

I knowed that was what they was here for because Priya had an eight-pound sledge slung on a strap over her shoulder. I noticed it because cold metal bonked my nose before she realized that we was wasting time and started to set me back from her.

"I knew we forgot something," I said. I have her one more squeeze before I let her let go of me, and we stood there for a second grinning at each other like fools until Tomoatooah cleared his throat real significant like.

"Right," Merry said. "How are you getting out again?"

We *had* thought of that. Tomoatooah held up a long red stick of dynamite. He said, "Fuse."

Merry's eyes got big. She stuck out a finger and touched it, gave it a little fingertip push. "That's better than sledgehammers."

Anybody who believes in stoic Indians or inscrutable Orientals never saw those two grinning at each other like a couple of rattlesnakes over a nest of baby bunnies. They was having so much fun I hesitated to interrupt, but Priya grabbed my hand and tugged at it. "Let's do this."

We crept through the door into a butler's pantry with a long breakfront along one side. It was full of crystal and silver plate and God knows what, sparkling in the faint light from outside. We paused at the mouth of it, realizing that the dining room—it was a dining room—beyond was lined with grand windows. But the house alongside was dark as well, and I figured what with more light outside than in, there weren't much chance of anyone seeing us.

Now we just had to blow up the machine without killing ourselves—or, by preference, any of Bantle's house servants, who—after all—just worked there. According to the Marshal, one stick of dynamite wasn't going to cause much collateral damage and it wouldn't—shouldn't—take the house down.

Priya gave my hand another squeeze and dropped it. "I know where Bantle's study is," she murmured. "You keep on. I'll get out the back."

She was gone, back through that door to the hall before any of us could so much as snatch at her shirt cuff. She moved soft as a cat, and I was just about to lunge after her when Tomoatooah caught my right elbow and Merry Lee caught my left.

"You'll get her caught!" Merry whispered.

I shook myself in frustration, but she was right. I didn't hear Priya climbing the servants' stair, but I knew she must be. And I imagined her sneaking past Bantle's bedroom and God knows what all else . . . maybe that Bruce Scarlet son of a bitch slept here.

The idea of him with his hands on Priya made me cold. What the hell could be so important in Bantle's study? Papers? Plans? Did it matter?

Yes. If Priya thought it was worth risking her life . . . it mattered a lot. I decided to trust her, even if the deciding hurt, and I wanted nothing so bad as to argue myself out of it. But the Marshal had let me come in here, and I imagined the look on his face then weren't too different from the one I was wearing now.

"We go on," Tomoatooah said. "We blow up the front of the house, she sneaks out the back."

I looked at him with respect.

He winked again, and this time I saw it clear. "Not my first raid."

Evidently.

We snuck into the front parlor through an open doorway big enough to carry two coffins through side by side. I guessed you had to get the piano into the parlor somehow. It was guarded by a heavy velvet drape, and once we brushed past that we was suddenly in more light than I'd expected.

Bantle's infernal machine cast its own glow, you see.

We'd caught that green spark through the pocket doors, and I'd expected . . . I don't know, some sort of hissing arc or a bottle of lightning.

It weren't nothing like that. Just a peaceful shining, green and orange in different places, like a chemical flame. Except without any sparking or flashing. It gilded the whole outline of the apparatus, and a complicated gadget it was. I expected . . . moving parts, I suppose, but the only one I saw was a cloth belt with a single twist in it. That ran between two rollers and a couple of tension rods, for all the world like the belt on a sewing machine except it was made of cloth—raw silk, I'd guess, if I was sewing it—instead of India rubber. The only sound was a whispery whirring from the thing running.

All around it was a forest of tall, narrow glass bell jars, each with some kind of component inside 'em. Little things, the size of my pinky nail, and I couldn't see much in the slow except they seemed to be intricately soldered with white and yellow and copper metal wires.

Some of those vacuum jars glowed with the green, and some glowed with the orange.

Merry leaned toward the thing, but not too close. "Static," she said, and suddenly I understood what that silk belt was doing. Well, maybe not what it was *doing* doing. But at least what it was doing, if you understand the difference. "Is that a Möbius band?"

"Don't touch it," I said. I remembered a machine I'd seen on a mountebank's wagon stage when I was a girl, a kind of metal sphere on a stick with one of those cloth ribbons stretching down beside it. He'd been able to lay his hand on it and shoot tiny tamed lightning from his fingertips.

His hair had stood on end. Just as Merry Lee's was starting to do, under the brim of her bowler hat. Mine was long and braided back, and so was most of Tomoatooah's.

Above us, a floorboard creaked. I jumped; Merry glanced over her shoulder; Tomoatooah looked up incuriously. He had dropped to his hands and knees and was inspecting the lower parts of the apparatus. Looking, no doubt, for a place to slide his dynamite.

So to speak.

Or, well, literally and not so to speak at all. Old habits die hard. I'm . . . mostly sorry.

Yeah, I'm trying to avoid telling you what happened next.

I was watching Tomoatooah and I probably should of been watching his back. So I was wrong about that, but it turns out I was right about the pocket door. When it rattled back, sharp and sudden, it made a noise like the whole front of the house falling off.

A newfangled electric light flared in that foyer, arc white, and when I blinked the glare from my eyes it was to see Peter Bantle strut into the room, flanked by Horaz Standish on one side and a short broad fellow with colorless hair, wearing overalls and a grayish complexion. I made a bet with myself that was that Bruce Scarlet, and I mostly ain't the betting type. There was three thugs behind 'em. One of those was my old friend Bill.

I didn't like one bit of the look he was giving me.

Bantle had that damned glove on, the harsh light sparking off its metal fittings. He had it balled up into a fist and was tapping it lightly against the palm of the leather range glove he wore on the opposite hand. Standish weren't carrying no weapon, but the man I thought was Scarlet had a big old wrench, and Bill had an ax handle. I couldn't see what the other two was carrying. "Oh, dear," Bantle said. "It seems somebody miscalculated."

Tomoatooah came up off the floor like a splintercat heading face-first for a redwood tree. He didn't make a sound, and he didn't do nothing to indicate he was about to lunge. He just went for Bantle with the directness I would of liked to have been able to muster, if I hadn't been losing a fight with panic. I was like a horse in a burning barn, the opposite of how calm and prepared I'd felt on the roof. I got stuck, unable to hear myself thinking over the pounding of my heart, which made it hard to decide what to do.

Tomoatooah, though—he acted. Practice, I guess, and Merry Lee was right on his heels. Tomoatooah barreled into Bantle and Bantle went down in a heap. Merry Lee had picked up a fireplace poker, and she went forward swinging. Sparks flew when Scarlet parried her forehand. My first thought was a spike of worry about the dynamite, but I couldn't see where it had gone. I hoped Tomoatooah had tucked it somewhere safe.

Tomoatooah kicked Bantle where it would keep him down and drove a fist into my old friend Bill's breadbasket. Merry was still fencing with Scarlet and keeping Horaz at bay with a pistol in her off hand. I hadn't even realized she was heeled.

Right about then, it started to sink in that maybe I should be doing something to help besides standing on the nice knotted rug staring like a strangled calf.

I should of borrowed Effie's gun.

There was a chair beside the fire, though—a mahogany Chippendale with a brocade seat cushion. Thought grieved my heart a little; I remembered the unkind fate of the striped silk settee and seized it up, rushing forward and swinging high. Bill was doubled over, having by now been relieved of his hatchet handle. How it was that that man stayed employed I'll never know, but Tomoatooah was swinging the handle ferociously at the next bruiser.

But the third one was coming up beside the Comanche, and he had a crowbar cocked over one shoulder. I saw him coming. And he didn't seem to see me.

I whirled that chair around and smashed it at him as hard as I could. It was well built and the wood was sound: it cracked at the joints and the caning broke under the cushion but didn't shatter or come apart. So I swung it again, and again connected.

This time I was left holding the back. And staring over into the stunned face of Tomoatooah, who was swaying slowly back and forth, staggering, hands out for balance in a way that might of seemed right comical if I'd seen a vaudevillian doing it on the opera stage.

I looked at the chair and I looked at the Indian, and I couldn't quite connect one to the other, though I'd apparently done it twice already. And then, that sick twist of understanding back in my gut like an in-law you can't get rid of and can't stand, I looked down at Peter Bantle.

Bantle was still curled up on the floor holding himself with his ungloved hand. But he was looking right at me over his *fucking* electric glove. And he was laughing silently, like a dog, while Tomoatooah fought him.

All the hesitation must of gotten burned up, because I slung that chair back up and whaled it at Bantle like I was swinging for a goose's stretched neck with an ax.

And Tomoatooah stepped right into the swing.

This time he went down—in a heap, and not even on top of Bantle where he might of done some good, but right beside him. Bantle grabbed his throat with the glove, and Tomoatooah arched up like a bronc trying to scrape a saddle off.

I screamed and scrambled back. Merry was still fighting, but now there was three on her, and I could see she was starting to get tired. It hadn't been *that* long ago Crispin and Miss Lizzie had cut the bullets out of her, no matter what she wanted to think—

Somebody big and soft bellied with hands like iron straps grabbed my arms from behind. I kicked for his crotch and got thigh. I caught a glimpse when he picked me up and shook me. My old friend Bill. Then Bantle was on his feet, staggering slightly but walking toward me, the glove outstretched.

Those other thugs had gotten their hands on Merry. She kept twisting, fighting silent like a coyote, but she was too outnumbered and outsized for it to do much good. I yanked at Bill, trying to go to her assistance, but he gave my upper arms a squeeze and I quit, gasping in pain.

Bantle sighed theatrically as he inspected me. "You're that same damned whore that confounded me the other time, aren't you? I do admit, I hoped you and some of your sisters might get a bit burned up in that fire, but you crawled out pretty well unscathed. Pity, but that can be fixed."

I tried to remember to breathe, because forgetting was making me dizzy. And was likely to set off another coughing fit, the way my chest was hurting.

"There weren't no pleasure in that," Bantle said, jerking his head at Tomoatooah. I didn't follow his eyes. I was too afraid I would see Tomoatooah dead on the floor. I'd rather look at Bantle, and I didn't want to look at Bantle at all.

"This, though," he said, "you ought to be charging me for."

He snapped his fingers, making a heavy blue spark hang in the air. Then he reached out for me with the glove. I couldn't look away. I couldn't of been more scared if he was holding out an angry rattlesnake—

"Wait, Peter."

I jerked my eyes away from the glove as if somebody had cut a rope. Horaz Standish had his hand on Bantle's shoulder. He wasn't holding him back, just . . . cautioning him, like.

And for a second, Bantle seemed to be listening. He turned toward Horatio.

"There just ain't time tonight, Peter," Horaz said. "Not to do a proper job of it. Not with the meeting and all."

Bantle's eyes caught the light all slick and gleaming—like they was extra-wet, somehow. "You gotta be fucking kidding."

"Put her away," Standish said. "Play with her when we get back. Let her think about it for a while."

I tried to catch Horaz's eye, to see if he was trying to do me a favor. But he kept his gaze on Bantle. His expression was all calm and reasonable. Bantle's hand started to sag.

Then Scarlet stepped up to Merry and without giving no warning at all slugged her in the belly as hard as he could. All his shoulder behind it, and hip. Merry made a sound like a squashed kitten and would of doubled up, except for the side of beef holding on to her arms. Her feet came off the floor, and the side of beef took a half step back.

She wheezed and puked all over the floor. She missed Scarlet, more's the pity. He'd stepped to the side like a pro.

"Cunt," he said conversationally. "What were you going to do to my Mesmeric Engine?"

He lifted her head up by the hair—her bowler hat had gone flying. With his other hand he fingered his belt, and I felt a chill. Even if Horatio talked Bantle off me, who was going to step in for Merry? I imagined one of my frail sisters tripping over Merry when she went to take the trash out, and I nearly puked, too.

"Fuck, Scarlet," Bantle said. "Mind the fucking carpet."

He turned around and slapped me hard across the face.

Bill must of got a lot of practice, because he let go of my arms and stepped back in the instant before Bantle connected. I ducked—I tried to duck—but it didn't work. There was a savage light, and the next thing I knew I was flat on my back on the rug, looking up at everyone from right beside the engine.

"Parshiviy!" Scarlet said. "Careful of the tubes!"

My ears rang. I smelled piss. A molar rocked in its socket and I tasted blood. Bantle stalked toward me. I wanted to scramble away, but I couldn't make my arms or legs twitch. There was a thin soft sound in the room.

I thought, *Priya. Run.*

Bantle stood over me, wrinkling his nose. "Well, that should lower your prices," he said. He crouched and grabbed my throat, squeezed. Not enough to make the world swim—just enough to make it go black at the edges. That thin, soft whine cut off. A moment later, I realized I had been making it.

He shocked me again. Not as much as last time, I thought. It hurt, and I smelled something burning, but I didn't fly across the room. I don't know how long he kept it up for.

Not long. Because when he let go—my head bounced on the rug—and my vision swam clear, I was looking right at the infernal machine. And from down here, I could see the long fuse on the dynamite Tomoatooah must of shoved up underneath it fizzing along, steady and slow.

I gurgled and tried to point. My hand didn't move, though my heel kicked feebly against the carpet. A second later, I thought better of it. Because Bantle was going to kill us all anyway. So why not let the dynamite do the job for him? It'd be faster, and it'd take him, too.

"What was that about the rug?" Scarlet scoffed from a long way away.

"My rug," Bantle answered. He sniffed. "You smell burning?"

"Yeah," Bill answered. "That little whore you just cooked."

"No," Bantle replied. He stood, and I cheered silently. There was no way he was going to spot the dynamite from up there.

Just to be sure, though, I made myself look away from the fuse. I could move my eyes, if not my head. I strained 'em after Bantle.

In time to see Tomoatooah pull his arms under him and get his hands flat on the floor. Nobody else had noticed—nobody else was looking at him. And I felt a horrible surge of hope that was like to bust my chest. I swear it hurt worse than the burns on my face—or the burns on my hands.

They'd all stepped over Tomoatooah. And now nobody was between him and the door.

I willed him to get up, knock over anybody who went for him, grab Merry Lee, and get out. That left me in the soup—dynamite soup—but so be it. There was less than an inch of slow match left.

I made myself look away from Tomoatooah, too. All the interesting things going on, and I didn't dare look at any of them in case someone should notice. You wouldn't expect that kind of irritation to get inside a girl's shoe when she's making her final peace, but apparently there's no cease in the world to petty frustrations.

My eye was drawn to Scarlet, anyway. He'd done hurting Merry for the time being, and he was stepping over me—fastidiously, so as not to soil his shoes—in his rush to get to his infernal engine and make sure we hadn't hurt it none. *Don't crouch down,* I prayed. *Start looking at the other end.*

But damned if he wasn't headed more or less for that stick of dynamite.

I tried to think of a distraction. I wondered if I could make a noise or heave a limb around to get him to come over and stomp on me some, and buy that fuse a precious few more seconds to burn. And I tried like hell not to look at Tomoatooah, nor the dynamite.

So because I was trying not to stare, I didn't see a damned thing when Priya stepped out of the shadows like an avenging angel and clubbed the big fool holding Merry over the head with something heavy enough that it didn't make a hollow melon thump but more of a wet thud. I did see him go down, though—you don't miss a noise like that—and I did see Priya straight-arm heave the heavy thing straight at Bill's head.

It didn't hit him, for a pity. He caught it—he'd turned because of the thud, too, I suppose. It was a cast-iron boot scraper—maybe she'd picked it up by the door?—and I have no idea how on earth a skinny thing like Priya managed to throw it hard enough that catching it knocked him two steps backward, though sadly not clean over.

Tomoatooah must of been biding his time, because he came up off the floor like he had springs for sinews, and I didn't even see what he did to old Bill except when it was over he was standing over the body with Priya's sledgehammer in his hands, the head dripping nasty. I must of lost track of Horaz, too—or maybe he skedaddled—because all of a sudden the only bad guys upright in the room were Scarlet and Bantle, and they was glancing one at the other like they didn't understand how the odds had changed so quickly.

Then Tomoatooah and Merry and Priya was side by side, black haired and wild like furies. Tomoatooah had that sledge, and Merry had picked up that iron poker she'd been waving around earlier—and in her other hand she had Tomoatooah's Colt.

Being a practical sort, she gave the fire iron to Priya and kept the shooter herself.

I managed to get my elbows under me as they came forward. Bantle checked the odds and ran like a bat out of Hell for the door into the dining room. *Damn,* I thought. *It's only one stick. He'll be out of range.*

"Get out," I croaked.

I don't know if they heard me. Because Merry aimed that Colt right at Scarlet's midsection and she told him, "You take a step, I drill you."

He stopped. "Drop the wrench."

It thudded to the carpet. I hadn't even seen he was still carrying it.

"Priya," Merry said. "You get Karen."

Priya was the obvious choice. Merry was still hunched over from that pounding, and Tomoatooah was listing a bit to one side. But I couldn't let them slow down enough to bring me. Not with the match—

Tomoatooah gave Priya a little shove with the side of his hand when she hesitated, obviously torn between going to me and looking out for Standish or Bantle coming up behind them. He turned to watch the hall.

Well, Tomoatooah knew about the dynamite, and he sure had a damn sight more experience with nitroglycerine than I did. If he weren't worried, I weren't worried.

"Hurry," he barked when Priya wavered another half second.

Okay, maybe I was a little worried after all.

But I'd delay her longer by putting up a fight than by helping. And honestly, I didn't want to die by being blown to bits with Bantle's infernal machine. So I did what I could, and she got me up, though I was the next thing to deadweight.

Reader, I fainted on the way out the door—Tomoatooah and Priya half-carrying and half-dragging me; Merry walking backward with that Colt level in her hand. I woke up three hundred feet down the street when the sky started raining glass behind us, as the Marshal reined Dusty in from a dead run just ahead.

Chapter Nineteen

I don't remember much of meeting up with Effie or the Marshal or of the ride back to Merry's place, except I did it on Dusty, with Marshal Reeves holding me into the saddle. I remember him asking about Bantle and about Scarlet. I'm not sure what he got told.

They got me up three flights of stairs, and Merry made a complicated knock to get us in. You'd think she'd have a key to her own door, but I heard the rattle of bolts and chains and then Aashini was peeking through the crack, frowning.

The door shut, there was more rattling, and then it was yanked wide open. We must of tumbled into the room like a shivaree, because she went jumping backward with a yelp, then scrambled up to slam the door after us. More rattling and bolts thrown, and the Marshal laying me very gently on a much-patched yellow couch. I heard cups clinking, and before I knew it I was holding a china cup with a mismatched saucer full of hot tea laced with sugar and rum. I didn't know if rum was the best thing for electrocution, but it looked like Tomoatooah had one, too, and he was only slowed down in drinking it by the steam coming off.

Effie was clucking over my face with cool cloths, and Priya was holding on to my hand. And all I wanted to do was forget the last hour . . . but I didn't think I could.

And I didn't dare ask Effie how bad my face was. I could tell from the way it hurt that there was going to be a scar. Or a lot of little scars, round like the ones on Priya's arms.

Well, I'd meant to get out of the seamstressing business sooner or later. I guess now was as good a time as any. And I kept telling myself that over and over, like it was going to make a dent in the hollow scared feeling inside me if I thought it often enough.

I wondered if I had enough money saved to get any kind of a start in gentling. If Priya still had my savings, I mean.

If she'd give it back to me.

Well, she was there now, and she was holding my hand. That was something promising. And we'd blown up Bantle's infernal machine. And maybe the man who built it, too, if we got lucky.

There. *That* made a dent in the hollow scared. Or maybe Priya rubbing between my shoulder blades was what did it.

Oh Christ, it hurt so much to cough.

I was thinking about that in a kind of not-too-discontented haze when my nose started working again. I tried to jump up, and Priya and Effie pushed me back into the couch. I wasn't in no shape to fight 'em.

"Oh Christ, Merry, your couch! I'm . . ." *soaked in piss*.

"It's seen worse," she answered, and brought me another cup of tea. Less rum in this one. I thought about Bantle's concern for his fancy rug, and Merry—who didn't have nothing—and how little she cared for what she did have when a friend was hurt.

Well, Bantle's rug was blowed up now.

And then I realized that I'd thought of myself as Merry's friend. Smiling made my cheek hurt like the skin was cracking leather.

Hell, maybe it was.

I realized I'd lost track of the men and lifted my head enough to see that the Marshal had gotten Tomoatooah into a battered armchair, his feet on an ottoman. He was fussing over the Indian and the girls was fussing over me. I started to spiral down that sucking hole of scared again, but Priya kissed my forehead and I remembered that my scars—whatever they turned out to be—weren't nothing on hers. We'd be fine. If she was sticking with me we couldn't not be fine.

I patted her hand and tried to sit up. When I did, Aashini was there. She didn't talk much, but I was getting the idea that she didn't miss much, neither. Because she had a pile of fabric in her hands, and when she shook it out I could see it was a man's loose flannel trousers and a check shirt and a knit wool cardigan.

She set them on the table beside the sofa. A moment later, she came back with a basin of steaming water and a clean, soft cloth. "Clean up?" she asked.

My heart about stopped at the kindness.

Her English wasn't as good as Priya's, which was a little re-assuring. Or maybe it would of been easier to deal with a whole family of creepy geniuses. It's hard to tell which way that would go. And it wasn't like Aashini ain't just as smart as Priya in her own way, though I didn't find that out for a few minutes. It's just that Priya's got that gift for languages.

"Thank you," I said.

Having the Marshal and Tomoatooah in the room bothered me—the Marshal turned his back ostentatiously and Tomoatooah never even glanced over, but I guessed maybe his people didn't fuss so much about hiding what preachers might call their shame, not being Christians and all. But all those months in a whorehouse and I was still self-conscious about stripping off in front of Priya.

Maybe she realized it, because when Merry and Effie started peeling my clothes down, Priya stepped off. She went into the coat she'd been wearing—she'd tossed it over the chair by the door in just the manner that would of made Mama chew her ear off—and started pulling stacks of papers she'd rolled and squashed into tubes out of the pockets and the sleeves. She turned around before Effie was quite done sponging me off— Aashini and Merry was holding one arm apiece to keep me standing—and I was too interested in what she was holding on to to remember to blush.

"Those from Bantle's desk?"

She nodded. "Everything from on top, and the top drawer." She settled down on the ottoman beside Tomoatooah's legs and started reading.

Those flannel trousers were the warmest and most comfortable thing I've ever put on. I suddenly understood why Priya might want to wear men's clothing all the time. Effie and Aashini let me sit back down again while they put the shirt over my arms, which was a good thing. They'd been doing more and more of my standing for me.

"It's safe," I told the Marshal, and he turned back around.

Effie took the dirty clothes and that basin of water away. I was warm and—aside from the bruises and burns—I was comfortable and didn't stink anymore. But something was still niggling at me. "Horaz said a meeting. What meeting?" I asked—Priya, mostly, as she had the pile of papers in her lap.

Priya, still flipping papers, frowned. "I don't think you're going to like the answer to that."

Merry looked like she already didn't like it, and she hadn't even heard it yet. "Tell us."

"There's a note here that probably relates," she said. She waved part of her pile with her left hand. "And a whole sheaf of sheets of figures I can't make head nor tail of—"

Aashini stepped over to her and lifted the papers from her hand. I caught a flash of red and black ink on creamy paper. She squatted down on her heels—close to the same chairside lamp Priya was using—and started flipping through them. Her hair fell forward across her face, her brow wrinkling in concentration behind it.

Merry said, "Tell me more about this meeting."

Priya continued, "I don't know where this is. Baskerville?"

"North," I said. "It's a logging camp by the Quaker River. They load the barges there and float 'em down to the Sound. And us. Or the port, anyway. They're always talking about building a seaport there—the river's deep enough, I reckon?—and skipping Rapid City entire, but it ain't happened yet. And there's already a seaport here, so the papers all say why spend the money?"

The Marshal snorted. "And the papers are owned by the same people as own the Rapid shipping, right?"

I shrugged, in the sort of way as allowed as he was probably right, but I didn't rightly know.

Priya pursed her lips. "Well, that's where we need to get to."

"Wait," I said. "What?"

She tapped the papers, seeming not to notice that we was all staring at her. "Bantle is meeting with some other person—Bantle calls him or her Nemo—at dawn. I get a sense that this person is foreign. Bantle has a note to bring a translator."

She made a helpless little gesture. That cold whirl was still inside me, but a kind of spark kindled in it. Curiosity—satisfaction? The satisfying excitement of a problem solved—or at least the solution glimpsed.

"Nemo," I said. I shook my head, but it wasn't from being confused. "From *Vingt mille lieues sous les mers* and *L'Île mystérieuse*!? He's the Indian submersible captain fighting the British by destroying their warships with the powerful drill mounted on the nose of his ship!"

Every single person in the room stared at me. Even Effie, and I'd have thought better of her. Apparently she hadn't been paying attention to the French lessons. "Jules Verne?" I asked. "No? Beatrice has the books—oh, they're *books,* people!"

Marshal Reeves pursed his lips in disbelief. "Bantle's meeting somebody from a book?"

"No," I said. "I think he's meeting a foreign agent that he calls Nemo. Probably because he's an Indian. Maybe an Indian who's fighting the British. And us."

"We need to go there," Priya said.

Effie looked at her. "We already broke Bantle's machine."

I tried to pitch my voice gentle. "Tomoatooah and me, we're not moving so fast, Priya—"

"But we need to *go there.* To the *meeting.*"

I took a breath. "But why do we need to go there?"

"To stop them." She said it like it was self-evident. "Whatever they're doing. It's no good for any of us."

I hated myself for thinking she sounded a mite hysterical. Especially as she had the best of reasons to sound that way when it came to Peter fucking Bantle. I knew I should be holding her stirrup. But I wanted to understand *why.*

"I have a few questions I want to ask Mr. Bantle about this Bruce Scarlet fellow," Reeves allowed in a leisurely fashion.

"Nothing Bantle's doing anywhere is good news," Effie said. She gave me a look that dared me to contradict her.

Aashini cleared her throat, and what had been on the brink of turning into a brawl got real silent real fast.

"These are accounts," Aashini said. "I can't be sure I'm reading them correctly. But it looks like Bantle's paying this Nemo for girls."

"I don't like the British," Priya said in a controlled monotone. "But I like anybody who would sell girls to Peter Bantle less."

"You might know this Nemo," I said. "When you and Aashini came over? If he's supplying the cribs?"

"We never saw anybody," Priya said. "Just the steward who brought rice. The men on the boat were white, anyway."

I had a short horrible inkling of what their passage might of been like. It curdled me.

"Wait," Aashini said in her soft, high voice. She brushed her hair back. "I read these wrong. It looks as if Nemo is paying Bantle, not the other way around. Or rather, they're paying him. But he's paying them twice as much."

Nobody said nothing for a long minute, but we all just sort of looked at one another.

"Why would an Indian agent be paying American pimps to take his girls?" Effie asked.

"Because he ain't paying them to take girls," Tomoatooah said. He cracked his eyes—he'd been resting them and I'd thought he might of dozed off, but I guess not—and ogled us as if we were all a pack of idiots. And maybe we was. "He's paying them to provide intelligence. Or perform sabotage." He sat up, painfully.

"Nemo could as easily be an agent of the colonial British powers, you know," Priya said.

"That's not how the book goes," I protested, but even as I said it I could hear how stupid it was.

"You think Bantle's a real stickler for literary accuracy?" Merry asked.

"No." I sat on my hands, because I couldn't step on my damned tongue. Anyway, they felt sore inside the dirty disarranged gauze wraps and pressing on 'em make 'em hurt less.

"I say we go," Merry Lee said. "Maybe we can find out something that will put a stop to Bantle. Once and for always."

I looked around the room. Only Effie looked the least bit dubious, and she seemed willing to be swayed. I sighed and reminded them, "We ain't getting there without a ship."

"Or an airship," the Marshal said after we'd stared at one another in dismay for a few more seconds.

And just like that, the penny dropped.

"I know a pilot," I said. "I know where to find him. Maybe he can get us there."

Of course, knowing a pilot and talking one into something were two different things. And I might of been exaggerating slightly when I said I knew one. But I'd *met* one, the very day before. And if I were lucky, he might even turn out to be daring.

I don't know if it was the colors on his airship and his uniform that made me think Mr. Captain Minneapolis Colony If That Was His Real Name Which I Doubt might be sympathetic to Priya, but I remembered Priya pointing them out and that they'd made her homesick. And they sure weren't colors that most white folk would put together to indicate their patriotism or whatnot.

And what the hell did I have to lose, anyway?

We took a streetcar back to the general vicinity of Mayor Stone's, and weren't we a gawker's paradise. Me with my burned face; me and Priya and Merry in men's clothes—at least Priya's and Merry's half-fit; Effie in what she thought of as a practical dress; Tomoatooah refusing to lean on anybody but just as plain needing to; Bass Reeves, a black man with his dapper coat and his gun on his hip and his silver star. Aashini stayed behind, tucked away at Merry's after a whispered fight with Priya. But even so, and even by Rapid standards, we was an assemblage.

I half-expected to get stopped by the constables, either because we looked like an escaped circus or because Peter Bantle had set 'em on us. But maybe on account of it was so early there was next to nobody about we didn't find no trouble. It's comforting when God lets you get away with something once in a while.

And a little unnerving. You start to wonder what he's got set up for you next and why he's softening you up, like.

We staggered up the hill to the mayor's yellow-and-sea-colored house, trying not to kill ourselves where the cobbles was icing. We weren't stupid: we went around to the servants' door. Miss Francina let us inside before we even had the chance to knock, and then her and Miss Lizzie and Crispin was all over us—all over me and Tomoatooah in particular.

I guess we looked rode hard, switched, and put away without a rubdown . . . and in fairness that's how I felt. Miss Francina kept hovering her long, graceful fingers by my cheek and then snatching her hand back until Miss Lizzie shooed her out to find "some brandy or something."

She held up a mirror for me, and I made myself look, though Priya had to hold my hand to get me through it.

It wasn't as bad as I'd feared. I mean, bad enough, sure, and the blisters was already rising. But I'd imagined two big red bubbled handprints by the way it hurt, and what I had on my cheek and throat looked just like the scars on Priya: a scatter of circles, sharp edged and as big as dimes.

Marshal Reeves just about let Miss Lizzie and Crispin get some aloe juice on my face before he pulled Crispin aside. I heard him say, "That pilot—I know you ain't no servant and

I hate to ask it, brother . . ." and then Crispin sighed and nodded and vanished up the back stair.

Madame beat Crispin and Mr. Colony down. She was still dressed, or maybe dressed again, because she was wearing a different gown than when I'd seen her last. It fitted, and I wondered where she'd gotten it.

Priya slipped a little bag into my hand, and a little book, too. They were both familiar, weight and heft, and that along with her sitting beside me did more to give me peace than any amount of Miss Lizzie's fussing.

Madame took one look at my face, sat down across from me, and balled her hands into fists on the scrubbed pine worktable. "I'll fucking kill that fucking son of a bitch," she said.

I had no illusions all her rage was on my behalf—Peter Bantle's fate had been sealed since he burned down Madame's house and killed Connie. But it was right sweet to see her flare up again. A good feeling that almost made me lose track how much my face hurt. And my knees. I'd almost forgotten about those, in all the adventures of the night, and now those blisters radiated pain again.

"I got plans in that direction myself," I answered. "Just as soon as Captain Colony gets down these stairs."

Then, all of us interrupting and talking over the top of one another, Effie and Priya and Merry and the Marshal and me filled Madame in on what we'd found at Bantle's house and what we'd done there.

She asked a few questions—smart ones—and said, "Well, that explains some things."

I waited.

"That pair of shitnozzles—I'm guessing they're trying to run the honest whores in Rapid out of business. Maybe in the whole Oregon Territories. If they corner the market, and they kick that money back to this Nemo fellow . . ." She shrugged. "I can see why he'd make an investment in 'em."

"Not to mention," Miss Francina said, "folks talk to whores."

Madame's mouth corner twitched, but she didn't say nothing. "What are we going to do about it?" Miss Lizzie asked.

There was another pause. Then, "I'm running for mayor," Madame said.

Miss Lizzie brought over the laudanum then. I held up my hand to give her pause.

"With what money?" I asked. Then I slapped my hand over my mouth, because I oughtn't of said that.

"I got investments," Madame said at the same moment Miss Francina said, "I got money in the bank."

We all looked at her.

She shrugged. "Banks fail. Houses burn down and get robbed. You pick your poison."

"And the Ancient and Honorable Guild of Seamstresses will back Madame," Lizzie said.

"We can't *vote*!" Merry yelped, like it had bubbled and bubbled until it couldn't help boiling out of her.

"No," Madame said. "But there ain't no law we can't *run*. And if Dyer's out of it, and the opposition is Bantle . . . well, without his infernal machine I think I got a fighting chance." She waved her hand around vaguely. "Besides, we need a new house, and this is a nice one."

"Mayor Stone's house?" I asked.

"It's not Dyer's house. It's the mayor's house," Madame said. "It comes with the job."

Miss Lizzie started to pour some laudanum into a teaspoon again. I stopped her again. "I ain't staying. I got a meeting to crash."

"Karen. Honey—"

Miss Francina cleared her throat. "She's a grown woman, Lizzie." Then she looked at me. "Unless you want me to go in your place, Karen honey. I wouldn't mind it."

"Ma'am," I said. And oh, I wanted to tell her, *Please. Go.* It had been a hell of a night, and my face—well, my face felt worse than my knees or hands, which was saying something.

But nobody was leaving Priya home and I wasn't staying behind if she was going.

And besides, I owed Peter Bantle something fierce right now.

"Thank you, Miss Francina. But this is my business."

I was interrupted in her turn by the tromp of man's boots in the hall. Crispin pushed the door open, and Captain Colony stepped through it behind him. He was in shirtsleeves and britches and boots, but his hair was slicked back and his eyes were only slightly bloodshot. He drew up short just inside the door.

"Now what are all you doing in the kitchen?"

I reached into the bag of money, found that Morgan dollar by feel, and slipped it into my bodice. Then I tossed my four hundred dollars in gold and silver to Captain Colony.

The bag clinked when he caught it. He looked at it curiously, his ponytail twitching over his shoulder when his head turned. "I haven't earned this."

"I want to hire you," I said. "We need to get to Baskerville before dawn, or not too much after."

He glanced at the kitchen clock. It said 4:37 and a hair. He said, "Sun's up around seven thirty? We could make it. But why?"

My mouth opened, then shut again. I didn't even know where to start.

Priya put her hands on the table and leaned forward. "Because if we don't, the whoremongers who enslaved me and my sister are going to meet up with somebody who is selling them more stolen Hindu girls like us, and we want to stop them."

He looked at her. His mouth did something, and he nodded. Then his hand moved, and the bag of coins lobbed back to me. I was too surprised even to move my hand toward it, so it thumped to the table in front of me and sat there while my heart sank so fast and so hard that the rush in my ears almost deafened me to what Captain Colony said next.

"Well, why didn't you say so?"

I blinked at him, dumbfounded. I'd always thought that was just a word, but it turns out to be a real thing and now I can say it's happened to me.

"Your money's no good with me, Miss Memery," he said. He glanced at the clock again. "But if you want to be there by sunup, you'd better drink that tea and button up your boots."

I don't rightly recall everything that happened next, except Effie had fell asleep in the corner next to Tomoatooah and we decided not to wake either one of 'em—Effie on account of she was so tired and Tomoatooah on account of how bad Bantle had shocked him. I got burned, sure . . . but we'd all been pretty sure Tomoatooah's heart had stopped. So he could snore all he wanted.

And it turned out that was plenty, thank you very much.

Crispin promised to wake him up and put him in a proper bed once we was safely away and he couldn't follow. And I could tell that him and the Marshal and Priya and Miss Lizzie only wasn't tucking me in next to him because Miss Francina was defending my right to go out and get my fool self killed if that was what it took to learn me.

I gave Miss Francina that purse and my diary, anyway, and made her promise to keep 'em for me. And she gave me a Colt six-shooter, and I didn't ask her where she'd gotten it.

"I'll never hear the end of this," Marshal Reeves said softly as we shut the door behind us. But I think he looked relieved as well as troubled to be leaving his friend behind.

So it was me and Merry and Priya and Marshal Reeves who got into the hack with Captain Colony and rode through the dark streets at a fast trot like to rattle our bones. They was supposed to be putting a kind of pneumatic tube system in to move people around Rapid, but it weren't there yet, so this was the fastest we could manage. We jounced along in silence, and I noticed Priya kept casting apprehensive glances at the eastern sky, and I couldn't do much to comfort her. So, while Marshal Reeves cleaned his nails with his fighting knife—a risk I wouldn't have taken on those springs—Captain Colony stared out the window at the Christmas candles that had begun flickering in people's windows as of the past day or two, and Merry caught the nap she'd been smart enough not to commence until we'd have to stop the carriage not to bring her, I edged over beside lovely Priya and took her hand.

"How did you know?" I whispered in Priya's ear, flicking my eyes at Colony. Of course she couldn't see me in the dark, but she understood me anyway. Because that was Priya.

"He's wearing *navaratna*," she whispered back. She waved at his hand. The gaudy ring with the stones in a wheel shimmered faintly even in the dark. "You'd say . . . 'nine jewels.' Ruby in the heart for the sun. Then diamond, most sacred. Pearl, coral, saffron garnet, sapphire, cat's-eye, topaz, and emerald. It's a very powerful amulet. He could have gotten it from a maharaja or maharani for some service or great friendship. And he wears green and saffron."

"You thought he might be a friend."

"He is a friend," she said. She leaned over and brushed my hair aside with her lips, then kissed the lobe of my ear. Such a shiver ran through me as I had only ever imagined, reading novels. "And so are you."

Chapter Twenty

I'd never been in an airship before. I expected quarters to be cramped, as I'd read they were on ships, but the salon was plenty big for all four of us, and there was coffee. Hot, too, from a gadget that brewed each cup as you wanted it. I drank four and then had to go find the head. *That* was tiny enough to suit my prejudices.

Captain Colony, of course, was in the control room. The rest of us tried to come up with a plan for a while, but we didn't know enough about what we was getting into to even begin one. Find Bantle and break his meeting up, have the Marshal arrest him and Scarlet, if Scarlet wasn't dead.

I drove the Marshal and Merry crazy walking in circles, jittering, but it had been coffee or collapse. Priya just kept handing me cookies. They was sugar cookies with peppermint icing, slightly stale. I ate every one she gave me, soaked in the coffee.

Mostly, we fretted and stared and tried to figure out how to sneak up on them. At least the airship was quiet and we figured we could have Captain Colony let us off down the beach and hike in.

"I hope they're out in the open," the Marshal said while his own third cup of coffee cooled between his palms. "Otherwise I don't know how we're gonna find them."

"It ain't a big camp," I said. "And this time of year, ain't nobody there but a caretaker, I'd submit."

The Marshal flashed his smile. Rain had begun drumming on the big gasbag overhead. It was strange to hear that, and nothing on the canopy of the gondola. But of course we hung in that gasbag's shadow, so there weren't no rain falling over us.

"You know much about logging?"

I wandered around the salon some more, smudging brass fixtures fiddling with 'em. The aloe juice was soaking through the fresh bandages Miss Lizzie'd wrapped on my hands, though they didn't hurt anymore. "Grew up in Hay Camp," I said. "I know a little."

He stared out the window into black overcast for a minute or two. "I asked Mr. Hayden that when Sky wakes up, he ask him to track down that Bruce Scarlet fellow. Or his remains. And put him under arrest if he can manage it, and he ain't already permanently arrested. But I'm thinking it might be within my remit to slap irons on Mr. Bantle, too, for conspiracy to commit murder."

He nodded, satisfied.

"Mr. Hayden?" I asked.

"Mr. Crispin Hayden?"

My face went hot as coals and I leaned on the brass railing I'd been finger-spotting. I'd never even thought to learn Crispin's surname.

Marshal Reeves, watching me, snorted. "Live and learn, child," he said. "Everybody's worthy of respect."

I went to fix another cup of coffee, trying to sort how I felt. Other than like a damned fool. I went and sat next to Priya and drank my coffee and wished I'd brought a book.

Fortunately, it was only another ten minutes or so to Baskerville. By the time we got there I could imagine there was a little gray through the clouds outside, but I knew I was probably imagining it. Down below, though, I could make out the narrow pale strip of the beach, so I stared at that—and just as I realized that the soft hum of the engines had changed a little, I also realized the blurred light-colored ribbon underneath was getting broader. Or closer.

"What's that?" Priya asked.

She pointed, but I didn't see anything but black. "What?"

"I thought I saw lights. Over there."

"That's ocean," I said. "Or Sound, anyway. I'd hate to be the ship's master out on this night. Maybe there's a lighthouse?"

There were lighthouses. A lot of them. All up and down the coast. It was as good a guess as any.

Priya reached out to touch Merry awake—it didn't take a shake or even a nudge—and the three of us clustered by the window. After a moment, the Marshal came over, too. I touched the cool butt of Miss Francina's Colt and I thought I'd just been pawing all that brasswork to keep my hand off the pistol. It was a comforting sort of coldness, smooth and heavy.

I wondered if I was going to shoot somebody tonight. And if it would be Peter Bantle.

I decided I wouldn't feel bad about that if it happened. And now I know that that particular delusion showed pretty well that whatever Miss Francina thought, I weren't too much of a grown woman yet after all. Time fixes that for most of us, though. More's the pity.

Worse pity for them who don't get either the time nor the fix.

I'd thought maybe we were going to have to slide down ropes or something else dramatic, and I would even have been looking forward to it if it weren't for the state of my hands and the ice freezing all over everything. Instead, Minneapolis Colony set that gaudy airship down on the sand like a feather. There wasn't even a thump when it landed. I had no idea then how it worked—Priya said it was something about canisters and vents and compressors.

Anyway, Captain Colony came back to wish us well and tell us he'd wait for us right here, unless he had to take off for safety. He said his real concern was ice weighing down the gasbag, but he had some way of heating it up to keep it from freezing. That didn't seem too prudent to me, what with the hydrogen and all, but I ain't no airship mechanic. I'm just a seamstress who can gentle horses.

If he had to take off, he said he'd not go far. He also said something to Priya in a language I didn't know; she laughed and answered.

On the way down the gangplank I looked at her.

"It was Hindi," she said. "He wished us . . . luck, I think I'd translate it. Good fortune."

"Well," I answered, "we're going to need it."

Then we were out from under the shadow of the gasbag, and the rain spiked down on us like needles of ice, sharp and cold.

We followed Merry and the Marshal up the beach in the thumping rain. It was sure enough graying by now, but when I looked back over my shoulder even that great, gaudy balloon didn't show up much as of yet. Ahead of us, we couldn't see a damned thing, neither—not the lumber camp, and not a glimmer of light. It was cold, and I didn't have mittens, and the coat I'd borrowed from Captain Colony was canvas and too big and already wet through the shoulders. The Marshal offered me his gloves. They was so big they didn't make no difference, so I handed 'em back. I'd pinned my hair up in a couple of braids, but they weren't standing up to the weather. I don't know if you've ever felt the frozen curls of your hair scratching around your cheeks and ears, but I can't rightly recommend it.

What I can recommend is somebody you love holding your hand in a black-ice storm. Even if you is both sneaking up a beach with the river—Miss Bethel would call it an estuary—hissing on your right side and the trees creaking like they're wont to shatter on the left. This'd be snow up in the mountains and rain down in Rapid, but here it was freezing and falling at the same time, and it weren't good. My feet was starting to crunch through a rime of ice when I put 'em down on the sand.

The sky was graying up some, but it weren't exactly what you'd call dawn. More just lightening. And we was all still pretty invisible in that gloaming, especially as we kept to the tree line and off the white sand of the beach. The mountains weren't out today, for sure, I guess is what I'm saying.

You could still kind of sense their presence, though, by the way those left-hand trees mounted up steep directly as they got beyond the river. Underneath 'em was nothing but hints of wet green dark and moss and dripping logs and fallen logs big around as a paddle wheel. I glanced longingly at the shelter, but trying to walk through that was asking for a snakebite on top a broken ankle. The tips of the trees was lost in the mist.

I swear to this day I did see a dark man-like shape ghosting between trees deep back in the shadows, and I regret to this day that I didn't have time to go look and see if it was a real

Sasquatch. In any case, I ain't never been so weather miserable in my life. And whatever I was feeling, it weren't nothing
on Priya, who just weren't acclimated. She shivered and minced
even though the Marshal hung his hat and his duster on her—
the duster dragged in the sand—until finally Merry and I chiv-
vied her into a kind of stumbling trot. It don't matter so much
if your skin gets cold if you keep your muscles warm, and it
weren't cold enough out for frostbite. But she could still freeze
to death if she didn't keep moving.

Hell, any of us could. I hoped we could get inside when we
got to Baskerville. Otherwise it was going to be a long walk
back to Captain Colony's airship when we was done.

I about cried with relief when we glimpsed a light. I don't think
we'd come more than a mile, though it felt like twelve. But there
was Baskerville looming up out of what was passing for morning, and it was shuttered up for winter just as it should of been.
Except for the loadmaster's stripped-log cottage alongside the
pier, that is—which glowed with a merry enticing light and
whipped a tangy banner of woodsmoke from its chimney up
through the whistling cold.

"Sons of bitches," the Marshal said, and I don't mind saying I sympathized. I wanted to bust that door down and go
take that fire away from them. It took more than a modicum
of self-constraint to hunker down and observe the situation,
and I know I weren't the only one as felt so.

"Are we sure that's them?" I asked. "I don't see no boat nor
no airship."

"Airship'd want to get up above the mess, if there were any
wait anticipated."

We huddled together, a bit, and that helped some. I held my
tongue, because I could about feel the Marshal thinking.

He thought as fast as he could, too, but Merry and I had joined Priya in shivering by the time he started talking.

"You two creep up," he said to me and Priya. "Get in that shed there."

It was just a lean-to against the back of the house, open on one side. But it was shelter, and I knew the Marshal was being kind to Priya and me. I was so cold I didn't even put up a fight about it.

He went on, "Looks like there's a rear door under that roof. Maybe you can hear what they're plotting at if you sneak up to it. Merry and me, we'll take the front. Miss Memery, you got you a six-shooter, don't you?"

I nodded.

He offered his two Colts out in each hand—one to Priya and one to Merry. He still had his Winchester across his back.

Merry took a pistol silently. Priya tucked her eggshell fingers into the sleeves of the Marshal's duster and said, "I don't shoot."

He shrugged and slid the pistol back into his holster. Freezing rain beaded on the oiled leather, which was when I realized that it had got light enough to see such things.

"You think Nemo is in there already?"

"I think given the weather, and that I don't see no boat tied up, I ain't going to assume either way. Now look—when I give a signal, I want you, Miss Memery, and you, Miss Swati, to make a good bit of noise in the shed and then run for the trees. Make it sound like you knocked something over on accident, then just light out. Zigzag when you run in case they open fire. Miss Lee and me will cut them off from the house, and when we've got the drop on 'em we'll demand a surrender. Are you all right with that? It ain't safe."

"What in life is?" Priya asked.

"What's the signal?" I asked.

"You know what a burrowing owl sounds like?"

I did, but Merry and Priya both took some convincing there even was any such thing. The Marshal and I took turns demonstrating—*who-heoo! who-heoo!*—until Priya succumbed to a fit of ague and nervous giggling.

"Right," the Marshal said. "I do that, and it means make a ruckus. You do it, and it means something's wrong, get out and regroup. There's no burrowing owls around here, so it won't happen by accident."

"What's your signal for get out?" Priya asked.

He pursed his lips, thinking. Merry watched him think for a moment. Then she put her hands before her mouth and made a fluted, echoing, ethereal cry.

"That's a phoenix," she said. "There's none of those around here, either."

"Good enough," the Marshal said. He looked around at us, shaking his head a little in . . . wonder? Disbelief at what he had to work with? Grudging respect? I couldn't say, rightly.

Then he said, "By the power invested in me by the Ninth Circuit Court of these United States of America, I'm deputizing each and every one of you ladies. You's my possemen now."

We stared at him for a minute. I don't know about the others, but me, I was wondering if this was the first time Irish and Oriental *women* was ever deputized as U.S. Marshals before. The silence started to drag a bit, I'll be honest, but I didn't know how to break it.

Then, "All right," Priya said. "Let's go."

Chapter Twenty-one

I don't know if it was the excitement that did it, but by the time we started our tiptoe across the icy, rutted skid yard to that shed Priya had quit shivering, but I was trembling like a marriage license in a young man's hand. The skid yard was wide and open—it'd be a field of mud in spring and hard-baked dirt come summer—and all I could think was how the sky was graying out fast now and if it were me holed up in that shack waiting for some agent of a foreign power whom I expected to slip me some ill-gotted gold I'd be spending a whole lot of time checking outside the windows. But they was hung with burlap coffee bags for curtains—I could make out the printing through the bubbled glass panes—and not a one on our side twitched.

Maybe Bantle and his fellows was staring out the front. One if by land, two if by sea. Or do I got that backward?

The lean-to was dingy and dark and a blessed relief. Just not having the freezing rain drumming on my head was benediction enough, but the side wall and slanted roof cut the wind, too, and in the stillness Priya and my new little burrow felt almost warm by comparison. We huddled against the back wall on the hinge side of that door, where it would shade us if it opened unexpectedly. She pulled the Marshal's coat out and I got under it with her. She weren't shedding no appreciable warmth.

I didn't care. She draped her arm over my shoulders and we crouched down, hugging our knees, and leaned in to the cracks between the logs to hear what we could hear.

There was some mud shoved in there in places, but overall they weren't chinked so good and it hadn't been reapplied recent. Little slivers of light shone out between 'em, honey warm and tantalizing. Priya and me, we tried to breathe shallow and not let our teeth chatter, because we could hear every footstep inside and sound travels in all directions. Except back up through the ceiling when your neighbor upstairs is getting up to acrobatics, if you know what I mean, but that's just the goddamn perversity of the universe.

I'd still maybe harbored a small niggle of worry that we'd come all this way and weren't going to find nothing except a winter watchman—especially when there was no means of transportation immediately apparent—but the first whisper of sound that filtered out with the warm air and firelight put paid to that. It didn't do nothing to ease the twist in my guts, though, because it was Peter Bantle's voice.

I flinched, and in flinching I noted that the icy rain had made my face stop hurting, because it started up again. Priya didn't cringe at all. The man who can make Priya cringe ain't been invented. And I believe the task would stretch even the Almighty's ingenuity.

Bantle said, "If that yellow son of a bitch ain't here in half an hour, he can whistle."

Did that mean Nemo was an Indian after all? Or was I wrong and he was Chinese?

Another voice cut in, more educated and more accented. "For what he is paying us, he may be being as late as he wishes. I for one do not care to go back out into that rain."

I glanced at Priya. She mouthed something in the dimness. It could have been *Scarlet*.

I nodded. I guess the son of a bitch weren't dead after all.

The third voice was familiar, too. Horatio Standish. "Why don't I make us some coffee, gentlemen? I brought cornmeal and flour and bacon. Figure if I start up a pan of grub, that'll bring him."

Some things are just universal.

Like the known scientific fact that the colder and wetter you are, the better bacon smells frying. I tell you true, if a woman could die of smells, I wouldn't be here today. There was scraping and mixing sounds, too, and sizzling. I thought even Priya was salivating, and she don't even like bacon.

We pressed up against the log wall and convinced ourselves that some of that warmth was soaking through it. I tried not to smell bacon while I was deciding if we should kick something over and run now—the conversation weren't too edifying—or if we should wait for Nemo to get here and try to scoop up the whole mess of 'em.

Of course, I was supposed to be waiting for the Marshal's signal. But he sure were taking his own sweet time about whatever preparations he had in mind. And I don't mind admitting I had an itch to hurry things along some.

I had just about decided that the sensible thing to do would be to slap irons on Bantle, Scarlet, and Standish—I felt maybe a little bad about Standish, but only a little; he did choose to associate himself with Bantle—and then for us to inhabit the cabin in our turn and lie in wait for this Nemo, when Bantle started in to talking again.

"Horaz, come over here and look at this."

There was a rustle of paper, some footsteps. I tried to press my eye to the chink in the wall and see what was going on, but there was nothing to be seen except light and blurs. I heard Standish make a humfing sound, and then there was nothing.

"Help me move this table," Bantle said. A great scraping followed, coupled with some muffled cursing I could not understand. In Russian, I thought, because that was Scarlet's voice.

If they was setting up the table and chairs, then they must expect Nemo to be coming any minute. Either that or they was getting antsy with waiting.

Well, I could relate. Still no owls. And less of my heart hammering on against the inside of my ribs, despite being huddled in a corner of that shed like a mouse in a loose box, hoping not to get stomped. Still, the waiting was like to be the death of me. I wondered if maybe Marshal Reeves had made his owl call, and we'd just not heard it through the rain and our eavesdropping on Bantle and his fellows. Maybe we should start our turn as bait—

The back door of the log cottage busted open so hard it bounced off my shoulder and knocked me on my rump. A harsh glare of light followed. I scrambled away, knowing that there was no way I could avoid getting seen but hoping maybe to distract from Priya. When I looked up, Horaz Standish was framed in the door.

He had a pistol in each hand, and both of 'em was trained at me.

I rolled on my side, thinking maybe I could sprint out the open side of the shed and make for the trees and maybe our plan could still work. And if nothing else, I could lead 'em off Priya. But as I gathered my legs under me, I came face to boot with Peter Bantle, standing with the rain dripping off the groove in his hat brim, scowling down at me. He had his glove on, and it was sparking and spitting. Me, I wouldn't have trusted that much electricity in the rain. The sizzle turned my stomach and made my insides feel liquidy and slick.

The burn on my cheek flared into fresh pain, just at the sight of it.

Bantle leveled a pistol, too, and sighed like I was the biggest exasperation he ever met. "Put the Peacemaker down," he instructed.

I just then realized it was still in my hand.

I know I should of leveled it and shot him where he stood. But I honestly think if I had, you wouldn't be hearing this story today. Standish and Bantle had me dead to rights, and even if I dropped Bantle, well . . . Horaz Standish's forbearance was unlikely to weather my shooting his boss.

I stretched out my arm and laid the gun on the packed earth, fingertip reach away.

Bantle shook his head. "You whores really are blamed fools. Get that other one out from behind the door, please, Scarlet?"

Scarlet crossed behind Standish, more's the pity—I would of liked him to foul Standish's line of fire—and went around the door. He was a medium-sized fellow only, compact, but his arms were as big around as one of Priya's thighs. And he was as strong as he looked; Priya kicked and fought as he drew her out, but she couldn't even shake his grip on her wrist. She bit him a good one—I saw blood—and he stepped on my leg fighting her, but before too long he twisted her arm behind her back and gave her the Spanish walk out of the corner.

She never said a word. But there was more light now, and she caught my eye. The toss of her chin told me she'd kill all three of them right now, if she had the means. Though I was chattering with the cold, I agreed with her silent threat 1,006 percent.

Standish lowered his gun. "These girls are soaked to the bone. Let's get them inside, before they freeze stiff."

"They'd be less trouble to me under such circumstances," Bantle said.

"I've got a use for at least one of 'em if you don't," Standish replied.

Bantle snorted. But he reached down—without holstering his pistol—and though I cringed away, he hauled me to my feet by the hair.

Chapter Twenty-two

I woke up with a drinker's head and the taste of vomit in my mouth, unable to feel my hands. It weren't dark—if anything it was too damned bright, and when I tried to open my eyes I slammed 'em shut again right quick, feeling as if somebody had driven an ice pick into my brain.

I hadn't got more than a glimpse, but I had the idea that I was in a bright, small room, maybe lit with electric arcs. I couldn't think of anything else that would make such a dazzling light, but I also couldn't think why anybody'd light an inside room with an arc. It was like killing ants with molten lead: significant overkill.

I moaned and tried to pull my hands down, to see if I could get some blood into them. Something rattled, and I realized they was chained up over my head.

I probably should of faked I was still out, I realized. But I had to vomit again, and I didn't want to drown in it. It took the sort of effort I'd usually reserve for mountain climbing—if I was a mountain climber, I mean—but I managed to get my shoulder down and my knees up, and toss my chuck over the edge of the narrow metal table I was laying on without either falling off it or puking on myself any more than absolutely necessary.

They'd chloroformed me. Or maybe ether. Whatever it was, it was turning my stomach something fierce. And I still couldn't feel my hands.

As I lay there, I came aware of a vibration coming up through the table. Like if I was on a train. But I couldn't hear the rattle of iron wheels on iron rails or the *ratcheta ratcheta* noise of those wheels rolling over the joints. Maybe a barge?

Either way, I was mostly surprised I weren't dead. Bantle'd proved in his own parlor that he had a taste for hurting women and that he wasn't about to draw the line at permanent, long-term hurt.

I pressed my burned face to the cool metal and sighed. Maybe he didn't like 'em once they was scarred up by his prior attentions. Or maybe he was just saving me for later.

That gave me a fresh well of sick. I tried to vomit again, but all I got for my trouble was hard stomach cramps and a thin, bitter streak of bile. Straining over the edge of the table made my shoulders hurt, and straining to vomit made my belly cramp, and I was feeling pretty miserable already when I realized that I didn't know where Priya was.

That fear you get for a loved one—that's a motivator like no other. Even though I couldn't feel my hands or lower arms, I scooted my butt up, angled myself sideways with my legs off the table, and leaned on the chain so I could use it for purchase to pull myself sitting. The room spun, all right, but I didn't dare fall over—and if I fell off the table I'd probably dislocate a shoulder, and then I'd really be useful for nothing.

I turned so the chain eased and my hands dropped into my

lap. I looked down at 'em, daring my eyes to open. It still hurt like hell.

But the hands were there, and attached, and a funny pale color. I tried to wiggle my fingers and got nothing—not even a shimmer. As I watched, they pinked up again a bit, though. I decided that was a hopeful sign, that blood was flowing back into them. I flapped 'em like a dying fish thumping its tail. They hit my legs like lumps of warm meat. When they bounced on my chest, I realized that the Morgan dollar was still inside my shirt, tucked against the top of my bosom.

No sign of Priya anywhere. I was in a little whitewashed metal room, on a steel table. My feet dangled over a puddle of my own vomit, and those were the only things anywhere near.

The metal walls made me think I was on a ship. That would explain the hum that was still rising up the table legs to numb my bottom. And why that table was bolted to the floor.

I was musing on that when the door swung open.

I braced myself for Bantle, but it was just Horaz Standish. I was ashamed of myself for feeling a spike of relief. He stood there, framed, with a bucket in one hand and a stack of rags in the other, and he looked at me. Maybe pityingly? His face was hard to read.

"Well," he said, after a minute. "You've looked better."

He came up to me and—stepping around the puddle of up-chuck on the floor—dipped a cloth in the bucket and wiped my face clean with lukewarm water. I bit my cheek not to scream when he touched the burns. He dropped the cloth on the floor, then repeated the process. He crouched down and wiped up the vomit, then washed the floor with rags.

When he was done, he washed his hands in the bucket, piled all the dirty rags back into it, and set it by the door.

I thought about kicking his head while he was down there, but somebody'd taken off my shoes, and it seemed like a lot of risk for a more or less Pyrrhic gesture. So I just watched while Standish cleaned up up after me and then came back.

"Before I unchain you," he said, "you ought to know that there's no escaping."

"We're on a boat," I said. "Where are we going?"

He laughed. "We're *in* a boat," he corrected. "A submersible ship. We're four leagues under the Sound, and all the hatches are dogged and pressure locked. You have no way out."

"A submersible ship?"

He smiled. "Think of it as a mechanical fish."

"It's the *Nautilus*!" I cried. "He really *is* Captain Nemo!"

Standish looked amused. "And Peter thought you weren't clever," he said. "Here. Hold out your hands."

I did, as best I could. I extended them, though they hung like dead flowers from my wrists. Standish unchained them, and I let them drop back down against my thighs. They lay against my lap like two warm, limp bladders. I tried to move them from the shoulders, and all I managed was to flop 'em against my chest and belly disgustingly.

Standish watched silently for a few moments. Then the pins and needles started and, after those, the pain.

I didn't scream. But I did say "*aaahah!*" loud enough for any-one to hear it two rooms over. And I did rock back and forth on the table, huddling my arms up to my chest and kind of shaking them.

It hurt worse than my burned face, and the rocking back and forth wasn't doing my splitting head any favors. Standish reached out and put a hand on my shoulder, ever so gently. "There, there, Miss Memery," he said. "The pain will pass."

And, more or less, given time, it did.

He touched my cheek gently—but not so gently the burned skin didn't smart something awful. I jerked away and hissed.

"Pity about your face," he said. "You were lovely."

And a lot of good it did me. His words still smarted, though I determined to do everything possible to keep him from noticing. I hoped he'd think my stung look was just pain. Christ knows I had plenty of it.

Besides, I never met more than one man in a hundred who was ever nice to a whore except out of pity or because he wanted something. Standish had the charm, sure, and I knew Priya said he was kind, by the standards of them as work for Bantle. But he wasn't entirely enticing me to let my guard down.

"Where's Priya?" I asked. I'd thought about keeping mum, not letting on that I cared. But who would I think I was fooling?

"I'm going to see her next. I'll let her know you were asking after her." He smiled. "I convinced Peter not to just kill both of you outright, you know. You owe me, Miss Memery."

Ah, there it was. I could do something for him. "What do you want?"

"Right now, I want you to rest and get your strength up," he said.

Well, that could sound as ominous as I wanted to make it. "I'll send someone with food presently."

That, however, couldn't sound ominous. My stomach rumbled, and I winced. I didn't want to admit to human weakness in front of any of Bantle's men.

At least I managed not to say, *Thank you.*

Standish took the bucket with him, and pretty soon the room only smelled faintly of vomit. I guess the air circulation worked pretty good, if he was telling the truth and we was in a submersible boat. In any case, it weren't pitching up and down with the waves the way a boat on the surface would.

The food came. The seaman who brought it was a white man, with high cheekbones and dark eyes. I tried talking to him, but he just shook his head and muttered, "No English," with a heavy accent. I might could have tried to brain him with the bowl, but then where would I go? Besides, there was another one in the corridor outside.

It weren't anything I'd eaten before—some kind of gritty tan grain, boiled, with turnips and mushrooms in it and a scrambled egg. I wondered if this were the sort of food Priya had grown up with. From her descriptions, I had expected more spices.

Unfamiliar or not, I ate it and didn't fuss. I figured if they wanted me dead they wouldn't waste poison when they could just drown me. And now that my belly had settled from the ether or the chloroform or whatever they'd used, I was ravenous.

I figured that since Standish hadn't mentioned Merry Lee or Marshal Reeves that maybe meant they'd gotten away clean. Which meant they was looking for us. Which meant I had all the reason in the world to stay alive and stay strong.

After I ate, I slept on that narrow table again, wishing I was wearing girl clothes. I could have used my top layer of skirts as a blanket, if I had any. And to cover my eyes from the glare of that awful, hissing electric light.

I was awakened by a terrible lurching and a horrible series of thuds that reverberated through the whole hull. I clutched the edges of the table to keep from being pitched bodily to the floor.

Well, of course I thought of Mr. Verne again and his *Nautilus*. Which was more like a narwhal, when it come right down to it—the *Nautilus* had a screw on its nose, a sort of augur that it used to rip open the bellies of enemy ships so they would founder and sink.

Maybe this Nemo had built his ship to be like the *Nautilus* in addition to taking the captain's name. Or maybe Mr. Verne has somehow heard about this Nemo and his submersible and put them into his book wholesale.

I hoped not.

I paced the room then, tried the door, tried to climb up to the ventilation shaft. I scrambled up, but it was too narrow for my shoulders. And I didn't hear anything down it but the deep hum of machines.

So I laid my head back down on my arms, then, 100 percent certain that I no longer knew what to think, and I hoped like hell Merry and the Marshal would come for us quick.

Some time went by. Having no clock and no light but the electric arc, I'd be hard-pressed to say how much time, except I was getting that desperate for a toilet. And that thirsty, too, because bodies is perverse and a trial. My face had settled into a sharp kind of itching, and I spent most of my time trying not to pick and peel at it.

I discovered I could use the polished steel of the table as a sort of clumsy mirror, and when I poked my face in it I could tell that those soft white bulges along my jaw was blisters. I didn't look forward to when they popped and peeled and left raw red behind 'em, so I tried not to poke at 'em too much. Anybody who's ever had a blister can tell you how well that went.

In what might of been the morning, the man with the dark eyes and no English brought me a bucket, a cup of water, and another bowl of mush. He had the decency to turn his back while I used the bucket, too, though at that point I wouldn't of thought much of dropping my trousers and peeing on his foot. If I could aim like a boy, I might of even tried it.

I drank the water and ate the mush, and he took the things away again. I commenced to my non-sleep pastime, which was pacing in circles around the table, twiddling my thumbs.

Thumb twiddling is harder than it looks, it turns out. Unless you go pretty slow, your thumbs have a tendency to brush together. But I got pretty good at it after what I figure was an hour or so.

Some more time later, Horaz Standish came back in.

His timing was good enough to make me wonder if there were spyholes in the walls, or those half-silvered mirrors you get in some whorehouses so people can spy on the clientele. Madame doesn't hold with such chicanery, but I know there's them that do.

I'd worn myself to a frazzle with the pacing, but every time I sat still for more than a moment the anxiousness started spinning around in me like an unhinged gyroscope until I felt like bits was going to start flinging off me in all directions. So even though I'd been watching the door like a mouse in front of a cathole, I still jumped half out of my skin when it opened.

He came in all mild, like before. But what I didn't like was that he had two big seamen with him, dressed like they fell out of a burlesque about the Happy Sailor, white shirts and bulging arms and little blue neckerchiefs and all.

They didn't look happy, though. Their hair was cropped off into brown-blond bristles. One had a cauliflower ear and a low forehead. The other was balding at the temples and had a flattened nose and was missing a couple of fingers. Neither one of 'em looked as if they was from India.

I turned to face them. At least the pacing had dried off the parts of my clothes that had still been wet and clammy when

I woke up. It's one way to keep warm. And it ain't too cozy in a submersible.

In my head, when I was thinking about this moment, I'd rehearsed all sorts of clever things I might say. I'd wracked my brains, trying to come up with some bit of badinage worthy of Calamity Jane. But I looked Horatio Standish in the eye, and all that came out was, "Can I be of some assistance to you gentlemen?"

"These aren't gentlemen," Standish said. "They're Cossacks."

Then he did something that purely blindsided me, though looking back now, I can't tell you that I know why I didn't see it coming. It was just that he was so polite, even working for Bantle. And in my defense, I was so busy being surprised by my realization that this was a *Russian* submersible, and that whoever Bantle was working for was a *Russian* agent, I didn't have much thinking space left over to be spotting other stuff in advance.

Horaz Standish pulled a riding crop out of his boot and slashed me once hard across the burned cheek with it.

Reader, I ain't never felt a thing that hurt like that before.

I rocked over sideways and then went down on my knees. Or would of done, except the table caught me across the floating ribs and the next thing I knew I was on the floor on my back, a cramp in my midsection I couldn't breathe around, and sticky-slick heat welling over the fingers I had clutched to my face. I stared up at Standish and his thugs, wondering if I was going to die of not being able to inhale.

Standish eyed the whip thoughtfully, gave it a snap as if he was shaking it off, and slid it back into his boot. "That's just so you have something to think about," he said. "For later."

He turned and said something in what I assumed was Russian that might of been, "Now help her up, lads."

So they did, and they were the only reason I stayed standing, because when they pulled me to my feet the world went black around the edges and nausea cramped me. I still couldn't breathe, and the idea of vomiting when I couldn't pull a breath in was so scary I started to yank against the sailors' grip. But I couldn't manage much more than a kitten thrash, and at least kittens have claws.

One of the sailors thumped me on the back—hard—and somehow that started me up breathing again. Released the cramp or something. The air came in with a whoosh and went right back out again on a scream. I ain't never been much of a screamer—but for that incident right then I made an exception. I gave another yank against the sailors, but I might as well have been pulling at iron bars set in stone. They were big, and as hard as a plowhorse's haunches.

I kicked at Standish, since they had my arms and all. He caught the ankle and gave it a fond squeeze before letting go of me again. "Don't worry, Miss Memery. We'll have plenty of time together later. Why do you think I argued so hard to keep you and your friend alive?"

He touched my bruised and burned and split-open cheek, and I tell you true—though I didn't mean to, I shivered. I thought of the girl in the alley, tossed in with the trash. I thought about Priya saying that things were always better when Standish was in town but that he traveled a lot. Because I realized something—something I should have comprehended as soon as he pulled that crop out of his boot. The Devil can quote scripture, after all. And monsters can say "please" and "thank you" same as any mother's son.

"How did you like the Indian Territory?" I asked. "Lose a cuff link there?"

His eyes narrowed. I might of regretted my bravado if it hadn't of been the only thing keeping me on my feet. I thought about this barn cat Da used to have that run off a brown bear once out of pure cussedness, and I made up my mind to be like her. Then he smiled and pulled out his crop again and tapped me lightly on the tip of the nose with it.

I flinched, all right. But then I made myself pick my chin up and smile right back at him.

"Oh," he said. "I'm going to like breaking you."

I had expected a long walk, sort of tromping through endless corridors. Instead it was just a few yards, and we did it in a sort of hunched-over shuffle because the corridors was that narrow and short. It was uncomfortable enough for me. I couldn't imagine what it was like for Ivan and Boris, the two Russian sides of beef. But in all honesty, I didn't mind seeing them suffer.

That short walk seemed long enough, with me dwelling on what Standish had said about breaking, and me thinking about my da and Priya and the ones you can't break. I didn't think I was one of those. But I wondered if I could make myself be, if I knew that no matter what he was going to kill me anyway.

Either Ivan or Boris stepped forward to open a hatch, and the other one guided me through it by my elbows. I'd expected . . . some sort of control room, I guessed. A bridge, right out of the illustrations for Monsieur Verne's book. But it was just a narrow room with a long table in it, and a lingering smell of onions and sour cream.

My stomach growled. Da would say that nothing in the history of ever has upset my appetite. And then he'd point out that Chinese recorded history is three thousand years long.

Endure this, I thought. *And you'll be seeing him soon. And Mama, too.*

Some would say a whore don't have no expectation of

Heaven. I'd say, if she gives value for cash, she's got a better shot at God's blessing than your average banker.

Jesus loved Mary Magdalene. He kicked over tables when He met a moneylender.

Well, that made me feel so much immeasurably better about everything that I was just about ready to trust to Providence and commend my soul into the hands of the Almighty—because whatever the preachers say, I know and you know that the flesh ain't His concern and He don't take no truck with what befalls it—when the door at the far end of the room opened up and another set of Boris and Ivan so like my own I could only tell 'em apart by hairline walked in, escorting Priya.

And it occurred to me that Da and Mama might be waiting for me . . . but whatever happened to Priya, if her religion was as right as mine, she was coming around for another cycle on her great wheel of being and me, I was going to Heaven or maybe Hell.

Well, dammit. If I had any say in the matter, I wasn't going anywhere without a chance at a good long life with Priya first.

She looked up at me, and even across the room I saw her mouth tighten. At least she didn't seem to be any more banged up than when I had saw her last.

I resolved then and there to do what it took to keep Horatio Standish's affections to myself for as long as possible. I wondered if I knew what I was getting into. Thinking about that poor girl cut to ribbons in the trash, I decided I probably had no idea.

I figured Standish must have a purpose for letting Priya and me see each other, so I kept my face as blank as I could. She stared at me hard, then let her gaze drop to her feet.

Boris and Ivan Mark Two brought Priya down to my end of the table. We stood side by side, not touching or talking or even acknowledging each other's existence, though it was all I could do not to lean toward her and soak up her warmth through my skin. She made me stronger and better just standing there.

That door she'd come in through opened again, and this time the person who walked in looked like a captain. He wore a black wool coat, double-breasted with silver buttons. A high collar embroidered with silver bullion and scarlet edging lifted his chin. His cuffs were embroidered, too, and his epaulets were gold, with a design of an anchor topped by a two-headed, crowned eagle on each one.

Definitely a captain.

He looked me up and down, and then Priya. Then he and Standish had a rapid-fire conversation that I understood exactly one word of—*prostitutki*.

"If you're going to talk about us," I put in, "it's polite to use a language we understand."

My da didn't raise no rude girls: I waited until one of 'em hesitated for breath.

The Russian captain looked at me. He was lean and bald on top, with white hair and a white beard cropped close to his pointed jaw. His eyebrows, though, was devilish black peaks over sparking eyes, and you could tell he knew he was handsome.

"Forgive me, miss," he said dryly. "I was simply asking Mr. Standish how it was that he intended to infect the two of you with his *Vibrio cholerae* without exposing my men to the bacillus."

His English was better than Miss Bethel's, and his lordly manner made me feel small and filthy.

Well, I might be filthy. But I weren't small. And even if I was, well, that barn cat still ran off that five-hundred-pound bear just by being a damned sight more invested in the outcome than the bear was.

"I bet you're what's been sinking the gold boats, aren't you? You really are Captain Nemo."

The captain looked at Standish all quizzical.

Standish shrugged. "It's a code name Bantle gave you."

"Ah," the captain said. "As in Monsieur Verne's books." He seemed quite pleased by the comparison.

That was about when what he'd said about . . . *Vibrio cholerae* started to sink in, and I realized exactly what was going on. My da didn't raise no dummies, even if I am a bit trusting for my own good sometimes. Still, Mama would say it's better to think the best of people and every so often get to be disappointed than always think the worst and die alone.

"Wait. You're going to use us to start a cholera epidemic. Which you plan to have kill off all the gold miners coming out of Rapid, and maybe even spread to Alaska. And then Russia can come take Alaska back."

"That's a brain that's wasted on a woman," Standish said.

I bit my tongue to keep from spitting on his shoe. If I had it to do over . . . well, quite frankly, I would of spat in his face.

I said, "Cholera is too catching. It kills too fast. Nobody still sick will make it all the way to Anchorage."

"You just leave the details to us, little lady," Standish said. "We have thought of everything. Our cholera bacillus is *encapsulated*."

The way he said it made me think he was quoting somebody and he weren't too sure what the words actually meant. I bet they had some kind of special breed, then. Something that could lie quiet before it spread and killed.

I nodded, then regretted it. "Well, you won't be able to flog me to death if that's your plan," I told Standish. "Dead people don't shit, and you know that's how cholera gets spread. It's in fouled water, from folks already sick with it."

Priya was about vibrating with indignation, but she held her tongue. "Oh, flogging you *nearly* to death will suffice for my needs," Standish said. "Besides, we need to keep you from talking. It's all in the service of a greater good."

He turned to the Ivans and the Borises and said something in Russian that was probably, "Take them away."

Because that was what happened next.

They put Priya and me in the same cell, though, and that's when I found out why she'd been so quiet while we was being . . . not interrogated. Assessed? Assayed?

Turns out, she spoke a little Russian. And she'd been memorizing what Standish and the captain said.

I'm afraid I weren't at my most helpful. Because when she told me—we was chained up to opposite walls—all I could think to say was, "You didn't say you spoke *Russian*."

"I don't," she answered. "Well, not much. I understand a bit more of it."

My Priya. None smarter.

Briefly, we caught up. I had more to tell her than she had to tell me, though she'd figured out most of it already. She was looking at that cut on my face—or worse, she was trying not to.

I figured it was best to just face up to it, so I ponied and said, "I'd rather it was me and not you he took a fancy to."

Her lips stretched. Somebody who didn't know her might have called it a smile. "You think it's him and not Scarlet. The killer."

There was enough slack in my chains to touch my cheek if I squatted down with my back to the wall. Touching it smarted. "I'm pretty fucking certain of it."

"He must have had the sense not to shit in his own well."

I guffawed, she took me so by surprise. That's what happens, I suppose, when somebody spends too much time around

Madame. You'd think Miss Bethel would be more of a civilizing influence, but I suppose there's only so much any of us can do to counteract Madame's level of artistry of language.

"I think he only likes American girls," I said. Then I thought about it and corrected myself. "White American girls. That's all he's done, that I've heard tell."

I poked the cheek again. It smarted again. I wondered if I would learn to stop doing that.

Priya thought about it and nodded. "Like them as only like black girls. Or blondes."

"Or whatever."

It didn't make me feel too much better about my prospects. Or her, either, from the sorrowful look she gave me.

But then, being Priya, she shook herself hard enough to make her chains rattle, and she started patting herself like she was looking for something. I watched, losing myself in the expression of concentration she wore. But finally she sighed in frustration and shook her head.

"For once, I wish I wore a corset," she said. "I could use a bit of whalebone now." She held up her wrist, showing off the keyhole in the shackle on it.

What kind of a submersible ship comes with a room equipped with hasps for chaining folk, too, anyway?

"How about a hairpin?" I asked.

"This isn't one of your dime novels, Karen my love."

The fact that she called me "my love" took every bit of sting out of the other thing she said. I sniffed and shot back, "A hairpin's what I have on offer. I ain't got a set of stays on, neither. Take it or leave it."

"Take it," she said.

I found one that hadn't slipped out of the mess of knots and undone braids my coiffure had become and slid it across the floor to her. It went wide, but she snagged it with a toe and pulled it to her. She sank down with her back to the wall, picked it up, snapped it in half to make two pieces, and went to work on the lock.

I wanted to talk, but I didn't want to distract her, so I contented myself with listening to the *scratch-scratch-scratch* of the pin in the lock and watching her concentrated face.

I don't know if you've ever looked at the face of somebody you love when you're in mortal fear for your own life and also theirs. But there's nothing lovelier nor more terrifying that I have ever seen.

I wanted to memorize everything. The way the too-bright light caught in her black amber eyes and cast the reverse of shadows there. The wrinkle of absorption in her smooth brow. Her lips pressed tight, then slowly slackening as she worked the hairpin deeper.

To keep from talking, I dug into my shirt and found the warm, slick surface of Marshal Reeves' silver dollar still tucked into the wrap around my breasts. They hadn't done a real good job of searching me, and at that moment I made up my mind that from then on if I lived I would always keep a penknife tucked inside my unmentionables.

I was leaning forward by then. I could tell from Priya's face that she was making progress and also that I shouldn't say a word. She was pressing one-half the pin down and sideways with the heel of her hand while raking the other half back and forth between forefinger and thumb. She held the shackle still against her thigh while she worked, and though it was cold in that little room, sweat beaded on her lip.

Mine too, for all I was only watching.

By her expression, she just about had it, too, when we heard a key scrape in the door lock.

I snatched my fingers out of my shirt collar like I'd been doing something to be guilty for. That little warning was just enough for her to curse, snatch the hairpin halves out of the shackle, and make 'em vanish into her mouth. I hoped she'd just tucked 'em into her cheek rather than swallowing. Even Miss Lizzie and Crispin ain't got no cure for a perforated bowel.

Then the door opened and in walked the captain with his dignity, flanked by one of the Ivans and the other Boris, making up a mismatched set. I wondered if they was like carriage horses and got used to working as a team in a particular way, so if you put the wheel horse to lead, or vice versa, confusion and wrecks result.

They didn't seem confused, more's the pity. Ivan came forward and unlocked Priya. He tossed the keys to Boris, and Boris came and unlocked me. Then each of 'em guided one of us to the door. "What's this?" Priya asked Ivan.

He shook his head.

The captain stood aside so we could be led out the door. "I thought you might enjoy to see the next events."

I managed to catch Priya's eye. She didn't look no more sanguine about that than I felt.

This time we had a slightly longer scuttle through the corridors, though still not far. I watched two seamen jump out of the way behind bulkheads as the captain came by, saluting like their lives depended on it. From what I've heard about how navies is run, they just about might have.

Then we came in through another little oval hatchway—more stooping—and the next thing I knew somebody was shouting an order and a roomful of people was spinning round in their chairs and saluting while still sitting. I guess I expected them to jump up and click heels and such, but I can see the sense in not doing so when you're all crammed into a room no bigger than a good-sized pantry.

The captain said something that I expected was the Russian for "At ease," and everybody—it was only three men, but in that little space it seemed like they had sixty elbows—went back to his job. The captain gestured to Ivan and Boris to take me and Priya over behind a railing. We stood crammed up against them there. I had the damned whitewashed pipe rail digging me in the belly and Boris' hard-on digging me in the ass. I guess it was a while since he'd seen a woman.

In fairness to old Boris, he couldn't help it any more than I could. And he was a perfect gentleman about it. No wandering hands, and no rubbing up on me, neither.

The captain climbed up to the only empty chair, which was in the middle of the cramped metal room full of gauges and pipes and Christ knows what. It was also up a little bit, like a coachman's seat. A wide pipe with two handles welded on to it hung from the ceiling over his head.

"Welcome to the bridge of my ship, *Os'minog*. You may find this interesting," the captain said. He didn't look over, but it must have been for us, because he said it in English. Then he barked something in Russian, and—

I grabbed the railing in both hands.

Silently, on what must have been well-oiled tracks, a couple of jointed metal shutters slid away from the front of the submersible, revealing the biggest single pane of glass I'd ever seen. It was curved, too, fitting the prow of the ship, and I wondered how the hell they had manufactured it. It was bigger than the glass mirror over Miss Bethel's burned-up back bar. Big as I imagined the windows in a lighthouse must be.

I gasped, and it weren't just from that. Because beyond it I could see a swirl of bubbles and the tossing waters of the Sound.

At least, I hoped it was the Sound and not the open sea. It was daylight and the storm had broke, though the clouds hadn't. Gray waves slapped against the glass, and it was hard to tell where they ended and the gray skies began.

But there was something black to mark the horizon, and as

we came up on it I realized it was a ship. And I had a horrible feeling inside me that I knew exactly why it was that the man Bantle called Nemo had brought us to his bridge. We were here to witness his crimes.

Is there nothing so awful that men won't use it to try to show off to girls?

The *Os'minog* glided through the sea, seeming silent from the inside. Only the soft hum reached our feet through the floorboards. It slid closer to the ship, and I barely noticed the stream of incomprehensible commands the captain gave and the quiet responses from his crew. We could read the lettering on the ship's stern now—*Daylily,* out of Seattle—and I couldn't believe they had not seen us. But even if they had, what could they do? It was a ship full of would-be gold miners and press-ganged dogs doomed to starve or freeze in the Yukon. It weren't armed.

I wondered if we'd use torpedoes or if, like his namesake, our "Nemo" anticipated ramming the civilian ship.

My question was answered when the captain uttered a gently voiced command and the man directly in front of him answered, "Da," and threw a very large lever.

A shiver ran through the *Os'minog* and then a shudder, and then through that forward portal it seemed as if the whole hull of the ship had twisted loose and was wriggling away, forward. There was a horrible skreeling noise and the ocean all around went white—a sea of foam—lathered and frothing. Something writhed in among it.

Tentacles. They was tentacles, arms like an octopus, only jointed metal and big as tree trunks, and instead of suckers they had big, jagged barbs or teeth like God's own bread knife.

"Christ on crutches," I whispered. "And His bastard brother Harry, too."

Priya grabbed my hand on the railing. I turned mine palm

up so I could squeeze hers. The *Os'minog* surged forward, and through the frothing water I caught a glimpse of men gathered at the railing of the *Daylily,* pointing, shoving, openmouthed.

There weren't nowhere they could run.

"Os'minog," Priya whispered. "Octopus."

I thought Ivan would give her a rattle to shut her up, but he didn't even seem to have heard. He and Boris was fixed in place watching just like me and Priya, but I somehow guessed the underlying emotions to be a mite different.

The submersible shuddered and bucked. I realized we'd latched on to the *Daylily.* Those huge arms was thrashing, denting the steamer's steel sides. I saw rivets pop, the plating buckle. A man fell past, arms pinwheeling, tossed from the deck. I couldn't look. I couldn't neither look away.

"Please God," I said. Priya muttered something in her own language. She squeezed me so hard my fingers went white.

The *Os'minog*'s arms was ripping through the *Daylily*'s hull, burrowing inside, dragging out bundles of cargo and tossing them into the snapping metal beak. It had to be some kind of a water lock, I realized: there was piracy going on here.

The man operating the arms made it look like a dance. He had slipped his hands into metal mesh gloves, and he moved 'em like the conductor in the orchestra pit at the big green opera house downtown. Every time his hand jabbed, a tentacle jabbed, too. Every time his fish clenched, a coil latched around some fixture of the *Daylily* and ripped it from its moorings, then tossed it out to sea. It was piteously awful and piteously easy, and my cut and burned cheek scorched from the salt of the tears leaking over it.

It was over soon.

There was a moment of silence, a moment of bobbing wreckage and bodies going still in the froth and oil slick of the present battle, during which the bridge grew hushed and I almost thought that these men quietly giving and following lethal orders might regret what they had done as a military necessity. When all eyes were on that forward port.

That moment ended when the captain, who had been leaning toward the scene of the massacre, congratulated his crew and gave the order to shield the port, stow the arms, and submerge. Then he stood up, and turned to us with the glow of a man well satisfied. "What do you think of my beautiful machine?"

I champed my jaw, my whole mouth wet with nausea. I couldn't talk. I shook my head.

Priya could. "I think you're a monster."

The captain smiled. "I so rarely get to share these triumphs with anyone who will appreciate them. But it doesn't matter what you see, does it, ladies? You'll never get the chance to tell anyone."

I drew myself up and found my voice. "You think President Hayes won't go to war to keep Alaska?"

"Your government has no resources with which to fight another war, currently. We can't drive the Americans out of Alaska. But we can make it too costly for you to stay. Who's to argue with a cholera epidemic? And once the country is vacant . . ." He shrugged expressively. "It's open to settlement, isn't it?"

"That's horrible."

"Ah," he said. "But my country is only using the tactics pioneered by yours. Have you not heard of the use of blankets tainted with smallpox against the native tribes of North America by the English settlers here?"

I didn't do much more, quite frankly, than gape at him. Which seemed to make him think the argument was won. He cocked one of those saturnine eyebrows at me and winked while my stomach writhed around inside me like I'd swallowed a pint of live worms.

"I thought you'd see it my way. Good evening, ladies." He added something in Russian to the seamen, who took us by the elbows and drew us away. I tried to think of something to shout after him, but words deserted me, and by now you'll know that that don't happen too much.

I was staggering when they pushed us down the corridor. I'd like to blame it on exhaustion and injury, but I think it was the pure horror of what I'd just seen dragging at my feet. So many dead. With no chance to do nothing about it. Even if they could swim, anyone who jumped into the sea and avoided the wreck and the killer arms and the thrashing would freeze to death in minutes.

At least I'll say this for Ivan and Boris. They wasn't any meaner than they had to be. And after Bantle and Standish and Nemo, that seemed near enough to a kindness, just then.

Chapter Twenty-three

Well, what happened next is that Priya stabbed Ivan in the jugular with half of my hairpin. It weren't real gold—it was plate over brass—and with the swing she put behind it, it went right in. Well, maybe it weren't his jugular. Maybe it was that big artery there under the ear, the one you slit hog slaughtering. Whatever you call it. Either way, he grabbed at his neck and went over sideways.

I felt kind of bad about Ivan taking it that way, him just being a workingman and in no ways in charge of the plan. But that didn't stop me from punching old Boris in the jewels when he turned around to see what was happening. Men look for the knee, you understand. So it's better to swing with a fist when you really need to nut one.

Boris doubled over with a wheeze, and Priya kicked him on the temple straight legged. He went down on top of Ivan.

We left 'em there and ran.

Where we was running to was anybody's guess, quite honestly, but I was thinking there had to be a hatch and it had to be *up,* and freezing and drowning in the ice-cold Sound was miserably preferential to being flogged to death, if you take my meaning, and hell if we popped that hatch underwater we might founder the whole evil octopus and sink it to the sea's bottom. It could join its victims there for all I cared, and that Russian Nemo with his perfect manners could go down with it.

And then I had my greatest stroke of genius since that ham sandwich with pickles that time.

There was a fire ax behind glass in the corridor—or gangway, or whatever the hell you call it on a submersible. With a sign next to it that I'm pretty sure read: BREAK GLASS IN CASE OF EMERGENCY in Cossack.

I took one look at that thing and put my elbow through the glass. It shattered really satisfactorily, and I don't know if it was sugar glass or I was just that tired of everything's fucking shit. I turned around to see Priya holding up a pipefitter's wrench as long as your arm. There was a panel open on the bulkhead behind her and some other tools were racked inside it, but none looked as fit for mayhem as that wrench.

"Next time, spare your elbow," she suggested.

Then I had an ax in my hand, Hallelujah, and somewhere not too far away a fire alarm started to shrill.

Submersibles must have some kind of strict regulations about fires on board, because the next thing I knew my ears were popping something fierce, and I felt like the floor—the deck, I guess—was shoving at my boot soles.

I looked at Priya and Priya looked at me. I said, "We're surfacing!" and she punched the air. Then she looked dubious. "We need to find a hatch. An outside hatch."

"Do you think this thing has a lifeboat?"

"I think we're going to find out." Grimly, Priya brandished the pipefitter's wrench. "I'll freeze and drown before I stay in here. Follow me!"

Men was boiling out into the corridors, but they wasn't expecting a couple of crazy Maenads swinging Christ knows what at 'em, and we left a trail of shouts and broken wrists behind us. Amazing how nearly any man will back down if you brandish an ax in his face.

I didn't feel none too bad about it, neither.

I was just fending one off behind us, and when I turned around Priya was gone. Panic stabbed me, but then her hand closed on my arm and pulled me into a side corridor. I was pretty proud of myself that I didn't even swing the ax at her when she startled me.

She dogged the hatch behind us and then took her wrench and shoved it through the wheel that locked the door. "That should hold 'em for a bit. Come this way."

"Do you know where we're going?"

She pointed at some writing on the wall. It looked like letters, sort of. But only some of them was the same as English letters. "Exit this way," she said.

I kissed her. And then stepped back suddenly. "I mean—"

"Oh, good," she said. "I wondered if you were just putting up with me."

"Yeah," I answered. "Because that seems likely."

She grinned, all full to bubbling over with the mania of adventure. "Come on!"

She led me up a ladder through a tube so narrow it made my breath come quick and shallow—and I wondered how the Ivans and Borises had even managed to squeeze their shoulders down it. Maybe they'd been lowered into the submersible young and fed up inside it, like when you grow a pear inside a bottle to make pear brandy on.

Then we was at the top. Priya spun the hatch and threw it open—

—and I realized just how fucking cold it was out there. Savage air poured down on my head as Priya climbed out, and I gritted my teeth and followed her.

We stood on a tiny deck, drenched in seaweed. Priya grabbed a pipe railing with one hand and crouched down to scoop a tiny, flopping fish back into the sea. When she stood again, she snatched her fingers back and blew on 'em. The wind whipped our hair and plastered what passed for our clothes to our shoulders. The submersible rolled in the valleys between waves. No lifeboats in sight. It was so cold I wanted to scream.

"What if they submerge?"

"With the hatch open?" She smiled bitterly. "At least we won't go alone."

I put an arm around her. She was the only warm thing in the world. "If they come up, we jump," I said.

She nodded. We didn't need to say it—that a clean, quick death by freezing was better than whatever Standish had in mind. And that as soon as we hit that water—well, there wasn't any ice in it. But any child in Rapid could tell you how fast cold water could kill.

There was drifts of rain and curls of mist all over, and would you believe it that my damned hair was freezing up again? Maybe Merry Lee had the right idea in cropping it all off. Christ, I hoped she and Marshal Reeves had made it clean away.

I hefted my hatchet. Giving up felt like . . . well, like giving up. In a situation like this, you'd think there would be something I could chop. Pity I didn't think I could get through the Os'minog's hull. That'd be a moral victory worth dying for.

Below, a steady clanging started to echo up the hatchway. Somebody throwing their weight against the dogged and jammed hatch below. It'd probably give eventually.

I decided that I wanted to kiss Priya again, and she seemed happy enough to kiss me back—happy being a sort of a relative, under the circumstances. But when I pulled my face out of her hair, I saw something that made me smile and say, "We ain't finished yet!"

She turned to see and laughed. There, out of all them dark clouds, burst the emerald-and-carnelian belly of Minneapolis Colony's vaudevillian dirigible, swinging down low and toward us. A dark shape dangled from a rope ladder fifty feet under the gondola, the familiar duster flapping like an eagle's ragged wings.

The only way I could be gladder to see something would be if it were my sainted da come down from Heaven to wrap me in his angel wings. A duster would do, though. A duster would do.

"Be ready," Priya said. The Marshal came on, wave tops licking at his boots as the dirigible plunged below the clouds. The roar of its engines rose over the wind, shattering the illusion that it moved in silence. I ripped my trousers off—ripped 'em nearly in half—and twisted them into a loop. We each stuck an arm through one end; there was no way one of us was leaving that deck without the other.

I hurled the ax out to sea, because it felt damned good to do it.

We climbed up on the railing and waited there, arms outstretched, balanced with our shins against the top rail. The wind blew through my cotton bloomers like I was naked. Below, metal rent. The hinges on the hatch giving way. Well, they *really* couldn't submerge now. But the Marshal was only going to get one pass.

I could see there was a tangle of net on the ladder around him and that he himself was roped in good. There would be things for us to catch on to, then, and we wouldn't pull him off. That pleased me. I'd hate to be the cause of the widowing of Mrs. Jennie Reeves and the orphaning of all the little Reeveslings.

I looked at Priya and felt a strange exaltation. Whatever happened now, there weren't no question what either of us wanted. I guessed I could die knowing that.

Then the Marshal was there, howling something that might have been instructions and might have been an animal cry purely formed of one half excitement and two halves being terrified. His hands grabbed at me and my hands grabbed the net. I felt a savage jerk as Priya missed, half-fell, was swept off the railing and then used the twist of flannel binding us together to right herself and grab again. Cord cut my burned palms. I screamed. My feet kicked free; then one toe caught in the netting. Priya swung beside me, a little lower. Marshal Reeves threw his arm around the small of her back. The relict Ivan surged out of the hatchway—guess he did fit after all!— and grabbed at my still-swinging sock-clad foot. I felt his hand on my ankle, felt the pull, screamed some more as he dragged at me, feet skidding on the decking. He fetched up against the pipe railing, took it right across the kidney, and let go.

We sailed on, under the beautiful green-and-orange belly of Captain Colony's delivering airship, with the gray waves hissing and tossing their forelocks below.

Some of that might be out of order. It's all a jumble in my memory. But I do remember that the last thing I saw before the wind twisted me away was Horaz Standish and Captain Nemo, standing on the tiny deck of their submersible, Ivan crumpled at their feet, staring after the three of us like a couple of cats that bumped heads over a blue jay and had to watch it sai-i-i-il away.

One or more of 'em might have shot after us, but if they did it was only with handguns and nothing came close enough to notice. We had other problems commanding our attention, anyway.

Somehow we made it up the ladder, me cursing my hands and my cold-numbed legs with every lurch. The Marshal was trying to help me without actually putting his hands on my fundament and hoisting, and Priya was shouting advice. We would have made us a regular slapstick, if anybody had been there to see us.

I think we only lived to the top because Captain Colony had the ladder on a winch, and the distance up kept getting smaller. Then Merry Lee was hugging and hauling and pulling me into the airship, and I'm not sure which one of us was crying harder.

The next thing I knew she had checked me over and sat me down and I was clutching a mug of sweet, milky tea between hands now wrapped in fresh (and freshly blood-spotted) bandages, trying to figure out how to work it past my chattering teeth. It was still damned cold inside the gondola from the hatches being open to effect our rescue, but just being out of the wind made all the difference and I figured if I could stop shivering long enough to get some of that tea inside me while it was still hot I might just be able to manage not to die.

Hugging the tea—and Priya leaning against my arm, sharing the same wool blanket—helped enough that I eventually managed to sip some. That done, I had enough control of my voice to ask, "How'd you find us?"

The Marshal slurped his own tea. "We tracked his exhaust pipe. We were trying to figure out how to force him to surface when you girls did that for us."

Colony, at the controls, shook his head. "I wish we could have got to him before he got to that ship."

We was all silent for a minute, and then I said, "Yeah."

Then I realized who I hadn't seen on the *Os'minog*. "Did you get Scarlet?"

Reeves shook his head.

Priya and me filled 'em all in real quick on what had happened, and that Standish was Reeves' man rather than Scarlet.

"Pity," Reeves said. Then he shrugged. "Well, I done harder things than get Horatio Standish back to Oklahoma. And you ladies done thwarted their cholera plan."

"For now," Merry said. She looked grim.

The Marshal said, "Before they captured you, they had to have planned on some other means of getting it into the city."

"If it were me," Priya said, "I'd get it into the water supply on a ship headed north."

"Or the expedition food," Merry Lee agreed. "Get it right out into the mining camps."

We was silent for a minute, contemplating that. It took some of the sting out of what might happen to Rapid . . . but it didn't lessen the threat to Anchorage and the Yukon none.

I finished my tea. It would do me more good inside than out, no matter how turned my stomach was. I was just running a finger around the inside to get the last of the sugar when Captain Colony called from the front of the bridge.

"There's worse news."

We're not cowards, none of us. But not a one of the three of us wanted to ask.

"He's gotten that thing under way again. And it's steaming for Rapid City."

When I shook my head, my hair slapped wetly on my ears. "I gotta get to my sewing machine."

Chapter Twenty-four

We didn't have no trouble beating the submersible back to Rapid—turns out there's some advantages to airships—and I'd like to say it was a pleasant flight, but in all honesty I don't remember a damned thing about it. Priya and me lay down on the couch for just a minute, watching the gray outside the window all featureless as fog. Which I guess it was, after a fashion. Or rather, fog is clouds.

And the next thing I knew, Merry was crouched down beside me and Priya, shaking us both awake. It was still daylight and the windows was still gray, but there was some texture to it now. As I watched—as we dropped lower, I guessed—the gray broke into streamers and billows across the top of the window, and then we was low enough to see the dirty cotton-wool texture of the cloud bellies up close. I wanted to reach out and touch 'em. They looked solid as ice, but I knew if I put a hand out it'd be just mist and cold between my fingers.

"We're landing," Merry said, somewhat unnecessarily, and left us with a pot of coffee while we rubbed our eyes and sorted ourselves. There was clothing laid out, all of it for a man twice my size, but beggars can't be choosers and there was a hank of cord to use for belts. I tied on a pair of Captain Colony's trousers over my wind- and rope-shredded bloomers and felt much better, all in all.

I'd fallen asleep with the Marshal's silver dollar in the hand that wasn't wrapped around Priya's. It was turning into a kind of talisman for me, and I tucked it back into my bindings—but not before sneaking it a little kiss. Priya saw, I noticed when I turned around, and I felt a little apprehension knot in my breast, but she just winked and smiled and went back to struggling a comb through her hair.

We had time. When I looked out the window now, I saw Rapid all spread out below us—ragged buildings and people small as ants—and so I led her to the window so we could both watch while I combed her hair. I braided it good and tight—a French braid—and then she did mine in a five-strand weave that used up most of the length and got it right up out of my way. Comfortable—and pretty, too.

By then the Marshal was awake, and Merry came back with sandwiches and cookies. The cookies and the bread was stale; the meat was potted; there weren't no green but pickles. I ate it like I'd never seen food before.

Amazing what sleep and food will do for you. By the time the little cigar and matchboxes below turned into proper houses and shops and men was running out on to the airfield to lash Captain Colony's airship down, I felt almost human again.

"You think Bantle's back here already?" Priya asked me.

I bit my lip. "Probably came back with Scarlet. I think we might have seen him, if he was on that *Octopus*."

We hired a wagon to bring us back to the mayor's house—Priya and me might have been able to walk it, but it wouldn't have been pretty—and it turned out to be a good thing, too. Because when we got up there, we could tell right away that something was wrong. There was constables going in and out of the front door, which was standing open, and neighbors finding any sort of excuse at all to be out in the street twisting one another's ears off with gossip. Marshal Reeves touched the teamster on the shoulder, showed him his badge, and asked him to keep driving. The teamster shook the reins over his mules and didn't speak a word.

Men are polite when you slip them a whole silver dollar for a twenty-cent job.

We kept rolling past, and I was proud of myself for managing not to scream when a man and a woman walked up beside the cart as if it was something they did every day and swung up beside us. A second later, and I was glad I hadn't disgraced myself, because it was Crispin and Miss Francina. Miss Francina was in the plainest dress I've ever seen her in, and Crispin was dressed like a laborer in flannel and a canvas coat. They settled in, and the cart kept rolling. "We hoped you'd come back," Crispin said before I could ask. "Things is bad, Miss Karen."

I looked at Miss Francina. She nodded, mouth and eyes tight under her bonnet. "Madame's in jail," she said. "The mayor too. Miss Lizzie and Miss Bethel."

"Who puts the mayor in jail?!" I asked.

I knew, though. Even before Crispin turned his head and spat. "Peter Bantle."

"He's declared martial law," Miss Francina said. "He's declared himself mayor."

"We broke his machine!" I felt betrayed by the whole damn universe. People were supposed to come back to *our* side when Bantle wasn't running their thoughts for 'em no more.

"I think he paid off the constables," Miss Francina said.

"Shit," I answered. "All that time we spent under one or another of those ungrateful bastards. You'd think it'd count for something."

She laughed—the sweet, girlish giggle that took ten years off her. "How do you think I got away?"

"The others?" I asked. Merry Lee and Priya were tucked back under the canvas cover, but I could see them leaning forward out of the corner of my eye, straining after every word.

"Beatrice, Effie, and Pollywog are all safe," Miss Francina said. "We've been taking it in turns to watch for you."

"Where are they?"

"We've been staying—well, the Professor knew somebody. He said I was hiding from a mean drunken husband." She held up her ring finger. A tiny diamond glittered there. "Crispin's my groom, and Effie and Pollywog are my daughters. We told the Professor's friend I had another daughter, too, and I was trying to get her away from my husband."

"What about Bea?"

"Well, that's my little girl," Crispin drawled affectedly. "She's a right fine lady's maid and don't you forget it!"

Gravel gritted under the cart wheels. His face fell. "I don't know how long we can stay there. And I don't know where Tomoatooah got off to, begging your pardon, Marshal."

"He got away?" Reeves' shoulders maybe eased a little under his salt-stained black canvas coat.

"Yessir."

"Then I ain't worried about him."

I was worried, though. "What about Signor?"

"Bea ain't let him out of her sight." Crispin nodded, satisfied. "But"—his face creased with worry again as he glanced over his shoulder—"I don't know what we're going to say about Priya, if we bring her back."

"Priya can stay with me," Merry said.

Marshal Reeves gave the teamster another dollar.

Miss Francina picked at the fingertip of one of her gloves. "We need to start thinking about how to get out of the city. And how we're getting Madame out of jail."

"We thought of making for Vancouver," Crispin said. "We could bail her, but I don't know if Madame would agree to jump bail."

"She won't," I said.

Miss Francinca nodded, of course. "Madame never ran from anything this side of a Kodiak bear."

It was the right thing to say. I remembered that damned barn cat and what I'd decided on the *Octopus*. And I remembered that if we ran there wasn't nobody to stop Bantle and Standish and Nemo from doing whatever the hell they liked.

And I remembered that the man paying off the teamster was a duly sworn and appointed lawman of the United States and Territories and that he hadn't revoked his deputizing of me yet. Which made me a duly appointed lawwoman, of sorts.

"The jail they got 'em in. It's the one in Chinatown?"

"Bantle's turf," Crispin said. "Of course."

"Not just his turf," replied Merry Lee.

"Ain't none of us gonna run," I said. "We're gonna fight."

The thing that stumped me most was what we were going to do to get the sewing machine back. But once Priya and Merry Lee and the Marshal and me explained the complex of problems to the others—this was after we paid off that teamster and left him behind, not anywhere close to anything that might be construed as a destination, and Merry Lee led us through byways to a room in Chinatown where she said nobody on earth was likely to bother us—everybody was agreed that we had to bring the fight to Bantle. And not just to bust Madame out of jail.

"How long do you think it'll take this submersible to reach us?" Miss Francina asked.

Marshal Reeves huffed through his mustache. "That'd be a question for Captain Colony, I'm afraid. I ain't no expert on steamship velocities, underwater or otherwise."

"Is the ship like to be a real problem?" I asked. "I mean, I figure they got the cholera on board, probably in drums of water, right? But all we gotta do is stop those from being shipped to Anchorage."

"What if they decide to release it here after all?" Crispin asked. "They could just dump it in a cistern down by the docks. Or at one of the cribhouses. Hell, Bantle's cribhouse. The sailors would cart the infection off to Anchorage inside their intestines, if what you say about them having some kind of . . . dormant and hibernating . . . variety is true."

I bit my lip. They could. And would. And no one the wiser until people started dying in droves.

Priya said, "If their plan needed Bantle to be mayor, then it wasn't ready to spring yet anyway. We might have rushed them by crashing their party."

"There's too much we ain't privy to," said Marshal Reeves. He hunkered down under his hat, elbows on knees. In his black duster, he could have passed for a raven skinchanged into a man and none too happy about it. "But that's the way of it. So we work from what we do know."

In the pregnant silence that followed, the careful tap on the door of the room that no one was supposed to be tapping on sounded like shotgun blasts. I jumped so high I near came down next to my pants.

The Marshal flicked his duster back from his pistols, but Merry laid a gentling hand on his elbow and he settled some.

"If it were the constables," she said, "they would just have kicked in the door. Besides, I know that knock."

She was right, it turned out. Because when she unbarred the door and opened it, beyond was Aashini and Tomoatooah. They sidled in, and Merry barred the door once more.

It was getting damned close in that windowless closet, and we had long since run out of places to sit. But after Priya and Aashini had finished hugging each other until I thought their ribs would crack, it transpired that the newcomers had brought a passel of steamed Chinese buns—chicken and vegetables— and a salty sharp sauce to slather on 'em. And they'd brought news, too, though that waited a minute.

I never did find out how Merry got word to Aashini where we were. But I hadn't understood a single word she said to her countrymen on the way in, neither, so that ain't too much of a mystery.

We settled again—cheek by jowl, at this point, and wishing for a breeze—and had recommenced arguing about whether to take on Peter Bantle direct like, and how to get our hands on Standish when he was somewhere under the Sound with the Russian Nemo, and whether we should just go bust Madame out of jail with dynamite five minutes ago.

That was when Tomoatooah started telling us about what he'd seen in the last day or so, which he'd spent spying on Bantle. Namely, that as of an hour previous when he'd tracked down Aashini at Merry's other safe house, he'd just come from Bantle's temporary lodging, where he was receiving visitors. To wit, Horaz Standish and an older white man, well dressed, answering the description of the Russian Nemo. They must have rushed right there as soon as the *Octopus* made it into the harbor—and it had to have made better time than Captain Colony thought possible, too.

Tomoatooah'd been with Aashini when the runner had come

from Merry Lee informing her of our whereabouts. They had sensibly decided that the best plan was for us to regroup and share information.

A useful fellow, that Tomoatooah. He was only saved from perfection by the fact that he told us these details through a mouthful of half-chewed vegetable bun.

"Where's the sewing machine?" I asked. "The Singer. The one I used in the fire."

"Still at the mayor's house, as far as I know," said Miss Francina.

Crispin said, "You aren't plotting what I think you're plotting, young lady."

I pasted my most innocent expression on. "If Nemo's here, his submersible must be in the harbor, right? Ready to pick him up? I can think of one way to end the threat of it sinking ships for good and all. And put paid to any chance of a cholera epidemic, also."

He spent a long time looking at me, and I spent just as long looking back.

"Besides," I said. "I bet after all Miss Lizzie's done to hot-rod it, that Singer can bust down a jailhouse wall pretty well. Don't you?"

Crispin frowned and stared harder. I smiled more. The stand-off only ended because Miss Francina put her chicken bun down on her knee, sighed, and said, "You know if we don't help her, she's just going to try to do it by herself."

Butter wouldn't have melted in my smile, I swear.

So it was Marshal Reeves who tore strips of black fabric into masks, which we snipped eyeholes in with Miss Francina's nail scissors—of *course* she had them in her reticule. We all tied them over our faces until we looked like a pack of cartoon banditos, and by then it was dark enough that we slunk out into the night. We split up, because that always works out so well for the heroes in the dime novels. Most of our party stayed in Chinatown but took off over the roofs under Merry's guidance toward the building down by the waterfront where Bantle processed his new-imported indenturees. Apparently, he was staying there until he got his parlor fixed.

My heart bled, I tell you.

Aashini had stayed behind, though Priya had had to twist her arm something awful to make it happen. She had a letter written out by Miss Francina and addressed to Mr. Orange Jacobs, who had been the Chief Justice of the Supreme Court of the Territory of Washington until 1875 and who was now the Territory's Delegate to the Congress of the United States, even if he couldn't vote there. In this letter was explained everything we'd learned about what Bantle and Nemo and Standish were up to.

So even if we all died, somebody would find out the truth and maybe be able to do something about it.

Merry Lee would have been the member of our company most specialized for second-story work, but as she was occupied, me and the Comache made do. He collected Adobe and Scout from the livery where they was stabled, and we made our way up the hill at a good trot. Not fast enough to draw attention but not slow, either.

The masks stayed inside our collars for now, tucked down like range bandannas.

We left the mares a street away, tied to a hitching rail, and crept around the back of the mayor's house. Tomoatooah lifted me through the window on the back porch roof while the constables milled about more or less uselessly below, and it was Tomoatooah and me who creeped down the servants' stair by stepping only on the edges of the risers, where the boards wouldn't creak. Most of the activity around the place seemed to have halted with suppertime. Though there was guards at each of the doors, the constant in-and-out had stopped and we moved through the shadows of the stairwell unobserved.

I knowed the Singer was in one of the rooms at the back of the house, and it was easy enough to figure out which one because the doorway smelled like rancid smoke. I made a face, but Tomoatooah was right at my shoulder, and we'd been through too much together for me to let him down. Besides, I'd be letting the whole city—the whole nation, and President Hayes to boot!—down if I didn't go through with it.

Tomoatooah patted me on the shoulder, and I pretended not to notice that his hand was still trembling some from the shock he'd taken. I hoped it would heal up, given time.

The door was already cracked. And the mayor's staff did a good job keeping the hinges oiled. We eased it open and greased inside.

The room loomed with shadows. There was some light from the outside—up here on the hill, they had gas lamps along the streets and some of the houses had electric arcs to illuminate their patios. One across the wide back lawn actually had a garden party going on—in the middle of winter, no less, with tall perforated stoves for heaters, and those lights glaring off everything. At least it was a clearer night than the day had been. And I reckon it gave those rich folk the chance to show off their furs.

I hoped they all caught pneumonia.

And there, hulking in the center of the room, was Madame's battered sewing machine.

Maybe it was the darkness, but the armature looked better than I had anticipated by a considerable.

The straps were hanging loose and the hasps were open, like they hadn't moved a thing since they pried me out of it. It still smelled like a fire in a cathouse, too. But I stepped inside and with Tomoatooah's help got it strapped on tight—and actually fitted properly this time. We'd decided we would fire up the steam engine first, and then once it came up to pressure we'd crank up the diesel, what with the diesel being louder.

Of course, that's when we discovered that the reservoirs was dry. Fortunately, there was a kerosene stove in that same room and a pump handle in the kitchen just one hall over. We filled the thing up with kero and water and we primed it and lit it. And then settled in to try to wait real quiet while the water began to heat.

The good news was it didn't make much noise while it was just coming up to a boil, and to pressure. Tomoatooah took advantage of the twenty minutes or so while I was trapped inside the thing in a rising state of anxiety to sit down in the corner with his rifle across his knees, fold his arms over the rifle, and take a nap. I just tried to stand still and concentrate on my breathing.

Finally the pressure gauge edged up into the green. I turned the valve, and the hiss of released steam and the thump of pistons wakened Tomoatooah. Shaky or not, he was on his feet in an instant.

A good thing, too, because *that* noise had carried far enough to alert the constables. Their boots was thudding down the hallway toward us while he turned the crank to spark the diesel engine. Their voices echoed through the empty house. We wouldn't make it to either door without stomping over the lot of 'em.

Just as well that had never been our intention.

I took three running steps toward the full-length windows and crashed through a pair of them, then out onto the porch. Boards splintered under the weight of the armature, so I kept moving, running, bursting through the rail. Tomoatooah was hot on my heels, and we thudded across the frozen ground toward the nearest hedge and a line of safe deep shadows before the first bullets started to cut the air.

Either a sergeant arrived or a cooler head prevailed, because there were only a few gunshots before the constables seemed to realize they were shooting toward a garden party full of rich folk and quit. First time the bourgeoisie ever did much for me.

By then Tomoatooah and me was among the trees, and by the time the constables actually got themselves organized to chase us I was flat out running and he was back up on Scout, leading Adobe—and we was long, long gone.

We expected a pursuit. But it didn't materialize immediately, and then we took to side alleys and thought maybe we'd eluded 'em for a bit. Not for long, though, because it turns out sprinting through the streets of Rapid in a sewing machine with one busted, stiff, grinding knee joint and a Red Indian for an outrider does draw something of a crowd. Fortunately, we was moving so fast that we stayed ahead of the interest, and inside of twenty minutes we had made it back to Chinatown.

Just in time to catch up to the gun battle outside the jailhouse. And—not too much later—for the gun battle to catch up to us.

I don't know whether one of our folk started proceedings prematurely or if Bantle and Standish and their boys looked out the window at the wrong minute and caught the Marshal and Crispin and Miss Francina and Merry and Priya slipping up on them. There wasn't exactly time to get a straight story out of anybody.

Tomoatooah and me came running up—well, he came running; I came thudding—and we heard the sound of gunfire from three blocks off, just where the plain brick facades started to

give way to ornate wrought iron painted in brilliant reds and
blues and greens and oranges, marking the boundary of Chinatown. We slowed down, then, under the big banner with
the bright gold characters I'd have to ask Priya to read to me,
someday.

If we both happened to live through this.

People was sheltering in doorways, huddled behind the corners of buildings, and scrunched down at the bottoms of the
walkway wells. Trying to stay out of the line of fire. I could
just make out the gray-painted clapboard of the jailhouse up
ahead and the bright licks of muzzle flash from inside it.

I figured the odds were good that they hadn't seen us yet
through the dark, and in the noise of that firefight they sure
hadn't heard us. It looked like at least some of our friends had
taken shelter in a side street opposite, and I couldn't tell if they
were returning fire. Or even who was over there: from this side,
all we could tell was where the people inside the jailhouse were
concentrating their fire.

Tomoatooah reined Scout back, which seemed like a good
idea to me. I wouldn't ride down a street toward shooters inside a building if I had any choice at all, either. He sidestepped
her into Passage Street, Adobe following, and I went with 'em.
We stopped by the side door of a block of apartments, with
five or six trash bins lined up beside it. The horses, I will say,
was damned calm about that hissing contraption I was piloting,
too. They seemed more nervous about the drop down to sidewalk level.

I looked down at my arms, shielded under the steel plates
at the front, and sighed. This one was going to be up to me.

I was grateful for all the time Miss Lizzie had put into tinkering with the thing, also. If I made it off this waterfront alive,
I was going to pay for an inventor's license and set her up in
business as a Mad Scientist.

But right now, Priya and close to half of everybody else I had ever cared about was down there somewhere being shot at, and unless I was much mistaken, it was my plan to bust out Madame that had gotten them into that position. I looked at Tomoatooah. He scowled back and unlimbered his Colt.

I said, "At least the constables ain't gotten here yet."

"I'll go around back," he offered. He hooked a thumb over that black rag mask and pulled it up to cover his eyes. When it was settled to his liking, he unhooked Adobe's reins from his saddle biscuit and dropped them on the curb. The horse snorted and dropped her head, like she didn't think much of this turn of events but was willing to play along.

"Well, I guess that makes me the distraction," I said, and picked up a metal trash bin lid in each one of the Singer's dented hands.

It would have been nice if I could have used those sunken side-walks to stay out of the line of fire, but there was one more drawback of them not connecting to one another underneath the roads. As it was, well, the darkness was my best advantage, and I was going to use it. And going to use every other thing I had at my disposal to get the attention of the defenders inside the jailhouse away from my friends.

Surely they couldn't be pinned down. If nothing else, that side street that was drawing all the fire opened out on the water-front at the back.

Would have been nice to have had a firearm, anyhow.

"So much for a nice quiet jailbreak," I muttered. Hefting my bin lids, I pumped up the pressure in the Singer again, and started to run.

For the first time since I can't remember when, luck was with me. At least for the next thirty seconds or so, as I bolted the

length of that street in the dark, inside the shuddering armature of that sewing machine.

I blessed Lizzie and Priya every step of the way. These things
ain't built for running—or climbing walls, or punching out of
burning houses, for that matter—but their tinkering had turned
it into the next best thing to a one-woman ironclad. The gyroscopes meant all I had to do was keep the feet rising and falling,
which given the dark and the uncertain footing was a blessing
and a half. And in that dark, I was three-fifths of the way
down the block to the Chinatown jail before anybody inside it
realized where that clanking and thudding was coming from
and that they should be concerned about it. Bullets commenced to rattle and spark off the stones around me, and one
or two ricocheted off my galvanized trash bin lids.

I thumped past the side street where the shooters inside the
jailhouse had been aiming before I arrived, and though I didn't
turn my head to try and peer through the dark at who was
there, I heard Priya's voice raised in a wild shout as I cantered
past. Sparks snapped from under my feet, and some of 'em was
from bullets and some was from the grippers on the Singer's
treads. That sticky knee still grated with every step, but I pushed
it through the motion and it got easier. Whatever was bent in
there must be wearing off or grinding loose. I heard somebody
running behind me, and more gunfire back there, and the barrage from the jail let up. A few shots still whizzed past me, but
they was unaimed, and from the flash it looked like somebody
was just firing out the window corner and hoping to get lucky.

A bullet spanged off the cage beside my face and something
hot shocked my cheek and ear. I thought it was just sparks,
and between the crop weal and the burns from the glove I
couldn't care much more than that if it were a bullet crease.
A big gun spoke to my left, and the flash at the window corner
stopped. I looked over to see the Marshal running, his Win-

chester at his shoulder. He'd shot right through the clapboard siding and got his man.

The wall of the Chinatown jail loomed up like a clapboard cliff. And to nobody's surprise more than mine, I jumped across the sidewalk trench like it wasn't even there and busted right through the jailhouse siding in a blizzard of spruce-scented splinters.

Contracted out to the lowest bidder, I bet.

I fell three feet on the other side, because the floor was lower than the road. The Singer caught and balanced me, though the joists creaked and bowed under the impact. I realized I'd lost the garbage lids somewhere. For a moment, I thought I'd be plunging through to the ground floor, but despite protest the planks held. There was a dead Russian—all right, fair enough, I assumed he was a Russian—slumped in the corner beside the window, the walls around him streaked and daubed in red. Looking at that almost gave me a second view of my chicken buns, but I kept my head together and the Singer kept me on my feet.

The cells were probably on the ground floor, I reckoned. What would be the belowground floor now.

I was pounding down the stairs, rounding the first landing before I realized that I should have picked up the dead man's gun. The banister tore off in the Singer's gripper, but the gyros saved me, and it was too late to turn back now.

There was gunshots at the next landing. I just kept running, remembering something some war-veteran john had told me about crossing battlefields, and how it was better to be the first man running through a gap than the second. Move fast, and keep on moving.

I missed my garbage can lids then, but I plunged down the

stairs with my arms raised in front of my face. I didn't hear or feel anything ricochet off the Singer, and—even better—I didn't feel anything slam into my flesh.

My foot went through a riser on the next flight. My left hand plunged into the plaster wall as I unbalanced, and it was sheerest luck that behind splintered lath and wads of horsehair, I found a stud. It cracked as the Singer's gripper closed on it, but it didn't shatter, and it gave me the leverage I needed to yank myself free. Then I rounded the final landing and knocked the door at the bottom right out of its hinges. It flew across the room and clanged into the bars of a cell, then tipped and fell to the floor with a crash.

For a moment, I stood panting, my ears full of the hiss of steam and the roar of the diesel engine, and had a look around the room. Madame stood inside the cell, back straight and shoulders back. No mere oaken door bouncing off the bars a foot from her face was going to draw a flinch from Madame Damnable.

Mayor Stone had flinched back onto the bench behind her. I didn't spare him much of a look, however, because what drew my attention was the sound of a shotgun being racked.

I looked toward it and found myself face–to–face with Bruce Scarlet, or whatever his real name was. The Russian engineer stood two steps in front of Horaz Standish, alongside the left side of that cell where the constable's desk was, and they both of 'em was heeled and standing over a pair of overturned chairs like they'd been taking their ease down here while the firefight raged out front.

They had me dead to rights.

It's one thing to run through a storm of bullets in the dark or when you're passing across a narrow passage and you know the bad guy's ain't got much time to aim. It's another to charge right at two men with a bead on you already, one with a ten-gauge street sweeper and one with a Winchester cocked and aimed at your eye.

Slowly, with a creak of stressed metal and a shower of plaster dust, I raised the Singer's scratched and dented arms.

The roar of a long arm beside and behind me near to deafened me, and I flinched from it so hard that if it weren't for the Singer's gyroscopes I would have pitched right over and sprawled. As it was, I staggered and twisted and danced drunkenly halfway across the room.

Buckshot pattered off the Singer's frame and something smacked into my hip and thigh. Madame hollered a curse that was probably exceptional even by her standards, if I could have made it out—but it ended with, "Horaz Standish, you obtuse son of a syphilitic bitch."

I also thought I heard Horaz yelp, but my ears was ringing so I couldn't be sure.

When I managed to drag myself upright, the first thing I saw was Bruce Scarlet in a puddle of sticky, stinking red, the top of his head clean gone.

Reader, this time I didn't manage to keep those chicken buns from revisiting daylight. When I straightened up inside the Singer—and discovered I couldn't wipe my mouth on the back of my sleeve because of the mica visor and the armature—it was to see Marshal Reeves grinning at me from behind his black strip of mask as he twisted Standish's arms behind his back and locked the shackles on. Horaz had a good big welt on his temple, and I noticed one of Madame's hard-heeled borrowed purple velvet boots lying against the wall.

Merry Lee came out of the busted stairwell door behind me, crouched down by what was left of Scarlet, and pulled a ring of keys off his belt. She didn't seem troubled by the mess. When she straightened up, I saw she was wearing a black strip across her eyes and the bridge of her nose, too, with a range hat pulled low to shade her features. If she'd had a bandanna tugged up to cover her face, she would have looked like a cow-boy kitted for a range war.

"Where's Priya?" I asked.

"Covering the exit," she answered.

Keys jingling, spattering drops of red (I looked at the wall), she jogged to the cell and fiddled with the locks until she opened it. Madame came out, hopping on her good foot and supported by Mayor Stone. At least he made a halfway decent walking cane.

Marshal Reeves strong-armed Standish toward the cell while Merry stood ready with the keys. That seemed like a fine idea to me, but I admit I was wondering where Peter Bantle and Captain Nemo was. I still made a point of looking Horaz in the face when they walked him past. "I hear hanging don't hurt so much as flogging to death," I told him when he curled his lip in a sneer. "It's humane, like."

He spat at the Singer's feet. He missed.

"Careful," I told Marshal Reeves. "He keeps a riding crop in his boot."

Reeves flourished it in his free hand. I hadn't even seen him relieve Standish of it, but I guess a U.S. Marshal gets pretty sharp at patting suspects down.

That door clanking shut was a very fine sound.

"Karen," Merry Lee said when she'd turned the lock and checked the door, "I saw Bantle running on down toward the waterfront when I came in. He was too far away to me to catch him, but—"

She waved at the Singer. *But you could.*

The gesture drew Marshal Reeves' attention, and I caught the flash of whites as his eyes widened behind the mask. His duster flared as he turned toward me.

But it was Madame who put her hand on the Singer's elbow and said, "Karen, you're bleeding."

I looked down, spotted the blood soaking through the cloth at my hip, and quickly looked away again. The good news was I had no lunch left to lose. "He just winged me," I said. "Don't hurt yet."

It would, I knew. But for now, I wasn't lying; the crop cut across my cheek hurt more, and my lungs was on fire. This was going to be pneumonia before too much longer and no mistake.

But that was a problem for if I lived through today. And right now, I was going to go get Peter goddamned Bantle if it was the last goddamned thing I did.

I busted three more stairs on my way back up again and jumped back to the road through the hole I'd left coming in. The Singer was making some horrible grinding noises through that damaged knee and around the hip joint, but it still moved and balanced. My jump back across the sidewalk gap left me dizzy with pain from the impact on the other side, though. Especially where it jarred my hip, and sent a fresh slick of wet heat down my thigh.

I turned in the road. I didn't see Priya or Tomoatooah, Miss Francina or Crispin anywhere. But I could see the waterfront from here, only a block downhill, and that was the direction Merry Lee had said Bantle had run.

I set off in pursuit.

Every step jarred my hip, and the hydraulics along that leg shrieked and smoked. I screamed through gritted teeth with every one of those first eight or ten strides as the armature dragged on my creased hip. Then my body seemed to resign itself to the abuse, and it started to hurt less. I picked up speed, running hard.

The sky, I realized a little dizzily, was turning gray. When I broke out onto Front Street I could see up and down the waterfront quite a ways in the gloaming, and out along the docks that floated in the quiet waters of the harbor.

And there was Peter Bantle—looking away from me, standing alongside a warehouse just this side of Commerce Pier, with Captain Nemo facing him—about two hundred yards away. Bantle waved his arms, and even over the clanking and growling of the Singer I heard his raised voice, if not his words.

Nemo wore a plain black suit rather than his uniform, but even at this distance I recognized him by that trim silver beard. He had a revolver in one hand, though that hand was down by his side, and I realized that *again* I'd forgotten to pick up a weapon. I was just an all-around terrible failure as a commando, and that was that.

"I found them!" I yelled, hoping somebody who liked me was close enough to hear. Then I lurched toward them at the Singer's increasingly unsteady run.

It weren't quiet.

Bantle paused in the middle of one of his better arm waves and turned toward me. "You son of a bitch!" he yelled—at Nemo, I guessed, rather than at me. "If you'd just agreed to take me with you we would have been gone by now!"

Bantle turned back toward me, pushing his coat back—to get at a revolver, I was guessing. I was gritting my teeth for another hail of bullets, too—

Then Nemo shot Peter Bantle in the back.

I almost tripped over the Singer's feet.

Bantle went down on his knees like he was falling through molasses. Nemo didn't seem concerned; he dropped the hot gun in his pocket, which didn't seem like the best idea, and turned his attention to a little black box that appeared in his other hand.

Bantle finished toppling forward. He ended up on his face, and his hat couldn't cover the stain spreading out underneath his head. I didn't gag this time; maybe I was already as sick of gore as it was possible for me to get.

Nemo thumbed a toggle switch on his box, like a little silver chessman, and a red light started blinking. I recognized the kissing cousin of the little box that has been supposed to let us know that Miss Francina needed a rescue when she was sneaking into Bantle's crib. The difference being, apparently this one was functional.

I had a real bad feeling I knew what happened next.

The dock beside me exploded into splinters as the *Octopus* lurched up through it, all its mechanical arms uncoiling explosively. I staggered sideways, but the Singer caught me. I most certainly did *not* scream. And even if I had, no one would have been able to hear me over the Pandemonium of shrieking metal and shattering wood. Writhing metal tentacles whipped overhead with a whistling screech, splinters scattering from their barbs, rattling off the metal cage that protected me. One whistled out toward Nemo—

He stood calmly, watching it come. I didn't think it would hurt him, somehow. This was his escape. Then he could just come back later when the heat had died down, or head up to Seattle or down to San Francisco, and work his evil plan over from scratch again.

And there was nothing I could do about it. Where on earth had I ever gotten the idea that the Singer would be any use against something like this?

A racing blur of black and white peeled from behind the warehouse, trailing the hollow cannonade of unshod hooves. I had a confused glimpse of Tomoatooah leaning low over

Scout's neck, her streaked mane whipping back as she ran. I froze in terror as a barbed tentacle whipped down. Scout dodged to avoid it, back feet where her front feet had been, and the road shifted under my feet with the force of the blow.

Then Tomoatooah had Nemo by the collar and was dragging him beside Scout. They charged toward me and suddenly those tentacles was writhing helplessly on all sides, slapping, trying to startle and herd the horse. One slammed down right before her, denting itself and shattering stone. Scout jumped it like she was born to steeplechase and pelted toward me, stretching out to a hard straight run.

Tomoatooah had somehow dragged Nemo up over his saddle. He stretched out toward me, something in his hand. I reached toward him. He hurtled past, Scout so close her lather splattered the mica visor. I looked down.

Three sticks of dynamite wrapped with tape, burning an inch of fuse, hissed in the Singer's claw.

"Holy Christ!" I shouted, and the *Octopus* wrapped a tentacle around my armature and whipped me into the air.

I slung hard against the straps, one direction and the other, and felt the thing's battered hip joint give—and then my hip wrench, too, torn or separated as the weight of the Singer's leg fell just on me. I think the force might have torn my leg off if the *Octopus'* tentacle hadn't been wrapped all around me, holding me together.

The barbs scratched and bruised, and there was a sharp pop as the thing squeezed—but the Singer's armature held. For now.

I screamed now, all right. And somehow, maybe just because the gripper locked until you intentionally released it, I held on to that dynamite. If nothing else, I figured, maybe if I was still holding on to it when it went off it might blow this thing's tentacles back down its throat. I wouldn't even have to be alive.

Which was just as well. I didn't relish getting blown up none.

The *Octopus* was thrashing around, still, splintering ships and dock, but it didn't seem able to drag itself out of the water. Maybe it was hoping if it broke enough things Tomoatooah would bring its master back.

I was just about to settle in for a nice refreshing faint, the world getting black and thick around the edges, when the *Octopus* whipped me around one more time and I caught sight of that big, snapping metal beak that the arms usually folded up to cover. And Reader, I had one of my very occasional good ideas.

I unlocked the Singer's gripper and cocked my arm back, bided my time until I was dangling near the maw and there was only a whisper of slow match left, and hurled that dynamite inside.

I made it, too. And either I timed that fuse right or the chomping beak itself detonated the dynamite.

A shudder ran through the thing, and a cloud of black smoke billowed from the beak. The *Octopus* started to slide backward, still thrashing—that hadn't been enough to torpedo it entirely, then. The arms were folding up tight again, closing over the beak. But not sealing as tight as before! The whole front of the submersible was twisted slightly askew, so it couldn't close itself up into a smooth, almost-seamless cone.

I wished them luck limping back to Russia like that, the sons of bastards. And I wondered for a moment why it was that I wasn't hearing the tremendous rasping and grating of metal, before I realized I wasn't hearing much of anything at all.

Then I was falling through the air, shaken loose from the barbed arm, and the ground came up and struck me—and the Singer—a prodigious blow.

———

I woke to find Priya kneeling beside me, reaching through the cage to touch my cheek and press my face. I squinted; her lips were moving. I couldn't hear what she said over the flat, painful ringing in my ears. But once she saw my eyes open, she smiled a dazzling smile.

Carefully, steadily, she unlocked the Singer's retaining bars and unbuckled the harness.

She caught me when I rolled out, too. Then she kissed me on the cheek like she didn't mind the blood on my face or the vomit in my hair. I couldn't stand; my hip hurt that much. But I was happy just to lay in her lap and let her stroke my hair.

After a bit, I decided I was probably even going to live, though I might regret it for a while.

Priya squeezed my hand until my eyes opened again. From watching her lips, I figured out what she said: "I need to confess something."

I looked at her, so serious, and a chill settled into my chest. It was going to be bad news, whatever it was. Nobody ever got told nothing good lying in the middle of the smoking ruins of a city dock.

Then she said, "I read your journal."

My hearing was coming back, but I must have heard that wrong. "You—wait, *what*?"

"Please don't be angry," she said. "I just . . . I missed you, and I couldn't find you, and I was scared. And once I started, Karen, I couldn't stop. You tell stories better than *any* of the ones we read in the library." She looked at me so earnestly I almost melted.

I opened my mouth. I closed it again.

She said, "What if we got Captain Colony to bring your manuscript back to Chicago? Or even New York? You know he said he knows writers. Maybe one of them would write a letter of introduction to a publisher. . . ."

She trailed off, looking at my face.

"That's not what you want."

"It is what I want," I said.

I struggled to get up, and after a minute she gave up fighting with me about it. Over her shoulder, I saw Crispin and Francina jogging toward us, the Marshal and Merry behind them. Tomoatooah was back there on Scout, and there was a bundle in a black coat over his saddle still.

I said, "But I thought . . . you'd want to go home." *Back to India.*

She stared at me like I was stupid, and then she smiled. "Aashini is going home," she answered, while she helped me sit. I leaned on her hard. "We'll get the money somehow. *I* want to stay with you. And I thought a book would help pay for your stable, and maybe I could keep fixing things. We can make something work."

The lightning of my heart hurt more than the buckshot in my wrenched hip. And the pain was a hell of a lot more welcome, too.

I dug in my shirt, inside the wrap binding up my bosom, until I found a warm disc of metal. It slipped, wet with sweat, but I dug it out and folded it in my fist. The fist was sticky with dried blood. I was a goddamn mess.

"I want you to have this," I said. "Marshal Reeves gave it to me. It's been . . . lucky."

She held out her hand hesitantly, curious, and I laid the Marshal's dollar in it.

She slid her thumb across and frowned. Then smiled. "She looks like you," she said, and grinned at me with all the morning sunlight caught in her bottomless eyes.

Epilogue

Mostly, I guess you know how it ended.

It was pneumonia. And it was a separated hip. And I still hear ringing in my ears when I'm in a quiet room, and I suspect I always will.

But it turns out the Federal Government actually takes a very kind view of folk who foil foreign plots against their sovereign territory. After the *Os'minog,* unable to submerge with her damaged hull, was tracked, rammed, and sunk off the Oregon coast by the USS *Amphitrite* we had a pretty nice reward paid in double eagles to divvy up.

Miss Francina took her share and what she'd had in the bank and rebuilt the parlor house better than it had been. Except Miss Francina listened to Bea and named the place the Hôtel *Ma* Cherie, even though Madame insisted that "mon" was better because "those fucking men think everything belongs to them anyway." Crispin's the manager now, and Miss Bethel runs the bar. The other girls all went back to work with her. I bet Bea's still sneaking Signor into her bedroom after closing.

It ain't all roses. Remember my old friend Bill? He runs Bantle's cribhouse now, and Merry's still in business busting girls out, more's the pity. But we got some legislation planned about that.

We gave Connie a New Orleans funeral, at Beatrice's insistence. Since Connie always kept her opinions on God to herself, we had to take our best guess.

The food wasn't as good as she would have managed.

Marshal Reeves and Tomoatooah had to sneak out of town to get his prisoner away from Sergeant Waterson, since our local constables wanted Horaz Standish, too. The Marshal and his posseman took Horaz back to Oklahoma in shackles, by way of the train. I read in the paper that he charmed Judge Parker so that Parker apologized when he sentenced Standish to swing.

Either way, Standish didn't live long enough to be extradited back to the Washington Territory. But the Marshal did ship Sergeant Waterson his remains, in a nice pine box.

Me and Priya paid for Miss Lizzie's inventor's license in return for her taking Priya on as a formal apprentice.

That's going well. So long as they don't blow themselves up.

I send the Marshal a letter once in a while. His Jennie reads 'em to him, and she writes me back. She says she'll ask Tomoatooah about a filly for me, when he gets around to getting Scout in foal. I just about think he might sell me one. Maybe I'll even take the train down there to get her when she's old enough to travel, and meet all the little Reeveses, too.

The house me and Priya bought together with our share of the reward has a nice bit of land attached, and Molly's going to need a stablemate once we're done teaching Priya to ride.

Mr. Colony took my manuscript to Chicago, and now you hold my book in your hand.

Madame ran for mayor.
    Unopposed.

Author's Note

Rapid City is not any one real place but a sort of Ur-place, a compilation derived of elements of historic Portland, Vancouver, San Francisco, and Seattle.

Madame Damnable is inspired by but not in any factual way based upon Seattle's legendary real Mother Damnable, Mary Ann Conklin (1821–1873), who is supposed to have run a city courthouse downstairs and a brothel upstairs in the same house on King Street.

The character of Merry Lee is very loosely based upon the exploits of heroic women such as San Francisco's Tye Leung Schulze (1887–1972), who was incidentally also the first Chinese woman to cast a ballot in North America, many of them of Asian heritage, who did what they could to help their "frail sisters" who were exploited, enslaved, and legislated against.

U.S. Marshal Bass Reeves (1838–1910) was a real person and is believed by some historians of popular culture to have been the model for the Lone Ranger. The real Bass Reeves, to my knowledge, never made it that far northwest of the Indian

Territory—but he did have a luxuriant mustache and a truly impressive number of children.

Tomoatooah, I am sad to say, is entirely a figment of my own imagination.

Brookfield, Massachusetts
10 May 2014

Acknowledgments

This book and its author owe a tremendous debt of gratitude to too many people to enumerate here—and a few I would be extremely remiss if I neglected to thank. These include Beth Meacham, editor extraordinaire; Jennifer Jackson and Michael Curry of the Donald Maass Literary Agency; copy editor Barbara Wild (who caught a couple of truly embarrassing errors and kept me honest the rest of the time); and Irene Gallo, Lauren Hougen, Ardi Alspach, Amy Saxon, and the rest of the art, production, publicity, and marketing people at Tor Books who do such incredible work in making me look good.

I've often said that it takes a village to write a novel, and this one was no different. While I was aided by and owe a debt of gratitude to the authors of the numerous books and Web sites on nineteenth-century feminism, the Wild West flesh trade, culture and history, the Plains tribes, and the history of the Pacific Northwest I have consumed over the past few years, I'd like to mention a few people who provided personal assistance. Catherine Kehl was very generous with her time in providing me with Chinese swearwords. Sheenu and Kay Srinivasan and Asha Srinivasan Shipman have been irreplaceable resources on Hindu religion and Indian culture. Mary Kay Kare, Caitlin Kittredge, and Cherie Priest were my tour guides to Seattle, and Jaime Moyer and Kelly Morrisseau took me all over San Francisco. Siobhan Carroll and C. G. Cameron provided Vancouver-related intelligence.

My colleagues and friends Amanda Downum, Sarah Monette, Jodi Meadows, Emma Bull, Stephen Shipman, and Jeff Mac-Donald were—as always—instrumental in maintaining my sanity during the creative process. I am also beholden to my mother, Karen Westerholm, and her spouse, Beth Coughlin, who excel both at sliding flat food under the door and at general moral sustenance.

I also wish to thank my beloved and brilliant Scott—partner, sounding board, backstop—whose support, love, tolerance, and understanding of the occasional vagaries of the writing and publishing process make everything that much easier.